THE HORIZON

Historical Fiction Published by McBooks Press

BY ALEXANDER KENT
Midshipman Bolitho
Stand into Danger
In Gallant Company
Sloop of War
To Glory We Steer
Command a King's Ship
Passage to Mutiny
With All Despatch
Form Line of Battle!
Enemy in Sight!
The Flag Captain
Signal–Close Action!
The Inshore Squadron
A Tradition of Victory
Success to the Brave
Colours Aloft!
Honour this Day
The Only Victor
Beyond the Reef
The Darkening Sea
For My Country's Freedom
Cross of St George
Sword of Honour
Second to None
Relentless Pursuit

BY DUDLEY POPE
Ramage
Ramage & The Drumbeat
Ramage & The Freebooters
Governor Ramage R.N.
Ramage's Prize
Ramage & The Guillotine
Ramage's Diamond
Ramage's Mutiny
Ramage & The Rebels
The Ramage Touch
Ramage's Signal
Ramage & The Renegades
Ramage's Devil
Ramage's Trial
Ramage's Challenge
Ramage at Trafalgar
Ramage & The Saracens
Ramage & The Dido

BY DAVID DONACHIE
The Devil's Own Luck
The Dying Trade
A Hanging Matter
An Element of Chance
The Scent of Betrayal
A Game of Bones

BY DEWEY LAMBDIN
The French Admiral
Jester's Fortune

BY DOUGLAS REEMAN
Badge of Glory
First to Land
The Horizon
Dust on the Sea

BY V.A. STUART
Victors and Lords
The Sepoy Mutiny
Massacre at Cawnpore
The Cannons of Lucknow
The Heroic Garrison

BY C. NORTHCOTE PARKINSON
The Guernseyman
Devil to Pay
The Fireship
Touch and Go

BY CAPTAIN FREDERICK MARRYAT
Frank Mildmay OR
*   The Naval Officer*
The King's Own
Mr Midshipman Easy
Newton Forster OR
*   The Merchant Service*
Snarleyyow OR The Dog Fiend
The Privateersman
The Phantom Ship

BY JAN NEEDLE
A Fine Boy for Killing
The Wicked Trade

BY IRV C. ROGERS
Motoo Eetee

BY NICHOLAS NICASTRO
The Eighteenth Captain
Between Two Fires

BY W. CLARK RUSSELL
Wreck of the Grosvenor
Yarn of Old Harbour Town

BY RAFAEL SABATINI
Captain Blood

BY MICHAEL SCOTT
Tom Cringle's Log

BY A.D. HOWDEN SMITH
Porto Bello Gold

BY R.F. DELDERFIELD
Too Few for Drums
Seven Men of Gascony

THE
HORIZON

DOUGLAS REEMAN

The Royal Marines Saga, No. 3

MCBOOKS PRESS
ITHACA, NEW YORK

Published by McBooks Press 2002
Copyright © 1993 by Highseas Authors Ltd.
First published in the United Kingdom by Wm. Heinemann Ltd.

Cover painting by Geoffrey Huband

Library of Congress Cataloging-in-Publication Data

Reeman, Douglas.
  The horizon / by Douglas Reeman.
    p. cm. — (The Royal Marines Saga ; no. 3)
  ISBN 1-59013-027-8 (alk. paper)
  1. Blackwood family (Fictitious characters)—Fiction. 2. Great
Britain—History, Military—20th century—Fiction. 3. Great Britain.
Royal Marines—Fiction. 4. World War, 1914-1918—Fiction. I.
Title.
  PR6068.E35 H67 2002
  823'.914—dc21

                                         2002010212

Distributed to the trade by National Book Network, Inc.,
15200 NBN Way, Blue Ridge Summit, PA 17214
800-462-6420

Additional copies of this book may be ordered from any
bookstore or directly from McBooks Press, Inc.,
ID Booth Building, 520 North Meadow St., Ithaca, NY 14850.
Please include $4.00 postage and handling with mail orders.
New York State residents must add sales tax. All McBooks
Press publications can also be ordered by calling
toll-free 1-888-BOOKS11 (1-888-266-5711).
Please call to request a free catalog.

Visit the McBooks Press website at www.mcbooks.com.

Printed in the United States of America

9 8 7 6 5 4 3 2 1

━━━━━

We have built a house that is not for Time's throwing.

We have gained a peace unshaken by pain for ever.

War knows no power. Safe shall be my going,

Secretly armed against all death's endeavour;

Safe though all safety's lost; safe where men fall;

And if these poor limbs die, safest of all.

Safety, Rupert Brooke, 1914

Author's Note

It was as long ago as the sixties, when I was writing the book called *H.M.S. Saracen,* that my late father really began to talk of his own experiences at Gallipoli and on the Somme. As a boy I had sometimes listened to him speaking about them to his close friends, who had shared the same nightmare of trench warfare, but he never mentioned them directly to me.

The first half of *H.M.S. Saracen,* which I read to him during the course of its writing, dealt with the ill-fated Dardanelles campaign, and it was that which encouraged him to speak openly about the Great War. He had served as a major with the Royal Engineers, as well as the famous Gurkha Rifles, but it was in his first experience as a very junior subaltern that he was to feel the true and brutal impact of war. Little more than a boy, he found himself in complete command of the remnants of a battalion at Gallipoli, and later, on the Somme with the youth of Britain dying in countless thousands on every front, he endured things which never left him. In his own way he passed some of his experiences on to me, and for that I am grateful.

PART ONE

Per Mare

1915

ONE

The smart two-wheeled trap stopped on the brow of the last hill, the sturdy pony steaming in the bitter winter air, irritated no doubt, knowing that a warm stable was so close to hand.

The groom held the reins lightly and glanced at his passenger. "Here, sir?"

"Just for a minute." Captain Jonathan Blackwood removed his hand from the man's arm and thrust it back into his greatcoat pocket. For these few moments he needed to get a glimpse of the great estate: Hawks Hill, where he had been born and had grown up with his brothers. There was an icy haze above the red-brick walls by the gatehouse; like a sequence in a dream, he thought vaguely. The distance helped to remind him of what it had once been like, when as children they had played and explored the old house and its maze of cellars and attics. It had been built originally as a fortified Tudor farmhouse, but had been added to considerably over the years. There was still part of a moat to one side of the wall, now a home for geese and swans.

Jonathan looked down at his uniform, that of a captain in the Royal Marine Artillery. The badges and marks of rank were the only things that distinguished himself and other marines from a regiment of the line.

For this was mid-January, 1915. He felt his body stiffen as he saw a tree bare of leaves standing alone by the roadside. Another memory. Did anyone here in Hampshire, or anywhere else in the country, know or guess what was happening out there across the English Channel? The war, which had already raged for five months; the war that would, it was confidently predicted, be over by Christmas, which had already ground to a bloody stalemate of unbelievable and horrific proportions. It was certainly no nearer to finishing than when the might of the German armies had crushed the first resistance of the French and then their allies, British regular troops commanded by the legendary General Kitchener.

The groom watched him curiously. He had been working only a short while at Hawks Hill but had heard stories of the Blackwoods. All had served in the Royal Marines except the first in the family to own this house and estate: Major-General Samuel Blackwood, still spoken of by the locals as "the last soldier," even though they knew little but rumour about him, as it had happened in the eighteenth century. All the Blackwoods had gone into the corps after that, although even members of the family did not quite understand the reason.

This was not much of a job, he thought; but the food was plentiful and he was with horses, something he knew well. He smiled grimly. Anything was better than being over there where this officer in the creased greatcoat had been.

Blackwood did not even notice the scrutiny. He was still staring at the solitary tree, almost black in this light, and shining in the last flurry of January rain.

He had seen a forest like that, but every tree had been blasted by fire and explosives. Stripped of branches and life, cut through by mortar and howitzer until there had been nothing, except the endless patterns of trenches which now stretched right across Europe from the Channel to the Swiss border. How *could* they know what it was like? How could anyone?

He cleared his throat. "All right, carry on, Marker. Let's go down." He heard the man's intake of breath, doubtless surprised that this youthful-looking officer should have taken the trouble to discover his name.

Closer to, the neglect and decay were more evident. Sagging gates, rusty and unpainted for years, weeds sprouting in the curving drive. Jonathan Blackwood bit his lip. Had all the childhood memories been another dream? There was a feeling about the house now, as if it were brooding, waiting for him. Parts of the estate and small-holdings had been sold off to pay the debts of Hawks Hill's last lord and master, Major-General Harry Blackwood, whose extravagances, grand dinners and balls had been the talk of the county and further. He had long been master of the local hunt, and to preserve its standards and impress others, he had spent more money than he could properly afford.

The wheels came to rest below the imposing entrance. He thought of his cousin Ralf, who had also lived here after the death of his father. They were about the same age, although Ralf was in the Royal Marine Light Infantry, a "red" marine as opposed to the blues of the artillery. But as one testy staff colonel had snapped, "There are only *khaki* marines until this lot's over, so don't you forget it!"

His mind returned reluctantly to David, his oldest brother. How quickly life had all gone, from youths to men with only brief leaves in which to know and understand one another. His middle brother Neil had been killed by a Boer sniper in South Africa. David, like his father before him, had been awarded the Victoria Cross. Two in one family, everyone said. Now both were dead. Jonathan tried to contain the sudden twist of anguish. It had all shown such promise. David had met and married Sarah, who had been betrothed to Neil before his death. She had been a happy, lively girl, the perfect foil for David's seriousness, and those experiences of his which she could never share.

The old general had also had an eye for the ladies, and as he had aged, the need to impress them had never faltered. Jonathan did not know how it had come about. It was said that the old man had challenged Sarah to a race. She was a good horsewoman, but the mount must have been too strong for her; she had been thrown at a ditch and was dead when the doctor reached Hawks Hill.

David had been away with the Home Fleet. It had all been over and done with when he had reached here.

He had always been a grave, self-controlled man in the face of tragedy, but this final time he could not contain his anguish. He had gripped his younger brother's hand and had spoken one word. *"Why?"* It still seemed to hang in the air over this place.

He climbed down and said to the groom, "I'll need you tomorrow. Bright and early."

The man nodded. "Mr Swan has got everything done, sir." When the captain did not reply he flicked the reins and the pony turned automatically towards the stable yard.

Jonathan thought of Swan, who had been David's Marine Officer's Attendant, and a whole lot more. Batman, servant, body-guard, friend. He was now in his forties, still a Royal Marine, but only in his heart. Curiously enough, he had been the first to learn of David's death when the postman had brought the news from the village.

But perhaps it was only right that he had been the first, a man who had been closer than anyone to David in Africa and then in China during the savage Boxer Rebellion. Then back to the fleet again, until that last link in the chain of tragedy which had left its mark on this house and estate had recalled him. After Sarah's death David had been given extended leave to help his father, who had suffered a stroke which had left him as helpless as a child. He had died soon afterwards, and the doctor had confided that the general's heavy drinking had not helped.

Jonathan walked into the familiar hallway with its fine, curving staircase. He heard Swan's hurrying footsteps and braced himself for the meeting.

Swan had been left in charge of the house after David had fired the steward. Like the empty gatehouse, carelessness and neglect were a sign of the times.

"I'm sorry, but this house is not open to visitors yet!"

Jonathan started. He had been so immersed in his thoughts that he had failed to see the man in a neat suit who was sitting at a small dark desk onto which, in other days, the general had thrown the visiting cards of callers.

Swan came out and Jonathan was shocked by his appearance. He may only have been in his early forties, but he looked ten years older.

There was nothing feeble in his tone however. "You calls the captain *sir* in this house!" He shot Jonathan a worried smile. "He owns it."

The official stammered, "I—I'm *very* sorry." He glared at Swan. "Er—sir." He tried again. "I thought you would have known about the proposed conversion of the house and buildings into a convalescent home for officers."

"I did know." Jonathan glanced around. The paler patches where paintings and portraits had once hung. Proud faces, the smoking walls of gunfire in battles from Trafalgar to the Crimea.

Each panorama had been careful not to show the true horror of war as he had seen it in France.

Swan said, "We've prepared the other wing, sir. Just like Major David wanted it." He waited for the government official to go and said doggedly, "I should have been with him. How could it have happened?"

Jonathan walked into the other room and tossed a dust sheet away from his father's favourite chair. It was already getting dark and it was not even four o'clock, and the rain was falling again, tapping on the tall windows; the sound which had frightened him as a small child. Was that why he still hated a thunderstorm, he wondered. Once he had been here alone, and when the lightning had filled the place with livid flashes and the thunder rolled against the hillside like an artillery bombardment, it had been as if those very pictures had come to life, men fighting their battles in miniature. He forced it from his mind and concentrated on Swan's despairing question. How could it have happened? From the first day, upon his entering the corps, the invincibility of the Royal Navy had been drummed into him as it was into every schoolboy in the country. The Royal Navy was the mightiest fleet in the world: it did indeed rule the waves, the sure shield every Briton accepted as his right. A source of pride, unchallenged since Nelson had fallen at Trafalgar.

But in times of peace when almost daily troopships had left Southampton and Liverpool unmolested to deal with trouble in obscure parts of the Empire, for "a skirmish" as the general had often scornfully described such campaigns, the dangers of all-out war seemed unreal. The minds of planners and peacetime senior officers ashore and afloat refused to change, so that when war with Germany broke out they found they had been outstripped. Jonathan had been on a short staff course, and had been astounded by the complacency still rife in those first months. Throughout the fleet, gunnery officers were still chosen for flag rank; others were largely ignored. As for tactics, the torpedo and the possible use of aircraft as weapons were discounted and thought vaguely ridiculous.

He looked at Swan and replied, "It was stupidity. There's no other answer."

He could see it as if he had been there. Three of the navy's big 12,000-ton cruisers, *Aboukir, Cressey,* and *Hogue,* had been sailing near—too near—the Dutch coast without an escort. Only a month had passed since the declaration of war. On that calm September morning between seven and eight o'clock a German submarine had closed with the cruisers and had sunk all three, with a terrible loss of life. David had been in one of them . . .

Swan watched him, unwilling to break the stillness. He had never known this Blackwood very well. There was much of Major David about him although he was taller, slim and straight-backed, with unruly brown hair and level blue eyes which were now deeply troubled.

His features were tanned and somehow boyish, although Swan knew he must be at least thirty; still only a captain but promotion was slow in the corps. Maybe he only looked young because he hadn't grown a moustache like so many Royal Marine officers. But there was fire too; Swan had been close to officers long enough to recognise it when that stupid official had challenged him.

"I'd like a drink, Swan."

Swan grinned, his apple-red face lighting up for the first time. "Course, sir. Got some good Scotch . . ."

"Then bring it, and I want you to join me."

Swan frowned. "Wouldn't be proper, sir. I knows me place."

Jonathan leaned back in the chair and watched the light dying outside.

"But this is your place, Swan. And I want you to be here when I come back . . ."

The picture refused to form. *Suppose I don't come back?* The Royal Marines would soon be in the thick of it. He pressed his eyes tightly shut. The place in France where he had been completing his course with a Home Counties regiment had almost been overrun. They had counter-attacked, and he had seen them die, not in dozens as their colonel had predicted, but in hundreds. In the twinkling of an eye: men falling, being blown to pieces, blinded in the ruthless exchange of fire and bayonet. They gained a few yards but lost it when the Germans had thrown in another assault.

When he opened his eyes again he saw Swan with the decanter and two glasses. He smiled, and the shadows fell away. "Good."

Swan said, "Cook's got something nice for your supper, sir."

Jonathan reached for one of the old general's finely-cut goblets and saw that his hand was shaking. But the Scotch was superb, one of the general's prize malts.

He said, "Here's to the Royals, eh?"

Swan watched him warily. "*Is* it going badly over there, sir?"

Jonathan held out his goblet again and stared at it. Was it empty already? Then he looked at the wall where one of the great pictures had been and said softly, "It's not a war, Swan." He held the refilled glass very tightly, and saw that his hand was steady. "It's sheer bloody murder."

Some time later, Swan picked up his own glass and tip-toed away as Jonathan's head fell against the chair.

He paused and looked back. With his face relaxed in sleep he was very like his brother, he decided.

Albeit for one night only, a Blackwood had come home.

. . .

Twenty miles south of Hawks Hill and the surrounding Hampshire countryside, the bustling naval port of Portsmouth
seemed to cringe under a blustery wind. The broad harbour,
usually so sheltered from all but the fiercest gales, was alive
with cruising wavelets that broke into cat's paws against the
sides of anchored and moored warships, while smaller craft
were tossed about in clouds of spray. Every kind of ship was
in evidence. Light cruisers, two elderly pre-Dreadnought battleships, and low-lying torpedo-boat destroyers, somehow
sinister with their raked black hulls, seemed to fill every buoy
and berth. Beyond them, poking above the dockyard jetties
and walls, were the upper-works and fighting-tops of many
more, being repaired, refitted, or constructed to prepare for
rising losses at sea.

At the top of the harbour and shining in spray like the
symbol she was, Nelson's old flagship *Victory,* painted now in
Victorian black and white, was a reminder, if one was ever
needed, that this was the home of the world's greatest navy.

But on this particular January morning the eyes of almost
everyone from sodden boats' crews to idlers on the walls of
Portsmouth Point or across the tossing water on the Gosport
side, were turned to the largest ship ever to appear. H.M.S.
Reliant, one of a new class of super battle-cruisers, seemed to
rise contemptuously above them all. There were other bat-
tlecruisers in the fleet; in fact they had been the only major
warships to have been committed to action with the Germans
off Heligoland Bight, when, in support of vessels of the Har-
wich Force, they had sunk three enemy cruisers in the first
weeks of the war.

But *Reliant* was something quite new and entirely different from her predecessors, and mounted six 15-inch guns in
three turrets, all of which could be trained on separate targets

at the same time. She also carried a formidable armament of
seventeen four-inch guns. But it was her size that awed the
casual onlookers, while to those who served such ships her
massive armament, 32,000 tons and length of nearly 800 feet
spoke of unprecedented strength. Big as she was, she retained
the graceful lines of a light cruiser. She had two funnels, the
forward one slightly taller than the other, so it seemed that
this huge ship was leaning ahead, as if eager to go.

Her abbreviated trials had been completed just before
Christmas, and now fully manned with a complement of 1,250
officers and men, stored, ammunitioned, her bunkers topped
up with oil, she was as ready as any untried ship could be.

Aft in his spacious day cabin the man who would control
Reliant's progress in a war which had already spread beyond
anything any of them had envisaged, Captain Auriol George
Soutter, stood by a polished scuttle and stared out at some
passing picket boats. In a comfortable green leather armchair
the captain of the dockyard, with a coffee cup at his elbow,
regarded him curiously. They were friends of a sort. The Royal
Navy was like a family and you usually ran into familiar faces
along the way. He had been a cadet and then midshipman
with *Reliant*'s captain, but there was little else in common.
Whereas he was comfortably round, as the result of too good
a mess life over the years, Soutter was lean and straight-
backed, young for his rank, younger still for the command
he had been given. But his face, now in profile, had an old-
fashioned look, and would not have been out of place with
Drake or at Trafalgar. Eyes grey-blue like the North Sea, a
tightness around the jaw which had developed on the pre-
carious climb up the ladder. From twelve years old, to this.
The other captain said, "What d'you think, George? You've
not had much time to get your people into shape. I know

they're all hand-picked apart from the last intake, but it's a hell of a responsibility, especially . . ."

Soutter turned from the rain-dappled scuttle and smiled at him. "Especially as after today, we are no longer a private ship—that what you were about to say?" Like all those who knew him, his friend had used his middle name. He had always loathed being called Auriol, and had been made to suffer for it as a cadet.

The other shrugged his plump shoulders. "Well, you know what they say."

"No. Tell me." Even his words were sparing, as if everything unnecessary had been honed away.

"He has just been appointed rear-admiral, and when he makes *Reliant* into his flagship, not too many hours from now . . ."

Soutter looked past him. "One hour, fifty minutes to be exact."

The ship's crest, hung between pictures of the King and Queen on the white bulkhead, was an upraised, double-edged sword surrounded by a victor's laurel leaves. *Reliant's* motto, *Gedemus nunquam,* stood out in bright gold below the naval crown despite the grey light. *We will never give in.* Rear-Admiral Theodore Keppel Purves would like that.

"Of course, I forgot. You served with him . . ."

Soutter's mouth relaxed slightly in a smile. *Oh no. You didn't forget.* "Under him. I was his gunnery officer in the *Assurance.* I doubt that he's changed much."

The other captain waited, but that was all there was. Gossip had it that Soutter and Purves had never really got on, and there had been talk of a court martial or something damned close. The lords of Admiralty obviously thought it did not count for anything now. Soutter had been given command of this, the largest man-of-war in the service, when many others had been praying for it. As for Purves, he was known to be ambitious—another Beatty, some said. If Beatty, who commanded the battle-cruiser squadron, got to hear about that, the tension would be between *them*.

A door opened and Drury, the chief steward, peered in at them. "Beg pardon, sir, the commander's respects an' the dockyard launch is 'ere." He vanished, his accent hanging in the air like a piece of London's East End.

The visiting captain reached for his cap and glanced at the cabinet which he knew contained Soutter's decanters. "Best be off then." He held out his hand. "Bit of a mess, isn't it?"

Soutter watched him gravely, recalling the wild cheering, the strident beat of the Royal Marine band when ensign and Jack had been hoisted for the first time above his *Reliant*. There was not much cheering any more. "Wish us luck." Soutter returned his handshake firmly. "We'll make them sit up when we join the fleet, or I shall know the reason!" He smiled, but it did not reach his eyes.

But it gave his friend confidence. He said, "I'll do my best to speed repairs—get the ships turned round without delay."

Soutter walked with him through the adjoining office and past the rigid Royal Marine sentry beyond the bulkhead.

He was thinking of the battleship *Audacious*, in which he had served for a brief period. In the first month of hostilities she had been sunk off the Irish coast, mine or torpedo nobody knew for certain. But a great ship like that, with far heavier armour plating than *Reliant*, gone in a moment. Only one thing was blatantly obvious: either way it had been a German submarine, even so far from base, which had fired or laid the fatal blow.

On deck, where a cold wind swept across the broad

expanse of perfect pale planking, all was as it should be. The officer of the day in frock coat and sword; probably for the last time, Soutter thought grimly. Duty midshipmen, their cold hands in white gloves, the boatswain's mates with their silver calls, all waiting to see the captain of the dockyard over the side where his launch pitched up and down at the foot of the long, varnished accommodation ladder.

Soutter glanced past the streaming White ensign at the quarterdeck rail and saw *Victory*, almost lost in the approaching drizzle, like some phantom ship. He heard the marines snapping to attention, the slap of hands on rifles with fixed bayonets. His own hand went sharply to the peak of his cap as the calls shrilled out. Nelson would have approved, he thought.

Commander Thomas Coleridge waited for the launch to stand away, with the dockyard captain staring up at the battle-cruiser before an onslaught of spray forced him to take cover in the cockpit.

Then he said, "I've been right round the ship, sir."

For a few seconds he and Soutter regarded each other like strangers. There had not been time enough to get to know one another much beyond the demands of duty and the need to pull a new ship into one company, if not yet a team. But as second-in-command Coleridge knew his responsibility, which was to keep his captain content and confident and to present the ship to him as a going concern.

"Good, but do it again before you pipe the guard and band."

Coleridge said, "I have some good heads of department, sir. We've been lucky. Later on it may not be so easy."

The grey-blue eyes hardened. "We shall worry about *that* later on." He deliberately turned his back on the dockyard and the busy signal tower with its crazily gyrating semaphore and the flags that were darting up and down as if the signalling staff had gone berserk.

Rear Admiral Theodore Keppel Purves would be up there now. It was exactly his style, watching his new flagship with the yeoman of signals' big telescope. Seeking flaws. Even as a captain Purves had never learned that all criticism and no praise did nothing to boost the morale of the lower-deck. Soutter refrained from mentioning Purves's custom to the commander. He was already nervous enough.

Coleridge saw a lieutenant and some seamen trying to catch his eye and hurried away.

Soutter walked slowly along the perfectly tarred deck seams, oblivious to the drizzle across his back. He was seeing this ship, *his* ship, as others would. More powerfully armed even than the battleships. He tried to thrust away the picture of the *Audacious* falling onto her side after the explosion. *Reliant* had done 31 knots on trials, faster even than the light cruisers. Faster than anything. Oil-fired, too. Every soul aboard would appreciate that, with the memories of the misery of coaling ships fresh in their minds.

Yes, this was a proud moment. He stared up at the masthead where Purves's flag would soon be flying. The greatest moment of his eventful career. He halted and looked down at a passing paddle-wheeled tug, from which some of the crew were waving at the glistening battle-cruiser. If he had one regret, it was that over there on the shore there was nobody to care.

Captain Jonathan Blackwood stood by a window in the adjutant's office watching the familiar activity on the square of Eastney Barracks. The parade ground was still too wet from the recent rain to allow any dust, otherwise it would have formed a cloud above the platoons and squads of marines as they stamped and drilled their way through one exercise after another, from the new recruits, stiff and awkward even at this distance, to smaller groups who were being instructed in the mysteries of the machine-gun.

Jonathan still could not believe the speed of events since his brief visit to Hawks Hill. He had reported here, as ordered, to discover that he was being sent without delay to the new battlecruiser *Reliant* lying in Portsmouth just down the road, although he was not, as far as he could understand, to join *Reliant*'s Royal Marine detachment. He turned towards the other door as it swung open and the adjutant, looking even more harassed than usual, beckoned to him and murmured, "The Colonel is ready to see you."

Jonathan went in and closed the door behind him. "Sir?"

Colonel St John Tarrier looked up from his littered desk. "Take a pew, Jonathan. Good to have you back with us."

He sat, and glanced at the ledgers, clips of signals and several large maps which covered the desk from side to side. He liked the colonel. A bluff, no-nonsense marine with steely eyes and a mustard-coloured moustache, Tarrier was one of the old school who had seen action just about everywhere that the Union Jack flew.

"Not back for long, it seems. Colonel—"

The colonel did not seem to hear. "Read your report from France. Sobering. Very. Can't have a stalemate for ever. Young officers and N.C.O.'s should be training now to take over the new army, not be thrown into useless trenches and slaughtered. We need leaders, not old duffers like me."

He seemed to recall Jonathan's comment and snapped, "Everything's moving fast. See that company drilling out there? Most of 'em as green as grass. It'll take more than the corps tradition to train *them* in a hurry. They're R.M.L.I., came over from Forton barracks a week or so back. I've been ordered to send the whole company aboard the *Reliant* in two days' time."

The mystery of his own situation was no clearer. "I'll bet her captain will enjoy that."

The colonel gave a brief grin. "He'll be hearing about it for the first time around now from Rear Admiral Purves. He's hoisted his flag in *Reliant*." He dragged out a much-marked map of the Eastern Mediterranean. "B Company is being sent to Port Said to reinforce the other Royal Marines already there." His finger moved away from the Suez Canal and halted at the Turkish coastline, to the narrow approach and entrance of the Dardanelles. "I expect you've heard the story, or most of it. The Turks have already made a few thrusts towards Suez, so a major operation is the obvious solution." His finger tapped the Black Sea beyond the Dardanelles. "If we can destroy the Turkish forts here and get our ships into the Black Sea, the fleet can bombard Constantinople and knock the stuffing out of 'em. Then, but only then, we can offer support to our Russian ally from that flank, give them heart when they need it most. The kaiser's army is making mincemeat out of the tsar's troops. It has to be done. If Germany forces Russia into some kind of armistice, the kaiser will bring even more men into play on the Western Front and we don't want that until we've made some progress."

In his mind Jonathan could see the explosions, the huge columns of earth and burned trees being blasted into the sky. Men running and falling, soundless as in a nightmare. Any progress there would be something, he thought, but he said nothing. As a very senior colonel who had been recalled from retirement to command here, Tarrier would not need much telling. It was said that casualty lists were to be posted throughout the country, instead of relying merely on those dreaded telegrams. *The War Office regrets to inform you that your son, or your brother, or your father. . . .* What would people think about the war then? It was not a matter of a few hundred, even a few thousand. Jonathan had heard it from officers he had met in France, reinforcements dragging their boots to the front line. In one attack, they had lost 20,000 men in three hours. Unless you had been there it was impossible to imagine.

"And me, sir?"

The colonel scowled as he heard voices in the outer office. More visitors. Requests, questions, apologies. It never stopped.

"I want you to draw your gear and tropical helmet and report back to me." He hesitated, making a decision about the officer facing him across his paperwork war. "There'll be a lieutenant-colonel in overall charge once you reach Port Said. He'll be sailing with you." He glanced at the wall clock. "Be on board now if I know Jack Waring. The marines will have to work as a team, all day, every day while on passage through the Med. Once the pressure is removed from Suez, new orders will likely be despatched. Some men will be posted to the ships already there, others—" He shrugged. "Who knows? In this damned war you can't plan for tomorrow, never mind a few months from now. I'll make sure your majority comes through." His eyes crinkled. "I don't want you to be outgunned by the R.M.L.I., do I?"

He walked with him to the door. "You've got the experience, and the men will look to you. Two V.C.'s in one family—well, dash it, man, who wouldn't? *Reliant* will probably be joining the squadron out there. It might be all over by the time she drops anchor. I can't see Johnny Turk standing up to a battering from all those broadsides." But he did not sound confident.

"One thing, Jonathan." The colonel rested a beefy hand

on his shoulder. "I am sending a subaltern with you. Bit young—too young, his mother would say . . ." He added harshly, "My son as a matter of fact. No favours. But keep an eye on him, eh?"

He roared, "Stop whispering out there, and *come in* if you must!" But it was too late. Just for those few moments St John Tarrier had shown himself as an ordinary man, who could still care and worry like any other parent.

Jonathan found himself outside in the damp air beside the busy, marching figures. Would this place ever be the same again, he wondered. The contests, the lively garden parties, with the ladies in summer gowns and the girls looking bold-eyed at the young officers in their smart uniforms. Would anything be the same, come to that?

"Squad, *'alt!*" A sergeant stepped out smartly and saluted him.

"Yes?"

The sergeant swallowed hard. "'Eard you was 'ere, sir. Cap'n Blackwood, right, sir?"

Jonathan waited as the man composed what he was going to say.

"I'm Sarn't Fox, sir. My brother was sergeant-major with your . . . er, Cap'n David. We was all sorry to 'ear about him goin' down in that cruiser."

Jonathan nodded, unable to speak. He should have been prepared. The corps was a family, and many of the marines, like their officers, came from generations of sea-soldiers. He recalled starkly how this sergeant's brother had commiserated with David when Neil had been shot dead in South Africa. The family.

"Thank you." He knew that the waiting squad of marines were staring with curious disbelief as captain and sergeant shook hands.

Then they saluted one another and as Jonathan walked away he heard the sergeant shout, "Now once again! When I says 'fix,' you don't fix! But when I says 'bayonets' you whips it out an' you whops it on, see?"

"Ah, there you are, sir!" Jonathan's Marine Officer's Attendant, Harry Payne, who had once presented himself to a recruiting party in Winchester, fell into step beside him. They had been together for three years and the arrangement worked well. Payne was a chirpy, sharp-witted marine who could do most things from polishing boots to reloading Jonathan's revolver faster than any man he had known. He thought suddenly of poor Swan at Hawks Hill, soon to be surrounded by the medical staff, the wounded, and the reminders of what he had lost.

"There's some packing to be done. We're joining the *Reliant*."

"All done," Payne replied cheerfully. "I've got your sunhelmet too. Must be going to the Arctic, I thought—you know what the quartermaster's department is like!"

Payne glanced contemptuously at the marching figures, back and forth across the square, while here and there small pillars of authority, the N.C.O.'s, stood and bawled out their commands.

"Good to be back, eh, sir?"

Jonathan stared down at him. Payne was quite short for a marine. "Is it?" Then he said, as if in response to a whispered word, "Yes, I suppose it is."

It came as a surprise. After what he had seen in France perhaps he had believed he would be too sickened to overcome it.

But as he had heard David say: *It is what I am. What I do.*

"After all, sir," Payne reflected, "you an' me'll be sort of passengers."

Jonathan smiled and saluted the sentry by the gates.

Payne had never served in a flagship before. It would certainly not be a pleasure cruise.

Payne glanced at him quickly. That was a bit more like it. He had seen that stupid sod Sergeant Fox stop the captain to speak with him and could guess what he said. He had already had more to put up with than most. New start, that was what he needed now. And a bloody great battle-cruiser should be safe enough.

TWO

Lieutenant-Colonel Jack Waring R.M.L.I. nodded curtly to Jonathan as he entered the Royal Marines' office and said, "You must be Blackwood. Sit down and we'll get on with it." Jonathan glanced at the other two officers, Captain Bruce Seddon who commanded *Reliant*'s own detachment, and a major he had already met in the busy days since leaving Portsmouth Harbour, whose name was Livesay, the hastily-embarked B Company's commander. He looked fed up, while Seddon was careful to show no expression at all.

Jonathan had seen the lieutenant-colonel several times, jabbing the air with an ebony walking stick as he pointed out something or other to the ship's commander. He seemed to be very friendly with the new flag-officer, Rear Admiral Purves, who was rarely seen in contact with anyone else. Jonathan had only once seen his cap on the upper bridge, set at a rakish angle, its double line of oak leaves gleaming like pure gold. He turned his attention to Waring and hid a smile. He was not called "Beaky" for nothing behind his back. His

nose was hooked and high-bridged, so that his eyes appeared
to be set in his cheeks.

Some plates crashed in a passageway and someone
shouted out with alarm as *Reliant* tilted her flank almost contemptuously into a deep trough. The sea was heavy, the
Atlantic crests curling and booming along the great hull with
the noise of wild drums. It said much for her builders, John
Brown of Clydebank, that even in the worst seas *Reliant*'s
decks were rarely awash.

The battle-cruiser was standing well out to sea, a wise precaution with one of her two destroyer escorts already gone
back to harbour with half of her bridge stove in.

The second destroyer was somewhere abeam, her low sil-
houette rarely in sight except from the bridge.

To know that the destroyer's small company was suffering
the discomfort of the heavy seas was little compensation to
most of B Company's new recruits, who were sick for much
of the time, and no threat from the toughest N.C.O. could
shift them. For this was the Bay of Biscay, angered perhaps
by the battlecruiser's invincible thrust as she parted each wave
like some giant cleaver.

Jonathan waited, expecting to see some maps, hear pro-
posals for the immediate future when they reached Port Said.

Lieutenant-Colonel Waring bit his lower lip so that his
dark, sprouting moustache seemed to put an edge to his dis-
pleasure.

"I am not satisfied, gentlemen. I am in overall charge and
you are my senior officers. And yet every day I find the
marines wasting valuable time with things which are not our
concern. I discovered some of them practising seamanship,
and up with the boats in their davits. And yet on Sunday at
Divisions I should imagine that even the padre was snigger-
ing behind his Bible!"

It had been quite rough at the time, and whereas the lines of seamen and stokers had swayed easily with the rolling hull, their voices roaring out, *"For those in peril on the sea . . ."* the Royal Marines had reeled against their rifles as if they had been paraded immediately after leaving a dockside pub.

"I will not have it, d'you see?"

Jonathan saw *Reliant's* R.M. captain watching him, despair in his eyes. It could not be easy to have over a hundred extra marines pushed into his limited space, and then to have Beaky Waring venting his wrath in this way.

He said, "May I comment, sir?"

Waring eyed him calmly—or was there a glint of triumph there? "Do so."

"It was largely my idea. I thought the constant repetition of rifle and bayonet drill was a bit pointless. These men will eventually have to know how to handle boats, to move weapons and stores with tackles . . ." He got no further.

"Of course! I was forgetting, Captain Blackwood, you have had experience of land warfare—I mean, should they decide to let us loose on the Turks." He paused, and Jonathan thought later that it had been like an actor making the most of his lines. "Three weeks, was it not?"

Major Livesay said bluntly, "More than any of us, sir. The last enemy I shot at was a Chinese pirate off Kwangchow."

"How interesting." Waring gave a cold smile. "May I suggest that your wretched company would do well to learn instant obedience, so that in the unlikely event they are asked to prove themselves they will have loyalty and discipline enough to provide what some of their officers obviously lack!"

They sat in grim silence, the sea sounds and the creak of steel through *Reliant's* great length intruding, as if the ship herself were listening.

"So arms and bayonet drills will continue." His head jerked

round. *"Well?* I said I was not to be disturbed!"

A small midshipman, with water streaming from his cap and teeth chattering, gasped, "The admiral's compliments, and would you join him on his bridge?"

The lieutenant-colonel glanced at his three officers and remarked casually, "Of course. Always a pleasure." As the youth turned to flee he snapped, "Is anything happening?"

The midshipman swallowed. "The second escort is leaving us, sir. Trouble in her engine-room. We are proceeding alone."

Waring nodded, satisfied. He said, "Double the sentries around the ship, Major Livesay, your best marksmen. Captain Seddon, rig two additional machine-guns where you think best. Unlikely to be a periscope about in this weather, but be ready at all times. I shall be along later to see how you have arranged things." He strode from the office, his words still hanging in the damp air like a threat.

Jonathan imagined the small destroyer, tossing about as her engine-room crew tried to put things right while their great consort vanished in a squall. No wonder they said destroyer men were the best. He was reminded suddenly of *Reliant's* captain, who had been in destroyers for some of his service. A good choice, he thought. Soutter, despite all the demands on his time, and unlike Beaky Waring, had made a point of welcoming him aboard.

Captain Bruce Seddon breathed out slowly. "Roll on Port Said!"

The major scowled. "It's fine for you. I'm stuck with him!" Then he looked at Jonathan. "Better get on with it then. I'll take young Tarrier, if that's all right with you?"

"Yes. Anything helps."

The colonel's son was still a month or so from his eighteenth birthday. His age was not so unusual when officers were in short supply, but Second Lieutenant Roger Tarrier

really was so *young;* there was no other way to describe it.
Like the day when *Reliant* had left Portsmouth and was passing the Isle of Wight. They had met a hospital ship, her elegant
hull revealing her as a peacetime liner, now painted white
with crosses along her side which would be illuminated at
night in case some German submarine commander should
mistake her for a supply ship. Her deck had been crowded
with khaki figures, their bandages and dressings clearly visible even in that dull fight.

The wounded men had begun to cheer, so that the sound
had mingled and become one great shout, while seamen on
the battlecruiser's deck had waved their caps in reply.

Jonathan had been talking with young Tarrier, and had
been shocked to see the tears in his eyes as he had said with
such obvious pride, "What courage, sir! They can still cheer
after what they must have been through!"

How could he explain that the wounded soldiers were
cheering because they were free of that hell beyond the wire
and the murderous shellfire? Whatever happened to them
now they could not be sent back. It was what they dreamed
about in the trenches. A wound, just enough to send them
home. A Blighty one, as they called it.

Jonathan seized a handrail outside the office as the sea
roared against the bilge, enough even to make this leviathan
shiver.

There would not be too many at dinner tonight, he
thought.

The girl was young and very pretty, her hair rippling in the
breeze, one of her shoulders almost bare as she moved her
feet in the stream. She was smiling; and he recognised the old
gamekeeper's house, with Hawks Hill in the background. But
the sun was too bright; he could not see properly.

"Cap'n Blackwood, sir!" It was Harry Payne, a large bull's eye torch trained on the pillow. "You're wanted!"

Jonathan rolled over in the bunk, his legs tangled in the blanket, his mind reluctant to admit it was only a dream.

He stared around, but apart from the dipped torch the cabin was black. Every scuttle and deadlight was sealed throughout the ship.

"What time is it, for God's sake?"

"Three in the morning, sir." Payne sounded wide awake. "Captain wants you on the bridge."

He swung his legs over the side and grappled with each item of news. For one terrible second he had thought that the ship had gone to action stations and he had failed to hear the alarm.

Payne was kneeling with his boots. "There's a ship of some kind in distress, sir. We have altered course a bit to have a look-see."

Slowly Jonathan's senses were returning. He could even feel the steep angle of the deck. *Reliant* must have turned broadside to the waves. What kind of ship?

"Is Lieutenant-Colonel Waring up there?"

Payne hid his grin in the darkness. "No, sir. I heard from the ship's colour-sergeant that the Old Man—beg pardon, sir —Cap'n Soutter wants to speak to you about mortars." Payne knew all about the lieutenant-colonel; the marines were moaning like whores at chucking-out time. Beaky would love to hear about this little lot.

Door by door, with a weary-eyed marine sentry at each one to close it behind him and slam the clips into place, Jonathan felt the same surprise as always at times like these. How could all these people, officers, ship's company and an additional company of marines, be here with him? Apart from sentries, there was not a soul to be seen.

The weather greeted him like a bucket of icy water, and as he climbed higher he caught the down thrust of acrid smoke from the two funnels. Faintly against the black water and the great wedge of foam rolling back from *Reliant*'s tall stem he could just make out the pale outlines of guns, black swaying shapes in oilskins, loose gear flapping on the signal bridge. He groped his way through the bridge gate and would have fallen but for someone gripping his arm.

"No place fer soldiers, sir!"

Another said, "He's here, sir."

Reliant's upper bridge was vast when compared with a cruiser. There was a faint glow from the ready-use chart table as someone ducked out of its protective cover.

"Steer south-thirty-west, sir."

"Very well, bring her round." Another figure came across the slippery grating and touched Jonathan's arm. "Sorry to wake you up. There's a ship in trouble. *Ciudad de Palma*, Spanish. According to the navigator's estimate she's about seven miles away. As a neutral she should be showing some lights."

Jonathan waited, feeling the strength of Soutter's presence. He sounded preoccupied, rather than troubled.

A voice suggested, "All her power must have gone, sir."

"Come with me." The captain turned to another officer who was standing by the main compass platform. "I'll be in the chartroom."

"Sir."

Inside the chartroom everything seemed different yet again. The gently vibrating top of the large table, the slight rattle of pencils and dividers kept handy where they would not roll onto the deck.

"Here we are." Soutter darted him a searching glance for the first time. "I've just heard about your brother. A great pity."

"Yes, sir. He was in the *Aboukir.*"

Soutter picked up the dividers and said absently, "He must have known my brother then. He was lost too when she went down."

Jonathan stared at him as he crouched across the table. Was that how it was—how it had to be? As the sailors sang at Divisions, putting their own words to the familiar hymn: *We're here today and gone tomorrow . . .*

He frowned and concentrated on the last wedge of Spanish mainland, the end of Biscay, the neat pencilled crosses, bearings and course alterations. Hardly what you might have expected from the massive, bearded Lieutenant Rice, *Reliant's* navigator.

Soutter jabbed the dividers down. "About here then. Pass the word—half speed, please." The navigator spoke into a brass handset and Jonathan felt the vibrations lessen, the motion grow heavier as she reduced speed. Soutter looked up, his eyes very grey. "We were issued with a new Mason mortar before we left Portsmouth. Unfortunately nobody aboard has any experience with the damned thing." He smiled, his old-world face suddenly much younger. "I believe you know all about the beast?"

"Yes, sir. They can throw a much larger line than the others. We use them for moving equipment across ravines and high escarpments."

The captain looked away, but not before Jonathan had seen the upturned hint of a smile. He said, "I am sure Colonel Waring would approve."

How did he know about Waring? And how did he find the time to concern himself while this great ship revolved and shivered around him?

Soutter said, "I've ordered the gunnery officer to give you his best men. A midshipman will guide you there, and will

then act as a go-between." He gave a slight cough. "It seems
likely I may be busy."

Somebody hissed a warning but it was too late. A broad-
shouldered figure in a greatcoat, the protruding collar of his
pyjamas already sodden with spray as he stepped into the
open bridge, roared, "Just what the *hell* is going on here?" He
lurched about, blind in the streaming darkness. "Fetch the
Captain!"

"I'm here, sir."

Jonathan felt the midshipman touch his arm. "This way,
sir."

He hesitated as the admiral bawled, "I didn't order a
change of course!"

"A neutral ship in distress, sir. May already have gone
down—the wireless was a bit broken up."

Rear Admiral Purves still did not seem to believe it.

"Neutral ship? What about it? Let some other vessel go to
her aid!"

The answer was flat calm, like a mill-pond. "There are no
others, sir."

Purves had to shout to make himself heard, while around
the two unmatched figures the watchkeepers listened, fascinated or embarrassed as their fancy took them.

"When we get into harbour, Captain, we shall see about
this!"

"It's all in the log, sir. Every detail." He glanced across.
"Still here, Blackwood? Cut along, there's a good chap."

Reliant's fighting top and the forward turrets shone in a
green light as a rocket exploded far ahead. Soutter saw that
the admiral had gone. But it was by no means over. He said
to the bridge at large, "Maybe we're in time after all. Pipe all
hands and clear lower-deck, if you please, Mr Fittock, and
close all watertight doors!" He waited for the order to be

passed, then snapped open the red-painted handset and pictured the noise and heat of the great ship's engine-room, far beneath his scrubbed wooden chair.

"This is the Captain, Chief. I may need some oil presently. There's a ship adrift, no power. Might have to take her people off."

"Aye, aye, sir. What ship, by the way?"

Smatter told him, and heard the engineer-commander exclaim, "I know her! Runs between Barcelona and the Canary Islands. Usually carries a lot of passengers—too many, but ye know about these dago ships, sir!" The line went dead, leaving the Chief's hard Glasgow accent ringing in his ear.

"Prepare the main searchlights." He tried to imagine a U-boat and discarded the thought. Not down here. Not yet, anyway.

Lieutenant Howard Rice, the navigating officer, bent over the chart-table again. If anything went wrong. . . . He shook his head and put it out of his mind, his pencil already busy on the chart.

After this, he was not sure that he ever wanted a command of his own.

Jonathan Blackwood found the gunnery officer's selected crew already gathered beneath the doubtful shelter of the aftermost fifteen-inch turret. The deck seemed to be strewn with wires and jacks, coils of line and a massive grass-hawser.

A rotund figure in streaming oilskin peered at him through the pattering spray. "Wallace, sir, Gunner (T)." He looked at the stooping figures around him. "Careful with the deck planking, Parker! The Bloke will do you in if you cut that about!"

Jonathan smiled, strangely excited at the prospect of finding and passing a tow to the Spanish vessel. *The Bloke*. The lower-deck's nickname for the commander. He guessed that the Gunner (T), a warrant officer, had not been away from the mess-decks for very long.

Torches were held close to the long mortar. It might work, but an ordinary line-throwing gun was more reliable.

As if reading his thoughts the Gunner (T) said, "We're too big for this sort of lark, sir. We'll get one chance, you see, there'll be no time to bend on different sizes of hawser. We'd likely cut the poor bugger in 'alf!"

"What's going on? Oh, it's you, Blackwood. Why wasn't I told?"

It was Waring, of course. No wonder he got on so well with the rear admiral, he thought; he even sounded like him.

"The captain sent me here, sir. He's going to take the ship in tow." A thought crossed his mind. "You should have been called when they cleared lower-deck."

"Hmm. Well . . ." Waring sounded less sure. "Tell me about the ship."

Jonathan caught the strong smell of Scotch despite the wind and sea. Waring had probably been too far gone even to hear the calls and the bugle.

"*Light*, sir!"

A solitary red eye glimmered across the surging water. Someone must have managed to light one of the oil navigation lamps. It was unlikely that the Spanish ship had any other kind.

"How are you managing, old chap?" It was Commander Coleridge.

Jonathan smiled. *The Bloke.* "Getting it sorted out."

Coleridge saw Waring for the first time. "Morning, sir."

Waring grunted, "Is it?"

Jonathan said, "I don't know how reliable this thing will be." He watched the chief gunner's mate make a few alterations to the elevating gear, saw the sudden bustle of figures along the deck where the stout wire had already been laid out. "I've never done this sort of thing before."

Coleridge showed his teeth in the darkness. "Neither has the skipper, not with a ship this size."

"We're turning again, sir!"

Coleridge said to Jonathan, "We're going around the other ship to take her starboard side under our lee. The chief is ready to spread some oil." He became very serious suddenly. "We don't have very long."

"If it fails?"

The commander rubbed his chin. "We'll try again at daylight."

An old ship, probably in bad repair, no power, and with the seas breaking right over her: it was unlikely she would last until then.

The midshipman called, "I can see her, sir!" His youthful voice was shrill with excitement and several of the seamen grinned at one another. It was more of a sensation than an actual sighting. The red light vanished as the great battle-cruiser passed around her stern, and Jonathan caught his breath as he saw waves bursting against the stricken vessel's hull like breakers on a reef.

The midshipman called again, "Can't see the starboard light, sir!"

It was all getting on the Gunner (T)'s nerves.

"Didn't you learn *nothin'* at that swell college, Mr Blarney? We're still on 'er bloody quarter!"

The youth fell silent, completely crushed.

Then one of *Reliant*'s huge searchlights seared across the angry crests and settled on the other vessel.

A handset buzzed in its case and a messenger called, "From the bridge, sir! *Stand by!*"

Jonathan crouched down on the streaming planking and wondered what would happen if the mortar jammed. It might blow up. He thought suddenly of the girl in his dream. If only it were true . . .

He saw the searchlight moving across the listing ship, laying bare some fallen derricks, and a lifeboat dangling from the snapped falls like a broken toy. Surely they hadn't been trying to lower it in these seas? A signal lamp was flashing, and Jonathan could picture Soutter watching every move, counting the seconds while his great ship forged closer and closer to the other vessel. Perhaps the admiral was with him now, properly dressed, in control of his anger if only for appearances. There was no signal from the *Ciudad de Palma*, although the searchlight clearly showed several groups of people crouched beneath a crumpled bridge ladder, or amongst the fallen spars and rigging.

Waring plucked angrily at his moustache. "What the hell's the matter with them?"

Nobody replied, and Jonathan saw a woman waving something white towards the towering battle-cruiser.

Calls trilled and a voice boomed through a megaphone. "Turn out first and second whaler! Clear the quarterdeck!"

The chief gunner's mate said thickly, "'Ere's the firin' lanyard, sir." He looked at the other ship and said quietly, "If we lowers boats, sir, we'll lose a lot o' men ourselves!"

Jonathan said, "Take cover, lads."

They needed no second warning, but some wag called out, "We'll pick up the bits, sir!" Another shouted, "Up the marines!"

Jonathan said to the chief petty officer, "You can clear off. No sense in—" But the seaman with the communications handset yelled, "Bridge, sir! *Fire!*"

In those split seconds Jonathan saw it all. The soldiers of

the Home Counties regiment in France, accents and dialects he heard every day amongst his own marines. Bright eager faces lighting up in the drifting flares, making jokes, scared out of their wits; going up and over the parapet, *the horizon* as the old sweats called it; some falling straight back into the trench, their grins fixed and still while the rest had staggered on towards the wire and the chattering machine-guns.

He felt the Gunner (T)'s fist close over his and together they dragged at the lanyard. Nothing happened, and then with a bang and a searing flash the rocket lifted away from the ship, the wire racing out after it with the sound of tearing metal.

Old Wallace forgot himself and banged Jonathan hard across the back. "Bloody good shot, sir! Right up an' over the bugger!"

Hope in a storm at sea will do wonderful things for those who have seen all hope fade. Now figures were darting about the Spaniard's deck, seemingly oblivious to the leaping spectres of water which tried to drag them down, when moments earlier they had been unable to move.

"There goes the second line, sir!"

Figures were stumbling from cover to watch as the big searchlight held its grip on the listing hull, while Captain Soutter used engines and rudder to con his ship slowly past, and more men scampered along the deck to keep the towing hawser from fouling anything.

Jonathan felt his limbs shaking. Would he have fired but for the old gunner's hand on his? As Lieutenant-Colonel Waring had sarcastically commented, he had only been three weeks with the army in France. Was that all it took? He had heard the army officers actually joking about it, that the average life expectancy of a new subaltern at the front was six weeks.

Jonathan felt the deck lurch very slightly even as the other ship passed clear of the quarter, ready to take the strain on the hawser.

"What was that?"

Old Wallace gritted his teeth and imagined he could hear the clang of the bridge telegraphs.

"We've 'it somethin', that's what. Of all the perishin' luck!"

Jonathan and the others clung to the guardrail and peered at the frothing water from the great screws.

They were slowing down. The searchlight vanished as *Reliant* altered course very slightly. If she had not, the other vessel might also strike whatever it was and the tow would part.

Commander Coleridge rejoined him. "You go to the bridge, Jono. Let the professionals take over down here. That was damned good."

"What did the captain just say to you?" It was strange, but he could not recall being given a nickname before.

"Submerged wreck. Probably sunk while it was trying to help our new companion back there. Our port screw is badly damaged." He cocked his head. "Lucky there are no U-boats about—they'd hear us all the way from Berlin."

On the bridge it was as if nothing had happened. The navigator was bent over his hooded table, the yeoman of signals was trying to see the tow with his big telescope. Messengers, boatswain's mates, marine boy bugler, everybody was as he had left them.

Soutter stepped from the gratings, his binoculars slung around his neck. "Nice shooting, Blackwood." He took a cup from a passing tray and waited for Jonathan to do likewise. "It was a near thing."

The drink was hot and thick: pusser's kye, the sailor's favourite for watchkeeping. Cocoa with a good mixing of custard power. It stuck to your ribs, they said.

"Port outer engine stopped, sir! Remainder at seven-zero revolutions!"

"Hold her at that. Tell the wheelhouse, I shall know more in a moment." He replaced the empty cup and said, "Bad luck, really."

Jonathan stared in the darkness. He could have been remarking on a disappointing over at cricket. But in some way he felt the captain wanted him here: a stranger, a passenger even. All they had in common was their loss when the cruiser had been torpedoed off the Dutch coast. And now this.

"What'll happen next, sir?"

Soutter studied the sky. A few stars showed themselves through the fast clouds. Soon it would be calm, but too late.

"Dockyard job, I imagine. I'll make a signal to Flag-Officer Gibraltar but we'll have to wait until Malta for docking facilities."

"And the eventual attack on Turkey, sir?" It was still hard to accept what had happened. The searchlight, the roaring hiss of the untried rocket, the woman waving a white cloth.

Soutter said levelly, "Probably just as well out of it. I'd rather rescue a few souls at sea than waste my own people on the impossible." He seemed to regret his confidence just as quickly. "So cheer up, Blackwood. Come and see me when. . ." He broke off as a small figure in white overalls stained with oil and grease stepped into the bridge. "Well, Chief, what's the bill?"

Jonathan knew he should go, but knew if he did he would always regret it.

Engineer-Commander Donald Kinross peered around the open bridge as if he disliked what he saw.

"Port outer has gone completely, sir, and I fear the shaft

is in a bad way. I canna really tell until I can work on it some more."

"Malta, then?"

The chief watched him, wiping his hands on his overalls. "Aye. Gib'll no be any use for this big lady."

He turned to go, to rejoin his men in their sealed engine and boiler rooms. The most expensive coffins in the world, as the Chief Stoker had described to them.

But he said, "You canna leave people to die, sir. Nobody'll blame you."

"Other people do." His tone hardened. "Thanks, Chief."

The chief vanished down a ladder, muttering, "We're no' like other people!"

The officer-of-the-watch lifted his face from a voicepipe.

"No injuries in the ship, sir."

"Very well, Mr Fittock. Pipe cruising stations and tell the galley to prepare something hot. They shouldn't have to wait for their breakfasts."

A midshipman crept closer. "The admiral's compliments and would you see him at eight bells, sir."

"Hmm. Yes, thank you, Mr Cullen. Tell my steward, will you? I'll need to get polished up."

He sat back in his hard chair. "Gibraltar then." He touched the gently vibrating screen. "Not yet, my lady. Not yet."

THREE

Rear Admiral Theodore Keppel Purves strode past saluting sentries and marched through the headquarters building with Galpin, his flag-lieutenant, almost trotting to keep up. He was

so angry that he had found himself here without remembering any detail of the journey in *Reliant*'s smart barge, and he
stared around with distaste. Gibraltar was unusually chilly,
with the top of the Rock shrouded in mist and low cloud on
this day which could have been a great moment in his life,
and would have been, had it not been ruined by a stupid and
avoidable accident.

Purves was 48 years old, and so newly promoted to flag
rank that he had the world at his feet, or thought he had, but
for Soutter.

The better weather which had immediately followed the
storm had brought other vessels to the scene: two Spanish
warships and a powerful tug. An unusually heavy presence
for an insignificant steamship, he thought. *Reliant* had slipped
the tow, and with the exchange of a few vague signals they
had left the Spaniards to manage on their own.

Purves had seen Soutter privately in his quarters. It had
been an unfortunate meeting.

He felt his temper mounting anew when he recalled the
captain's impassive face, as he had told him that he would do
his best for him should there be a court of inquiry.

Soutter had remarked, "Like old times, sir." Then in a
harder tone, "I will stand by what I did. That ship would have
foundered without aid."

"Don't you realise, Captain Soutter?" Purves could hear
himself now, his voice rising by the second, oblivious to the
stewards listening from their pantries. "Our passage to Port
Said will be delayed because of this—because of *you*, damn
it!"

And so it would, no matter what happened to Soutter. The
fleet in the Eastern Mediterranean was going to attack the
Narrows and so destroy the Turkish batteries and forts which
were said to dominate the straits. With a fleet like that, backed

up by the French for once, nothing would stop them. There were some great names already at Mudros: the new battle-ship *Queen Elizabeth* with her fifteen-inch guns like *Reliant's*, the crack battle-cruiser *Inflexible*, which had proved herself already in her victory over von Spee off the Falklands. There was also a mixed collection of older battleships drawn from the Channel Fleet with destroyers converted to sweep for mines, plus all the necessary supporting vessels required for such a daring operation.

Purves stopped dead, so that Galpin almost bumped into him. "Well, *I'm* not taking the blame!"

Galpin started. "Quite right too, sir!"

A lieutenant came towards them and smiled. "Rear Admiral Purves, sir?"

Purves glared. "I am, and I wish to see—"

The lieutenant glanced at a clock. "Oh, yes, sir, but you have been so quick—not even a guard mounted for you—"

Purves waited, sifting through his words in search of sarcasm or as close to it as a mere lieutenant would dare, then he said, "I came ashore to see the flag-officer in charge. I do not have an appointment."

The man looked baffled. "Then you didn't know, sir? An invitation was just sent out to *Reliant* when she anchored."

Purves took a grip on his thoughts. "I left in something of a hurry."

"Well, come along, sir, he's waiting to see you. If you will follow me?"

Purves whispered, "What is the fool talking about, Galpin?"

"Apparently they were expecting you, sir."

Purves glanced at himself in an ornate mirror. Perfectly fitting uniform, the gold lace, one thick stripe and one thin, the oak leaves around the peak of his cap. An imposing figure, tall, broad-shouldered, with a face once handsome; a man's man with an eye for the ladies. In this war there was no saying what he might achieve. He recalled Soutter's quiet defiance. What kind of idiot at the Admiralty had caused their paths to cross again? *Like old times, sir.* We'll see about that, he thought.

The Flag-Officer Gibraltar was a full rank higher than Purves, a man who could be hard or easy-going as the situation demanded, who dealt impartially with everyone from dockyard workers to impatient captains whose needs were always a priority at this strategic fortress. Whoever held the Rock controlled the Mediterranean.

The vice admiral got up from his desk and shook Purves's hand. "By Jove, it's good to see you!" He took Purves's arm and guided him out into feeble sunshine where, beneath a broad veranda, the bay and dockyard were spread out like a giant model. "I see you have the water-lighter on your port quarter. Good thinking. Any enemy agent curious about *Reliant*'s reason for being here might otherwise get too close. The sea is clear enough hereabouts . . . that damaged screw would soon attract attention."

There was a huge telescope mounted on a tripod at the end of the veranda. *Reliant*'s entrance had been watched all the way.

The vice admiral smiled. "Cunning idea of yours to dismiss the tugs I had in readiness. One would never believe anything untoward had happened!"

Purves met his gaze. Was this a softening-up process before the hammer fell? The water-fighter and the refusal to use tugs had both been Soutter's ideas. He said flatly, "Would you mind telling me what this is about, sir?"

"Call me John—or Sir John if it makes you easier. Of course, you'll know nothing about it—I had forgotten. Here they've been talking of little else!" As the story unrolled Purves's mind reeled from the incredible to the impossible. The old *Ciudad de Palma* had gone to the assistance of a capsized coastal vessel, and herself had been smashed by the biggest waves her master had ever experienced. He had apparently given up all hope until *Reliant* had found them.

The vice admiral dabbed his eyes with his handkerchief and chuckled. "What we have since discovered was that one of the King of Spain's favourite nephews—a young rascal if you ask me—was on board, an unofficial passenger who makes a habit of this sort of escapade." A white-jacketed steward entered silently and began to lay out some glasses. But the vice admiral was still enjoying it, reliving it, and would tell all his friends later about Purves's utter consternation.

"Yes, my dear chap, a message from His Most Catholic Majesty Alphonso XIII no less, thanking the Royal Navy in general and you in particular! Whitehall will be extremely pleased. Things have not been too cordial in their dealings with Spain. Our ambassador was summoned by the king in person. . . . So what do you think about that? Can't do your future any harm at all, I'd have thought."

Purves swallowed the cool wine but barely noticed it.

"And now, old chap, this other thing you were coming to see me about." He rocked with silent laughter. "No wonder you had my staff on the jump!"

Purves put his glass down very carefully and watched the steward refill it. He was not certain whether to laugh and share his relief, or to tell the vice admiral about his clash with Soutter.

His voice was quite calm again as he said, "I thought it might save time, sir, if I discussed the docking arrangements at Malta?"

Then he sat back, relaxed again, in control. After all, if

you shared the blame, you might as well share the reward.

At dusk on the same day as her arrival, *Reliant* weighed anchor and moved into the calm waters of the Mediterranean. She had three destroyers as escorts, and even at her much-reduced speed she made a splendid spectacle as she turned and headed due east for the 990 mile passage to Malta.

Once the hands had been dismissed from their stations for leaving harbour, and the Royal Marine Band had gone through its entire repertoire of jaunty marches and old sea songs, most of them were unwilling to go below and miss the last sight of the Rock with its scattered lights glittering like fireflies in the sunset.

Jonathan stood by the davits of one of the whalers. He had been to Gibraltar several times, so that it gave him a strange feeling to hear the young marines of B Company calling excitedly to one another while they pointed at the fading shadow of the land. Pride at what they had helped to do, and above all the exhilaration of youth which even Waring's drills could not bridle for long. Very few of these marines had ever been out of England before; many had never left home until they had enlisted with the corps. But the rough seas of Biscay, the danger of collision, even the damage to their own ship was in the past now, something they had shared, and which in turn had drawn them closer together.

It was a fitting moment, he thought. Like the walls of Hawks Hill and the vivid painting of battles fought and lost, the Royals had been in so many campaigns, and yet the honour they displayed on their helmet plates and badges was *Gibraltar*, which they had taken from the enemy.

The street vendors and beggars would soon discover the youth and innocence of these marines when they reached Malta. Then what? On to Port Said as planned? Most of the officers seemed to think they would be too late for any action there. Some were genuinely anxious that they might miss it altogether, at least the bombardment.

He wondered what had really happened between Soutter and the rear admiral. Was everything as normal as it now appeared? Or were there still true differences?

He had seen the rear admiral walking along this same deck just minutes before weighing anchor. Amiable, speaking to seamen and marines alike, his fine cap tilted at the now-familiar angle, asking names, where they came from. It seemed to make quite an impression, but when he had passed Jonathan the smiles and the easy chatter had gone, as if it had all dropped off like a carnival mask.

A bugle blared from the bridge. *Men under punishment to muster.* Soon it would be calling the cooks to the galley, then supper throughout *Reliant's* crowded mess-decks. The sea routine of a capital ship. He tried to think of Port Said and what might be waiting there, but around him this great ship, now in total darkness, refused to release him. A lot of men scoffed at the idea that ships lived and had character. Jonathan was not certain what he believed.

He thought too of young Roger Tarrier, the colonel's youngest son. *As I once was.* He moved to the guardrail and stared at the gleaming water, moving so slowly, for this ship anyway.

But why? Because it was expected, because of duty or family pride; was that why he and others like Tarrier had followed the tradition?

"All on your own, Jono?" It was Coleridge. The Bloke. "Come down and have a gin. I can tell you about the King of Spain!"

Jonathan turned from the side, mystified by the remark.

But behind his back, the ship was still there. Waiting.

•   •   •

The damage sustained by *Reliant*'s port outer shaft was less than had been feared, but while the ship waited for the new propeller which was being sent with all haste from England, an almost holiday atmosphere prevailed. With the ship in dock, and the limited facilities the yard had to offer, local leave was the order of the day. There was not a street on the island where you would not run into men with H.M.S. *Reliant* on their cap tallies, or marines who saluted their officers with a kind of knowing smirk.

The weather improved, the sun shone, and but for the ranks of anchored troopships in Grand Harbour, their rigging adorned by endless khaki washing hung out to dry, the war seemed like part of another world. In the Eastern Mediterranean the assembled fleet had bombarded many of the Turkish defences, with some success according to the reports. But the channel was known to be sown with lines of anchored mines, of a German pattern which could be relied on to explode even if brushed by a passing vessel.

Despite the massive bombardment by the heavy ships, whenever minesweepers had attempted to enter the channel they had been deluged with heavy gunfire of every calibre, so that they suffered casualties and serious damage and achieved very little.

And all the while, the enemy were flooding the peninsula with reinforcements, guns, men, and engineer: who were said to be under the instruction of German field officers.

On March 18th the battle-cruiser, re-stored and with all repairs completed, moved out into the crowded anchorage with the aid of tugs, and was, as Commander Coleridge had said, "Ready for anything!"

Rear Admiral Purves left his hotel and rejoined his flagship. The band played, his flag broke at the masthead, and the soldiers who lined the rails of the troopers watched the ritual with wonder and frustration at their own enforced idleness.

The next day found *Reliant* steaming at half-speed with her escorts ahead and abeam, heading south-east by south, Malta and its cheerful markets and other temptations already far astern.

Jonathan was on the upper bridge with the watchkeepers, the nerve centre of any warship, looking down at the squads of marines who were lying prone on the forecastle, their rifles protruding a few inches over the side, waiting for the order to open fire as soon as the nearest destroyer released some of her makeshift targets. It was unlikely they would hit anything, but it made a welcome change from inspections, drills, and more inspections.

"Morning, gentlemen." Captain Soutter walked into the bridge and returned the commander's salute.

Lieutenant Rice, the navigator, carefully rolled away the cover from the chart-table and a boatswain's mate waited to repeat the captain's first order of the day, should he choose to give one.

They all waited for the captain to follow his usual routine but he stood quite still, one brown hand resting on the back of his tall chair, his eyes in deep shadow beneath the peak of his cap.

More feet on the bridge ladders, and then Lieutenant-Colonel Waring with the two other senior marine officers climbed into view, their faces as surprised as those of the watchkeepers.

Jonathan glanced round as Quitman the gunnery officer arrived; then lastly the engineer-commander, almost unrecognisable in his proper uniform with clean white cap cover, entered the crowded bridge and gave Soutter a casual salute.

He felt a sudden chill in his spine. Except for the pay-masters, and the many junior and warrant officers, these men were *Reliant*'s heads of department. What had happened? He could tell by the commander's expression that he was as much in the dark as the others.

Soutter turned to the yeoman of signals. "Pass the word, yeoman. I want all the bridge staff to pay strict attention to their duties. I will personally see anyone who fails, be it as lookout or as tea maker, at the defaulters' table."

Nobody smiled. In fact, when the first shots echoed up from the deck there was not even a blink. Jonathan thought how far away the rifles sounded.

Captain Soutter glanced around their tense faces and then said, "I thought you had all better know without delay. You can sift the information through your departments and parts of ship as you will, but better truth than rumour." He looked briefly at the rear admiral's white flag, crossed in red with its two bright balls as it strained out in the steady breeze, its cleanness made more obvious by the funnel smoke.

"I have just seen Rear Admiral Purves." There was no emotion in his tone. "I have to tell you that the attack on the Dardanelles, the minefields and Turkish forts, which was carried out yesterday, failed to crush the enemy's defences. Despite the gallant behaviour of our people and the combined efforts to force home the attack, the fleet was forced to with-draw." He looked up suddenly as two flags, an acknowl-edgement to one of the destroyers' signals, darted up the yard and then dipped again. Afterwards Jonathan recalled that glance. It was clear on his face like a shaft of real pain.

He continued. "The operation was costly. The battleships *Ocean* and *Irresistible* were both damaged by mines and shell-fire, and were subsequently lost. The French battleship *Bouvet* suffered the same fate, and their two battleships *Suffren* and

Gaulois received very severe damage and were put out of action. Our own fine ship *Inflexible* also struck a mine, but is thought to have been still afloat when this news was released." He glanced at his watch. "There will be other losses, gentlemen, and the minefields and the forts will still be there."

Coleridge exclaimed, "What will they do, sir?"

"They?" The smallest shrug, nothing more. "The Admiralty and the general staff will have to think again. And with each turn of our screws the Turks have more time to prepare. You all saw the troopships at Gibraltar and at Malta. They will have to storm the peninsula which still commands the Dardanelles. Down the years fighting sailors have achieved much. But until the British soldier, or—" he shot the captain of *Reliant*'s marines a glance, "the Royal Marines can plant their flag alongside their boots on enemy territory, there can be no victory."

"Orders, sir?" Coleridge looked dazed, shocked by the incredible losses in only half a day.

"No change, Commander. Port Said as before." He looked suddenly at Lieutenant-Colonel Waring. "You can call off the shooting gallery, Colonel." He saw the argument in the other man's eyes. "It's all right, you know—the admiral agrees with me." His voice had a sudden edge. "It seems likely we shall need all our ammunition before long!"

He gave a curt nod. Dismissal. But to Jonathan he said, "You stay here if you like." He climbed onto his chair and settled himself where he could reach his powerful binoculars. In a matter-of-fact tone he added, "You know, Blackwood, Nelson once confided that no wooden man-of-war could succeed against a properly sited shore battery. I don't suppose anyone listened to him either, until a costly lesson was learned."

Jonathan watched him, fascinated. This terrible news, which had shocked them all and which would go through the ship like a ball of fire, had somehow left the captain removed. He was already assessing it. Seeking solutions.

He asked, "May I ask what *you* think will happen, sir?"

Soutter turned easily in his chair, but did not reply directly. "I was reading the second part of your report, when you returned from France." Jonathan started. That part had been top secret, to give private scope to his own observations, with suggestions if he had had any to offer. Soutter smiled. "I see it in your face, Blackwood. All secret stuff. But I do still have a few friends." He shaded his eyes as a solitary gull floated around the masthead, its cry lost in the roar of *Reliant*'s great fans. "Another poor Jack," he remarked absently. Then he changed again. "You said in the report that you thought the terrible losses at the front were because nobody could accept stalemate, yes? That the general staff knew of no solution, no fresh tactics that would prevent such casualties. That was brave of you. I'll wager it raised a few temperatures in high places . . . Perhaps stalemate might be the solution after all. We are not fighting the Zulus or the Mahdi's fuzzie-wuzzies, and this is *not* the thin red line, either. The Germans are brave, resourceful and, it has to be said, well led for the most part. We on the other hand. . ." He shrugged. "Well, in answer to your question, I believe an all-out landing of troops will be considered, and very shortly too. A month or two ago, we could probably have taken and held the Dardanelles with 20,000 men." He sounded bitter and unusually angry. "But Lord Kitchener would not release more battalions from the Western Front when it might have made all the difference. Winston Churchill obviously believed in the strategy of it, or did, before these latest losses." Soutter leaned back in his chair, his cap tilted over his eyes. "You can cut along, Blackwood."

Jonathan smiled. What he had said that night when they had rescued the drifting steamship.

It was a strange bond between them, he thought, as he made his way down to the deck where two squads of marines were using their pull-throughs to clean out their rifle barrels.

A corporal called them to attention but Jonathan said, "Carry on—stand easy."

The corporal said, "Just heard, sir, about them ships. Terrible, innit? I got a mate in the old *Inflexible*. Hope he's all right."

A young marine called out, "When will us get a chance at them murderin' Turks, sir?" The corporal glared at him but said nothing.

They did not seem to mind talking with Jonathan, perhaps because he was R.M.A. and not R.M.L.I. like them. But they were all khaki marines now, as the old warrior had pointed out. In any case they all did the same basic training, and when required performed the same duties. It never occurred to Jonathan that they actually liked him. An officer with two V.C.s in his family, but one who could still stop and speak to them, or offer advice.

"You'll get your chance soon enough. Barlow, isn't it?" Something his brother had always impressed on him. Remember names; it's all they own in the corps!

The young marine flushed. It made him look about twelve.

Another asked, "Where's Port Said, sir?"

The corporal had had enough. "Never you mind, Petit! It's where we're goin' an' that's all you need to know!"

Jonathan smiled and walked on. So young and eager to fight, and yet most of them had no idea where they were going or why. After Malta and their first sight of the Rock their appetites for adventure and more foreign places were well and truly whetted. They probably thought it would be all camels and mysterious dancing girls in veils. If so, they were in for a shock.

He had glanced at Lieutenant Rice's charts on the bridge. About another 1,100 miles to go before they reached Port Said. At this economical cruising speed it would be another five days before *Reliant*'s big anchor splashed down. He thought of the other marine officers, most of whom were as junior as the men they commanded. It might be a good thing to become acquainted with them. He paused to watch a gull rise from the sea—another poor Jack, as the captain had remarked. Surely the spirits of dead sailors could find another form in which to reveal themselves, he thought.

Some seamen with paint pots and brushes passed him, so he turned away to conceal his face from them. Why should he get to know them? After Port Said he might never see them again. Like Soutter and this ship, it was an experience, nothing more.

High above his head, the captain was sitting in his small sleeping cabin abaft and just below the bridge. Somewhere he could snatch some rest, or in this case find a temporary haven from curious stares and the gritty taste of oil fuel.

His steward had provided some cold beef sandwiches and a chilled half-bottle of hock. He always knew. Never too much mustard, and always a perfect cut-glass goblet.

Soutter smiled to himself. The captain's perks. He thought too of the news from the Dardanelles. He knew many of the people who must have died by drowning or explosion when they had tried to force that narrow, deadly channel. He opened a drawer in his small desk and took out his leather-bound personal log. As he did so he saw his wife's photograph looking up at him from the silver frame he still carried. He lifted it out and placed it on the desk, searching her pretty English face for something—some hint, some warning. He had been expecting her that day when *Reliant* had commissioned, the proudest event for any captain, especially with a ship like this one. Nobody had said anything afterwards, not the members of Parliament who had been there nor the port admiral. He had seen a small girl in white silk being hustled away, the bouquet of flowers she had been going to present to the captain's lady still clutched in her hands.

Soutter had sent his steward Drury to the house they had been renting, but it was no accident or unexpected illness that he came back to report. There had been just a short letter.

Do not try to trace me. You have the ship you dreamed of. Now I must find another.

Another what? A separate life? A lover, whom she had been concealing from him during the first grinding weeks of the war?

But for this ship, he thought he might have gone out of his mind. *Daphne.* He glanced around the gently vibrating sea-cabin, angry and guilty that he might have spoken her name aloud. She had always seemed so pleased when he had returned home from whatever ship he was serving, and their lives had been so full for the weeks, or the days, before he went away again.

A lot of his contemporaries had married into the service, the daughters of senior officers. It never did any harm to marry somebody who already knew the navy's ways, the ache of long separations.

He had met Daphne at a reception in Hong Kong when he had been on the China station. A doctor's daughter who was staying with her parents there at the time.

What might happen if by chance they met?

He thought of his brother, who had died when the *Aboukir* had been torpedoed. "Treat her gently," he had said. "She's not like the others, you know. She's a proper person, not out of the mould like some."

Had that been what had made her leave him?

The handset buzzed and he picked it from its hook.

"Captain."

It was Quitman, who was in charge of the watch. "Signal for you, sir. Being decoded now. Top secret and Immediate."

Soutter looked at his untouched sandwich. *Reliant* even had her own bakery, and fresh bread was always available.

He pictured Quitman, very earnest and intense, a true gunnery officer.

Quitman said less confidently, "Shall I inform the admiral, sir?"

"Not yet. Have your assistant bring it to me first." He put down the handset and thought about Quitman, the words *Top secret* and *Immediate* standing out in his mind in huge red letters.

He glanced at her face and then thrust the picture into the drawer again.

The assistant O.O.W., Sub-Lieutenant Whittaker, entered the small cabin and stared owlishly at his captain. Soutter took the sealed folder and opened it with a silver paper knife, his grey-blue eyes moving along the signal flimsy printed in their chief operator's heavy hand.

Then he looked up and saw the young officer try to extinguish all curiosity. "My compliments to the commander, Mr Whittaker. Ask him to take over the bridge. I have to go aft to see the admiral."

Outside in the bright sunshine again Captain Auriol George Soutter, who hated his first name, paused to stare aft along his ship, past the four-inch guns and the long barrels of Y turret to *Reliant*'s unending white wake in a flat calm sea.

There was to be no visit to Port Said after all. *Reliant* was to alter course and head direct for the small island of Mudros where she would join the other ships of the bombarding squadron which had been repulsed so bloodily; and that was only yesterday.

His jaw tightened and he made his way down a steep ladder to the deck below.

He hoped Rear Admiral Purves would be satisfied. He was not going to be too late after all. Instead he, the ship and all her company were to be thrown right into the middle of it.

He saw some of the new marines drilling under a reedy-looking subaltern and remembered what Blackwood had written in his report.

But by the time he had reached the admiral's quarters right aft beneath the quarterdeck, his mind was clear of everything save what he must do. He was the captain, and nothing else could matter.

FOUR

"All present, sir." Captain Soutter glanced around the expectant faces, *Reliant*'s heads of department gathered here as they had that day at sea when he had told them of the losses in the Turkish minefields.

The main chartroom, large though it was, felt like an oven, and with the battle-cruiser lying at anchor even the modern fans and air ducts could do little to ease their discomfort.

Through the open scuttles Soutter could see the rocky out-thrust of Mudros Bay. What a god forsaken place, he thought. Now, crammed with troopships, large men-of-war and supply vessels, it looked more like a refuge than the launching point for an invasion. Ashore it was no better.

Tents in neat lines covered every available piece of ground along with hastily rigged field hospitals, red crosses on their sloping canvas roofs, machine shops and cook houses: an army preparing itself.

If only they could get back to sea, Soutter thought wearily. But week had followed week in this dreadful place, with only rumour to feed their hungry minds.

Now at least that was over. He watched the papers in the rear admiral's strong hands and saw Galpin, his flag-lieutenant, also staring at them as if to seek out his own fate.

Rear Admiral Purves stood quite still, his fingertips resting lightly on his papers, which he had now laid on the chart-table.

"Gentlemen, the day we have all been waiting for is almost upon us." His resonant voice carried easily above the sounds of fans and other ship noises. "At dawn in a week's time, on the twenty-fifth of April, the attack on the Gallipoli Peninsula will begin. The British Army will land at these points— V, W, X and Y beaches," he tapped the chart with a ruler, "at Cape Helles, led by the King's Own Scottish Borderers. Halfway along the peninsula the Australians will land at Gaba Tepe. That's where we come in." The ruler moved back again. "On the British right flank, the French division will be put ashore at S beach, Morto Bay."

Purves pulled out another sheet of paper. "The Royal Marines will of course be in full support." He waited as the marine officers grinned at one another, then said sharply, "We shall be taking part in the bombardment of Turkish batteries and forts, and anything else which might prove a real danger to our advance. The day after tomorrow the troopships will disembark their soldiers, who will be put aboard the escorting naval vessels without delay. *Reliant* will take on board another company or so of Royal Marines, contingents released from ships of the squadron." His eyes settled on Lieutenant-Colonel Jack Waring's sun-reddened face. "As senior R.M. officer you will naturally be in command."

Waring brushed his moustache with one finger and gave a fierce grin. "Proud, sir. Very!"

Soutter saw Purves watching him. "Sir?"

"Anything you'd like to add? I know the *ship* is in good hands!" He laughed, but there was no warmth in it.

Soutter said, "We shall be towing extra boats when we leave here, as will other ships in this section. Picket boats will be used to tow the unpowered craft once they have left the safety of the ships." He saw an unspoken question on the navigating officer's bearded face. "We shall remain a thousand yards offshore, although it is quite likely that the marines will not be ordered into the attack at that early stage."

Captain Jonathan Blackwood was right at the back of the silent figures. He could feel the marine officers' disappointment at Soutter's last remark. The marines were keen enough, but like their young platoon commanders they had almost no experience. Some of the older N.C.O.'s could be relied on, but Soutter's words were still fixed in his mind. A thousand yards offshore, at best in pitch darkness, at worst in sunlight like this under the sights of those same Turkish batteries. If Waring had any doubts he did not reveal them.

A few questions came from the various officers, but they were mainly concerned with individual departments. Quitman the gunnery officer wanted to know if they would have any spotting aircraft. Purves replied that there might possibly be two; more he could not say. He sounded as if he thought Quitman's concern was a waste of time.

Purves said abruptly, "Our job is to get the troops ashore and keep Johnny Turk's head well down until they're safely in position. I am sure that the army staff will know exactly what they're doing."

Reliant's captain of marines asked, "What about the possibility of German submarines being sent through the Mediterranean to support their ally?"

Purves glanced meaningly at the clock. "It would take weeks, even if they could get here. By that time the fleet will have forced the Dardanelles and then on to Constantinople, what?"

He paused on his way to the door. "Remember at all times, gentlemen, this is the flagship, *my* flagship, and I want—no, I *demand* that each and every officer behaves accordingly!" They parted before him as he strode stiffly out.

Soutter beckoned to Lieutenant-Colonel Waring.

"May I make a suggestion, just in case your people should be required?"

Waring looked at him coldly. "I am banking on it, sir!"

"Then forget the present arrangements in the various contingents. They will all be under your command. Why not mix the younger marines among the more experienced ones?"

Waring seemed to enjoy it. "As you say, Captain Soutter, all under my command. I think I can be relied upon to handle such matters!"

Soutter saw Coleridge looking for him and snapped, "Then do as you damn well please!" He walked away, his back turned to hide his anger, with himself as much as with Beaky Waring.

There was a burst of cheering from beneath the bridge. It was through the whole ship already. Soon every man on the island would know.

Jonathan moved to follow the others but Waring blocked his way. He had heard some of the exchange between colonel and captain, and could guess the rest.

"Ah, Blackwood. I shall want you to take over as adjutant. With all these extra men I want someone with a bit of seniority. They don't know you like their own officers, and I think that's all to the good. Get familiar with them and they take advantage, and any kind of softness I will not tolerate." He seemed to expect some sort of argument, but when Jonathan remained silent he said, "The admiral was right. This is the flagship. People will be looking to us!"

That night, his head throbbing from excitement and heavy drinking in the mess, Jonathan climbed to the upper bridge in search of some cooling breeze from the sea. The bridge was only shadow, the superstructure and funnels merely darker shapes against the thousands of tiny stars. He could hear the muted stammer of Morse from the wireless room, the occasional scrape of feet from a lookout or the duty signalman. A door slid open and shut and he heard the commander's shoes on the scrubbed gratings, which would soon be baking in the sun again.

"Can't you sleep, Jono? That was quite a party! Like peacetime again." He laughed and felt for his cigarette case in his mess jacket. Then he stared across the screen to where a hospital ship lay like a phantom in her white livery. "That couldn't be thunder, could it? That would just about put the lid on any landings."

Jonathan climbed up beside him, glad of the darkness.

"No. Not thunder." He remembered the bombardments in France: on and on, until he could neither think nor even be afraid. It had been beyond even fear. "It's guns. Our ships or their coastal batteries." It was like a threat, a terrible warning. Someone had told him that in southern England on quiet nights, they could hear the roar of artillery from the Western Front.

He thought of Rear Admiral Purves, of Beaky Waring and

the captain, recalling Soutter's comment that the peninsula could have been seized and occupied with few casualties if they had not delayed so long, and the reinforcements from France had not been denied him.

He was reminded of this fine ship's crest and motto: *We will never give in.* He spoke aloud.

"So be it then." But when he looked, the commander had gone, his cigarette still unlit.

In his mind he saw Hawks Hill as it had been in that dream, with the girl dipping bare feet in the stream. But there was no stream just there.

He found that he could still smile, despite the far-off thunder. No girl either.

The mood quickly passed. Nor would there be, after all this.

It was midnight, with just a gentle offshore breeze to fan the faces of the officers and men on *Reliant*'s upper bridge.

Captain Soutter was in his chair, his shoulders swaying only slightly to the ship's slow, corkscrew roll; he could have been asleep. Commander Coleridge stood on the opposite side, close to the hooded chart-table from which Lieutenant Rice's considerable buttocks made a hump against the pale paintwork. Like interlopers, Lieutenant-Colonel Waring and Jonathan Blackwood, his new adjutant, watched the sea beyond the bows. The ship might have been steaming quite alone on some vast ocean: it was almost unnerving to realise that she was only a part of the fleet of transports and their escorts heading towards the Gallipoli Peninsula. Between decks *Reliant* had somehow absorbed all the extra marines who had arrived from other ships, as well as two companies of soldiers of the Australian Infantry. Despite the overcrowding and a cheerful rivalry between the Australians and the

Royal Marines they had made the most of their time on board. If needed, they would disembark under cover of darkness and transfer to the clutter of boats towing astern of every major warship in the fleet.

This tense stillness contrasted starkly with the very moving moment when they had weighed and steamed slowly from Mudros Bay. As they had passed abeam of each waiting transport and her mass of waving khaki figures, *Reliant*'s Royal Marine Band had formed a smart square on the quarterdeck, and after playing the national anthem of all the allies had broken into some lively marches, to the obvious delight of the madly cheering soldiers.

Jonathan had snatched a few moments' rest during the day, although like most of the officers he had given his quarters to the soldiers. Now, in retrospect, it seemed like another ship. The troops were being mustered by their own officers, sections checked and checked again.

After leaving Mudros *Reliant* had steamed west and around the island of Lemnos as part of a deception to confuse the Turks before the final rendezvous was made.

It was one of the few occasions on which Soutter had displayed his anger.

"What kind of 'deception' is that? Most of these troops have been transferred from Egypt. The Turks will likely know the exact strength of every regiment!"

The navigator had told Jonathan quietly that the Turks would know anyway; they would have calculated that the attack would come between the waning of the old moon and the rising of the new. He recalled Rice's white teeth grinning through his beard as he had added, "The Royal Navy isn't the only one with navigators, you know!" There was something very reassuring about the massive, bear-like lieutenant.

He shivered, and yet his spine was wet with sweat. He

probed his feelings. Fear, then? But he felt nothing, only the old need to get a move on, for better or worse.

He had watched the ship's own midshipmen, and there were fifteen all told in the gunroom ranging in age from children to self-possessed young men, who waited the chance for examination and promotion to sub-lieutenant. The first proper step up the ladder. They had stained their white uniforms into something like khaki, and were hung about with revolvers and water bottles, which only made them look younger.

He wondered about the other ships: some were said to be carrying horses and mules. That at least seemed like a note of confidence. Somewhere astern was another battle-cruiser, H.M.S. *Impulsive*, the sister ship of *Inflexible*, which had struck a mine on that first attempt to force the Narrows. Seven years older than *Reliant*, with eight twelve-inch guns of the former design, her captain had nonetheless boasted that his was the best gunnery ship in the fleet. Jonathan had heard little about *Impulsive*'s Captain Vidal, other than that he was known as an iron disciplinarian and had been a midshipman in the same class as Soutter.

Soutter stirred. "Have all the soldiers been fed again?"

Waring said, "Yes," curtly. It sounded like "Of course."

Somebody whispered, "The admiral's comin' up, sir!"

Soutter slid from his chair and turned as Purves and his flag-lieutenant loomed into the darkened bridge.

Purves looked around, picking out shadowy figures and their immediate functions.

"I have had a signal from the flag." He sounded angry and subdued.

Soutter said, "So we're not going in after all, sir?"

Purves must have known that everyone was listening but did not care.

"The Australian Infantry are to go on their own and join up with the rest of their division on the beaches. They all know what to do." He suddenly exclaimed, "God damn it, Captain, what about our marines?"

Waring bobbed forward. "*We're* ready, sir! Just give the word!"

Purves stared across the screen, seeking a place where the sea joined the sky, but it was still too dark.

Soutter said, "Perhaps Admiral de Robeck believes they are too inexperienced."

Purves almost choked. "What about these damned colonials then? Rounding up sheep is more in their line, I'd have thought!"

"Ready to alter course, sir."

"Very well." Soutter sounded almost disinterested. He did not even turn as the order was passed down to the wheelhouse, and a whiff of funnel smoke alone betrayed the change of course.

Jonathan moved closer. It was much as he had expected; hoped perhaps. The marines he had spoken to were trained to the hilt for barracks or parade ground, but they were not the hard men his brothers had known and led or those he had seen in action himself. It took time. But there was no time. The doubting was over. It was now, for the soldiers anyway.

Purves said in a more level voice, "*Reliant* will remain ready to offer covering fire if needed, as will *Impulsive*."

A boatswain's mate stood back from a voicepipe. "Permission for tea to be brought up, sir?"

Purves glared and strode to the ladder.

Soutter smiled privately. Purves had probably gone to get something stronger. He had not done too badly already.

"Permission granted."

Waring strode about, his boots clicking on the wooden gratings.

"Waste of time! My men will perform as well as anybody!"

Jonathan watched him warily. "Shall I tell Major Livesay, sir?"

"*No.*" He stared at the captain's chair. "I shall reserve that pleasure!"

Soutter said, "I'm not happy about slipping the tows. The time has been altered to four-thirty. That's about four hours' time right, Pilot?"

Rice sounded surprised. "It'll be nearly daylight."

"Another point which someone in high places has missed. We're now ordered to slip the tows at three thousand yards, not one."

Lieutenant Fittock, who was officer-of-the-watch, said helpfully, "Maybe the big ships would present too good a target, sir?"

"I hope the soldiers appreciate that." Soutter came to a decision. He touched the commander's arm and said quietly, "I'm going down for a shave. You know what to do."

"Aye, sir. Main and secondary armament stand to, then clear lower-deck. The landing parties can assemble aft and amidships. They've got quite used to it. Then at first light the people will go to action stations."

"And then?"

Commander Coleridge heard the muted cries of army N.C.O.'s and the sudden clatter of weapons being gathered so that they would require no further sorting. "Sir?"

"*Then* you can tell the chief yeoman of signals to hoist battle ensigns."

He seemed to notice Jonathan for the first time, and smiled. "Can't you stay away, Blackwood?" He became serious and confidential. "You go around the marines yourself when—"

Jonathan thought he was about to add, "When Waring's finished." But Soutter said, "Try to keep their spirits up." He turned sharply as some of the Australian soldiers broke into a wave of laughter. "You know how it is." He moved to the inner ladder and Jonathan asked, "Are we going to be needed after all, sir?"

For a brief instant he imagined he had tested their relationship too far. Soutter was staring at him in the darkness. Then he answered, "You never doubted it, did you?" and was gone.

Later, as Jonathan walked though the crowded mess-decks where the marines were huddled amongst their carefully prepared kit, he felt their disappointment like something physical.

One looked up and asked, "Why not us, sir? We're as good as them Aussies any day!"

Jonathan gripped his belt until the pain steadied him. *Are you so eager to be killed before you've learned properly how to defend yourselves?*

He spoke slowly and saw others pressing closer to hear him. "It is out of our hands. But we are Royal Marines, and must be ready *at all times.*" He saw their eyes watching bleakly. He was doing no good. "If we are called . . ." He hesitated and knew that the wrong word now would he seen as deception; and if Soutter was right, they would need to trust each other in a way they had never known before. "We will stand together, because that is our way." He nodded to one of the sergeants and tried to place his name. "I want our men at the guardrails when the boats are cast off. Let them know we are all proud of them." He waited, feeling the sudden tension around him. "For after today, many of those same men will be gone forever."

The mess-decks were still silent as he walked away, until

the blare of a bugle and the trill of calls between decks brought them to their senses again. They seemed stunned, as if their lives were no longer in control, and something enormous and terrible was about to take over.

Rear Admiral Purves, slumped in the captain's bridge chair, rested his chin in one hand while the watchkeepers stood restlessly around him.

He said, "Time?"

The navigator replied, "Two-thirty, sir."

Captain Soutter levelled his binoculars over the screen and stared into the darkness. The ships astern and abeam had already turned in one huge arc in a south-easterly direction towards the peninsula and yet the sea could have been empty.

Purves leaned over the arm of the tall chair. "Better get on with it."

Soutter moved nearer to exclude all the others in the crowded bridge. "Another half hour, sir?" He was almost pleading. "The boats will be overloaded as it is."

Purves leaned back in the chair and said, "The sea's good and there's been no sign of trouble. Keep to orders."

Soutter clenched his fists in the darkness. "Stop engines."

After a moment or two the four great screws stilled and the ship tilted uneasily, like a wild animal sensing danger.

Soutter said, "Carry on, Tom."

The commander waited, wanting to help, but very aware of the admiral's brooding shape.

"Aye, aye, sir."

On deck he found most of the marines silently observing the carefully rehearsed operation as the way went off the great ship. The boats were warped alongside where the troops waited in squads and sections, their officers moving amongst them to pass final instructions.

Coleridge found the senior army officer and they shook hands without any emotion. Jonathan Blackwood watched as the first troops clambered down the prepared wooden ladders and into the waiting boats. Just a few jokes in the darkness, a grin or a handshake for friends about to be separated, the dull clink of muffled weapons. A few of the marines called down to the pitching boats, "Keep yer 'ead down, chum!" and "See you in the pub!"

Lieutenant-Colonel Waring strode along the deck and barked, "Can't you keep these people quiet?" He jabbed at someone with his stick. "Take that man's name!"

A marine corporal muttered, "Stupid prick!" Then he saw Jonathan beside him and stared at him anxiously.

Jonathan turned away. Embarrassed or angry? Probably both.

Then very slowly the boats were allowed to drift astern until they formed dark clusters on their tow lines, the steam pinnaces already puffing smoke as they prepared to take over the work as soon as the prescribed position was reached.

Jonathan felt the deck tremble and watched as the over-loaded boats fell further astern until they were moving safely after the parent ship. Hidden in darkness other ships, men-of-war and transports would be doing the same, preparing their armada of small boats: David and Goliath.

Coleridge put down a deck telephone and remarked, "The Old Man's not pleased." He saw Jonathan's uncertainty, or sensed it. "Come up with me—we'll not be opening fire until daylight. I think the captain likes to have you around. No strings, you see?"

They reached the upper bridge as orders were repeated or passed down to other parts of ship.

"All engines slow ahead, sir, revolutions seven-zero."

"Course south-fifty-east, sir." That was Rice.

Below the bridge, the director control with its powerful range finders and gun sights squeaked slightly and swivelled towards the port bow. Like a giant medieval helmet, Jonathan thought, inside which Lieutenant John Quitman and his team were preparing their three main turrets, to support an advance or to cover a retreat. To a gunnery officer like Quitman it was not emotion but arithmetic that would win the day.

A signalman said in a hushed tone, "Land, sir! Dead ahead!"

Soutter raised his glasses. It was more of a hint than something solid. But he had studied his charts well, with Rice at his side. He had formed a true picture of what awaited them. A grim line of hills with more beyond them, crisscrossed with ridges and gullies now merely vague shapes outlined by the remaining stars.

Each minute felt like an hour, and when a man coughed or dropped something the others glared at him, hating the interruption of their innermost thoughts.

Purves said casually, "We can slip the tows now, I think."

Jonathan was standing just behind the chair and could sense his anxiety. It seemed to hang over him along with the smell of whisky.

Soutter did not turn. "Too early. Another half hour—right, Pilot?" As he walked to the opposite side of the bridge he said, "Remember what you said about orders, sir."

The time dragged on, the ship barely moving, or so it appeared. The stars continued to fade, and far ahead in deeper shadow the land waited, crouching. Yet there was no sound, no sudden alarm. The chief yeoman trained his big telescope like a gun and remarked, "Maybe they're all asleep."

"Time, sir!"

Soutter walked to the bridge wing and peered astern. "Tell the quarterdeck. Slip the tows."

There was no confusion as obediently the boats fell away, forming into their own separate flotillas with every pinnace towing four hulls, each of which was crammed with khaki figures. In the powerful lenses Soutter could see the pinnaces forging ahead but seemingly still stationary. The boats under tow were so overloaded that they appeared to have hardly any freeboard.

"Director control, sir!"

Soutter walked to the forepart of the bridge and took a telephone from the boatswain's mate.

"Captain. What is it, Guns?"

Quitman's voice sounded tinny. "I can see the land quite well, sir. Three thousand yards. All quiet."

He handed it to the seaman and said to Rice, "A nice piece of navigation. Right on the pin!"

Rice showed his teeth but leaned under the chart-table's hood to hide his thoughts. The Old Man rarely praised anyone for doing his job. It was what they were here for, something he expected. So he was worried about something.

"Gunners' party request to start hoses, sir?"

"Granted."

On either side-deck from forward to aft they had already laid out endless curls of leaking hose. When the water was pumped through them then it would trickle across the immaculate planking, which might otherwise shatter to splinters when the big guns opened fire. The decks were sun dried, like tinder. The commander would have something to say if that happened.

Soutter was at the compass. "Alter course, Pilot, steer south-ten-west." He watched one of the pinnaces as it appeared to turn away when *Reliant* altered course, twisting in the dull light like an unmanoeuvrable snake. *Too slow. Too slow.*

He heard someone by the big searchlight give a quiet cheer and looked up to see the huge curling shapes of the extra white ensigns, paired at each masthead and at the gaff.

She must make a brave sight, he thought. He heard the admiral remark, "Well, it's up to them now." Nobody answered.

Jonathan took a pair of binoculars and peered astern. He could see the other battle-cruiser *Impulsive*, her long guns already trained to port where the land rose and fell in a hard undulating line. Other ships were beginning to appear too, some elderly River Class destroyers spaced out ahead and abeam. They were all converted for minesweeping, but looked somehow vulnerable against the land's menacing backdrop. Much further to seaward, and only because of her white hull, he could just make out the one hospital ship which had been selected for this section of the landings.

Soutter looked round as Second Lieutenant Tarrier all but pitched headlong through a bridge gate.

Tarrier found Jonathan and said breathlessly, "Colonel Waring's compliments, sir, and would you see him about arranging a kit inspection for all contingents?"

Soutter said dryly, "Your colonel's making quite a name for himself."

Jonathan found he could smile as he recalled the corporal's angry comment. "I think he is, sir."

Soutter smiled too and afterwards Jonathan remembered it. Like conspirators, he thought.

"Firing, sir!"

Purves twisted round. "What? Where?"

Then they all heard it, the crackle of rifle fire, the urgent stammer of machine-guns.

Jonathan heard Soutter say, "In the log, Pilot. Our people are ashore."

Rice pulled one of his many pencils from his pocket. He said, "Four fifty-three exactly."

Jonathan watched them, recalling the soldiers in France. Synchronising their watches, discussing it calmly like the captain and his lieutenant. They could have been commenting on the arrival of a train.

Purves said, "Take up our bombarding position. Make to *Impulsive: follow father.*" But his voice was humourless.

Jonathan knew that the battleships and battle-cruisers would each take their selected positions for targets already clearly defined. They would lay down a barrage whenever requested, from a range of 10,000 yards. It would certainly demoralise the enemy and perhaps give the troops time to dig in, even drive the Turks from any commanding positions on high ground.

He saw the two forward turrets moving smoothly, the four long barrels rising and dipping slightly as Quitman and his spotting officer prepared to fire their first bombardment in anger. *Reliant's* main armament could drop a salvo at the rate of six tons a minute on a target at twice the agreed range. It was a sobering thought.

He raised the glasses again. The light was a little brighter, but coming from the east it held the shore and the beaches in darkness. But there was already haze over the water and it was impossible to see what was happening.

Soutter said, "Send the hands to breakfast in watches. A good meal. Then pipe Up Spirits. I know it's early, but I am sure that Rear Admiral Purves will agree." He faced the admiral like an antagonist. "Fight on a full belly—it's Jack's way, eh, sir?"

Purves twisted his neck to listen to the firing ashore. It had intensified within the half hour. The Australians and their New Zealand companions were in action.

He said gravely, "A foothold on enemy territory, gentle-men!"

Jonathan touched Tarrier's arm and felt him jump as if he had been shot. "Come along. I expect my man Payne has already magicked up something for us."

He saw the marine boy bugler moistening his lips as he prepared to sound the stand-down.

It was amazing, Jonathan thought as they clattered down the ladder. Breakfast and an unexpected tot of rum, Jack's way as Soutter had remarked; steaming along into the hazy shafts of first sunlight, and picking their way over the trick-ling hoses while the big battle ensigns streamed out in the breeze. And after that, a kit inspection for all the marines. Names to be taken, Waring poking any untidy gear with his stick no doubt. He stopped by a guardrail as the deck quiv-ered to a sudden increase of revolutions. It was like madness, the very normality of it. And all the time, just over there, men were fighting and dying. Bullet and bayonet; no quar-ter for either side.

"What is it, sir?" Tarrier was watching him, his eyes fill-ing his face.

"I was just thinking. It's like leaving them behind. They've come all this way to fight and now we're leaving them." He shook his head. "But I expect somebody, somewhere, knows what he's doing."

But he thought of Soutter's face when his request to close with the shore had been denied. He had been ashamed too.

"I'm glad I've been seconded to you, sir." So simply said. *So young.*

Jonathan touched his arm again. "You may not be later on. Now come on and have breakfast, then we can all really enjoy the kit inspection!"

As the bugle blared its orders watertight doors and hatches

opened and men streamed out, blinking in the sunshine and the glare from the placid water.

The tension was no more: the talk for the most part was of the extra tot of rum. It had already become a direct order from the admiral.

Faintly, but without a lull, the firing continued until it was lost completely in the roar of *Reliant*'s fans.

FIVE

For two whole days the battle-cruisers *Reliant* and *Impulsive*, like the other ships of the bombarding squadron, moved slowly up and down the embattled peninsula, the air cringing to the deafening roar of their broadsides.

News of success had come with a laconic message from the Australian major-general ashore. He had stated that despite the large number of casualties when his men had splashed and struggled up the beach, the first Turk to receive a Dominion bayonet had died within half an hour of landing.

The firing had been almost continuous, and it was known that the Turks were rushing in reinforcements and heavier guns to block any further gains.

It had become almost impossible to move casualties out to the hospital ship and other transports by day because of enemy artillery, so the work was done at night, each pain-laden boat groping through the darkness until they could find a refuge for the wounded.

Jonathan Blackwood had sensed a change amongst the young marines. From the initial excitement and comradeship their mood had become resentful and bitter. Lieutenant-

Colonel Waring had already carried out his threat to punish any insubordination without mercy. At the end of the second day as cease-firing was sounded on bugle and turret-gongs alike, Jonathan could feel the hostility all around him as the marines stumbled out into the dying sunlight. For during action stations, and because the majority of the marines had no proper shipboard duties, they had been confined to the sweltering mess-decks with watertight door and scuttles tightly sealed around them. At best they were sent in small sections to join the damage-control parties; at worst they sat and stared at the deckhead as the hull shook and quaked to the roar of guns, and smoke filtered amongst them to remind them of their useless isolation. It was a wise precaution however. One small Turkish shell had exploded against the port side and blasted a whaler to fragments in its davits. Two seamen had been cut down by flying splinters, and Jonathan had seen the startled exchange of glances amongst his men until the wounded sailors' cries had faded into the bowels of the ship.

He stood and sucked in the evening air, watching the forward guns returning slowly to their fore-and-aft position, their long muzzles burned and blackened by the heavy firing. A few seamen were digging out shell splinters from the deck where *Reliant* had received those first casualties, one of whom had since died.

Despite the Turks' counterattacks and their fanatical determination to drive back any sort of advance, *Reliant*'s role in the bombardment must have played a tremendous part in forcing the enemy if not into retreat then under cover, where they could do no harm to the stream of men and supplies being landed on the shell-torn beaches. Each of *Reliant*'s big fifteen-inch shells contained 20,000 bullets, and throughout the bombardment the distant hills and gullies beyond had smoked and erupted like volcanoes coming to life.

Jonathan climbed slowly to the upper bridge while the grimy sailors stood down from their secondary armament, exchanging white grins in stained faces: they looked shaky and dazed, and he was not surprised. The constant roar of guns, even when you were not on the receiving end, seemed to curdle a man's brains. How much worse for the enemy, he thought.

The atmosphere on the bridge seemed relaxed by comparison. The admiral was leaning against the side, his binoculars following a series of vivid flashes on a hillside. Soutter sat on a step, his uniform dappled with paint flakes like snow. The others reached out gratefully for fresh tea as it was hauled through the bridge gates. Jonathan glanced at the sun-reddened faces, the regular British sailor in each one of them, contemptuous of every other nation's bluejacket.

Soutter sipped his tea and half listened to Lieutenant Rice speaking into the wheelhouse voicepipe. He saw Jonathan and waved the tea fanny towards him.

"Warm work, Blackwood. You should have been up here—the fleet really hit the enemy where it hurt."

Jonathan contained his reply by sipping the tea, which was scalding hot despite its meandering journey from the galley. He had wanted to be here, but it had been necessary for him to be with his men, to show them he was sharing it.

Uncannily, Soutter seemed to read his thoughts. "Hard, was it? I can understand how they feel."

Purves said harshly, "God, look at that mad fool!"

It was one of their own steam pinnaces, and through the binoculars Jonathan saw it zigzagging wildly in what appeared to be a great hail storm, but he knew the hail was rapid fire from a cleverly sited machine-gun. A destroyer glided through the smoke and after firing at the shore at what seemed like point-blank range allowed the pinnace to resume its journey.

"Senior officer on board, sir!" That was the chief yeoman.

Purves snapped, "What sort?"

The yeoman lowered his glass and added heavily, "There's some wounded as well."

Soutter said, "Inform the chief boatswain's mate. Tell the surgeon to have his crew ready." He glanced at the bearded lieutenant. "Slow ahead." He crossed stiffly to the compass, like a man who had not moved for hours.

"Port ten. Steer south-seventy-east."

Rice passed the order and watched the ticking compass. "Midships, steady." Unlike a smaller warship the wheelhouse was deep down behind heavy armour, and Jonathan could barely hear the man's acknowledgement up the bell-mouthed pipe.

He felt the ship slowing down, her superstructure and funnels like painted bronze in the sunset.

Down on deck he could see the party already gathered to take the pinnace's lines, and the surgeon's white coat as he gestured to some men with stretchers.

The yeoman said, "One of the wounded is Mr Portal, sir."

Soutter acknowledged it, his head cocked while he listened to the beat of engines. The face formed in his mind. A cherubic midshipman with freckles. He had celebrated his sixteenth birthday when they had been in Malta.

The yeoman added, "Don't recognise none of the others, sir."

Soutter said, "I think *you* should see the midshipman, sir."

Purves seemed uneasy. "Why? I'm the last person on earth that young man will want to see just now."

Without looking Soutter knew the boat had at last reached

Reliant's side. Just in time. It would soon be too dark to see anything.

"When they've hoisted the boat resume course and speed, Pilot." He turned his back to the rear admiral. "He is the only one of my officers who has seen anything at close quarters, and besides . . ."

"He may not live, is that what you were going to say?"

"Something like that."

"Hooked on, sir!" There were far-off shouts and the squeal of calls as hands were piped to secure the pinnace once it had been hoisted to its tier.

Commander Coleridge appeared from the shadows. "Will I take over, sir?"

Soutter glanced at his admiral. "Yes. I shall go."

Jonathan watched the rear admiral but he said nothing.

Soutter said, "Come with me, Blackwood. It may be useful." Down on the wet decks where the leaking hoses were still doing their work he added, "I'll just speak with our visitor." He introduced himself to a tall soldier who wore a bush hat and a colonel's rank on his filthy uniform. "Rear Admiral Purves is on the upper bridge." He beckoned to a midshipman. "This officer will take you to him."

The soldier looked around as if he could not believe *Reliant*'s air of peace and orderly routine.

"My God." He spoke quietly. "So this is the ship that was pounding those bastards for us!" He sounded all in, beaten.

Soutter said, "I shall not be running any boats tonight. We're taking up our cruising station with *Impulsive*." His arm shot out. "This man will take you to my quarters aft when you have done with the admiral. My steward will look after you."

Jonathan could sense the soldier's torn emotions as a distant explosion echoed against the ship.

Soutter asked abruptly, "How is it going, Colonel Ede?"

The man stared at him through the gloom. "You know me, Captain?" When Soutter said nothing he shook his head. "It isn't."

He glanced at the stretcher bearers as they vanished into the superstructure. Jonathan thought he might be comparing them with his own casualties.

Soutter persisted, "What does the general say?"

The colonel touched the midshipman's arm. "Lead on, sonny!" He was obviously eager to meet the admiral, more so perhaps to find some brief sanity in the captain's quarters. He began to move off and replied calmly, "He's gone; they've all gone. I'm in command now."

He vanished after the midshipman's white patches and Soutter remarked, "I wonder how the other beaches are getting along."

Jonathan followed him through a steel door into the ship's warm interior and her familiar, oily smell.

The sick-bay was ablaze with light, the white-enamelled cots swaying very easily as the ship headed on her new course.

Soutter waited for John Robertson, the fleet surgeon, to leave his work and join him. He was a tall, imposing man with long and unfashionable sideburns and a severe manner.

Soutter said, "I want to see Mr Portal." He glanced at a cot with several sick-berth attendants stooping around it.

"I *must* be allowed to do my work, Captain." There was anything but welcome in his tone. "I'd not interfere with yours!"

"It is interfering with mine already, by my very being here. We're five miles from the enemy coast and I'd be little use if anything unpleasant were to happen."

Curiously, Jonathan felt that these two men very much admired one another despite their apparent hostility.

Robertson became very business-like. "The boy's taken some splinters." He touched his own stomach with a large hand. "They did nothing for him ashore. He's in great pain but I shall do what I can." He looked steadily into Soutter's eyes: "To make the end peaceful."

"I see." Soutter removed his cap with the oak leaves around its peak.

Robertson shook his head. "No, keep it on, Captain, for the boy's sake. Just be yourself. It'll make it easier."

The fleet surgeon looked at Jonathan and shrugged. "Otherwise we're pretty quiet here." Soutter had reached the side of the cot. "Although I have a feeling that all that is about to change."

Midshipman Timothy Portal looked even smaller than usual as he lay propped up in the cot. Jonathan stood a little apart from the captain and watched as the midshipman stared at his visitor, his mouth tightly closed against the pain.

"Very sorry, sir."

Such a faint, quavering voice and yet Jonathan had often seen him skylarking with his friends in harbour or during a make-and-mend.

Soutter said, "Well, you got back, didn't you? That was bravely done. I shall come and see you later on when you've rested." He reached down and took one of the boy's hands. "What was it like? If you're strong enough, I'd be grateful to hear from you."

The boy stared at him, his astonishment holding the pain at bay.

"It was a terrible mess, sir." He peered at the hand on his own, the cuff with the four gold stripes on it which he had probably only seen at Divisions or when running errands to the bridge. "There was a gully." He screwed up his eyes to remember. "Men everywhere, dead and wounded piled up, and all the while they were shooting." His voice was becoming weaker. "Shooting. My cox'n and stoker were killed outright—and when we went to find somebody I saw the beach. Stores, ammunition—dead men everywhere—all scattered about or crying for help. But nobody came—"

The fleet surgeon wiped his hands angrily on a towel. "I think that's enough; sir. I'll send for the chaplain."

"I'd rather you did not." His gaze lingered on the pinched white face, the grimace of agony, one eye drooping even as he watched. "Give him what you must, but spare him that hypocrisy. He is a brave young officer. Let him die knowing that."

Robertson watched them leave. Soutter carried them all. He glanced round at his petty officer. The midshipman's father was a friend of the captain's too. *"Yes?"*

Another sick-berth attendant was drawing a white curtain around the cot.

"He's gone, sir. Best way, if you ask me."

Robertson walked away. "I'll surely remind you of that, Essex, when your turn comes!"

He relented slightly and beckoned to him to enter his private office with its shelves of vibrating jars and bottles. Then, reaching down, he pulled a bottle of Scotch from a drawer. "Have a dram, Essex. The last you'll get for a time, I shouldn't wonder."

But he was thinking of Soutter's face, his hand on the boy's dying fingers, and of the marine officer who had been here with the captain.

Was that why Soutter had brought him? To see what to expect when the marines were put ashore?

He shook himself angrily. "Get this place prepared, Essex. I'll have a word with the commander about taking over the storerooms through the bulkhead."

But the picture persisted, and the dying midshipman's words, *crying for help, but nobody came,* seemed to hang in the air like an epitaph.

Lieutenant-Colonel Jack Waring's eyes seemed to spark from either cheek as he stood, hands on hips with his back to the fireplace, and waited for the last Royal Marine officer to find a seat. None of the navy was there: the commander had sent word that even when off-watch the ship's officers were to vacate the wardroom, in order that the Royals might hold this formal meeting.

There were about fifteen officers present, ranging in seniority from Major Livesay, commanding B Company, and Captain Seddon of *Reliant*'s own detachment, to the lieutenants and subalterns from the various ships. Some of the officers knew each other quite well, others were total strangers who would soon be required to trust one another with their very lives.

It was strange to see the wardroom like this, Jonathan thought, a place usually rife with complaints and laughter, the ship's officers' home until fate or Their Lordships decided otherwise. In the silence he could feel the gentle pulse of the great engines far below his chair, and saw the easy sway of the long curtains that divided the mess as the ship ploughed steadily into a light swell.

Waring's sleek hair shone beneath the deckhead lights as he gazed severely at the faces of his officers.

He said, "You will all know our new orders, gentlemen. We are taking our place—our rightful place—in the line, in positions already seized and held by the Australians and New Zealanders."

Jonathan glanced at the tall Australian colonel who sat next to Major Livesay, and yet seemed completely isolated from them all. He had seen him during the day pacing the deck amongst the busy sailors, or watching a bombardment from the bridge, where he had been able to pass valuable information to the gunnery officer about the most suitable targets. When the six great guns had hurled themselves inboard on their springs he had remained there, had not appeared to flinch while the smoke and dust had eddied around him.

Waring raised his black stick and pointed at the big map which had been hung beneath the portrait of the king.

"Once we have taken over these positions, the Australians can fall back to rest." He gave the colonel a thin smile. "They will be secure enough in our hands!"

Jonathan looked at some of the others. Young eager faces, some nervousness which showed itself in tightly-clenched fists, or quick whispers to a friend as if for reassurance. But that was usual enough before any real action.

He saw young Tarrier busy with his notepad as he sketched out this small section of a formidable coastline.

It would have made more sense to bring the senior N.C.O.'s to this meeting as well. Now they would all have to be told separately by their platoon commanders, and Jonathan had seen for himself how orders could lose their meaning once they had run the full length of the chain of command.

And there was the debonair Lieutenant Wyke of the third platoon, touching his small fair moustache with one knuckle. He seemed at ease, relaxed, and just before this meeting had been heard discussing the merits or otherwise of the girls at the London Pavilion, the popular music hall in Piccadilly, with his second-in-command Charles Cripwell, who looked as if he should still be at school.

"The drill is much as before." Waring was obviously excited. "The men have already rested and they will be fed as soon as a last weapons inspection has been carried out. We will then disembark to the boats provided, and be towed as near as is prudent to the beaches. By first light I want every man in position, kit stowed, magazines loaded, and ready for action—do I make myself clear?" His incisive voice lingered in the warm air. "The fleet will continue to provide support beyond us and as far as the enemy supply lines, so the rest is up to us."

The tall Australian officer stood up, as if he had been waiting, perhaps, to be asked.

Waring snapped, "You wish to say something, Colonel Ede?"

"I do." Then he faced the watching officers and gave a brief smile. "Just a couple of points that are never in any drill book. Like most other serving officers I know and admire the reputation of your corps—as I believe Kipling described them, 'soldiers and sailors too.' But this is a different sort of campaign for you to fight. It certainly is for me. I think that many of my men were contemptuous of the Turks—thought of them as a cross between brigands and aborigines, something to stamp on and still have time for a beer." He leaned towards them. "So that you don't make the same mistake let me tell you: Johnny Turk is one of the most deadly fighters I've come up against. They attack when they have no chance—when they run out of ammo they'll stand bayonet to bayonet till one falls. Their weapons aren't a scratch on ours and in many cases their rifles are single-shot relics." He had their full attention now and Jonathan could feel all of them hanging onto his words. Ede continued in a contained voice. "We fought our way into our present position just three days ago. Not a week or a month, but three days. I don't know what the hell is happening on the other beaches but in that time I've lost a battalion. My men have been fighting day and night, no chance to sleep. We can't even bring in the wounded—Turkish snipers are everywhere." The power seemed to drain out of him. "Just be careful. The Turk is a brave and dedicated enemy, not some kind of native." He looked hard at some of their faces. "Think how you would feel if you had the Germans coming ashore in England, shooting their way up the beach at Dover. You'd fight like men possessed if that happened. Well, see it from their point of view and you'll have a better chance of survival." He was about to turn away when he saw Lieutenant Wyke holding up his hand. "Yes?"

Wyke's rather affected drawl seemed in stark contrast to the colonel's blunt and abrasive manner.

"But we *are* getting reinforcements, sir."

Ede said coldly, "So they tell me." He studied the young lieutenant's sunburned features for what seemed like a minute and then said, "By the time this war is over, millions may have died at the rate they're going. The Dardanelles, you and me, we'll be forgotten. So when you take your fellows into battle don't waste them. Lead them. Don't let them die for nothing."

He turned sharply for the door with only a brief nod to Beaky Waring.

As the curtains fell again into position Waring remarked, "Well, that was all rather disappointing, wasn't it? A bit of sour grapes, I suppose."

Several of them chuckled.

Waring continued, "Tell your men as much as you think best. But no heroics. We are here to do a job in the great tradition of the corps. That we shall do. Carry on, gentlemen."

The chairs scraped, and they all stood up while waiting stewards and messmen darted through the curtains to prepare the tables for supper.

Jonathan turned as he heard Waring speaking with the

officer commanding *Impulsive*'s marine detachment. He was a grim-faced acting-captain named Peter Whitefoord who had made a lot of notes during the meeting. Waring said, "You will lead in the first boats, Captain Whitefoord." He watched him searchingly. "Yours is the honour. After all, *Impulsive*'s detachment has been together longest—not all fingers and thumbs, what?"

Jonathan walked into the passageway where some of the ship's officers were already waiting to reoccupy their wardroom. He heard Waring's braying laugh and thought of his dismissal of the Australian's quiet warning. Tarrier walked beside him in silence.

Jonathan glanced at him. The next hours would be the worst. He said, "Go round the platoon commanders, Roger." He saw him start at the casual use of his name. "Impress on each of them the importance of drinking water. Stop them from using it all up before we get replenishment. You can tell them the order's from the colonel, if you like."

"Is it, sir?"

Waring had not touched on the subject, even though there was nothing definite about the water replenishment lighters in the prepared orders.

He smiled. "Would I lie?"

Jonathan went to his cabin and looked around, imagining the Australian officers who had slept here. Were they still alive, or lying out there waiting for help which never came?

His M.O.A. Harry Payne had laid everything out. Revolver, extra ammunition, and two water flasks. The old campaigner. A true blue marine.

"After midnight then, sir?"

"How do you feel about it?"

Payne paused in his polishing and stared critically at the

belt buckle. "Me? I s'pose I feel all right, sir. Not much I can do about it, is there?"

Jonathan folded the writing case, which Payne had put ready for a last letter home. He had nobody to write to any more.

Payne watched him gravely. "I've got a bottle of the good stuff in me kit, sir." He forced a grin. "In case it's going to be anything like that last little lot in France."

Jonathan smiled. Payne was pure gold, as old Jack Swan had been for David. Maybe they would end up just like that: like dog and master, each fearful that the other would die first.

"Nothing could be as bad as that, my friend." He seemed to hear the Australian colonel's words to the debonair Lieutenant Wyke. *Don't let them die for nothing.*

Payne glanced up at the deckhead as the engines' regular throb slowed, and then stopped altogether. Jonathan could picture it as if he were up there on deck. The great ship already in darkness, her upper works black against the sky. Discreet and without fuss, and with so many of *Reliant*'s company at their evening meal, anxiety and emotion would be at a minimum. Through the maze of decks and watertight compartments, he thought he heard the brief lament of a bugle, but it was so muffled it could have been part of a memory.

The engines' vibrations began again, churning out the ruler-straight wake which would carry them all to the enemy's shore.

In that same wake, Midshipman Timothy Portal would still be falling through the black depths where he would remain forever undisturbed.

He looked at Payne and knew he was sharing his thoughts. Sixteen years old. It had not been much of a life for him.

· · ·

Lieutenant Christopher Wyke leaned over the guardrails and
stared impatiently at the swaying mass of boats alongside. He
reached out and seized the arm of his second-in-command.
"Hurry them up, Charles! They're like a lot of old women!"
The second lieutenant scrambled down one of the dangling
ladders, probably remembering the Australians who had done
this very thing only a few nights ago. The colonel's revela-
tion, too, that casualties of battalion strength had fallen during
the same period.

Wyke saw Jonathan in the darkness and said, "*Impulsive*'s
detachment have been off-loaded, sir. I'm just disembarking
the H.Q. Platoon. We've got some horse-boats apparently."
He sounded disdainful, as if horse-boats were hardly fit for
Royal Marines.

Jonathan joined him by the tail and looked at the strange
oblong craft. They would carry more than cutters or whalers,
but it was just as well that the sea was almost flat. The noise
seemed incredibly loud. Voices that urged or controlled the
scrambling marines like horse trainers; clinking equipment
and the occasional gasp of pain as somebody's heavy boot
crushed the fingers of the next man down the ladder. But he
knew from experience that at this distance from land the
sounds would be lost in the sigh of the sea, especially along
this rocky coast.

Lieutenant-Colonel Waring was everywhere at once, strid-
ing up and down amongst the waiting sections and squads of
men, his voice demanding and irritable. Always close by, his
M.O.A., loaded down with pack and extra equipment, was
finding it hard to keep up with him.

"Ah, so here you are, Blackwood!" It sounded vaguely
accusing. "Are our H.Q. people in the boats yet?" He saw
Wyke and snapped, "You should be with your men!"

The battle-cruiser's vast stretch of pale planking was emptying more quickly, and Waring muttered to nobody in particular, "That's more like it. Swank and swagger, not a horde of bloody moaners!"

One of the ship's lieutenants found them by the guardrails.

"The captain's compliments, sir, and he wishes you luck."

Waring dismissed him with a curt nod. *Luck!* He sniffed. "Hardly that, believe me!"

Another tall figure loomed from the darkness. It was the Australian colonel.

"I won't be seeing you until your men are in position. The admiral's sending me ashore in his own barge so that I can prepare for your arrival." He glanced at the faint stars. "Seems quiet enough."

Jonathan heard a marine murmur, "The admiral's barge, eh, Tom? Doesn't want it filled with the likes of us!" And others, invisible, chuckled.

Jonathan saw the Reverend Simon Meheux standing by some empty davits, his surplice flapping in the breeze. All his other darker clothing merged with the night, so that he appeared to be hovering above the deck. Jonathan had always thought him a rather ineffectual sort of man, who was slow to offer an opinion in the wardroom. Apart from religious matters, he occupied himself more with writing long letters to his superiors about the need for better instruction and education concerning the Church in general, than with the sailors he was supposed to serve.

Another small drama happened even as he watched the next file of marines clambering down the nearest ladder. A man removed his sun-helmet and stepped out of the ranks as the chaplain was passing.

"Would you bless me, Father?"

Meheux seemed startled. "I am not a Catholic, my son. But be assured, God will be with you when you need him!" He hurried away as if afraid of becoming involved.

Sergeant McCann, a massively built man with square hands like a pair of spades, rapped out, "You'll need more than God to 'elp you if you breaks ranks again, *my son!*"

Colonel Ede said, "Sorry we didn't have time to speak together, Captain Blackwood. I know your family's history. We could certainly use a few more officers like you."

Jonathan said, "Like them perhaps, sir. Not like me, I think."

Ede was staring at him as if his eyes could pierce the darkness without difficulty.

"I think you're wrong." He glanced at Waring but he was speaking sharply to another officer. "I've seen too many bloody heroes just lately. Death or glory, but mostly the former. Those days are gone forever."

A midshipman murmured, "The barge is ready for lowering, sir."

Ede nodded and they shook hands. Afterwards Jonathan remembered it: hard and rough like the man, but warm too. A man you would follow to hell and back if need be.

"Has he gone?" Waring gave a brief smile. "It's all been too much for him—that's what's wrong with these people, Blackwood!"

"Ready, sir!"

Jonathan glanced around and saw off-duty seamen watching them. Deep in his heart he must have known it was to be like this, and now it was time. He felt untried, unready.

Waring snapped, "Off you go, Blackwood. It is the custom, you know!"

Jonathan climbed down, his body already soaking with sweat. Apart from the awkward sun-helmets none of them had been issued with light tropical clothing and they were still wearing thick serge tunics and breeches. Once ashore in the bright sunshine it would be torture.

Payne was waiting in the crowded horse-boat, and some witty marine, safe in the darkness, whispered, "We must be all right, lads—the colonel's with *us!*"

Two cruisers were already towing their clusters of boats, the hulls merely shadows, their size revealed only by their bow-waves.

Silence closed over the boats as they were warped astern of *Reliant's* pale shape until they were moving again, the boats squeaking together, the water splashing dangerously over the gunwales.

Waring crouched with his shaded torch and took a quick glance, at his map. Then he and the other officers checked their watches, as if to put a seal on the task ahead.

When at last the main tow-lines were cast off and the steam pinnaces took the strain on their assorted charges, Jonathan felt the sudden sense of loneliness like something physical. Men he had come to know in the day-to-day routine of a big warship, faces in the mess, cheering at the makeshift boxing matches and skylarking on the passage out from Portsmouth, the sweating tolerance at the drills and inspections. Now that had all been discarded, and the towering funnels and tops of *Reliant's* outline had already vanished into the night.

A lot of men around him would be thinking that. Like the marine who had asked for a blessing, had risked the scorn and the ribbing of his mates, because he needed it.

Once, the boats swayed and banged together when the towing pinnace swerved hard over. Later as they ploughed past a stationary pinnace with its towed boats drifting out in all directions, Waring demanded to know what was wrong.

The pinnace had broken down, and the towed boats, with most of *Impulsive*'s marines crammed aboard, were unable to proceed.

Jonathan heard *Impulsive*'s marine captain yell, "The snotty says we'll be moving very soon, sir!"

"If not, I'll send someone for you!" He brandished his black stick. "Can't hang about here! *Plan Two!*"

Jonathan felt Tarrier close beside him. "Will it make any difference, sir?"

"It shouldn't. Major Livesay will lead, that's all."

The drifting boats were soon lost astern, and Jonathan realised that the pinnace had been the one which had carried Ede and the dying midshipman out from the beach. Perhaps he should mention it to Waring. The pinnace might have been damaged by rifle fire, and her present crew might not know how to restart it.

He peered at Waring's erect shadow and dismissed the idea. It was too late.

Payne touched his arm and whispered, "Look, sir! The land!" His round Hampshire accent was somehow comforting as the rugged wall of cliffs loomed out of the night sea.

Waring grunted, "If there's nobody here . . ." But there was. A shuttered lamp flashed from very low down on the small beach where they were supposed to get ashore. Colonel Ede had kept his word, and had reached it first and without incident.

"As soon as we're in our H.Q., Blackwood, we'll get a wiring party on the move. Rig field telephones that we're used to. I don't want any of their stuff!"

Then he waved his stick above his head. "Pass the word, Sergeant! Prepare to beach!"

Blackwood strained his ears above the noise of sea on

sand, the clatter of tackle as their pinnace cast off and thrashed astern clear of danger. Nobody had fired a shot. The silence was almost painful.

"Now!" Waring clambered over the square bows as the horseboat crashed onto the sand, with some marines leaping into the shallows to steady it, and others helping the next boats on the tow to punt their way in towards what appeared to be a narrow crescent of beach hemmed in by fallen rocks.

"Take charge!" Waring stamped his boots free of sand. "Sergeant McCann, scouts and pickets at the double!"

A corporal was leading a shadowy figure from the rocks, the guide sent by Colonel Ede.

Jonathan heard the men getting into some kind of order and wondered if Major Livesay's contingent had got ashore yet on the other side of the beach. God, he thought, the cliff was even higher than he had imagined. It might take longer than hoped to get all their equipment up it to the Australian positions.

The anonymous guide said thickly, "Took yer time, didn't you?" He gestured with his thumb. "Follow me close an' do exactly what I say!" Then he was gone, with Wyke and his platoon sergeant stumbling behind him.

Waring snapped, "Uncouth lout!"

Jonathan loosened his revolver and watched the men clambering past him. They had practised this sort of thing in their field training. He looked up at the cliff, the pale stars so far away. But it was not the same. This was enemy territory. He saw a young marine unclipping his water bottle, and seized his wrist. "Not here, and not yet!" The youth stared at him but hurried on, too breathless to speak.

Reliant would be far away already, and tomorrow she might be required to offer covering fire.

He walked carefully after the last section and thought he heard the next steam pinnace panting towards the beach.

Tomorrow? It was today.

Six

The Australian infantry captain rearranged a thick blanket across the entrance of what was obviously a natural cave and turned up a solitary oil lamp.

"Colonel Ede's sorry he couldn't wait to get you settled in, but he'll be starting the stand-down in half an hour."

Jonathan sat on a packing case and stared wearily at the cramped place that was to be their headquarters until the Australians took over the line again. It had been a long, hard climb from the beach, their guide reaching out in the darkness like a blind man as he waved them into silence, or told them to duck when crossing a clearing. Even he had seemed surprised at the lack of firing, although several times they had heard the impartial clatter of machine-guns to the north.

The trench, which had been hastily hacked out after the first Australian advance, twisted and turned across the ridge, and would, the infantry captain explained, give a perfect view in daylight.

Jonathan heard the marines hurrying to take up their positions, confused and alarmed at the speed of the takeover. The Australians looked exhausted, and like this captain were dirty and unshaven, their uniforms cut and torn from climbing the rough terrain or dropping down hillsides to avoid sniper fire.

He asked, "Will they attack tonight, d'you think?"

"Unlikely. They'll wait until we've pulled out. They know your lot are new to this game. My guess is that they'll try to retake this position tomorrow."

So the stealth and the secrecy had been for nothing. Colonel Ede had warned them about that too. It was wrong to underestimate the Turks.

The curtain moved and Waring's burly figure ducked into the light. One glance took in the field-telephone and the marine who was working on it, the litter of empty meat tins and bottles: a battlefield slum.

"Not very satisfactory, is it?"

The Australian said curtly, "Not my fault, Colonel."

Jonathan was afraid the man would leave, and yet there was so much he needed to know.

"What about prisoners? I didn't see any enclosures on the way."

The captain accepted it like a peace offering. "No prisoners here. A bayonet is the best way of settling an argument."

Waring was staring at a makeshift bunk. "What about him? Shouldn't he be getting ready with the others?"

"No, Colonel, we'll take him when we go." He took a cigarette gratefully from Payne and lit it with great care. "It's our brigade-major. Got too eager to see the enemy positions. Sniper got him bang through the head." He added reflectively, "Not a bad old bird, so I thought we'd take him down with us." He looked at his cigarette and his hand, which was shaking suddenly as if with fever. *"Christ."*

Second Lieutenant Tarrier came into the cave, swallowing hard. "All in position, sir." Despite his sunburn he looked deathly pale; like the dying midshipman, Jonathan thought.

"What's the matter?"

Tarrier licked his lips. "Corpses. Just over the parapet. The stench is terrible. I never thought . . ." He retched and ran from the cave.

The Australian said, "Poor little bugger. He's seen nothing yet, believe me."

Some of his men came with a stretcher and rolled the dead officer onto it, but not before Jonathan had seen the bloodied bandages wrapped carelessly around his head, and one out-thrust hand, tightly clenched as at the moment of impact.

"Ask permission before you come in here!" Waring was getting angrier by the minute. The soldiers ignored him and tramped out into the darkness.

There was a sudden crack, and the Australian opened out a stained map and spread it on another empty case. "That's the gully leading to our next position, here." He pointed with a grimy finger. "A fixed rifle, we think, and a sniper fires every so often when he figures someone might be using it." He gave a strained grin. "Good thinking. It's the only one we *can* use."

A marine poked his head into the lamplight. "Major Livesay is here, sir."

"I'll come at once. Officers' meeting in thirty minutes."

The Australian crossed his legs and looked at the empty bunk and the black stain beneath it.

"I must say, I don't care much for your colonel."

Jonathan smiled. "I'd like to hear what might be of some help. Most of my men are new recruits. They were supposed to continue their training at Port Said, but . . ."

The man nodded. "*But.* What a lot of wars have hinged on that word." He leaned forward and put his hand on Jonathan's sleeve. "When they come at you, you must show them you're not going to run, see? They'll attack all along the defence line, regardless of losses, and if they're allowed to get near enough they'll pitch bombs into the trenches." He added with sudden bitterness, "We don't have any bloody bombs, of course!"

"Nor do we."

"We make our own until supplies start coming through. Cocoa tins, bullets, short fuse—you know how it is." His hand pressed down harder. "But don't let them get that close or you're done for. Order your blokes up on the parapet and face them with bayonets, clubs, axes, anything you can find. There are plenty of spare rifles around here. Their owners don't need 'em any more. Get your officers to use 'em. That fancy pistol of yours is a dead—" He grinned again. "If you'll pardon the expression, giveaway. Johnny Turk always picks off the officers first. Then there's drinking water . . ."

"I've already passed the word about that."

"Good lad." He was probably three or four years younger than Jonathan but spoke with the authority of a veteran. "There should be a lighter coming into the cove tomorrow." He glanced at his watch. "But then, the war was supposed to be over by Christmas." He stood up and patted his pockets. "Last word on the subject of prisoners and then I'm off. Don't let the bastards take any of your men." He looked at him steadily. "They'll send 'em back to you, a piece at a time."

Jonathan watched him, fascinated despite his chilling words. This man wanted to go, get away from all of it, but something stronger seemed to be holding him back.

"This is the narrowest part of the peninsula, and to the left front is Sari Bair, the biggest ridge hereabouts. It commands the whole area. It's only four miles across the peninsula to the narrows. Get to there and we've cut the bastards in half." He stared at the map with angry, reddened eyes. "They put us down here to do just that. I'm only a soldier, but I tell you now, it can't be done."

An Australian sergeant leaned through the entrance. "Ready for the off, Ben?"

"Too right." He shook hands solemnly. "My name's Duffy— My dad builds boats in Perth. Look us up some day if we both make it." He was gone as if he had not been real, a spectre from some other time and place.

Waring and Major Livesay pushed in, and after dusting off one of the empty crates they sat and compared their maps.

Livesay mopped his face and neck with a piece of rag. "God, what a place. Cross between a slaughterhouse and a cemetery!" He nodded to Jonathan. "All our guns are in position. Lines have been rigged to the next trench, and I have two sections of men digging out deeper defences. Tomorrow we'll get a line run down to the beach, maybe two in case of accidents."

Waring listened in silence as Jonathan related what the Australian captain had told him, his face expressionless and only his sprouting moustache giving any hint of irritation.

"Officers with rifles and bayonets?" He sounded shocked. "This is not the French Revolution!" Then he smiled, like a schoolmaster with a slow-thinking pupil. "*Impulsive*'s contingent will soon be with us."

Livesay seemed uneasy. "They may not have been able to get under way again, sir. Or one of the ships might have towed them back to the squadron."

Waring looked pleased. "You've got to *think*, Livesay!" He tapped his forehead. "That's how you survive and win." He yawned. "I've already sent a pinnace to find them and bring them in."

Livesay stared at him and then at Jonathan as if for support. "But—but, sir, they'd never arrive before dawn even if the pinnace found them without delay. They'd be coming ashore in broad daylight!" He stared through the crudely curtained entrance as if he could see it. "Up that cliff? They'd never stand a chance!"

Waring lay down carefully on some sacking. "Must get some shut eye. Call me if anything happens." Before he closed his eyes he looked over at Livesay and tapped his forehead again. "Think, man—it's all you have to do." Then he was instantly asleep.

Jonathan and Livesay left the cave together and stood on what felt like broken boards while they allowed their eyes to grow accustomed to the darkness. The steep cliff and the rocky barriers that ran behind the defence line cut out every sound of the sea, and it was quiet, and somehow eerie. Finally Jonathan could see the faint outlines of sentries posted along the firing step, their sun-helmets showing clearly against the stars. He thought of the man from Perth and said, "I would have the men remove their helmets, sir. To any sniper they must look like enormous mushrooms, even in the dark."

"I'd better have a word with the colonel about that," Livesay said, and reconsidered immediately. "No, dammit, he's asleep." He beckoned to a corporal and told him what to do, then added, "I don't like this place, Jono. Not one little bit. It's not proper soldiering. Sitting ducks, that's what we are!"

They all looked up as a flare burst high over the ridge and lit the barren landscape like a desert.

Jonathan climbed up beside a sentry and stared across the undulating gullies and scattered rock formations. A corpse lay near the trench, its staring eyes like glass in the drifting glare. Others lay beyond, and the sour stench of death was everywhere.

To the young sentry he said quietly, "Watch the corpses, Tucker." He recalled what David had told him about the Chinese corpses in the Boxer Rebellion. The dead were the dead, but there they had moved imperceptibly until they were close enough to fall on the thin line of marines like crazed, screaming dervishes. "Just in case."

"Yessir."

Jonathan sensed Payne beside him. He was holding out a silver cup. "Here, sir." Jonathan felt the Scotch burning his empty stomach. How could men eat when they knew what to expect? It must be like that before climbing to the gallows, he thought. But even then you had some dignity.

"Thanks. I needed that."

Payne said gravely, "No, you don't, sir. Not like some."

Jonathan saw Payne place a spare rifle close at hand. So even he knew about that. He thought of Waring's shocked response. *Officers with rifles and bayonets!* He had made it sound like an act of treachery.

The flare had extinguished itself and there was only darkness again. What did it mean? A signal, a warning? Who could tell?

He leaned his back against the rough side of the trench. At least it was cool. He would not have believed it possible at one time, but in seconds his head had lolled in sleep.

Payne tilted the silver cup to his lips until a solitary drop of Scotch ran down his tongue. Then he screwed up the flask and collected his own rifle.

He looked at the stars. Fainter already. Never mind, captain, he thought. We'll stick together, and we'll be as right as rain!

"Here, sir, something to wet your whistle."

Jonathan suppressed a groan and waited while his reluctant senses returned to life. "What is it?" Surely he had not been asleep. He was still slumped against the side of the crude trench, every bone and muscle throbbing a separate protest. Not *asleep.*

"Char, sir. The Aussies left us a fair supply of water when they pulled out. Wouldn't float the old *Reliant* but it'll keep us going for a bit."

The tea tasted bitter, and there could have been more milk and sugar. But it was like pure champagne, and Jonathan could feel the tension easing in his limbs.

"Colonel's coming, sir." Payne busied himself with some invisible task as Waring's ramrod figure, followed closely by Major Livesay and Lieutenant Wyke, strode along the winding trench. He saw Jonathan and gave a stiff nod.

"Time to stand-to. It'll be light within half an hour. Remember what I said—space out the N.C.O.'s and make certain that the machine-gunners know their sectors." Wyke hurried away, calling for a corporal.

Waring rubbed his chin with his stick. "I've been thinking." He turned his back to the parapet and glanced at the shadowy humps of rock through which they had climbed from the beach. "We should have an observation post there, with another wire running down here and to the beach party." He did not even blink as the heavy rifle cracked out again. The hidden sniper with his fixed sights could have been the only Turk on the peninsula, except for the gaping corpses. Waring looked at Jonathan. "Well? What d'you think? You're something of an expert in gunnery matters, what?" He sounded more irritable than usual, Jonathan thought; and it was rare for him to ask for an opinion.

"I agree, sir. From there I might even see our ships."

Waring's mood changed. "So you intend to go yourself, do you? Add another V.C. to the family collection?"

Jonathan unclenched his fists slowly. "That was unfair, sir."

Waring gave his braying laugh. "You're too serious by half, man!"

Payne was shaking out some mugs and suddenly Jonathan saw his outline for the first time. It would soon be dawn. "I'll leave now, sir. I'd like to take Tarrier with me." He expected another argument but Waring was already getting out his binoculars as he snapped, "Stand-to. Make sure the H.Q. platoon is in position and aware of the high ground on our left front." He saw Wyke staring at him and added harshly, "And get those men to replace their helmets! The place is a shambles!"

Jonathan asked, "Ready, Payne?"

"As ever, sir." He handed him one of the forbidden rifles and grinned. "Don't forget your bundhook. I've checked it—full magazine, one up the spout, safety catch on."

Figures were showing themselves along the trench, and Jonathan could feel the sand between his teeth. Just as well about the tea. You couldn't kill a raging thirst with neat Scotch.

Tarrier faced him, his eyes like dark holes in his face. "Won't it be dangerous, sir?"

There was no answer to that.

Jonathan climbed over the back of the trench and walked quickly towards the shadowy rocks, his rifle held at the port across his body. He heard Payne fix his bayonet and work his rifle bolt just once. The rest was instinct. By the time they had reached the cover of the rocks it was already much lighter, the stars almost gone, the slope and the nearest gully beginning to take shape like some aerial photograph.

Tarrier almost fell as he slipped on loose stones, and pointed at the edge of a pale crater. One of the fleet's shells had left its mark here, when the Turks had been driven from this ridge as the first landing parties had surged ashore.

There were several rifle shots and Jonathan heard Tarrier's sharp breathing as he ducked down amongst the rocks. Payne said reassuringly, "Not shooting at us, sir." He added to himself, "Not yet."

"God, I can smell the sea!" The words were torn from Jonathan's throat. Somewhere to the south-west *Reliant* and her consorts would soon be calling the hands. Order and cheerful discipline, a good breakfast and some of the baker's fresh bread. Could life become so basic that that was all that really mattered?

"Watch out, Mr Tarrier!" Payne's bayonet moved like lightning and steadied above a shallow depression where two figures lay, arms outflung, rifles glinting very slightly in the strengthening light.

Payne grimaced. "What a stink! Still, we'll get no trouble from *them*."

Despite the warning the young second lieutenant still stood looking down at the corpses, the rifle fire and lurking danger momentarily forgotten. It was very early, and yet the sound of buzzing flies, the stench of decay seemed to dominate this place, staining the clean morning.

Jonathan watched the boy, remembering how he himself had felt when he had seen his first smashed and mutilated corpses. These must have been coastal lookouts and had probably been caught in the first naval bombardments. The rocks were star-marked with shrapnel, and one of the Turkish soldiers had been almost decapitated. There was a broken heliograph near his legs, used to warn the shore batteries of the warships' approach.

Tarrier asked hoarsely, "What do we do, sir?"

Payne clambered down and tore the water flasks from the two mutilated soldiers and said, "Empty. Bloody useless." He swatted some flies away. "We'd better get a move on."

They climbed up the slope and all at once the sea was there like an endless, dark blue backdrop. Closer inshore the water was in total darkness, and only a few early gulls swooped over the hidden beach where they had stumbled ashore.

Jonathan knelt down and took several deep breaths. He thought of the average sailor's belief, like a private prayer. *Just get me to the sea, and somehow I'll get home.* The soldiers he had known so briefly in France had had no such comfort. Each dawn on the firestep, the rim of the parapet above them: the horizon. No hope of a friendly ship at the end of it. Just up and over the top, into the wire, into the guns.

He shook himself and peered over the last scattered rocks. He heard Payne humming softly to himself as he took up a position behind and slightly below him. Maybe he didn't care about the sea.

Tarrier said tightly, "Sorry, sir. I don't seem to be able to get used to it."

Apologising again. Like the young midshipman with Soutter before he had died. Jonathan pulled out his binoculars and felt the warm metal, smooth in his fingers. They had been his father's, but they were still better and more sharply focused than most modern ones.

He said, "You've only been out here for a dogwatch, Roger." *What can I tell him? You never get used to it if you are a human being. Or should I tell him to be like Beaky Waring?* He would never break under any disaster. His code of conduct was as much a part of the man as his pig-headedness. He said, "No half measures, Roger." It was strange how hard his voice sounded. "It's kill or be killed. They're the enemy. As people they don't exist."

Payne rested his rifle against a slab of stone and peered down at the defence line: a rough scar which vanished on either hand, marked all the way by shell craters and discarded equipment. Dug by the enemy, taken by the Australians. The light was stronger, and he thought he could feel warmth on his cheek. He could see the vague shapes of other corpses. All along the line, some right up to the trench where the marines were hidden from view. Beyond and disappearing into shadows and morning mist were the undulating gullies: a useless, empty desert.

Something flashed from a far hillside and he thought of the sprawled corpses, the army of buzzing flies. Another heliograph. Up in those foothills the Turks would have found the sun before anyone. Another signal from the unseen enemy.

Crack. A sniper somewhere. Payne wriggled round as his captain called, "Listen! What the hell is that?"

Payne backed up the slope to join him, his rifle in the crook of his arm like a watchful gamekeeper.

Together, hatless, they knelt on the hard stones and stared across the dark placid water.

It came again. The bright, cheerful toot of a boat's whistle.

Payne gaped at Jonathan in stunned disbelief. "It's *Impulsive*'s lot, sir. They're coming in."

Jonathan stared around desperately. They had got the pinnace restarted, and with another to assist were making straight for the beach.

Payne said, "We must warn them!" But they both knew it was already hopeless.

Jonathan began to get to his feet, and ducked again as a rifle cracked out from another hillside and the heavy bullet flung grit into his face.

Payne adjusted his backsight and said, "Keep down, sir. They know we're here." More bullets cracked over the rocks and ricocheted across the cliff like maddened hornets.

Then, as if to a signal, the hills reverberated to the sharp crash of artillery and the quiet morning air was ripped apart by the staccato rattle of machine-guns.

His breath rasping in his lungs, his knees and elbows raw from their rocky cover, Jonathan crawled farther until he could see over the lip of the cliff, even as smoke drifted thickly into the sheltered beach. He forced himself to watch as one steam pinnace received a direct hit and was blasted to fragments, its towed boats flung about in disorder as men pitched overboard, torn apart by splinters or dragged down by the weight of weapons and kit. The sea's face was boiling, churned into a million feathers as the hidden machine-guns raked slowly back and forth, smashing men and boats alike until the water near the beach was bright red. The other pinnace exploded, its brass funnel flying into the air as another shell found its mark. A few pathetic survivors had reached the shallows, and for the briefest of moments it seemed their despair and courage had saved them. Then the machine-guns began again, catching them, flinging them down into the water or onto the smoking sand. Jonathan found that his glasses did not even quiver. It was as if he must remember every hideous moment.

Two last khaki figures had almost reached the shelter of the cliff when one of them swung round and fell, an arm outflung, and probably calling to his friend. The other marine hesitated and turned back. Just seconds. *What were they thinking?* The wet sand leaped and spattered and the bullets ripped over them yet again. And then, at last, there was only silence.

For hours the naval bombardment continued. Along the twisting trench the marines lay or crouched, with their bodies and faces pressed against the sun-heated rock or the bullet-riddled sandbags.

When the onslaught on the Turkish positions had begun,

some of them had cheered and waved like madmen as salvo after salvo had roared overhead like express trains. If anyone raised his head to watch he could see the tons of earth being hurled into the air, the hills and gullies hazy with green lyddite smoke as shrapnel joined forces with high-explosive shells and ranged the enemy positions in a torrent of death. Whether the bombardment was in retaliation for the slaughter of *Impulsive*'s landing parties, or because of information received by the flagship, it had given them heart. It was vengeance for the marines who still drifted in the sea, or lay on the bottom with their unused weapons and equipment.

Jonathan sat with his back against the firestep and tried to prevent his mind from cracking, forcing himself to remember every detail of what he had witnessed, checking to ensure that his cringing brain still recalled the right order and content of each horrific picture.

He did not know what he had expected of Waring when he had made his report. Dismay, remorse, guilt even, for ordering the boats to continue inshore without support or the cover of darkness.

In fact Waring had said very little, only, "At least we know what we're up against." And, "It proves the need for faster and better communications."

Major Livesay had said quietly, "I knew most of those chaps. I still find it hard to accept."

What had he meant? That the useless slaughter could not have been so complete as Jonathan had described it? Or that Waring's callous reaction was beyond belief?

At noon the bombardment finally stopped. It was as if each man had been rendered deaf, or some great door had been slammed shut. Dazed, dust covering their bodies and sunburned skin, the marines stared at one another like strangers. Sergeant McCann, his walrus-like moustache curled at the ends and stained dark with tobacco, moved slowly along his platoon, speaking to some of them, growling an occasional threat at anybody who had failed to clean his rifle after the grit and drifting smoke had settled: the ideal, no-nonsense N.C.O., who would always obey orders and would see that they were carried out by those in his care, no matter how young and inexperienced. Squatting behind his heavy machine-gun, Private Bert Langmaid moved its crank handles slightly and made certain the long fabric belt of bullets did not catch on any obstruction. Langmaid was one of the hard men, tough and insubordinate, who had been put into the new company to stiffen it with his experience, but mostly because every officer he had served had wanted to get rid of him. He and Sergeant McCann had a wary respect for one another, but any comparison ended there. Langmaid had been made up to sergeant and had been broken to corporal twice. Now he no longer even wore those chevrons as some record of his service. He had received punishment that would have broken most men. But not Langmaid; he took it like a challenge and had kept his contempt for authority intact. A weary commander had once asked him why he was in the corps at all.

Langmaid had displayed his crooked teeth, victims of too many fights to remember. "Cause I likes it, sir. It's wot I does best."

He was squatting there now, eyes slitted against the glare, large and untidy like a badly packed kit-bag. His two assistants were mere boys by comparison, who looked on the machine-gunner with as much fear as awe.

Next in the trench was Barlow, the one who had shown such eagerness to Jonathan aboard *Reliant*. A youth with a scrubbed, pink face which refused to tan, he was leaning against the side of the trench, his rifle gripped in his fists while he repeatedly licked his dry lips.

Jonathan looked away. He really did look no more than twelve. It was rumoured that he didn't even shave as yet.

Next to Barlow was Corporal Ned Timbrell of the third platoon, with a pointed foxy face and deep-set eyes like black olives. A reliable N.C.O., and one with his sights set on promotion, no matter what it might cost. Like Langmaid he had a violent past, but Timbrell's was private. It had to be. He had once been a young waterman working on the London river at Blackfriars: it was so hazy now that he could scarcely recall it in exact detail. He had got into a brawl outside The Flying Horse with a warehouseman he barely knew. They had both been drunk, but not so much that Timbrell had not seen the knife in the other man's fist. The scar was still on his left shoulder, but the force of the blow had allowed him to turn the man onto his own blade. In the terrible silence he had stood alone on the wet cobbles, the corpse leering up at him in the light of a gas lamp. With great care he had lowered the body into the dark, fast-moving current. The Thames had been on the ebb and moved swiftly to hide its secrets as it sped down to the Pool of London.

There had been no report of any suspicious death, perhaps because they were almost too commonplace for mention. Shortly afterwards Timbrell had gone down to Portsmouth and enlisted. That had been eight years ago. He was safe.

Lieutenant Wyke stumbled over loose stones and the broken packing cases that had been laid over them like duckboards to make movement at night less audible. "What now, sir?" He sat down heavily and ran his fingers through his fair hair.

Jonathan thought of the Australian infantry captain who

had described the ordeal of his men when they had taken and held this miserable place. "I think they'll attack. Soon." He shaded his eyes to watch Private Geach as he crouched down with the youthful Barlow and offered him what looked like a toffee. *Kids.* Geach was a Yorkshireman who had given up work on a farm and taken to the Royal Marines like an old sweat. The others had pulled his leg about his broad dialect, and the "Hey-oop, then!" which was his regular greeting.

Wyke was watching him narrowly. "But the bombardment, sir. Nothing could live through that."

The air quivered to one heavy explosion and everyone crouched down, teeth gritted against the shock.

But when it came it was far away, like thunder on the hills. That must be the big gun the Turks had mounted on the high ground, he thought. It fired again, with the same muffled result.

He said quietly, "There's your answer, my lad. They must be firing at our ships." In his mind's eye he could see them: the flags darting up and down the halliards, the semaphore arms wagging from bridge to bridge as the admiral ordered his squadron to safer waters, from which the big ships like *Reliant* and *Impulsive* could concentrate their fire on the enemy's heavy gun. But while they were doing that they would be unable to support B company or anyone else.

The sudden clatter of machine-guns shattered the dusty silence and men covered their faces as bullets cracked amongst the stones and torn sandbags. Interspersed with it they could hear concentrated rifle fire.

Lieutenant Wyke replaced his sun-helmet and unfastened the flap of his holster. "Where the hell is it coming from?" He sounded quite calm now that they were under fire.

A runner panted along the trench and halted when he saw the officers.

"From th' Colonel, sir. There are enemy soldiers on the ridge, left front."

"Very well. Pass the word to the next section." He watched the man pound away, pausing only to give a thumbs-up to someone he recognised as he passed.

Second Lieutenant Cripwell polished his binoculars and trained them on something to adjust them better. With great care he climbed onto the firestep, his chin almost touching the rough edge of the trench.

Jonathan turned as someone shouted, "Get down, you fool!" There was a sharp crack, like an axe splintering bone, and Cripwell seemed to pivot round like a puppet before he pitched down amongst them.

In those seconds Jonathan saw it like a small fragment of war: the staring marines, their stricken young faces unable to move or cry out. One, the Yorkshireman Geach, was splashed with bright daubs of the blood that had spurted over him.

Cripwell, the young subaltern whom he had heard discussing the ladies of the music hall with his platoon commander, who had tried to talk like a man of the world, had been killed instantly. The heavy bullet had struck his sun-helmet and punched a hole through his skull before he had even been able to scream. He lay at their feet, staring at the clear sky, his brains and the white chips of bone already alive with flies.

Wyke knelt but Jonathan snapped, *"Not now."* He saw the lieutenant staring at him, his face hurt, even angry, but that no longer mattered. He shouted, "Be ready! Stand-to, marines!" They tore their eyes from the dead officer. Already he was nothing: unreal. His mind again tried to rebel against what he saw. He was nothing. *Dear Mr Cripwell, I have to tell you, with regret, that your son . . .*

"Take over, Mr Wyke!"

The lieutenant swallowed hard and then drew his revolver. *"Marines! Fix bayonets!"* Along the trench and around the bend which was supposed to protect the occupants from splinters, the sound was like a prolonged hiss of steel, as they dragged out their bayonets and slammed them onto their rifles.

A marine close to Jonathan was saying with every breath, "Oh, dear God, protect me." It was like a chant.

"Here they come!"

They all heard the baying yells and cries, mingled together like one vast inhuman voice.

Jonathan took the rifle and snapped on the bayonet. He saw Payne watching him, his casual salute with one finger to his helmet: the face in the background of so many paintings at Hawks Hill and around the world.

"Face your front!"

Stumbling like old men they climbed onto the firestep, their rifles and shining bayonets probing over the edge in a long serried line. He swallowed dryly. If his voice broke now . . . He did not dwell on it.

"Range one hundred yards! *Steady, lads!*" He made himself stare unwinkingly at the oncoming, zigzagging mass of Turks, as he had at the carnage on the beach. Was that only this morning?

"Take aim!" He thought of his brother David, his stories of the fanatical Boxers who had believed themselves impervious to bullet and bayonet.

Sergeant McCann jabbed one man's shoulder with a broad thumb and the marine cried out with alarm.

McCann rasped, "Take yer safety catch off, Clark!" Then he climbed up beside him and took aim.

There was a broken, overturned cart by some forgotten corpses and Jonathan had already judged it to be about one hundred yards from the trench. The first charging figures dashed past it.

"Rapid fire!"

The insane chatter of machine-guns and the rapid crack of rifles sent a tide of bullets sweeping across the barren land and into the Turkish soldiers.

McCann bellowed, "Reload! Remember what you was taught!"

Langmaid licked his lips while he swung the heavy machine-gun from side to side, pausing only to allow one of his crew to drag another belt into place. It was as if the enemy troops were charging into some invisible barrier, he thought. Running and screaming one second and then slipping and falling in heaps, their comrades clambering over them only to add to the pile as the carefully-sited guns swept back and forth like reapers in a field.

Bolts were jerked open, torn fingers scrabbled for fresh clips of ammunition. Some of the marines were sobbing as if they had been running and were too breathless to know what they were doing.

"Cease firing!"

Jonathan jerked the bolt and ejected a spent cartridge. The enemy were falling back.

"Keep down! *Cease firing!*" Some of the marines had to be prevented forcibly from shooting at the dust and swirling smoke. The enemy had gone. Melted into the ground. Only the crawling wounded and the piled corpses proved what they had done.

There was a solitary crack and then a voice echoed around the bend of the trench. "Stretcher bearer!"

McCann said heavily, "Bloody snipers!"

Jonathan handed the rifle to Payne and looked at the line

of exhausted men. And the Australians they had relieved had been on their feet here for four days and nights.

He glanced round and saw that Cripwell's body had been dragged away, and somebody had flung sand over the mess from his shattered skull.

Second Lieutenant Tarrier was scrambling over some rubble. When he saw Jonathan the terrible strain seemed to fall from his face.

"How are things at H.Q., Roger?"

Tarrier fell against the trench by his side. "We fought them off! I never thought . . ." He could not go on.

"They'll come at us again. Be ready for it." He watched the warning going home. "We're outnumbered. They'll keep up the pressure and make certain our people get no rest." He saw Tarrier's eyes flicker as a stretcher was carried past. A pair of dirty boots protruded from beneath an old blanket and blood was running down a dangling arm to show that it was already too late. Another marine, hatless and carrying his dead friend's rifle, followed in the rear, his young features like stone: someone who had aged within the hour.

"Fall them out in sections, Sergeant. One cup of water." He said sharply to the men nearest him, "*Sip* it. Don't take it in one swallow!"

Langmaid peered from his gun. "Wot does them Turks drink, sir?" He winked at Corporal Timbrell. "I reckon if we takes their next trench we might get a wet or two, eh sir?"

Jonathan felt his mind reeling. He said, "Coffee, Langmaid, not much else, I'm afraid!" He could hear himself laughing, but the laughter seemed disembodied, not his own. The others were all grinning up at Langmaid as if he had said something hilarious, the break in the tension coming like another kind of madness. Eventually he said, "When we get back to Mudros I'll do what I can." He walked along the trench and heard someone call out, "Good old Blackie!"

If only they knew.

He stopped dead, then ran back to the position he had just left as the cry was passed along the trench.

"Stand-to! Here they come again!"

Some of the marines had not moved, and could only stare at him as if they were shell-shocked.

Hatless, half-blinded by the sun, Jonathan jumped onto the firestep and shouted, "Face your front, damn you!" He added brutally even as he worked the rifle's bolt, "I can't carry you forever!"

Then he took aim at the oncoming Turks, their bayonets flashing through the rolling dust. Without looking he knew his men had taken up their positions. He shut them from his mind and yelled, *"Rapid fire!"*

SEVEN

Reliant's chief yeoman of signals lowered his long telescope and reported, "From *Impulsive*, sir. *Have sustained some damage and ten casualties. Will return to Mudros as instructed.*" He closed the telescope with a snap. "End of signal, sir."

Captain Soutter walked from his chair to the opposite side and watched the other battle-cruiser's lean shape shorten as she altered course to port. He allowed his binoculars to fall to his chest. He had seen the black pattern of splinter holes along *Impulsive's* hull below B Turret, which moments before had been firing onto the peninsula and the Turkish support lines. The shell had come from nowhere, then a pair had almost bracketed *Impulsive* before she could take avoiding action. With her armour plate sacrificed for greater speed and agility, it was lucky she had not received a direct hit, and as Quitman the gunnery officer had commented from his control position, the Turkish guns were much more powerful than before.

Soutter saw the rear admiral coming out of the chartroom, his usually immaculate white cap-cover smudged with smoke and oil. Purves had been in contact with the fleet's flagship, and was evidently not pleased with the way things were going. The news of the total destruction of *Impulsive*'s landing parties had shocked everybody, and Soutter could well imagine how his old friend Captain Vidal must have taken it. His men and boats, Royal Marines, midshipmen and sailors, wiped out in minutes. With communications so bad it might be weeks before the blame would be laid where it belonged, and then it would serve no purpose. And all the while the ships maintained their bombardment of the enemy positions: tons of high-explosive, shrapnel and even the lighter armament, to offer protection to the troops and marines ashore. But still the Turks counterattacked, and the casualties continued to mount by the hour.

Boats' crews repeatedly risked their lives to carry the wounded to safety but the hospital ships had been badly allocated, so that some lay almost empty and others, like the nearest one, were already full. In desperation the boats were offloading the casualties into warships, and even *Reliant*'s sickbay was overflowing. Bandaged, shocked, maimed and dying: it was pitiful to see them being hoisted on board.

Soutter looked at his superior as he heaved himself into the captain's chair.

"Any news, sir?"

Purves glanced at him. "Reinforcements are on their way. Next month the Australian Light Horse will be arriving from

Egypt." He added savagely, "The admiral was careful to point out that their horses would be left behind!"

Soutter did not have to consult the chart or the map sent from the flagship. The ships had been able to hold the enemy at bay, but only because they had closed the range during the day, and retired in the hours of darkness. But the new Turkish guns, which were probably on or near the all-commanding ridge of Sari Bair, would soon prove a real threat to any large warships that came too close. Even the old Russian ship *Askold,* popularly known to the troops as the "Packet of Woodbines" because of her five spindly funnels, had narrowly escaped one of the enemy's big shells.

Soutter said, "The marines *must* be supported, sir. They've been in action almost without a break since *Impulsive's* landing parties were massacred. These are not seasoned soldiers—by rights they should be in Port Said continuing their training, doing guard-duty on the Canal."

Purves glared at the *Impulsive.* Smoke was drifting from her wounds as well as from her funnels. "Do you think I don't know? As far as I can tell it's the first ridge on the left front of our positions which is the real threat. That's where the snipers and enemy machine-gunners are. Our marines cannot advance while that ridge is in Turkish hands." He waved vaguely at the two blackened muzzles immediately below the bridge. "Our guns could wipe them out in a single day if we could stand closer inshore. Their heavy artillery has put paid to that!"

Soutter's glance fell on the navigator as he entered more calculations in his log.

He could find no fault with the admiral's comment. To order the gunnery officer to open fire at a more realistic range, perhaps ten or twelve thousand yards, was like passing a sentence of death on the marines as well. No range-finder was that accurate, especially when the guns had to fire into rugged territory which was poorly described on the chart.

He said bluntly, "Well, sir, they won't be able to hold on much longer. The Australian 4th Brigade can offer some support but they are hard-pressed, too. The Royal Marine Brigade on the other beach has had so many casualties I think they may be withdrawn for regrouping at Mudros."

Purves turned and gazed at him calmly. "You always were a canny dog, Soutter. You show an excellent grasp of the facts, but you manage somehow to avoid the one true issue."

Soutter met his eyes with equal hostility. "I imagine that, as we are in command of this inshore squadron, the admiral has put the decision in your hands, sir?"

Purves did not reply directly. He appeared to be watching their nearest escort, a small destroyer regularly deluged with spray as she zigzagged abeam of her massive consort.

"Lieutenant-Colonel Waring is a very experienced officer."

Soutter wondered how he would present it if the worst happened. *If?* There was little doubt now. He thought of the grave-faced R.M.A. captain, the one officer who had given heart to the inexperienced marines. Was he still alive? Soutter had seen the wounded for himself. Left too long without proper dressings or water: men and boys driven to the edge of despair and anguish and then beyond even that.

And their own captain of marines, Bruce Seddon, who enjoyed playing whist with the commander: what of him?

He said, "I was not impressed with Colonel Waring, sir."

"I have known him for some years." Purves sounded less certain. "A fine record."

"He has no experience of a war like this." Soutter added bitterly, "Who has? I am not suggesting that Colonel Waring lacks courage. At Omdurman or Trafalgar I am certain he would have distinguished himself."

Purves tugged his cap over his eyes and said angrily, "I didn't make the damned rules. I don't suppose anyone in England cares a jot for this campaign in any case. Damned civilians—they want to be safe behind their fighting men. I've no time for them!"

Soutter thought of his quarters down aft, of the clean bunk where Colonel Ede had found peace for the first time since the landings at Gaba Tepe. Those hard-won beaches had already been rechristened by the army and were now called Anzac Cove, a name written in blood.

Just to lie there for a while without every eye on the bridge upon him; to drink too much like the red-faced man who was now sitting carelessly in his chair. As soon as he thought of it he knew he would do neither.

Purves muttered, "There's another R.M. battalion on its way to support Waring. If we waited one more day, two at the most, the new battalion would relieve them, at least to get some rest."

Soutter almost felt sorry for him. Almost. "We can't afford it, sir. If the Turks overrun those positions it would take an army corps to fight its way back. Even then they might be repelled."

Purves pulled out his watch and beckoned to his flag-lieutenant, who was hovering nearby.

"Warn the wireless office. Signal to the Flag, coded and Top Secret."

Soutter walked to the gratings and climbed up to obtain a better view of the shore. Even above the noise of his ship's fans and a winch near Y Turret, he could still hear the far-off clatter of machine-guns and dull explosions, guns or bombs he could not tell. There was so much haze and smoke it seemed the whole coastline was smouldering. He heard Purves dictating the signal, his voice quite empty. Very soon now that smouldering would burst into flames.

Tomorrow the ships would repeat their bombardments, each to her allotted sector, but the shells would be at extreme range to fall on the enemy's support lines or reinforcements on the march. And this time there would be no need to avoid the one ridge ahead of Waring's men, because by then the marines would have stormed and seized it, or they would all be dead.

He glanced curiously at the marine bugler who was always in attendance: one of *Reliant's* own detachment which was over there somewhere in the smoke. Then, angry at himself and ashamed at the intrusion, he looked away. The youth was standing rigidly at his position but he had heard Purves dictate the signal and his eyes were shining with tears, which he made no attempt to staunch.

Soutter seemed to hear the words he had read at the last Divisions before leaving Mudros, as if someone else were speaking them aloud on the bridge.

And there shall be no more death, neither sorrow nor crying, neither shall there be any more pain: for the former things are passed away . . .

Lieutenant-Colonel Jack Waring glanced around the command dugout, the cave now hated by everyone who visited it. In the flickering light from the small lamp his eyes shone like stones as he watched his companions. They looked as if they would drop once they found somewhere to sit or lie down. Their eyes were staring, and flickered with alarm at each unusual sound, the far-off crack of a sniper's rifle or the thud of a grenade on the northern sector of the cove where Australians and New Zealanders were still holding out.

Jonathan Blackwood sipped a cup of brackish water but barely tasted it. The attacks had continued for most of the day, as soon as the big warships had retired out of range of the Turkish guns. The Turks had come across the dusty landscape in yelling waves, to be met by the company's murderous machine-gun fire and the endless bark of rifles. Each time the enemy had retired, leaving piles of dead and wounded, and each time the marines, gasping from thirst and exhaustion, had prayed it was the last.

Then, just before dusk had drawn its copper glow over the ravines and gullies, they had attacked once more. At the critical moment one of the machine-guns on the left flank had jammed, and even as a corporal had rushed to clear the stoppage a grenade had exploded in the trench. The place had been too confined to allow the crude bomb its full effect, but the explosion had killed Second Lieutenant Dane of the second platoon and five other marines, who had been ripped apart in the blast. Jonathan had recalled the Australian captain's warning and had yelled, "On the parapet, lads! Fight them off!"

And in the light of an early flare and the dull copper sky, the marines had scrambled up from the firestep and onto the parapet, firing blindly through the smoke, until with their magazines empty they had faced the enemy for the first time, bayonet to bayonet. Anger mixed with fear was a terrible combination, and when the Turks had broken under the ferocity of the defenders' steel, some of the marines would have chased after them, their minds unhinged by the pain and savagery of battle.

All told they had lost twenty men and two officers including the luckless Cripwell. The remainder were barely able to stand and stared at the lip of the trench; they no longer wondered how they would die, only when.

Waring said crisply, "A bad day, but it might have been worse. I have had a message from the beach. More boats will be attempting to land supplies and ammunition tonight. With luck some of the wounded can be taken off too." He looked at their dulled expressions. Captain Seddon of *Reliant*'s marines had his wrist in a sling, after seizing a Turkish bayonet to ward it off while he waved an empty, useless revolver. Livesay's head was in his hands, his fingers dark with dried blood, his breathing heavy and painful.

Young Tarrier was peering at a map, but stopped when Waring said, "We are getting support in 24 hours, from the new Royal Marines division at Mudros. The Australians will also send fresh troops once they have regrouped."

They all looked as Tarrier asked hoarsely, "But how can we hold on, sir?"

Waring eyed him with cold dislike. "We must defend our sector of the beach until we are relieved. *Hold the line.* There is no alternative course open. We have the sea at our backs, and few would survive retreat once the enemy retook this defence line."

Livesay said wearily, "It can't be done."

Waring snapped, "And what do *you* think, Captain Blackwood?"

Jonathan glanced at the lamp's flickering, smoking wick. What a story this cave could tell. One day.

"The fleet can't drive the Turks off that ridge without causing heavy casualties amongst our men. No naval gun is that accurate. We need a proper system of spotters ashore." He tried to clear his brain. What was he saying? It no longer mattered. At daylight the enemy would attack again, knowing that the defenders could not survive another day. The lucky ones would die instantly. The others, like the man he could hear sobbing and pleading outside in the trench, would linger, alive and aware. He had lost a hand and a foot when the grenade had exploded. Better he had died: his pitiful cries for help were having a damaging effect on his listless companions.

Waring touched his moustache. "Suppose we commanded that ridge?"

Jonathan said, "Is that what *they* expect, sir?"

Waring shrugged. "Something of that sort. If we took it we could prevent frontal attacks and allow the squadron to concentrate their fire on the enemy support lines." One hand tapped impatiently on the stained map.

Jonathan said slowly, "Eight hundred yards across open ground, and then up to the top." The others were watching his lips as if they had all gone suddenly deaf. "The Turks haven't attacked us at night." His mind was grappling with the immediate problem. He had witnessed it in France: the night raids, unlike any field training or staff college, unlike anything orderly or civilised. Grim-faced Tommies arming themselves with sharpened entrenching tools, knives and nail-studded clubs. They had become part of the mud and dirt that were a soldier's lot. Methodically, ruthlessly, and without hope, they had gone out under the flares and through the wires to extend their positions, to kill or to die.

"If there was a diversion . . ."

Waring's eyes glittered from either cheek. "The boats coming into the cove—they'll provide a tempting bait."

Major Livesay seemed to emerge from his despair like an angry bear. "Bait, sir? Sacrifice our own people?"

Jonathan rubbed his own reddened eyes. "It's our only chance. Choice does not come into it." He did not look at Waring: he knew the triumph he would see there. Even in the face of death Waring would not alter.

Waring said, "That's settled then. Pity we've no light machine-guns, but once our people are in position a party can carry one of the others up to the ridge. That'll dampen their fires a bit if their flank is under our guns for a change!"

Major Livesay said dully, "I shall go, sir. I'll take only volunteers."

Waring was already studying the map. "You will detail the *right men,* Livesay. Volunteers are not always the best material." He glanced up and gave the major a twisted smile. "Besides, if you rely on volunteers, you'll likely be tackling the ridge on your own!"

He gave his humourless braying laugh, which brought an instant response of shrill curses from the dying man outside.

"Keep him quiet, somebody." Waring looked at Tarrier. "I want a runner sent to the beach with a message to be transmitted to the ships. Pick a good man. I don't want him down there in the gully with all the other corpses!"

Jonathan found that he could watch the colonel without anger, and it surprised him. The navy had been requested to perform this thing, and Waring, the callous, arrogant bastard that he was, would carry it out, no matter what.

Waring added as an afterthought, "As second-in-command I think . . ." His glance fell on Captain Seddon who was rocking quietly back and forth and holding his bayoneted hand. "On second thought." He smiled at Jonathan. "You go. As a gunner you might be of some use up there, what?"

Jonathan shrugged. "Who else, sir?"

Waring frowned at his abruptness. "Lieutenants Maxted and Wyke. Pick the N.C.O.'s yourself."

Livesay lurched to his feet. "*I'll* deal with that." He hesitated by the blanket curtain and said, "What time shall we move out, sir?" His face was stiff. A man already dead, Jonathan thought. He was married, with two boys who would doubtless end up in the corps. But at this moment his family would still believe him to be safely in Egypt with nothing more dangerous than the mosquitoes to deal with.

"Report to me when you're ready."

Waring watched him leave and remarked, "I suppose that's why he was given a company of green recruits!" Waring's M.O.A. entered and after searching through a heavy pack produced a full bottle of White Horse. "Drink, Blackwood?"

Jonathan would have given almost anything for a glass of Scotch. He seemed to hear Harry Payne's voice in his ear. *You don't need it, sir. Not like some.* He heard himself reply, "Later, sir. When it's done."

He walked out into the darkness and watched another flare light up the gullies where the sunset had disappeared.

He heard voices calling faintly from the long slope of no man's land which separated their shallow defences from the nearest ridge; men dying even while he stood there. As some of his own had done. Thankfully they had managed to recover their bodies from in front of the trench. God alone knew when—or if—they could ever be buried. If you showed your head for more than a few seconds you were dead.

He found the two detailed lieutenants crouching on the firestep, Maxted who commanded the second platoon quietly smoking a cigarette, the glowing tip cupped in his fist. He was probably thinking about his second-in-command, who had been ripped apart by the grenade just hours ago. But for his body blocking the way, Maxted would have been the casualty. He seemed a good, serious-minded lieutenant; and Wyke, whose own second-in-command had been killed on this same firestep, was his usual laconic self.

"Any chance of some leave after this, sir?"

Maxted gave a soft laugh. "Where to, for God's sake? Mudros-on-Sea?"

Wyke did not hear him. "Just to saunter along Piccadilly again . . . order a bottle of champagne at Hatchett's and dance the night away with some fabulous girl!"

Maxted stubbed out his cigarette and said, "On *your* pay?" He laughed again, a sad sound in this place, and added, "Sorry, Chris. I forgot your father is a major-general."

Jonathan climbed up and stared across the dark emptiness. In daylight and the sun's pitiless glare it was different, a panorama of war, its cruel nakedness always there to stop a man's heart. But now in the cooler air there was only the smell of it. Smoke, lyddite, and the dead. He heard the two lieutenants talking quietly below him, with the resilience of youth that made them feel invulnerable. They had already accepted that men they had known, closely or at a distance as demanded by the corps, were gone. Even if a corpse lay beneath an old blanket or strip of canvas, it was not the man.

He heard Major Livesay's boots in the trench and knew he was coming to gather his raiding party together. There were too many officers going but without them, if the worst happened, the force would be headless, its determination gone before anything was achieved.

Payne climbed up beside him. "Got this off one of them Turks, sir." Even in the darkness, the long trench-knife seemed to shine.

Jonathan gripped his arm. "You've not been out there alone, man?"

Payne wiped his mouth with his sleeve. "Safe as houses, sir."

If Waring ever discovered what he had done, Payne would face a court martial or worse.

Jonathan sighed. "All gone, have they?"

"Think so. I saw that flare, though: I reckon they know about the boats coming to the beach." He added heavily, "Like they did about us!"

Jonathan eased the knife down into his boot. Payne knew everything.

Major Livesay asked uncertainly, "Ready?"

Jonathan joined him with the others. "The sooner the better, sir."

They were momentarily alone, the other dark figures somehow apart.

Livesay said, "If anything happens, old chap . . ."

"Yes. Do the same for me, sir." It would not help the major to know that Jonathan had nobody else, whereas Livesay had everything to lose.

Sergeant McCann came up. "With respect, sir, if we gets cut off, there's barely enough of our lads to hold the line."

Livesay nodded vigorously, hardly hearing what he said. "We know that, Sergeant."

McCann seemed satisfied. "We'll show them bastards, sir!"

They stood in line along the firestep, their hair ruffling in the breeze, their helmets discarded, no matter what the colonel might say about it. Then up and over the parapet, the horizon that now reached out into unending blackness.

Nothing stirred, and even the wounded had fallen silent. It was as if the whole of the peninsula was holding its breath for them.

Livesay had drawn his revolver, but the lieutenants had armed themselves with rifles and bayonets and were spaced out along the untidy line of men.

Livesay bit his lip until the pain steadied him and said, "Forward, marines—good luck, lads!"

Jonathan felt the safety catch with his thumb. Livesay's encouragement was puny compared with what was expected from them. But its very simplicity was perhaps all the more inspiring.

Major Andrew Livesay held up his hand and the long extended line of men came to a shuffling halt on either side of him. He could hear some of the marines gasping for breath as if they had advanced with full kit and at the double. *Fear.* He tried to calm his own breathing, and when he lowered his arm he could feel the sweat beneath his thick tunic like ice rime. Despite their slow and stealthy approach their footfalls and the sound of an occasional stumble in the darkness had seemed deafening. But no flares had burst overhead and the machine-guns had remained silent, and all the more menacing.

One of the scouts was returning, his rifle and bayonet at the high port as if he were taking part in an exercise. It was Corporal Timbrell.

"Nothin', sir." He sniffed the damp air. "Corpses by the cartload, theirs or Aussies I didn't wait to find out." He waited in silence, watching his officer without curiosity. He had done his part, and had left another marine up ahead as a picket in case they were approaching an ambush.

"I see, Corporal." Livesay rubbed his chin. "I see." He saw Jonathan coming out of the darkness. "Ah—what do you think we've covered?"

Jonathan sensed the major's uncertainty. "About halfway. Four hundred yards at a guess." He stared ahead but the slab-sided ridge looked no nearer. He had heard what Timbrell had said: just as well it was so dark. The stench of corpses, burned scrub and a few shell-blasted trees had been with them all the way. He turned to look at the trench, the scattered rocks beyond, but there was nothing. It was as if they had fallen from the sky into some unknown landscape.

Surely the enemy must know they were in this fought-over desert?

Livesay said, "Better get on. Tell the others." He saw Jonathan stride away, unhurriedly or so it appeared, and wondered at his calmness. Livesay was in his forties, old for his rank, and for several years had held settled administrative posts, the last being at the training barracks. After sending off the recruits to their various ships and battalions, he might have stayed in Port Said or even Cairo. Enjoying a mess life of sorts again, showing the flag. He felt himself shiver. But not this. He was not trained for brutal murder. He cursed Waring and his stubborn dedication, even Blackwood for defending the colonel's stupid plan. They would never get back, and if they were taken prisoner . . .

Corporal Timbrell said, "They're ready to move, sir."

"I know that, damn it!"

Timbrell's eyes widened in the darkness. In the corps, you obeyed, and you did it better than any line-soldier. But Timbrell had never considered that an officer could be afraid. The realisation swept over him like a tide-race. God, you could smell it!

Timbrell peered round for the burly Sergeant McCann. Did he know? He swung away and hurried toward the brooding ridge again, his bayonet hovering occasionally toward some sprawled body. Things darted away from his boots and Timbrell grimaced. Rats. Dozens of them.

On the right flank of their wavering line, Jonathan stepped carefully over a piece of splintered wood. Part of a cart, an ammunition limber, another relic of war. Would it ever be clean again here? He sensed Harry Payne beside him as he had seen him many times, eyes everywhere, lips always pursed in a soundless whistle. He thought suddenly, vividly of Hawks Hill in the perfumed green of spring, so different from this baking hell, so different from the other days. Wounded and shell-shocked officers sitting in the early sunshine, or merely staring into space like those he had seen at Portsmouth. Men who had lost their pasts in the trenches and had no future to recognise.

He tensed. A sound, a smell—what was it?

Out of the stony ground itself a figure sprang into the air, as if one of the corpses had come to life. He heard Payne gasp as the figure jumped onto his shoulders and pulled him down. Too stunned to move, the nearest marines stared with disbelief, and one shouted, "He's got a knife!"

Jonathan ran to help but sprawled headlong when his boot caught in some tangled wire. His rifle clattered across the dry stones, but he managed to reach out and seize the soldier's belt.

With a sob he dragged the Turkish trench-knife from his boot and drove it into the man's ribs with such force that he could feel the pain lance up his arm as the blade glanced off bone, then went in to the hilt.

Two other marines dragged the Turk from Payne's back and Sergeant McCann thrust down with his bayonet to end the last choking cries.

"All right, Payne?" Jonathan helped him to his feet, and for a moment longer they clung together like drunken squaddies emerging from a wet canteen. Payne could barely get his breath. Then he groped in the darkness and recovered his rifle, and said hoarsely, "Told you that knife would come in handy, didn't I?"

Livesay was there now, peering round, bent almost double as if he expected a fusillade of shots.

"What's happened?"

Jonathan looked down at the man he had just killed. Only a thing. He said, "I think he was a sentry. Either that or he was stalking Corporal Timbrell and didn't realise this lot were behind him." He heard Livesay's rasping breath and tried to help. "Just as well you ordered a halt back there." He was surprised he could speak so easily about it. The madness.

Livesay pressed him further. "You mean he's the only one here?"

"Until he's relieved. Or maybe he'd fallen asleep. After all, who would expect a depleted platoon to advance on the Turkish army?" What the hell did it matter, he thought. The Turk was dead, and nothing had happened.

Someone exclaimed, "Look, sir! A flare!"

But it was far away, probably a small one fired from a pistol.

Payne said, "The buggers have taken the bait. The supply boats must be standing into the cove."

Livesay whispered, "Thank God! We'd better advance, Blackwood!"

This from the officer who had protested to Beaky Waring: *Sacrifice our own people?* What had happened to that man?

Payne handed Jonathan the evil-looking knife. "All nice an' clean now." He found it hard to express his true feelings. "Ta, sir. For what you did. I thought I was done for good an' proper that time!" He peered after Livesay's shadow until it was lost in darkness. "Well, you lives and learns."

Jonathan cradled his rifle across his arm. "Couldn't manage without you!" He heard Payne chuckle. In this terrible place, while they moved slowly away from the last man to die, the sound was the warmest thing he had ever heard.

Jonathan leaned on his borrowed rifle and waited while the marines, in small squads, clambered over the lip of the ridge and fanned out in three directions.

Made it. We made it. If he was out of breath it was because of the last part of the climb. He almost wished it otherwise. He could feel the dead Turk's blood already hardening on his fingers but sensed only disgust.

Lieutenant Maxted crunched across the loose stone and sought out Major Livesay.

"One prisoner, sir. An N.C.O. of some kind. He was sleeping beside one of their old Maxim guns." He was quite matter-of-fact about it. "No other machine-guns though. They must have carried them down to rake our supply boats."

Livesay stared around with increasing desperation. "If only there was a moon, some sort of light!"

They all turned as sporadic firing echoed against the ridge. Sergeant McCann said, "'Ere we bloody well go!"

Jonathan asked, "Any grenades, John?"

Maxted tore his mind from the sound. "Sorry, sir. Yes— there's a crate of them in one of their dugouts."

Livesay came out of his thoughts as well and snapped, "Take Sergeant McCann and issue them to each squad. Just in case . . ." He did not finish.

Jonathan watched Maxted hurry away. Thank God he had not noticed Livesay's uncertainty. But when dawn broke. . . . He said, "Issue rations, sir?"

"Ah—yes, of course. Squad by squad, but have every sector manned." He flinched nervously as a corporal called out, "The heavy machine-gun's here, sir!"

There were several derisive cheers as the lump-shaped Langmaid and his assistants stumbled into the defence line, and two others dragged the ammunition belts after them like shining snakes. But there was relief in their voices as well. Once it had been hopeless. Now, with the heavy machine-gun and some grenades at hand, they had a chance, and it put new life into them. They might even get the ancient Maxim to fire.

Livesay said, "They can have a tot of rum with their rations. I—I think we should have some too."

Jonathan glanced around but Payne had already vanished. He recalled when he had been resting in a ruined village on the Western Front, behind the support lines but not far enough to shut out the endless roar of artillery. Payne had disappeared then also, and had eventually returned with a dead chicken and some sticks of freshly baked bread.

His shadow loomed towards the two officers now and he handed a mug to the major before offering Jonathan what he knew was the familiar silver cup.

Livesay swallowed deeply. "God! That's the stuff to give the troops!" He gestured with the mug. "Leave the flask, Payne, there's a good chap."

"Sir." Payne seemed to be waiting for his reaction. "All right?"

The cup felt cold in his bloodied fingers. It was Scotch. The wheres and hows meant nothing to Payne, or to Jonathan himself now either.

Livesay was saying, "When we get some daylight we'll know better what to expect."

Jonathan ignored the meaningless comment but heard him refilling his mug. How many was that? He would be useless when the time came. The Scotch might hold his fear at bay, but it would not kill it.

He said, "Go and get yourself some food, Payne." He held out the cup. "And thanks."

Payne grinned. "Told you, didn't I, sir?"

Jonathan looked at Livesay's outline. He must stop him from thinking about the enemy counterattack, as attack there surely would be once they had discovered what had happened. There were more muffled shots, and the sound of a different machine-gun. But not Turkish; more like the one Langmaid was tinkering with while his crew dragged sandbags closer to give him some protection.

Jonathan said, "You once served with Captain Soutter, I believe, sir?"

Livesay wrestled with his reeling mind. "Yes. And Rear Admiral Purves, for good measure. Why?"

"I was wondering why they dislike each other so much. It was something that happened aboard the light cruiser *Assurance* in the North Sea—that's all I know."

Livesay tilted the flask over his mug but it was empty. Savagely he flung it against the sandbags.

"I was in command of the marine detachment. Purves was the captain and Soutter the gunnery officer." He was feeling his face as if it hurt him. "Peacetime, of course, but we all knew it was coming. It was a night exercise off the Danish coast—we were showing no lights as I recall." His words were slurred, angry. "Anyway, we ran down two fishing boats and some men drowned. Soutter was the officer-of-the-watch. at the time, and was ordered to face a court of inquiry. Could have been the end of him . . ."

He was losing the thread of his own description and when Jonathan prompted him he snapped, "I mean a court martial,, man!"

It made no sense. Soutter careless, even incompetent? A man who handled both himself and *Reliant* with such discipline and control; and yet was not ashamed to reveal his own pain and pity for a dying midshipman.

Livesay lurched to his feet. "But Purves interceded, spoke up for him. He was well-connected even then. The matter was dropped. So just forget it, will you?"

Jonathan propped his head in his hands and felt the dried sand on his scalp. A bath, a swim in some impossible river. . . . He looked up and saw Lieutenant Wyke standing in silence, his fair hair ruffling in the light breeze from the sea.

"Have you seen Major Livesay, sir?"

"He's gone to relieve himself." He could sense Wyke's anger and something more, despite his level voice. "What is it?"

"The prisoner escaped, sir."

Jonathan stood up slowly, sensing there was worse to come.

Wyke said, "The sentry must have released his arms so that he could feed himself. The Turk garrotted him with some wire. I'm not quite sure when."

"Who was it?" But he already knew.

"Private Barlow, Sir. He was only seventeen."

"Yes." The one who had looked about twelve. What a way to end. "I'll tell the major if you like."

Wyke said in the same inexpressive voice, "No, sir. He's my company commander. But thank you." They heard Livesay coughing nearby and as he turned to go he added, "But I wish to God *you* were."

McCann joined him and said harshly, "Some of the lads want to go after that Turk, sir. If I got my 'ands on that bastard I'd . . ."

"It wouldn't help, Sergeant. We'll need every one of them when it's daylight."

McCann seemed to force his mind away from the murdered Barlow and said, "It would take an army to get us off here, sir."

"They've *got* an army." He saw some shadowy figures carrying the limp body down into a shallow depression at the end of the ridge. One of them would be Geach, his friend from Yorkshire. *Hey-oop, then.* He could almost hear it.

"This is a fine bloody mess, Blackwood!" Livesay came out of the darkness, his breathing worse than before. "I shall get to the bottom of it, believe me! How could anyone be so stupid?"

The stench of whisky was almost physical. Jonathan said, "He paid for it. Sergeant McCann was ready to kill the prisoner when he found him asleep."

"I know all about that! I told him as I tell you now, we'll not fight with their barbarous methods! We did not make this war but we'll surely fight it by the rules, dammit!"

"There are no rules, sir."

Lieutenant Wyke hovered nearby. "The firing has stopped, sir."

"What?"

Wyke replied calmly, "Either the attack failed, or the boats took a different course. Maybe they returned to the ships."

Livesay strode this way and that. "Then it'll be our turn next!"

Jonathan said, "The enemy will probably know we're here if the prisoner has reached his unit. They'll take their time, put out their snipers before they begin an attack."

"Quite the expert, aren't you?"

Jonathan ignored the sneer. How could a man alter so much? It was as if Livesay's enemies were here on the ridge instead of out there in the darkness.

"We'll stand-to in an hour. Change the sentries and . . ." His voice trailed away.

Jonathan saw the lieutenant's quick nod. Wyke and Maxted had already dealt with it. After the last few days they could not afford to forget anything.

He leaned against the sandbags and stared hard into the darkness. Suppose there were to be no relief force? It would be here that they would all die. He waited for the realisation to move him, but it left him like a stranger.

Just over there, at no more than 800 yards, Colonel Jack Waring would be gathering his resources. Preparing to fight to the last man. And what about young Roger Tarrier, whom he had promised his father to look after? *There are no rules.* The words came back as if to mock him. The only water available was what each man carried, and most of that had probably been drunk. Enough ammunition, but only just enough. He heard the scrape of entrenching tools and knew that the youth Barlow was being laid to rest.

And how will I behave?

In the darkness someone laughed and Jonathan turned to see who it was. But there was nobody.

He unbuttoned his holster and took out the revolver.

Only one thing seemed certain. These men, some no more than boys, were worth fighting for, if necessary dying for, if only to shame those who had put them in this hellish place.

Not because it is expected of me, or because I was trained, perhaps for this one hopeless battle. But because I care.

"Time to stand-to, sir."

Jonathan opened his eyes, from mindless rest to instant readiness. He looked up at Lieutenant Wyke's face, covered with a fair stubble that somehow made him look younger.

"You shouldn't have let me sleep." He allowed Wyke to help him to his feet, aware of the marines moving into their positions, bent almost double as instructed in case of snipers.

He saw Payne standing by the Turkish Maxim gun with Langmaid and some of the others, who were stacking ammunition where it would be safe from any stray bullet. Langmaid was saying, "I done most of my training with the old Nordenfelt. Good gun in its way, and you could still crank off a 'undred rounds a minute from every barrel. But a Maxim, I ain't so sure."

Payne grinned. "I can manage it, Bert. Once a gunner always a gunner, that's what they say."

Jonathan turned as Livesay approached him with Lieutenant Maxted. The major looked at his officers, his face pale in the first lightening in the sky.

He said, "Have the ammunition shared. One grenade per

section." He winced as a machine-gun rattled into life, but not in this part of the cove. Troops were on the move, theirs or ours it no longer mattered.

Jonathan took out his binoculars and wiped the lenses with his handkerchief. He saw a marine shake his water bottle and stare at it with surprise. His friend offered his own and he took a quick grateful swallow: men finding strength when they had none of their own to offer.

He moved his glasses with great care, his jaw tight from strain as he waited for the crack of a sniper's rifle. There was no other ridge within range of rifle-fire which was higher than this, but they all had to be careful.

Livesay said thickly, "Minimum fire. Tell the N.C.O.s I doubt that the escaped prisoner saw how many men we have, but the enemy will try to draw us out." He saw the untidy machine-gunner watching him and added with unnecessary sarcasm, "Make sure *your* people know how to keep the barrel casing filled with liquid—at least the barrel must be kept covered at all times. These water-cooled weapons need a lot of care."

Langmaid bared his teeth and looked at his assistants, each young enough to be his son.

"I told 'em to piss in it if need be, sir." He added rudely, "They should be good at that!"

Livesay turned away as if he had not heard, or maybe he was too used to Langmaid's insolence to care. He was peering at his watch, even as the first faint light topped the ridge and the great ships steamed into their positions, fifteen-inch guns high angled, battle-ensigns streaming above the lingering shadows.

Crack! A heavy bullet smacked into the sandbags and Jonathan saw the grains trickling across his boots. Good shot, but the angle was too extreme.

Gunfire like distant thunder made the ground quiver, and seconds later they heard the shells tearing overhead. Men cringed and covered their ears.

Wyke said uncertainly, "Wrong direction, sir."

"Turkish ships over there in the Narrows, snug behind their minefields." Jonathan felt the bitterness again. The Narrows, which the fleet had tried to force with such terrible losses. Now the enemy were firing right over the peninsula in the hope of hitting some of the attacking ships.

The response was deafening, and Jonathan guessed that the battleships and battle-cruisers, *Reliant* in the van, were nearer than they had expected. There was a buzzing drone overhead, like a lazy bee on a summer's afternoon, and he knew it was one of the spotting aircraft sent to estimate the range and bearing of the anchored Turkish warships.

He imagined the gunnery officers, fingers itching to fire, turrets moving smoothly beneath them as the information was passed to the crews, while more massive shells were swung into position. High-explosive and shrapnel to turn the support lines into a smoking ruin, but first concentrating on those enemy ships.

When it came it was still a shock: the devastating scream of shells followed by the echoes of the explosions. Again and again while daylight strengthened and showed the drifting smoke, and at last the glitter of the sea beyond the defence line.

It was ironic, Jonathan thought, the Turks had been caught out by some last-moment plan in unloading stores and reinforcements. But had there been new support, Anzac or marines, they could have crossed to the enemy lines without a challenge.

The bombardment began in earnest, the ridge shaking violently as if a volcano was about to erupt.

Livesay said tersely, "Fire the signal. Otherwise they might still drop a few on us."

Wyke raised his arm and fired. Seconds later, two pearl-like flares of bright emerald green were taken by the breeze and drifted slowly towards the cove.

Jonathan leaned on the sandbags and rested his forehead on his arm. They would all see the signal and know that a handful of marines had achieved the impossible. Nothing could move in no man's land now without being caught in lethal cross fire from the trenches and the ridge.

He picked up the rifle and worked the bolt to load it. And the ridge was where the enemy would come. There was nowhere else to go unless they were prepared to face the murderous bombardment from the sea.

The officers glanced at one another, as if trying to remember something before it was too late. Only Livesay stood apart and alone, his face like death as he blinked at each scream of shells.

"Here they come!"

The officers turned and scattered. One shell or grenade could kill all of them.

Livesay yelled, "One hundred yards! Independent! *Fire!"*

The instant clatter of the heavy machine-gun, followed at length by the old Maxim, sent more echoes bouncing around the ridge and through the nearest gully where so many dead still lay untended and forgotten.

Jonathan wiped his mouth and watched Turkish soldiers ducking amongst rocks; some of them must have been on the move for hours, and had almost reached the ridge.

The machine-gun swept over them and he saw them fall like bloody puppets, or try to turn and run. The cliff-top line came to life and the machine-guns swept out from the trench where he had said good-bye to the Australian from Perth whose father was a boat builder.

Caught in the open, the Turks were mown down on every side. But others had taken positions in the larger rock falls, and as a marine stood to fire down a sniper's bullet spun him round, his face almost shot away. But he did not die, and the others stared at him with horror as he thrashed at the ground with his boots while his fingers clawed at the blood and torn flesh where his eyes had been.

The Maxim jammed and Jonathan shouted, *"Get down, Payne! Never mind the bloody gun!"*

Payne turned, his eyes watering in the first proper sunlight. Then he grinned, and re-opened fire as the stoppage was cleared.

But soon he had no more ammunition, and seizing his rifle and fixed bayonet he loped across the rubble to join Jonathan.

"God, look at 'em!"

Dead and wounded Turks lay everywhere, some turning over as if regaining life as more bullets ripped across them.

But they were still coming, yelling and screaming like madmen, their bayonets jabbing at the air as they scrambled up the side of the ridge while snipers pinned down the defenders.

A corporal named Cowell picked up a captured grenade, one of the new German types that resembled a potato masher, and his mind visibly grappled with the unfamiliar weapon before he pulled out the cord, and stood to fling it down the slope. Then a bullet smashed into his chest like a hammer and he fell by the sandbags, the grenade hissing out sparks beneath his leg.

Sergeant McCann snatched it up with a curse and flung it

over the edge where it exploded instantly, cutting down a running group of soldiers like a scythe.

"Over here!"

Jonathan ran down across the depression and saw several Turks clambering over their own dead, firing as they came, meeting the marines' bayonets until they were driven back or killed. Four marines also lay dead, while another crawled blindly over their bodies pleading, "Don't leave me, lads! For Christ's sake don't go!" A crucifix dangled from his neck, and Jonathan knew he was the man who had asked the chaplain for a blessing.

Wyke was firing his rifle, and then drew his revolver as more heads bobbed amongst the rocks. Langmaid left his gun and snapped his bayonet onto a fallen rifle.

"No more ammo, sir!" In his big fist the bayonet looked like a bodkin. Steel clashed against steel and the marines yelled encouragement to one another, with little time to reload. And all the while the great shells roared above them, while by comparison in this forgotten place they fought like ants.

Wyke was down, his face shocked with pain and with blood soaking one arm. A Turkish soldier rose above the sandbags and stared at the fair-haired lieutenant, then took careful aim with his rifle.

Jonathan saw them, motionless like crude statuary: Wyke on his knees while the Turk trained the bloodstained bayonet at his shoulders. Dispassionately he watched the face swim above the Webley's foresight, then he squeezed the trigger and felt the revolver buck in his fist. In France they had joked that a Webley could stop a charging man in his tracks. He broke the revolver and felt insane laughter tearing at his brain. The man had gone: there was only a feather of bright blood where he had been standing. So what they said was true . . . He fumbled for six fresh bullets and continued to fire. Around him men were cursing and dying, and as though in some horrific dream he heard McCann bawl, "Fall back, lads! Reload!"

Despairing, mad with thirst and pain, the remains of the platoon, no more than a dozen, closed ranks while the wounded crawled or were dragged to join them.

There was a sudden lull as even the naval bombardment ceased. Jonathan felt a hand on his bloodied boot and saw Wyke peering up at him with pleading, desperate eyes.

He stooped down and heard him whisper, "Shoot me now. I'm done for anyway." Then the silence seemed to penetrate even his pain-shocked brain, and he stared at the sandbags and sprawled corpses and gasped, "What's happening?"

Maxted ran down to them and, as if to prove something he did not himself believe, tossed his rifle to the ground.

"The bastards have gone!" He crouched by Wyke. "I wish you could see it!"

Jonathan and Corporal Timbrell approached the edge of the ridge, ready to drop flat if a sniper marked them down. He had to wipe his eyes several times before he could see beyond the pall of thick smoke.

In long, extended lines the Royal Marine Light Infantry was advancing through the piles of corpses, with bayonets shining: they even appeared to be in step. Behind him, Payne said hoarsely, "Jesus, it's the relief brigade from Mudros. I never thought . . ." He could not finish it.

It seemed an age before a lieutenant and some forty marines reached the ridge, some men averting their eyes as they saw the great patterns of blood, the gaping dead, some in uniforms identical to their own and with familiar ranks and badges.

The officer found Livesay and saluted. "We apologise for

the delay, sir. The Australian 4th Brigade broke through and we joined them."

Livesay said dully, "We held them off." He stared around with a strange, resentful expression, as if cheated of the death he had come to expect.

The relief force was already scattering among the rocks, and some light machine-guns were being set up.

The young lieutenant made another attempt when he saw Jonathan. "You may recall your men, sir. Lieutenant-Colonel Waring has ordered you back to the line."

Jonathan said, "These *are* my men. All that are left. Bring some stretchers, will you?"

Again he thought of the Australian infantry captain. Needing to leave; compelled to stay. He walked slowly from place to place, staring at each youthful expression frozen in the instant of death. He must never forget.

Payne followed him anxiously. Men called out in small voices as they were lifted into stretchers: Waring must have sent one for each man in the platoon. They would not need many of them now.

Somewhere a bugle sounded, and from another world the rapid fire of guns and rifles shattered the dusty stillness. Then Payne felt something like relief as his captain holstered his revolver and walked unhurriedly after the stretcher bearers.

While men fought and died along the adjoining landing beaches, the remains of B Company and the other marines were ferried in pinnaces out to *Reliant*. There were no cheers this time.

At dusk, the Turks counterattacked and the ridge changed hands again.

EIGHT

Jonathan Blackwood stood by the covered cockpit of a fast-moving pinnace and narrowed his eyes against the sun's hard reflection on the pristine whiteness of the hospital ship, which had arrived three days earlier and had been loading sick and wounded around the clock. Against the rocky headland of Mudros Bay and the shimmering Aegean beyond, she somehow managed to look at peace, and remote from all the suffering and death within her. So clean, he thought, her hull lined with a green band interspersed with huge red crosses, and lights on brackets which would establish her identity. as a hospital ship even at night, if she should glide into a U-boat's crosswires.

There were a few wounded men in the cockpit with medical orderlies in attendance, their own tunics even more blood-soaked than those of their charges, and Jonathan had been aware of their curiosity, and perhaps their resentment. His own stained and torn uniform spoke for itself, but some might want to know why and how he had escaped unscathed, when so many others lay back there on the peninsula.

The ship loomed closer, her name, *City of Singapore,* clearly visible across her elegant stern. Even her port of registry, Liverpool, evoked a small picture of busy streets and the cool presence of smoky rain: a half-forgotten world, unreachable as a dream. But there were few faces at the guardrails where passengers and emigrants had once stared out at the many and varied ports on the long haul to Australia.

He had seen Waring before coming out in the pinnace to say good-bye to Wyke: Waring at least seemed to possess boundless energy. He had announced that he had been promoted to full colonel, in a tone which suggested he had been expecting it, but sooner. Jonathan still wondered how he had managed to find the time to have his new rank attached to his uniform.

"And you, Blackwood, have been granted your majority, so you'll be staying under my command, for the present anyway."

He had felt no particular elation. Once he had thought of promotion as something exciting and desirable, something to be proud of. Maybe all that lay back there in France or across that placid strip of water to the ridge with its stench of death.

Major Livesay was not going on to Port Said, nor was he staying here. Waring had remarked absently, "The admiral is putting him up for a decoration. I've seconded it, of course. He'll probably be given some training role with new recruits— you know the sort of thing. The rugged hero from the front!" It seemed to amuse him.

Livesay had already left in a homebound cruiser. He had not even said good-bye to his own men, or what remained of them.

"Stand by in the bows, there!" The midshipman blew on his whistle and the engine surged noisily astern. Tackle and hoisting gear were already hovering by a great open port in the ship's side, while a scrubbed accommodation ladder trailed skywards.

An orderly said, "You can use the ladder, sir." He sucked his teeth. "None o' this lot'll be walkin'!" As one of the men in stretchers opened his eyes, he patted his arm and grinned. "Not yet anyway, eh mate?"

Jonathan looked away from the young soldier's face, the

terror draining from his eyes as the memory came back. "Safe," he whispered.

Jonathan swung himself onto the accommodation ladder and touched his hat to the saluting midshipman.

Safe. The man had one arm and only one foot.

Halfway up the ladder he paused and looked across at the anchored warships: *Reliant*, smoke stained and resting momentarily beneath her spread awnings, *Impulsive* close by, her wounds made good until they could use a proper dockyard, her marines' mess-deck still empty. He continued up the side, surprised that the climb did not tire him. The pinnace was already making for the shore again, the sea bubbling astern in a curving wake.

Another orderly watched him step aboard, his eyes searching for a label and an identity, some classification of injuries and religion, should the worst happen.

Aware of the professional scrutiny, Jonathan said, "I want to see Lieutenant Christopher Wyke. He was brought aboard yesterday." He thought of all the wounded men he had seen laid out in the many huts and tents on the island. Those who survived their wounds and the surgery would be gazing over at the *City of Singapore* as if she were some kind of miracle.

"Not a relative, are you, sir?"

"No. I'm Captain—" He hesitated; the new rank seemed so unfamiliar. "Major Jonathan Blackwood. He's one of my officers."

The man's expression changed. "He's going to be all right, sir." Then he said, "Told me about you, sir. What you did."

Jonathan closed his mind as someone began to scream. The orderly showed no emotion. In his work it never ceased.

He said, "In there, straight down to B-Deck—they'll put you right when you get there. Don't be too long, sir. The Old

Man's going to weigh anchor after the next lot's brought out. Get away before the Jerry U-boat gets here."

"What U-boat?"

The orderly grinned. "Sighted a week ago, they tell me. Steerin' east—that's here at a guess!"

Jonathan forced a smile. "Nobody tells us anything." He heard an incisive voice say, "Want the boat to take this one back. The captain knows all about it." He glanced at a blanket-shrouded shape on a stretcher. No miracle for him, after all.

Twice he lost his way during his descent, encountering only lines and lines of silent cots and a tangible sense of pain and endurance.

"Can I help you, Captain?"

It was so unnerving to hear a woman's voice that he found himself staring at her. "B-Deck?" She was darkly pretty, the sort of face you saw in the West Country or Ireland.

"This way." She caught his arm as, with disbelief, he recognised a face and moved towards the bunk. "Not him, if you don't mind, sir. He's too drugged to know you anyway."

He looked down at the huddled figure, the mass of bandages, the staring, empty eyes. It was Bruce Seddon, *Reliant's* whist-playing captain of marines. Waring had mentioned it with his customary callousness. "Seddon's wound deteriorated. Gangrene . . . well, what do you expect in that pigsty? I ordered him to leave with the pinnace but he insisted on staying with *Reliant's* people . . . said it was a matter of pride or something equally feeble. I told him it was conceit, and he should be able to tell the difference." He had shrugged as if it were of no importance. "So they took off his arm. Not much use to any of us now, is he?"

They descended another ladder and she pointed at a curtained, watertight door.

"Thank you, Sister. I'm sorry I was taken aback just now. I—"

She regarded him gravely: such a young face, he thought, too young for the horrors she must see.

"I think you should be coming with us, Captain." Someone was ringing a bell, and she added only, "Take care." Then she was gone.

He found Wyke propped up in a bunk, his arm bandaged and splinted. It had been a near thing: the bullet had passed through it, chipping the bone, but an inch or two the other way and it would have been his heart. He was pale and seemed exhausted, probably from the drugs they had given him, but his smile was so genuine and full of surprise that Jonathan was deeply moved.

"It does me good to see you sitting up like this, Chris." He rested one hand on the blanket and realised that it was still badly bruised. The corpses, the insanity of battle while they had clashed and fought with the enemy bayonets and blasted them with their own grenades. The nightmare. He knew Wyke was remembering it, too.

He said, "Major Livesay has gone home."

"I know, John Maxted told me. And about your promotion too . . . congratulations, sir."

Maxted would miss him, he thought: he and Wyke had always been good friends although they were poles apart, Maxted a first generation marine while Wyke's family, like the Blackwoods, had always been in the corps, and his father was a major general.

He felt the deck quiver slightly. Deep in the *City of Singapore*'s bowels the engineers were testing steam pressure. Eager to be off.

"I just wanted to say that I was proud to have you under

my command, albeit temporarily. And when you're well again I hope you do have that night on the town you were talking about, with a very pretty girl." Wyke was watching him intently, the pain, the drugs, the memories forgotten. "Raise a glass of champagne to us out here, will you, Chris? I have a feeling we're going to need that extra bit of luck."

He disengaged his fingers from Wyke's without consciously recalling the handshake.

Wyke said faintly, "I won't forget, sir. And if you find yourself in England with nothing to do—"

"I know. Piccadilly." He stood up. There was no point in prolonging it. "My regards to your family."

The hospital ship weighed at dusk. He watched her illuminated red crosses until she passed the headland, while *Reliant*'s bandsmen marched and countermarched to the bright music of "Highland Laddie" and "Bonnie Dundee." The bandmaster came from Fife, so it was hardly surprising.

Then the lights and crosses vanished, and he made his way down to *Reliant*'s wardroom, unable to shake the conviction that she should have gone accompanied not by stirring reels and marches but by a lament. For all of them.

Captain Auriol George Soutter was standing by an open scuttle in his spacious day cabin when his steward Drury announced that Blackwood had arrived. He closed the polished scuttle, tired of the ceaseless rumble of artillery and naval gunfire from across the glittering water.

When he turned to greet his visitor some of the tension was gone from his face, and his smile was genuine.

"Sit down, Major Blackwood. Scotch? A nice Islay malt, perhaps?"

Jonathan sat in a chair beautifully upholstered in green leather and tried to relax. He had been busy since the *City of*

Singapore had steamed out of Mudros Bay; Waring had seen to that. More marines would be arriving very shortly, both from Chatham and Portsmouth, some recruits but not all of them. Fresh officers too, "as green as grass," Waring had commented. "We'll soon change all that!"

He took the tumbler from Drury and looked across at the captain. Strained to the limit. It was there in every gesture.

Soutter said, "A lot of changes."

"Yes." He let the fine malt whisky run over his tongue. Sergeant McCann was promoted to sergeant-major, Corporal Timbrell, the Londoner, had been made up to sergeant. He had seen the pleasure and pride on Timbrell's foxy face and wondered why he still felt no satisfaction at his own promotion. He was losing young Roger Tarrier, who had been ordered to relieve *Reliant*'s one surviving Royal Marine officer so that the latter, who had commanded the marines' gun crews in Y Turret, could take over Seddon's work. Tarrier's quick promotion to acting-lieutenant, to be quarters officer for two of the ship's great guns, would do his career no harm. But Jonathan knew he would miss the youth's simple honesty all the same.

He said, "There's to be a new R. M. battalion to work in liaison with the Royal Engineers, and a Gurkha battalion."

Their eyes met, each thinking the same. There was to be no letup, no acceptance of stalemate, despite the casualties that mounted with each advance or counterattack. Another landing was even now being planned to take the pressure off the Australians at Anzac, where the whole front was devoid of depth and proper communications. Only the previous day the Australians had launched a determined attack on a vital crest line, similar but far larger than the one Jonathan's own men had taken. The cheering infantry had driven the Turks back and eventually cleared them completely from the ridge, but because of poor communications the advance had not been reported to the bombarding squadron, and the cruiser H.M.S. *Bacchante* had opened a murderous fire on the ridge, still believed to be in enemy hands. The bombardment had forced the Australians from their captured trenches, only to be cut down by machine-gun and sniper fire.

Soutter said at length, "And now I'm losing *you*."

Colonel Waring had insisted that he needed Jonathan as his adjutant. The C-in-C had agreed.

"I shall miss the ship, sir. I know marines are not supposed to care—"By Sea, By Land" and that kind of attitude—but I've been happy in *Reliant*."

Soutter eyed him gravely. "Naval Intelligence is convinced that a German submarine is on its way here." He did not mention how Rear Admiral Purves had scoffed at the idea when the rumour had first filtered through. *Impossible! No submarine could reach this far without refuelling!* "You may as well know, Blackwood, that the Admiralty, or Lord Fisher to be precise, is going to withdraw the battleship *Queen Elizabeth* . . . to prevent his finest man-of-war from being sunk, of course."

Jonathan was not sure whether he had expected it or not. After the appalling naval losses when the fleet had attempted to pass through the Turkish minefields and force the Narrows against well-sited shore batteries and without support from the army, the doubt had always lingered. Apart from the lightly-armoured *Reliant*, most of the capital ships were outdated, relics as he had heard Purves call them. The *Q.E.* as she was affectionately known, was the newest and most powerful battleship in the fleet, if not in the world. To lose her would be a disaster; to Lord Fisher, who had done more than anyone to force this hopeless campaign into action, it would be something personal.

Jonathan said, "What about the troops ashore, sir?"

Soutter was on his feet by the scuttle as more explosions made the hull tremble.

"They will have *Reliant* and *Impulsive*, and some monitors to offer full support when the new landings are launched."

But Jonathan recalled the great fleet which had hurled tons of explosives ahead of the first landings. The soldiers had come to rely on those guardian ships for everything: to see the most powerful of them sail away would damage morale even more than their own lack of progress had done. They would still have the monitors, flat-bottomed warships with a broad beam out of all proportion to their length, which because of their shallow draught could manoeuvre right inshore. Once in position these floating gun-platforms could use their huge guns, high-mounted in a single turret, to provide support for the army. But they were not the *Q.E.*

Soutter added, "I feel badly about it. It's like a betrayal."

Reliant would be leaving Mudros at first light for another long-range bombardment. Soutter had already pressed the admiral to plead with the C-in-C to oppose any such withdrawal, but communications with Purves were now almost impossible. He had found the rear admiral lying on a couch in his day cabin, more drunk than sober. Soutter could still feel the anger running through him like fire. Purves had been drunk on that other occasion when *Assurance* had run down the fishing boats in the North Sea, and had been prepared to swear that he had not ordered the navigation lights to be switched off or that Soutter was merely obeying those orders. But unknown to either of them, there had been a witness, a youthful sub-lieutenant who had been prepared to give evidence before any kind of court. So Purves had changed his tune and offered favourable evidence instead on his gunnery officer's behalf, and the looming clouds of war had dampened any further interest in Soutter's court martial,.

Purves had stared at him angrily. "What do you care? I certainly don't! If Fisher or any one of Their Lordships or Churchill himself for that matter want to withdraw some ships I do not intend to create . . ."

Soutter had left, swinging the door shut so hard that the marine sentry had jumped with alarm.

Maybe there was a U-boat, and maybe not. If it existed it was taking its time. But the Germans were already heavily involved with the Turks and the man who commanded their army was a Prussian general, Otto Liman von Sanders, and most of his field commanders were his own.

"You know that I'm soon to lose my second-in-command?"

Jonathan nodded, wondering why Soutter found it so easy to talk to him. He had heard that Coleridge, *The Bloke*, was being given his own command: he knew too that Soutter had insisted he accept the promotion even though it deprived him of a very competent commander, and one who had been with the ship since the day she had been launched.

Soutter was saying, "I suppose I'll soon break in the new boy, whoever he turns out to be. And leaving *Reliant* might take Coleridge's mind off poor Bruce Seddon—they were quite good chums, I understand."

More memories: the pretty nurse with the dark hair poking from beneath her veil, Seddon staring at him, numb with shock and disbelief although death was everywhere and wounded men lined every deck; and more, many more would be brought out from the peninsula every day until this agonising contest was settled.

A sub-lieutenant was ushered into the cabin. "The commander's respects, sir, and a boat is alongside to take Major Blackwood ashore." He was at great pains to look at neither of them.

Unexpectedly, Soutter held out his hand. "I'll not come up—I hate farewells. We shall meet again, I have no doubt." His grip was firm and very hard, like the man.

On deck the air was hot, and without much movement. Jonathan shaded his eyes to look at the far-off flashes, listening to the guns where men fought in gullies and dried-up streams with bomb and bayonet, among the forgotten corpses and the army of rats. The hotter it got the more hellish it became. Dirt, infection, lice: the soldier's lot. He grimaced. *Ours too.*

He considered Soutter's bitterness, and remembered something Coleridge had told him concerning Soutter's wife. Why had she left him? Was this ship nothing more than a rival to her? Could she not share her husband's pride?

He found them all waiting to see him over the side: the commander, the bearded navigator Howard Rice, Quitman the gunnery officer and of course, young Roger Tarrier. People he had come to know and respect in so short a time. Then it was over and he was in the pinnace, staring astern at the crouching ship, her White ensign quite limp like a salute. Living faces, dead faces, his young marines—on that hard-won ridge, the telegrams reaching their homes. And *Reliant's* motto: *We will never give in.*

Nor had they.

Speculation about the *Queen Elizabeth's* future ended abruptly a few days after Jonathan left *Reliant*. For the first time since the campaign had begun, the enemy made a daring and reckless attack on the bombarding squadron by sea. A Turkish destroyer, the *Muavanet-i-Miliet*, manned entirely by officers and seamen of the Imperial German Navy, managed to avoid the patrols and then torpedoed the battleship H.M.S. *Goliath*. She was hit by three torpedoes and sank in minutes, with the loss of 500 lives. The attack was completely unexpected, and more of her company could have been saved had not the other ships wasted valuable time in taking what they imagined was avoiding action against the much-talked-of German submarine.

The *Q.E.*'s recall from the Dardanelles was immediately signalled, and seeing his campaign frustrated and in ruins Lord Fisher resigned from the Admiralty. As Sergeant-Major McCann was heard to remark, "Pity we're not allowed to resign when things get a bit nasty!" His outspoken bitterness was shared by the entire force of men assembling for the new landings.

They were still stunned by *Goliath*'s loss when on May 25 Otto Hersing, one of Germany's most successful submarine commanders, arrived off the Straits in his U-21.

Hersing had proved himself both skilful and quite fearless in the early months of the war, when in the same submarine he had broken through a destroyer screen off St Abbs' Head to torpedo and sink the cruiser H.M.S. *Pathfinder*, even though the weather had been bad and there had been a real risk of the boat porpoising and breaking surface to face the destroyers' combined gunfire.

Rumour had not exaggerated but he had not come directly to the Straits: he had first called at the Austro-Hungarian base at Cattaro in Pola to carry out repairs and refuel after his long passage from Germany. On that first day, while cruising submerged off Gaba Tepe, he sighted another great battleship, H.M.S. *Triumph*, a veteran in every sense, and fired just one torpedo. That was all it took, and even as the huge vessel began to heel over Hersing dived beneath the hull to avoid detection. All but seventy of *Triumph*'s men were picked up, as the attack had happened in bright sunshine, but the dismay and humiliation remained to haunt the fleet.

Most submarine commanders would have been content with one battleship, but not Otto Hersing. Two days later off Cape Helles where *Reliant* had carried out several bombardments another battleship, the *Majestic*, suffered the same fate, although she was surrounded by antitorpedo nets and patrol craft. Hersing waited for a small gap to appear between the protective boats and merely fired through the nets. In the confusion there was great loss of life.

The officers and men of the fleet were profoundly shocked. In the campaign so far the C-in-C, Admiral de Robeck, had lost six battleships and most of the souls who had manned them.

The signal was repeated around the fleet: all major warships were to take shelter in Mudros Bay, and the bombardments of Turkish positions were to be given over to the monitors and destroyers, with their very limited armament.

As the newly assembled Royal Marines battalion and part of the re-formed R.M. brigade were put to work, training and drilling in preparation for the next landings, each man was very aware that he was to be sacrificed for the same ships which now lay at anchor.

The soldiers and marines worked in the sweltering heat, laying wire, stabbing at dangling dummies with their bayonets, hacking out makeshift trenches and carrying out firing practice on the ranges. Even Beaky Waring must have learned a hard lesson on the peninsula, Jonathan thought. He had been heard to rasp at one of the new lieutenants as he drilled his men in the sweltering heat: "Train these men to *fight*, sir! They are not mounting guard at the Palace!"

And every day, with terrible regularity, the boats arrived at Mudros with their wounded and dying piled on bottom-boards, some of which were completely awash with blood.

One week followed another, with bad food, flies and dysentery taking their own toll of the men who waited and listened to the hunger of the distant artillery. Finally Waring sent for Jonathan.

He was found standing by a trestle-table in his tent, his huge nose shining in the reflected glare through the canvas. He had grown leaner, and, if possible, less tolerant, and between them there now existed a sort of truce which had arisen out of necessity.

"Thought you should know, Blackwood. I've just had the signal. It's to be at Suvla Bay, four weeks from now. It's here on the map but I've never heard of the damned place. . . . We'll call an officers' meeting when I know something more."

Never heard of the damned place. In four weeks' time everyone would have heard of it.

He tried to imagine Wyke in some smart cafe or bar, raising his glass to them, but the comforting picture eluded him. All he could see were those dead, youthful faces.

Was that where it would be? He had thought Livesay marked for death, but he had been wrong.

Maybe it's my turn now.

Waring said savagely, "I'm going to have a drink, Blackwood. What about you?"

They regarded one another warily, and then Jonathan heard himself reply, "Yes, sir. Better make the most of it."

NINE

The remainder of July passed swiftly, and a general apprehension at the total lack of news made the perpetual training
a misery. The assembled divisions of troops, Royal Marines
and contingents from Australia, New Zealand and India somehow endured the appalling conditions, and food which even
the sturdy Gurkhas found inedible.

Then, in the midst of final preparations, Brigadier-General
Sir Charles Nugent arrived to take charge of the regrouped
battalions and the mixture of recruits from England. A short,
strutting figure with a full military moustache and a breast of
medals which were for the most part unrecognisable to the
new men, Nugent wasted no time in summoning his senior
officers.

The meeting took place in a large tent normally used for
serving meals to the many wounded who daily waited and
prayed for the next hospital ship, and "Blighty." Jonathan
attended, with the company commanders and the two C.O.'s
of the Royal Engineers, as well as the Gurkha detachment,
and the crowded tent was soon like an oven.

Like all marines he was wary of serving under an army
general, despite the corps's martial origins. On the Western
Front it had too often been proved that senior officers had little understanding of the marines or their skills and traditions,
and failed to deploy them to the best advantage. They had
been used as replacements for men killed in the line, only to
fall themselves in an alien environment and separated from
their own. He watched critically as with his staff the brigadier-

general strode into the tent, and stared piercingly at the assembled officers.

"Sit, gentlemen." A sharp, nasal voice, changing to an angry muttering when he realised that there were not enough chairs.

He was perfectly turned out, Jonathan thought cynically, boots and Sam Browne polished, glove-tight uniform pressed and devoid of the ever-present dust. His batman must have his work cut out.

Nugent got straight to the point. "This is a very mixed force, gentlemen. Under my command it will soon overcome any disadvantages. Suvla Bay is our objective. You have all received your instructions and have had time to study the maps." His eyes moved amongst them. "We shall seize the Anafarta Hills which overlook the bay, and from there we will join with other brigades to establish a front across the whole peninsula north of Anzac. We will then be able to divide the Turkish army. To the south of Suvla Bay the Anzac divisions will break out and advance towards us." He smiled quickly but without warmth. "The Turks will be made to fight on two fronts at once. The rest is up to you, gentlemen."

Jonathan glanced at Waring's grim profile. It was an impressive buildup of troops, but it seemed likely that the enemy would already know the place, if not the exact time of the landings.

The remainder of the original landing force, recruits almost to a man, had become hardened veterans, which was obviously to the good. There was hope, too, of much improved communications, unlike the last onslaught. The Royal Engineers would see to that.

Another advantage was the arrival at Mudros of new self-powered motor barges. Each was armoured and claimed to be bullet and splinter-proof, and Jonathan thought how different the landings at Anzac and Cape Helles might have been if they had been available then, instead of sending men to face machine-guns and shrapnel in towed whalers and cutters.

Each boat, or "Beetle" as they were nicknamed, carried a hundred men, and had a bow-ramp like a small drawbridge so that troops could disembark on the shore ready to move inland without delay.

There was the usual concern about the enormous weight of equipment each man would carry: full pack, mess gear, blanket and groundsheet, the new snub-nosed Lee-Enfield rifle and bayonet, plus all the ammunition each one of them could manage. Drinking water was also essential, vital to the entire operation, but lighters had been prepared on another island and would be readily available. *They said.* He smiled to himself despite the tension around him. Once he would have accepted almost anything. Now he believed only what he saw.

Brigadier-General Nugent was saying with emphasis, "This whole campaign can be brought to a successful conclusion, and Constantinople will fall to us. The enemy's pressure on Russia will be reduced, and we can continue to drive them back on the Western Front."

An army major murmured to his companion, "Continue? First I've heard of it."

Nugent became very grave. "The general officer commanding, Sir Ian Hamilton, has relayed a message, a fine one I think, which over the years to come will inspire every one: *'The faith which is in you will carry you through!'*"

Waring snorted angrily. "What's the use of that, I ask you? They don't need faith. All they want is ammunition, support and competent leadership!"

The general's eyes singled him out in spite of the crowd.

"What name, sir?"

"Colonel Waring, sir!"

There was total silence while one of Nugent's staff officers held out a notepad and whispered something. Nugent said with a change of tone, "Ah . . . a Royal Marine."

Waring faced him hotly. "I think the record of the brigade here, and my makeshift battalion in particular, can speak for itself, sir!"

It was like watching two duellists, Jonathan thought.

Nugent asked quietly, "Do you have any complaint or criticism of the plan to take the Anafarta Hills, Colonel—er, Waring? If so, I am sure we would all like to hear it."

Waring was unmoved, and touched his bristling moustache with one knuckle as Jonathan had seen him do so often.

"If we cannot take the hills, sir, *we* will be fighting on two fronts, not the enemy!"

"'Cannot' is out of the question, Colonel. It must be done. It shall be done." He glanced over their faces. "We attack on the sixth. The Royal Navy will be giving us full support."

Now the reason for Soutter's bitterness and sense of shame became clearer. He had known then that apart from the destroyers and hundreds of Beetles and small auxiliary craft, the main naval support would be offered by two elderly cruisers, *Endymion* and *Theseus*, which had been built during the 1890s, and were completely out-of-date in weapons and armour.

That afternoon Jonathan watched the final preparations for embarking this huge army of regulars and volunteers. Now that a decision had been made and passed to every company and platoon, the atmosphere became almost cheerful as the lines of tents were broken down, and the walking wounded gathered critically to look on.

Perhaps the Turks would be stretched to the limit and

could no longer face attacks from two flanks. He recalled the Australian colonel who had made the comparison between the enemy defending his homeland and their own emotions if the Germans had been smashing their way up the beaches of Kent and Sussex.

All these men, and many more on the island of Imbros where another armada was preparing to head for the enemy shore. Would these islands ever see such an army again, and how many would ever live to see England once more? Voices all around him, from the north of England, Scotland and the Dales, the round accents of the West Country and townies from the London Territorials. The youth of a nation, of a commonwealth.

Lieutenant John Maxted found him on a bluff, contemplating the seething activity on the bay.

"I've had a letter from Chris Wyke, Sir!" He became more subdued. "Came with that last hospital ship."

Jonathan smiled. "How is he?" It was suddenly important. A familiar face in that other world.

"He's well, sir. He's getting some leave—expect he's had it by now! Sends his best wishes to you and his chaps." His eyes clouded over. "What's left of them."

They stared down at the Beetles and launches, the dust from marching lines of khaki.

"Did he have that champagne?"

"Didn't say, sir. But he wishes us luck."

Jonathan glanced at his watch. "Go and tell the Colonel that we move in thirty minutes." Waring would still be seething about the slight to his Royal Marines. It would never occur to him that he had had exactly the same contempt for the Australians.

"And, John . . ."

"Sir?"

"It's not a battalion this time, it's the whole bloody army. Safety in numbers."

It was a lie, and perhaps the lieutenant knew it. But he seemed to cheer up immediately and strode away saying, "I'll bet he did have that champagne, lucky bastard!"

Harry Payne appeared, seemingly from nowhere. "Starter's orders, sir." He handed Jonathan his revolver. "We'll be at Battalion H.Q. then." His eyes crinkled in a sly grin. "That should be well back from the firing line, if I'm any judge!"

They walked down the crumbling slope towards the beach, and the sea.

The eventual disembarkation of the first troops did not begin until ten-thirty on the night of August sixth. Each company and platoon commander had a fixed mental picture of the bay, opening up ahead of the flotillas of boats with hornlike headlands at each end. At the top of the bay was a strange narrow strip of sand which separated a large salt lake from the sea itself. And beyond that lay the real objective, the line of the Anafarta Hills.

Yes, they all had it fixed in their minds; but in broad daylight it might seem very different. To the south-east of the bay there was supposed to be a small hill, Lala Baba, which although only shown as two hundred feet high would easily command the beach, as an air reconnaissance had reported that there were strong trenches. Lala Baba was to be the first hinge of the attack. Waring was thunderstruck when told at the very last moment that there had been a change in the plan. All three brigades of the Division were to have been landed on selected beaches on the seaward side of the hornlike Nibrunesi Point. Instead, this brigade was now to be sent directly inside the bay to land on the long sandspit which separated it from the salt lake. There was no consultation, and Waring had muttered angrily, "Afraid the Turks will beat them to the hill! They just don't *think!*"

The sea was quite choppy and the Beetles were tossed about like leaves. Jonathan guessed that the boats were overloaded anyway, the men crammed together like sardines, barely able to move because of their weapons and equipment. Occasionally faces lit up in the fierce glow of gunfire while the warships fired at enemy flashes without any knowledge of their accuracy. The southern beaches were laid bare by the brighter glare of shrapnel as the Turkish gunners fired over what were probably prepared and sited positions.

It took longer than expected to guide the Beetles and their attendant launches with towed supply boats through the entrance of the bay itself. In the first rays of pale sunshine Jonathan saw the huge drifting clouds of smoke, as the landings and the defences showed themselves for the first time. It sounded as if the main landings outside the bay had gone well, and the troops were probably digging in to await the next counterattack.

The sunshine spilled over the distant line of hills and filtered through the smoke. Jonathan steadied himself and trained his binoculars on the sandspit and at the pale outline of the dried salt lake beyond it. There would be casualties; he could already hear the officers shouting instructions from one of the leading boats, the rasp of steel as bayonets were fixed, with great difficulty with men packed so tightly. But once on that sandspit they could cross and find cover until the next order to move forward.

Lieutenant Maxted gasped, "God, what's happening, sir?" A leading Beetle had slewed round and another only narrowly missed colliding with it. Jonathan felt his skin go cold. Something unnoticed, unforeseen, and it was happening right now. The beach could not be reached; the steep shallowing of the water was too much even for these boats.

Waring blew his whistle and shouted, "Signal our boats! *Steer south!*"

Breaking away from the original formation of floundering craft, Waring's flotilla turned heavily and headed towards the beach to the south-east. Jonathan stared abeam and saw the soldiers abandoning their boats and starting to wade ashore, all advantage of cover and speed denied them as sniper fire and machine-guns cut them down in dozens, then hundreds as they straggled onto the sandspit, already exhausted and without proper supervision. But Lala Baba had been taken in the early morning. Later Jonathan heard it was the work of the Yorkshires and the West Yorkshires, who had charged up the hill and forced the enemy to fall back. As the light grew stronger he saw many Turks lying along the shore of the salt lake, cut down even as they retreated. Piles of khaki corpses marked every foot of the fierce attack.

Gasping for breath, the marines abandoned their boats and dragged themselves below the cover of Lala Baba. If the hill had not been captured, it was unlikely that any of them would have lived. Dazed and wheezing like old men, they watched the havoc on the sandspit until more covering fire from the ships forced the enemy to fall back again from their defences. Snipers still marked their targets, and many more men fell before the rest of the division could dig in or find cover.

In short, shambling rushes they eventually crossed the salt lake, while shrapnel burst overhead, cutting down some of the men who had never been under fire in their lives.

And all the while, more and more soldiers and supplies were being landed. The sun rose higher, and the attack lost its impetus. Men fell asleep; exhausted, they lay like the dead around them despite the humming drone of sniper-fire, the bang of shells. Eventually a runner found Waring, his eyes red-rimmed, his hands cut where he had thrown himself down to avoid an enemy rifle.

Waring snapped tersely, "From Brigade. We're to attack the enemy's position here . . ." He unfolded his map and sand drifted from it like dust. "Hill Ten. A strong position apparently." He peered round for his own runner and added scornfully, "The army have fouled it up again!"

It took another hour for the changed instructions to be passed to Waring's company commanders, all of whom were found except one whose Beetle had received a direct hit from some light artillery and capsized. It was unlikely that there would have been any survivors. The weight of their packs and ammunition would have seen to that.

"We shall go around the *other* side of the salt lake, Blackwood. Longer but firmer." Waring pointed suddenly, his voice furious. "Stop those men drinking all their water! *Take their names, you dolts.*"

The distant gunfire intensified by the hour. It was probably from Anzac where they would be trying to break out through the enemy lines, the other prong of the attack which would cut the Turkish army into halves.

Jonathan lay among the rocks and levelled his binoculars on the distant hills. All the names he had learned by heart, with their rolling objective bathed in sunshine: beyond reach, without hope.

It was dusk of that terrible day before they had reached a position where they could fire on the enemy redoubt. Hours of running and ducking when some hidden marksmen probed the ground for them, or shrapnel exploded and tore around them like deadly hornets. By this time the battalion had lost two officers, a sergeant and a hundred killed and wounded, the latter abandoned until help was sent. If it ever came.

Jonathan saw another side of warfare at its most savage. A corporal caught sight of a sniper, wrapped in rags, and lying by an overturned waggon like a pile of rubbish. With a scream the corporal, normally a quiet man, flung himself at the hidden Turk and before the others realised what was happening impaled him on his bayonet. He saw some of the young marines including a few like Geach, who still grieved for his dead friend, display a similar madness as they surrounded the writhing sniper, stabbing him repeatedly until long after he was dead, and their bayonets were red from point to hilt.

Eventually they were all concealed and Waring snapped, "A Company will attack—the rest will supply covering fire. Then B Company." He peered at Jonathan and bit the chin stay of his sun-helmet. "Then *our* H.Q. platoon." He added dryly, "C Company will remain here to cover the retreat—that is, if we get that far!"

The rattle of machine-gun fire and the crack of rifles were directed at the other side where the British infantry were pinned down, and had, according to the terrified runner, suffered many casualties.

During a brief lull when they guessed the infantry had fallen back to gather their remaining strength for another attack Waring said, "When they advance, we shall begin!" For a moment his eyes looked tired and he muttered, "Give me a division and I'd soon show the bloody army!"

On either side of him the crouching marines shifted their arms and gripped their weapons more tightly as the firing began again.

Waring put his whistle to his lips then hesitated, and

shouted, "Remember this: you are *Royal Marines,* not a bunch of mothers' boys! Colour-Sarn't Grensmith!"

"Sir!"

"You go across with B Company in the second attack! I want that flag up there where everyone can see it!"

"Understood, sir!"

Waring blew sharply on the whistle, and while their newly acquired light machine-guns crackled from either flank, the marines charged like madmen up the slope.

Shots flashed from the hidden parapet and several fell, including Major Vickers, the company commander. The others scrambled forward, yelling like men beyond help and reason, while the enemy were held down by the rapid fire from their companions.

Waring shouted, "Ready Company B!" He blew another blast and the next line charged from cover.

Waring was staring wildly, but managed to say in almost a normal voice, "It's not the first time in their history that the Turks have had their artillery pointing the wrong way."

He stood up and took out his revolver, his eyes fixed on the bright colours of the flag as it floated lightly in the last of the sun's rays.

"H.Q. Platoon *advance!"*

There were no more shots from the parapet, and when they clambered over to be greeted by the gasping but jubilant marines Waring said curtly, "A flare for the infantry, Sergeant! Tell them they can come in now!" He gazed impassively at the flag, still gripped in the colour-sergeant's dead hands where he had planted it in a sandbagged emplacement even as he fell.

Jonathan saw the carefully dug defences suddenly laid bare by the signal flare. *Only the dead lie here.* As they had on that other ridge. He turned as Waring said, "Better have a look round before the general gets here, what?" He gave his braying laugh. "The Turks don't drink, do they? Pity!"

A deep bunker was abandoned, two lamps still showing in the gloom. Waring sat down and laid his revolver on a wooden table. "Not what one might expect to see here of all places, what?"

Jonathan heard Harry Payne whistling outside the entrance and turned to see Waring's discovery. It was an English Bible.

He heard himself yell, *"No—don't!"* His voice sounded like a scream. Then Waring opened the Bible, and even as Jonathan flung himself to the ground the book exploded with a tremendous bang. Metal and fragments from the walls and table cracked around him and he heard Payne calling his name through the dense smoke, then his words were lost in deafness.

How long he lay there he could not tell. Seconds, a month? But his hearing was returning, and when he moved his body very slightly there was no stab of agony.

Someone brought a light and he retched as he saw Waring, still slumped at the punctured and splintered table. The front of his uniform was shining red in the lamplight. Jonathan felt Payne holding him even as he was trying to drag himself away.

I command now. It was like a hammer beating out the words in his brain. Waring was still sitting here. But he was headless.

Boots clattered in the entrance, and an army lieutenant-colonel stared past them at the hideous corpse as if he thought it was a trick of the light.

Then he said slowly, "You can fall back and rest your men, Major. We've been reinforced. After what you did. . ." He could not go on. He tore his eyes from the corpse. "Lose many?"

Sergeant-Major McCann called from outside, "Seventy, sir!"

The army officer was staring at Jonathan.

"Was he a friend of yours?"

Jonathan wiped his eyes with a dirty handkerchief. "Hardly that. Always making remarks about my family's decorations. Well, he'll get a Victoria Cross for what he just did. He'd like that." He pushed outside in the gathering darkness, which came so suddenly here, and was glad his young marines could barely see his face, or know how near he had been to breaking down completely.

The other officer offered helpfully, "I'll detail some men to take your wounded back with you."

He shook his head. "The Royal Marines take care of their own." And for one wild moment he thought he could hear Waring's last braying laugh.

At the end of a week's fighting the forces landed at Anzac and Suvla managed to join their line. But that was as far as it went, and no further advances could be made in the face of fanatical Turkish opposition. The marines had grown dazed and depressed by the savage change of circumstances. To the soldiers in general there came a hopelessness which made every elusive objective unimportant.

There was so much stupidity, so much incompetence. Men driven half mad with thirst wandered down to the beach from the firing-line, oblivious apparently to the real risk of snipers and shrapnel fired from inland. The water lighters lay close to the beach, but nobody had considered supplying any receptacles so that when water was pumped ashore from the lighters the men found they were expected to direct a hose of some four inches in diameter into water bottles with quarter-inch holes at the spout. More water was wasted than drunk, and some of the thirst-maddened infantry, their blackened tongues hanging out like dead men's, hacked holes in the hoses and drank deeply rather than stand in an endless queue.

And the dying who lay out in the open all day could neither be reached nor treated. Not even a Red Cross flag could save the stretcher bearers from the many hidden marksmen.

Into September, the weather was already showing signs of deteriorating. Advance, gain a few yards at a terrible price only to lose the blood-soaked land in the next enemy counterattack. And at each dawn they could see the same span of the Anafarta Hills, as far away as they had been on that first morning.

By the end of the month Jonathan wondered how much longer the bloody stalemate could continue before a decision was made to evacuate the peninsula. Even in these bitter days there were those who found the time to censor every letter that the disheartened troops tried to send home, and he was convinced that nobody in England knew the true situation here. Perhaps nobody cared.

The battalion was reduced almost by half, either dead or wounded, and on every front it was the same. It was rumoured that Sir Ian Hamilton was to be recalled, and another general sent out in his place. Nobody knew any more how many had been killed or wounded. There were so many different units, so many nationalities. Even Maoris had been thrown into the cauldron of war.

On the first day of October, less than six months after the first landings at Anzac and Cape Helles when all their naval guardians had been there to protect an army, Jonathan was slumped in the command dugout, still dazed from an attack the previous night. On the left flank the infantry had beaten the Turks back, and had charged on to retake some high ground which had already changed hands a dozen times.

A Royal Engineers signals section, wearing their familiar blue and white brassards, were sharing the line with the remaining marines, and one dashed into the dugout. "One of the ships has opened fire on that ridge, sir!"

Jonathan stared at him. Like that last time and all the others when shells had fallen short, or been fired by mistake at their own men.

He ran to the field-telephone but the soldier said, "Cut, sir. Won't work. I daren't send a linesman down there with all this lot going on."

It might have happened to his own men. He snatched up a pair of yellow and red semaphore flags and saw Lieutenant Maxted staring at him, while Payne put down his rifle as if to protest.

Without waiting for events to change his mind he climbed over the rear of the trench and said harshly, "Fire a flare! Any bloody kind you've got left!"

Then carefully and deliberately he began to semaphore his signal to the destroyer firing over the beaches. The sea was so calm that he could see her full reflection on the water.

A signal lamp winked over the gently-moving water and all firing ceased, and with immense relief he was about to turn when a shell exploded somewhere behind him. He was flung face down on the loose rocks, and as consciousness returned he could hear his own cries as the agony closed around him like a white-hot metal trap.

Men were holding him, but nothing made sense: Harry Payne was wiping the hair from his eyes and muttering, *"Please God! Not now!"*

He knew Maxted was kneeling beside him and wanted to

tell him what to do. All the company commanders were killed. But all he could see now was his own blood, hear his breath rasping in his throat as he tried to breathe. An authoritative voice interrupted, and through the mist of agony Jonathan could vaguely make out the red tabs of the brigade major.

"Who is in command of this battalion?"

And Lieutenant Maxted's hoarse reply. "I am, sir."

"Give me an 'and!" That must be Langmaid, the oafish machine-gunner. McCann was there too.

But suddenly the pain was too much, and there was only darkness.

In the weeks that followed he did not know if he would live or die; nor did he care, in those few blurred, terrifying moments of understanding. He became part of a nightmare, where the villains were the hard-eyed surgeons in their blood-ied coats, and the only peace was the oblivion of drugs. He lost all sense of time, and waited only for the dreaded agony's return to torment him: even drugs could not soften the pain of the probes that explored or reopened his wounds where shell splinters had struck him with the force of axes.

He could not recall being moved, only that he was on some sort of ship with many others on stretchers. He had felt tears on his face, and was angry with himself when a nurse had dabbed them with a cloth. *Going home. Going home.*

But after an eternity of pain and the awakened torture when the soiled dressings were changed, he was moved again. Not into an English winter but into sunshine, where he had managed to discern palm trees.

When he recovered his senses again he was in a clean bed, and soon the surgeons came once more to examine him.

He was in the Royal Military Hospital in Cairo: a great

building full of pain, where men died of their wounds or struggled to survive against the odds. Harry Payne came each day to see him, and the staff allowed him to sit beside the bed, just to reassure himself that his officer still lived.

And while Jonathan fought his fiercest battle, the war in Gallipoli drifted to a close.

Payne told him some of it. How they had made one last attempt to break through the enemy's line. It had failed, and in four days' fighting the army had lost another 11,000 men, killed, maimed or simply vanished. By January a complete evacuation was carried out by the navy at night, with a mere handful of gallant defenders remaining to the end to conceal their intentions from the Turks. Then even they had been safely lifted off, and without the loss of another life the army was carried to safety. *An heroic failure,* Jonathan had heard one surgeon call it.

Payne told him that the battalion's survivors were being sent back to England. He was careful not to mention that when the ships had lifted the troops to safety, they had left behind that other army of a quarter of a million souls: the army of the dead.

In February Jonathan took his first steps, cheered by an unknown soldier with only one arm.

In March the matron came to see him where he sat staring out of a window; he had been watching an army officer who had spent the entire morning saluting his own shadow on the wall. There must be thousands like him.

She said severely to Payne, "Get this officer's kit ready." Then she rested one hand on Jonathan's shoulder. " We need the bed."

She softened very slightly. In her work neither compassion nor hope came easily, but she had been the only one who had expected him to live. She said, "Major Blackwood is being taken to the ship." She saw his emotion and added, "Now you *are* going home."

Eventually he said, but only to himself, "In time for the spring."

It was over.

PART TWO

Per Terram

1917

TEN

The overloaded train gave a great shudder and came to a halt, steam spewing over the edge of the platform to hang motionless on the damp, bitter air. Major Jonathan Blackwood rubbed some condensation from the window with his greatcoat sleeve and looked for the name of the station. It was a slow train from Southampton, stopping at every halt, and sometimes redirected into sidings to allow the progress of more important ones.

It was strange how each stop seemed like the one before. Usually crowded with khaki figures, clinging to their loved ones for those final precious seconds, when before there had been nothing to say. Red-eyed women with cheerful soldiers, the new recruits going off to join their first active-service units. And the others in stained khaki, their eyes empty, expressionless. *Going back.*

This station had a little cottage attached and there were colourful paper-chains across one window, for it was not yet Twelfth Night in this new year of 1917.

He let his head loll against the cushion and tried not to look at the two women who had shared the compartment with him all the way from Southampton. One young, the other older, obviously mother and daughter, pale-faced, and somehow lost in their drab black clothing. They had most likely been to one of the many military hospitals which ringed the great port where daily the white-painted ships unloaded their wounded. For many it was only a brief moment of refuge.

There had been another passenger who had sat opposite him peering at each station: eager, fearful, despairing, it had all been there. An infantry lieutenant from the Hampshires, an arm missing and one side of his face cruelly scarred. At a guess he was about twenty, but like most of them, he looked much older.

Where had 1916 gone? Jonathan often tried to piece the last months together even as his mind fought against the memories. The long and painful voyage from Egypt in the hospital ship . . . It had all nearly ended after only a few days outward bound. He had shared a small ward with several other wounded officers, a group who managed to smile at one another on each morning call. The survivors. Then one morning a cot had been empty. He had heard the ship's engines stop often enough to know that another sea burial was imminent.

But the memory that still chilled him was that of a routine night, when his particular doctor had come to inspect the dressings. This had become less painful, and Jonathan had wondered, and wondered still, how close he had been to death on that terrible day on the peninsula.

A nurse had entered, not even glancing at his nakedness as he lay face down in the cot. Like the others, she had done and seen everything. In response to her whispers the doctor had said irritably, "Very well, I'll come—but if he's playing up again I'll forget my calling for a few minutes!" He had patted

Jonathan's bare shoulder and murmured, "Back in a tick, old chap."

He had lain there, feeling the engines pulsing through his body, listening to the occasional rattle of bottles and jars as the ship had altered course. Malta tomorrow; after that Gibraltar, and then the Atlantic, and England.

His companions had either been asleep or taken along the upper deck to exercise and he was alone, and he recalled that the doctor had removed his white coat and gone out displaying his full rank, no doubt to quash the patient who was "playing up." He had obviously not fastened the bulkhead cupboard and when the ship had rolled very gently the door had fallen open. On the inside there was a full-length mirror, something of which Jonathan had been deprived throughout the long months in hospital.

Gasping with stiffness and the pain of exerting muscles he had forgotten how to use, he had clambered down from the cot, and waiting for the ship to dip into a slight swell he had let the momentum carry him across the deck to the open cupboard.

He had stared at himself as though at a total stranger, but with some relief: he was thinner, but no worse than the others who had been at the Dardanelles. With great care he had manoeuvred himself around, clinging to the shelves and dangling white coats, hating his weakness but determined to see the cause of all these months of suffering.

Even today he hardly knew what he had been expecting. Scars, blemished skin, but not this. The sight of his back had filled him with nausea and horror. At least six jagged wounds from his left shoulder to his buttocks, stamped deep into his body like crudely made stars. How could anyone, even a nurse, bear to see them?

The rest had been a blur, and he had hit the deck heavily.

He had heard voices, urgent or angry. "Why was this man left alone?" And there had been blood too, from one of the wounds breaking open.

He shifted his body now against the seat and saw the women glancing at him. Did they blame him for being alive when their own man had lost the fight?

His back was still painful, and he was conscious of walking very straightly as if that would prevent its return. He recalled one of the doctors had laughed when he had taken his first lengthy stroll at Plymouth. "You look as if you're ready for the barracks square!"

A whistle shrilled and he saw the guard waving his green flag. The beast gave a jerk and then began to glide out of the station, and the air was very cold suddenly; he guessed that every window had been lowered for that final handclasp, the brave smile that might have to last a lifetime. He closed his eyes again.

As his recovery had progressed he had found to his surprise that he was able to interest himself in that other war beyond his own desperate fight for survival. There had been a great naval battle off Jutland, in which the leviathans of the Grand Fleet and the German High Seas Fleet had grappled bloodily for the first time: the news had been vague when it had reached the hospital in Plymouth. British losses had been greater, but the Germans had not lingered to suffer probable destruction. It was not until much later that Harry Payne had told him that one of the vessels lost had been the old battle-cruiser *Impulsive*. Like others of her class, she had blown up in one huge fireball after being straddled by the German gunners. There had been no survivors, and Jonathan wondered if Captain Soutter's friend, Vidal, had still been in command.

One thing had become starkly clear: the nature of the war

had completely changed while he had been away on his mindless journey. When he had left for the Dardanelles he had
seen it as a contest fought by amateurs, with a set of outdated
rules for guidance, but in a matter of months the war on land
and sea had become one of barbaric savagery. U-boat warfare
had become a sink-on-sight affair, with no thought given to
crews or passengers when the torpedoes had turned the
ships into infernos. U-boat commanders who had previously
shown mercy no longer took the chance of being caught on
the surface while they allowed apparently stricken sailors to
get away in their lifeboats; too often the "victim" had been
an armed Q-ship with a separate crew to man her guns behind
mock deckhouses, waiting for the submarine to draw nearer
for a kill.

The war in France and Belgium was beyond belief in its
unprecedented ferocity and horror. Casualty lists on the Western Front, even allowing for strict censorship, were appalling.
It was nothing to gain an advance of a mile, or not even that,
and pay for it with 20,000 lives. As the armies grappled in
wire and mud, under bombardments and air attack, a new
dimension was added: phosgene gas, which left men coughing out their lungs or completely blinded. Flamethrowers,
too, made life at the front into hell itself.

The main armies had taken to wearing steel helmets, from
the German coal-scuttle shape to the Tommies' soup-dish,
which would not have looked out of place at Agincourt. There
had been so many head injuries that it should have come
much earlier. And after endless delays the government had at
last introduced conscription, in a desperate attempt to fill the
growing gaps, the steadily mounting losses. There had never
been a shortage of volunteers, youngsters inspired by patrio-
tism or bravado to join the regulars in the front line; but now

so many of the latter had already fallen in battle when they might have been usefully employed to train the conscripts, if only the act had been passed in time.

Jonathan remembered as if it had been yesterday being taken out in a car for the first time by a medical officer making his rounds, visiting some of the smaller, makeshift hospitals and dressing stations. Passing through a typical West Country market town, with its flintstone church and broad market square, he had noticed a crowd of people gathered by the church wall peering at a bulletin board. The doctor had watched him thoughtfully.

"Casualty lists." It was all he had said.

"But how can they get all these names distributed around the counties?"

The doctor had driven on, his face like stone. The Royal Marine major with the serious features had still been a long way from complete recovery, but he had happened to believe that it had been worth the struggle to keep him alive and sane. It would have done his morale little good to explain to him that the long list of dead and missing had all been from this one sleepy little town.

But Jonathan knew now. He had returned to light duties at Plymouth, helping an elderly lieutenant-colonel who had been given the task of working new recruits into companies and battalions. He had been glad not to be ordered back to Portsmouth, not yet anyway. Too many missing faces, too many curious stares. And then had come the news: he was to be awarded the Distinguished Service Order for his behaviour at Gallipoli. His father would have been proud of it; but out there every man in the line had deserved a medal of some kind.

Another familiar station passed, and he thought suddenly of Harry Payne, his constant companion, his crutch. Payne would have been getting off this train at Winchester in time to spend the last of the holiday with his parents and family, but he had already gone. A week or so ago he had got the news: his youngest brother had been reported missing, presumed killed, in Flanders. Jonathan had found him packing his kit in his quarters, bitter and angry and smelling strongly of drink.

He had stared at Jonathan wretchedly. "Don't like leaving you in the lurch, sir." He had almost broken down again as he had attempted to explain. "Young Titch thought the world of me, you see. I blame myself. He only joined up because of me. And now he's gone, poor little bugger, just like all the others!"

Jonathan had found himself reluctant to go straight to Hawks Hill. There would be nothing there to draw him or keep him, just another place full of broken men. He had spent Christmas at a house on the edge of the New Forest with the family of an old friend in the corps.

He could not recall ever drinking so much, and his head still throbbed savagely. When the surgeon had warned him that the pills did not allow for too much alcohol he had been right.

A ticket collector was coming through the carriage, a red-faced man with a walrus moustache who resembled Sergeant-Major McCann.

"Winchester in a few minutes, Major Blackwood." He beamed. "So pleased about the D.S.O., sir." He glared around challengingly as several civilians turned to stare. "Pity more don't join the Colours!"

His round Hampshire accent reminded Jonathan again of Payne. How many there must be like him. A name on a notice board like the thousands up and down the country.

"Someone meeting you, sir?"

Jonathan shivered. He seemed to feel the cold so much more than before.

"Not sure."

"Nice to be home anyway, sir." He ambled away, warning some of the passengers that their journey was almost over.

Nice to be home. He stared at his misty reflection as it raced past bleak, bare trees and great spans of open fields. Where was home now? Left back there on the peninsula, or in the barracks with its constant reminders: stamping boots, the maniac screams of drill-sergeants, the mess dinners and the maudlin sentimentality that usually emerged after the second round of port.

There were a few little cottages now, a child with a dog at a level crossing waving up at the train. The place where Jonathan had been born and which he barely knew would not be far away.

He stared at his hands as they began to shake, then thrust them into his greatcoat pockets. Tonight, would he lie in peace or would the nightmares reach him even here? Like the one in which the dugout was brightly lit by artillery fire and then in total darkness, and all the time Beaky Waring sat there laughing at him. Sometimes headless, sometimes alive as he remembered him. The boats with the bottom-boards covered in blood, the dying midshipman holding his captain's hand, and the marines stabbing at the writhing Turkish sniper. Would it never leave him?

"Winchester! Winchester!"

Doors were banging open and people were rushing this way and that searching for the welcoming face, the first grateful hug.

He looked around. The compartment was empty.

And all at once, he knew he was afraid.

•   •   •

"Major Blackwood, sir?"

He turned and saw a smart, burly corporal in leather gauntlets throwing up a salute.

"I've got a motor car, sir." Without waiting he picked up Jonathan's cases and added, "We telephoned the R.T.O. at Southampton to make sure you was comin'."

Jonathan fell into step with him and wondered why someone had taken the trouble to arrange transport. It was only ten miles to Hawks Hill. Surely he would have managed to get a lift from some trader or carrier.

The car was a large, impressive one, painted khaki with a red cross on the door and R.A.M.C. underneath. It was strange to think of the Royal Army Medical Corps being at the old estate. He remembered how the soldiers in France had joked about it, telling him the letters stood for *rob all my comrades.*

"Ready, sir?" The corporal had a tentative air, as if he were more used to dealing with difficult or abnormal men. Jonathan wondered which he was. He glanced around at the shifting groups of soldiers and busy porters, officers with their girls, a policeman giving directions to an old lady. Even the friendly bustle of Winchester railway station unnerved him: being surrounded by strangers, away from the only world he knew.

The corporal held the door and he climbed stiffly into the car. "Be a bit strange for you, I expect, sir?"

"Strange?" It came out too sharply. "Sorry. I think I know what you mean."

The corporal relaxed and put the car into gear, driving with great care around the many obstacles and across the old cobbles of the station approach. He had noted the way his passenger held himself, and was not surprised. His own commanding officer had told him about Jonathan Blackwood when he had checked with the R.T.O, at Southampton, and certainly the whole countryside around the Hawks Hill estate seemed to know of the decoration he was about to receive. He glanced at Jonathan's profile. So that was what a hero looked like, he thought, a man on the edge.

It seemed to run in the family, though: he had heard about the two Blackwood V.C.s when he had been posted to the place, almost before he had unpacked his kit. He particularly liked the story about the old general; bit of a lad to all accounts. A groom had told him that the general had left a few brats behind when he had died, and quite a pile of debts as well.

Jonathan remained unaware of the corporal's scrutiny. He was staring at the winding road ahead of the car, the bare trees that almost touched overhead, the little wooden platform where farmers left their cans of milk for collection and servant girls waited to beg a ride into town. Two farm workers stepped aside as the big car roared past. They did not even give it a glance. It made him feel even more alien and uncomfortable here.

He found he was clenching his fists again as he saw the familiar gates of Eastwood Farm, where as a child he had played with a boy he could scarcely remember now. Broad, curving fields, ploughed with a precision worthy of *Reliant*'s navigator, each sharp crest still glistening with the hard frost. A frozen sea.

He bit his lip. He had forgotten the navigator's name.

More cottages now, and then they were rolling through the little town of Alresford where his mother had occasionally shopped. He found himself wanting to look at his watch, but he did not want to show his agitation. Surely they had not reached Alresford so soon?

The driver remarked, "Not long now, sir."

"I don't suppose I'll recognise the old place."

The car stopped and the driver leaned forward on the wheel to watch a line of ducks sedately crossing the road.

He said, "It's quiet. What they need." His C.O. had told him not to talk about it, but how could he say nothing? His passenger had been there, been through it like so many he had driven from one station or the other, or had seen being taken away, denied any hope of recovery.

He swung the big car around another bend and listened proudly to the engine's powerful response. They said it had belonged to a peer of the realm who had wanted to "do his bit." His lip curled in a smile. I wish it was mine, he thought.

"I know one thing, sir. The old fellow up at the house went mad with joy when he heard you was comin' home."

That would be Jack Swan. "I'm glad he's all right. I should have written." Jonathan reached out and gripped the corporal's arm suddenly. "Here! Stop just here!"

He climbed down from the car and felt the bitter air penetrating his greatcoat as if he were naked beneath it, and his breath was like the engine's steam over the station platform, but he stood unmoving, gazing across at the main gates of the estate, or where the gates had once hung. They had been removed to make room for wider lorries and ambulances, as was the case at so many other old estates taken over by the armed forces. But the gatehouse looked clean now, and freshly painted, and there was a soldier in blancoed belt standing attentively by the entrance. Part of the old moat was still there; he could see it through the pair of oaks that guarded the driveway as they had for over a hundred years. Somebody had been thoughtful enough to break the ice on it, and the geese and ducks could have been the same ones he had always known.

He glanced round at the driver. "I—I'd like to walk, if you don't mind, Corporal."

"I'll bring up your gear, sir." Afterwards he thought the major had sounded as if he was dreading these last few minutes.

The sentry threw up a salute as Jonathan walked past. Like a ramrod, with only his eyes moving to follow the tall, solitary figure. It was pretty rare to see one walking alone, without an attendant orderly or nurse.

Jonathan paused to stare beyond the great house. It was like forgetting the navigator's name. He could scarcely believe this was the same place. Where the vast flower beds had been there were long wooden buildings with what looked like a new boiler house nearby, presumably to supply heat to them, and temporary structures everywhere, some with red crosses on the rooftops, in the unlikely event that a German airship might lose its way and fly over this remote corner of Hampshire.

It was almost exactly two years since he had gone from here to board the *Reliant*. Two years. It seemed a lifetime, an eternity.

He quickened his pace and heard the big car growling up the gravel drive behind him.

The army certainly took care of the old place, he thought. White-painted stones to guide vehicles at night, a Union Jack flapping damply from a mast in the middle of the old croquet lawn. He felt his heart beat harder as he saw the house's imposing entrance. The place was deserted, an earthbound *Mary Celeste*, and yet he had the strong feeling that eyes were watching him, observing him like a specimen. Up the steps, then into the enormous entrance hall. The fire was blazing and there were some Christmas cards on the marble mantel. A sergeant was sitting at a desk, and stood up when he saw him.

"You'll be Major Blackwood." He looked uncomfortable. "Sorry about all the clutter, sir."

At that moment Jack Swan came in through the side door, his eyes nearly vanishing in the crinkles of a huge smile.

"It's so good to see you again, Major!"

Blackwood hugged him tightly and saw the sergeant was watching them curiously. The car's driver opened the doors with his back as he carried in the luggage.

"There's a fire lit in each of your rooms, sir. A nice single malt ready an' waiting!"

The memory triggered something, but it would not form properly. Then the sergeant said quietly to the driver, "Lend a hand, Bert." Then in a controlled tone, "Now you know you shouldn't be here, Captain Beamish."

Jonathan turned and saw a young man in a pale blue coat like a dressing gown, and felt his blood run cold. Like the one he had worn in Cairo and at Plymouth.

The man stared at the sergeant, his eyes completely blank, then he said in a small, broken voice, "I want to go home." He seemed to notice Jonathan for the first time, and probably in his tortured mind imagined he was one of the doctors. "Tell them, please! I want to go *home!*"

"Come along now, Captain Beamish." The sergeant sounded relieved as two nursing orderlies hurried in from another door, where the old general's gunroom had been.

Jonathan did not resist as Swan took his arm. It was suddenly important that David's servant did not feel that he was shaking. He glanced back but the place was empty, and the sergeant had returned to his desk.

"Yes, I think I could do with a drink, Swan." He tried to smile but it would not come. "Several."

For those few terrible moments, he had been face-to-face with himself.

Jonathan paused halfway up the hillside, on the path that led higher still to a leafless copse. He was breathing hard after a lengthy stroll around the fringe of the estate, but not so hard as when he had first arrived here.

Ten days of walking, eating alone in his rooms, and often drinking too much, to awake in front of a flickering fire. It never seemed to go out completely, and he guessed that Swan was trying to take personal care of him. He had tried to avoid the long huts and the secluded places where men walked, cut off completely from those around them, men who sometimes stood shaking, unable to move until somebody led them back into the warmth. Shell shock, something which the hard men joked about. It was not funny to see it at close hand.

He himself found it difficult to sleep properly, with the nightmares always lying in wait to torment him, and sometimes he thought that he had been reduced to playing a part; that he was really no better than those desperate, lost figures who stumbled around the grounds. He had tried to come to terms with it, to deal with it by remembering the complete pattern of events. Instead, there were only unanswered questions. What had become of Major Livesay's prospects in the corps? And young Roger Tarrier; had he overcome his youthful naivety and settled down aboard *Reliant*?

On his long walks, with his greatcoat collar turned up over his ears, Jonathan had probed every angle of memory. There were voices too. *Who is in command of this battalion?* Perhaps the brigade major had been scared as well. But Lieutenant John Maxted's reply had not even quivered. *I am, sir!*

Places were always in the background, but sometimes hazy in the smoke of war. Suvla Bay and the salt lake; Anzac where the dead had lain rotting because of the snipers. Achi Baba and the Anafarta Hills, which had killed so many and had defied even the bravest to the end.

He had received a letter from Christopher Wyke. He was completely recovered from his wound and had been promoted to captain. It had been a curiously stilted, uncertain letter, as if Wyke could not believe that their comradeship and interdependence could be a lasting thing, and thought their closeness was merely a passing figment of battle. His father, the major-general, had hinted that there was a new appointment coming up for Jonathan, and after he had read the letter, he had wondered if Wyke was trying to warn him or prepare him for something.

Swan had spoken scornfully about one of the theatres he had visited in Winchester. Chorus girls dressed as squaddies, marching down the aisle in fake uniforms which left *little to the imagination,* Swan said darkly. For an old Royal Marine to be so shocked it must have been bad. Swan had told him that the girls had been careful to pause in their prancing march whenever they caught sight of a man in civilian clothes.

Jonathan had already heard the song in Plymouth.

Don't delay, go today,
Make your daddy glad,
To have had such a lad . . .
Tell your sweetheart not to pine,
To be proud their boy's in the line.

"I nearly walked out, sir, 'specially when some young idiots started to cheer!"

Jonathan smiled to himself. Harry Payne would probably have started a fight.

He groped in one pocket for his pipe. He had got out of the way of smoking it at Gallipoli, when even a puff of smoke could have betrayed his position to a sniper, and then while he had been in hospital the simple mechanics of it had seemed too remote and improbable: rather like this walk. It was only half past three but darkness was not far away. Then silence would close over Hawks Hill once more. His rooms were in the rambling east wing overlooking the moat, where sound carried because of it, and like the hospital ship stopping her engines in the night while a burial was carried out he had often woken to hear vehicles coasting down the driveway, like undertakers. He deliberately took out his pipe and began to fill it, his fingers stiff with cold. Then the petrol-filled lighter which had been fashioned from two French greatcoat buttons emblazoned with the fiery grenade. He watched the pale smoke drifting towards the copse. He could not remember what he had exchanged for it. Just a bearded French *poilu* with eyes squinted against the sun, but the rest of it was lost in his mind somewhere.

A twig snapped and he swung round instantly, his hand going to his hip where his revolver would have been. It made him sweat in spite of the cold air, to discover that the nearness of danger had armed him with senses which even now refused to quit.

He saw that it was a woman, coming down the other path towards the houses and outlying farm cottages from where he had started his walk. She wore a long, dark green coat with a fur-lined collar which, like his own, was turned up to her ears. There was a tartan scarf over her head and her hands were invisible in her pockets.

She was watching him all the way, as if to guess what he was doing.

Jonathan called, "It's all right, I was just walking."

She halted and faced him. Even in the dying light he could see she was pretty, even beautiful, with dark hair that poked rebelliously from beneath the scarf, and grave, steady eyes that could have been either blue or grey.

He said awkwardly, "Thought you might think I was one of those poor chaps from the hospital."

She waited for him to move and then fell into step beside him. She was quite tall, which the long green coat emphasised, and might have been, he thought, in her middle twenties.

She answered abruptly, "Oh, I know who *you* are, Major Blackwood. I grew up with tales of your family." She glanced at him. "Not going too fast, am I?"

He replied indirectly, "I'm getting used to it." Then he said, "I still don't think you should be using this path. It will be dark soon."

"I thought perhaps you imagined I was trespassing?"

She made him feel clumsy, out of his depth, and he retorted, "I have no say in things here at the moment."

They walked on in silence, their feet squeaking on wet grass. Once, on a narrow part of the track, she overtook him, and he saw that she was wearing long laced boots, which like the hem of her coat were heavy with mud.

He asked, "Where *are* you going, if it's not an impertinence?"

"The hospital. I work there some of the time."

Dogs were barking noisily ahead at one of the cottages. The sound gave an edge to his voice. "I'm sorry. I've spoken to hardly anyone here."

She pulled her scarf closer around her throat. "My name is Alexandra Pitcairn, by the way." She glanced at him and saw the memory come alive.

"The doctor's daughter." He had stopped and was frowning. "I saw you once at a party—something at Eastwood Farm. I remember your father very well. I was on leave, the last one I had before war was declared." It was all tumbling out of him and he could not stop. And all the while she stood watching him, without impatience or curiosity, as if she shared the pictures forming in his mind.

It was suddenly as clear as polished glass, and he said, "There was a young subaltern there too, from the Rifle Brigade."

"He was killed at Loos."

A huge dog rushed out of the gloom, and for an instant Jonathan thought it was going to attack her. But she bent down with her hand outstretched as the dog pounded up to her, and it panted with excitement as she pulled its ears, murmuring something he could not hear.

"I—I'm very sorry. I didn't . . ."

She stood up and said, "How could you have known? You've been away, doing things for King and Country."

Her tone was cool, detached, and he guessed she was like the women on the train. *Why him? Why not you?*

A figure walked past and called out, "How do, Major? Good to see you up an' about again!"

It was the head groom, coming up from the stable where he kept his pony and trap.

"Thank you, Marker. Glad you're still here."

They walked towards the outflung shadow of the great house and then she said, "I must leave you now, Major."

She seemed to hesitate, then she said, "I hate and loathe this war. What it does, what it destroys. I work here when I can—they need all the help they can get. It never stops."

Jonathan asked quietly, "The soldier from the Greenjackets. Was he . . .?"

She put one hand on the side door. "I'm not sure what

might have happened." She pushed open the door and light spilled over her hair. It was the colour of dark chestnut.

She stood watching him, sensing his despair. "You see, I was in love with your brother David." She gave a quick smile. "But he never knew I existed."

Jonathan followed her, and hesitated by the massive fire-place where he had seen the shell-shocked Captain Beamish.

Then he made up his mind and walked after her. She paused outside another door and closed it behind her. Jonathan heard her say, "Well, here I am, Malcolm—I told you I'd come!"

Jonathan did not hear the reply. He was staring at the notice on the door. *All the patients here are blind. Please do not discuss it.*

A different sergeant was sitting at the reception desk, a dark quiff of hair plastered to his forehead. He stood up and clicked his heels.

"Good walk, sir?"

"I was speaking to Doctor Pitcairn's daughter, Sergeant." What was the matter with him? People might get the wrong impression. But she had been in love with David. It was incredible. *He never knew I existed.*

The sergeant walked round the desk and held out his hands to the fire.

"Oh, our Angel—that's what we calls 'er, sir." He saw the uncertainty on his face and said gently, "She teaches them poor lads Braille. Gives 'em heart. Most of 'em 'ave nothing else left."

He became suddenly businesslike as one of the orderlies clumped in.

"She's just gone in, Harry." He looked at the corridor meaningly. "Just 'ang about till she's finished."

As the orderly opened the door with its warning notice,

the sergeant said to Jonathan, "It don't follow that because a bloke's been blinded that 'e's automatically a gentleman, if you gets my meaning, sir?" Then he reached into a drawer of the desk. "So nice talkin' to you, sir, an officer wot's seen an' done the things you 'ave, an' that—I forgot to give you this." He pulled out the familiar buff envelope. *Orders.*

"Thank you, Sergeant." He would have a drink, maybe two, and then he would open them.

But all he could see was the hurt in her eyes, the sting of her tone when she had told him about her love for David.

Perhaps she had been the girl in his dream, whose face had always been unclear. Of one thing he was certain: he could never forget her now.

ELEVEN

Harry Payne slipped off the tailboard of the farm cart and waved to its driver.

"Thanks, mate!"

The horse trotted away and Payne stood watching it for some while, remembering what this great estate had once looked like when the general had ruled the place. More to the point, how it must have been before the old fellow's extravagances had taken their toll.

He knew the soldier on the gate was staring at him curiously and automatically straightened his shoulders, testing the weight of his neatly stowed pack and all the other clutter that hung about him. There was even more now, he thought grimly. A steel helmet on his pack, and an anti-gas respirator for good measure. It had been bad enough at Gallipoli: he remembered seeing the soldiers floundering in the sea as their equipment had carried them to the bottom. With this little lot they would not have got even that far.

He hoisted his Lee-Enfield rifle on its webbing sling and walked towards the gateway. To many he might look like just another soldier, but Payne was a true professional and proud of it, despite all that had happened. His cap was tilted at a jaunty angle, the R.M.A. grenade shining like gold, while his boots gleamed like black glass.

The soldier said, "Your guvnor's not back yet."

Payne strode on. They knew everything here, and gossip was rife amongst the staff. It probably helped to take their minds off the patients and the cruel reminders of a war they had not shared.

He grimaced. Not yet, anyway. They would be calling up schoolboys if things got much worse. He thought of his young brother, who had lied about his age and had signed up with the corps. Payne could have stayed in Winchester for a longer period; Major Blackwood had said so. He always thought of everyone but himself.

But Payne had been surprised to discover he was glad to come back, even to this place with its human derelicts.

His father had been in the corps, with a few uncles as well. He had died of fever while serving in a gunboat during some godforsaken campaign in Africa long before the war. It had been hard for his mother to manage, so she had married a local fishmonger. His lip curled with contempt. A mean bugger to all accounts, although he always had enough brass to spend on booze at the King's Head with his cronies.

God, his mother would miss young Titch. He had been the apple of her eye. Perhaps in some way he had reminded her of her man. Payne had two sisters, both married and making good money, one in a munitions factory, the other stitching uniforms. His mother would be doubly lonely now, he thought. And he had noticed that his stepfather had removed the picture of his real father from the parlour.

His stepfather had remarked on one occasion, "The armed forces are no way to find a proper living—I did tell you that, Flo."

Payne had retorted, "Most of them are *dying* at the moment, Mr Green." He could never bring himself to call him anything else. But he had refrained from making it worse. His mother, so frail and troubled, would only suffer for it.

His boots crunched up the winding gravel driveway. Even they sounded angry. No, he had not been sorry to get back. The major had sent a message to explain that he had had to go to London. Never a moment's peace. *I'll bet he's been going over it all again while I was in Winchester.* He almost smiled. He had done enough of that himself. *Where to next, I wonder?*

Maybe they would get a ship together. Whatever it was, he would stay with the major. When was he coming back, tomorrow? He would clean his kit for him, if old Jack Swan hadn't already done it. He was as pleased as Punch to be "back in the regiment" as he called it, doing things for the Blackwood family.

"Take that man's name, Sergeant-Major!"

The voice scattered Payne's thoughts and automatically he stamped to a halt, his fingers opening in readiness to salute.

But it was one of them: a tall, gaunt man who was hobbling across the wet grass leaning on two sticks. He looked wild and outraged; and Payne waited patiently to see what would happen.

"You—what's your name?" He peered at him searchingly.

"Don't you usually salute when you see an officer?" He gestured with his head towards his shoulder. "Don't you recognise my rank?"

"I'm sorry, sir." Payne felt a sense of hopelessness closing in. It was so cruel and unreal. The man with the wild stare was wearing a dressing gown with no piece of uniform at all. Payne had stood in the line with Blackwood and seen awful things, men screaming and dying as they had fallen to splinters and bullets. He had even felt the agonised breath of a Turkish trooper when they had clashed, bayonet to bayonet on that crumbling parapet; seen his eyes roll like marbles as he had wrenched the bayonet from his ribs and kicked him away. But this was something he could not fight, and he found himself thinking it was a mercy that Titch had been spared this living death at least.

"I've met your sort before, you know!" The man in the dressing gown gave a desperate grin. "Think that because of a war we're going to allow all the standards to go to blazes, what?"

From one corner of his eye Payne saw a white-coated orderly emerge from a door and then stand stock-still as he saw their drama.

"Where is that bloody Sergeant-Major?" He swung round angrily and one of his sticks slipped to the ground.

The orderly called in a matter-of-fact tone, "I'll take over. Leave it to me!"

But keeping his eyes on the man in the dressing gown, Payne lowered himself beneath his pack and equipment and retrieved the fallen stick.

"Here you are, sir." He was careful to be very formal, as he would have been with Colonel Waring. "Sorry about the salute, sir. I don't know what I was thinking of."

The man snatched back the stick and snapped, "Well, in future . . ." Payne was unable to watch as he suddenly burst into tears.

The orderly murmured, "You were lucky, mate. He can be a bit difficult." He took the man's arm and added, "Come along now. Time for some coffee."

But the other pulled his arm away and turned to stare at Payne. His face was streaming with tears but he managed to call, "Smart turnout, that man!"

Payne waited until they were swallowed up by the buildings and continued on his way to the stable yard, beyond which was the cottage he would share with Jack Swan.

He was still brooding over the encounter, and was not prepared for a woman's voice calling him by name.

"You must be Harry Payne! Mr Swan told me all about you."

"Not too much, I hope." It gave him time to recover himself.

It was not a nurse as he had expected, but a tall girl in a green, fur-collared coat. Her long chestnut hair was hanging quite free, and when she smiled he believed she was the prettiest thing he had ever laid eyes on.

"And who might you be, er, miss . . .?"

She said, "I'm not miss, I'm Alexandra Pitcairn. My father's the local doctor. I work here in the hospital when I can."

She brushed some hair from her eyes, and her smile was gone.

"I was in the house just now and I saw what happened, what you did. I suppose you're quite hardened to it, obeying orders, fair or otherwise, without question?"

"You get used to it, miss." What was she working up to?

"That officer with the two sticks . . . he probably led a lot of men like you to their deaths in the name of duty."

It was not a question, and Payne waited for more. She had a low, almost husky voice. Local girl, not like some of the snooty, affected officers' wives he had met.

She said abruptly, "I'll show you your room. I was helping Mr Swan get it ready for you." Then she added in her strangely direct manner, "I was very sorry to hear about your brother. I can imagine how you feel."

Payne remembered his stepfather's boozy grin when he had left, the falseness of his handshake. It would wipe that smirk off his face to have to stand on the firestep, shoulder to shoulder with his mates.

As they walked she asked, "What about Major Blackwood? Is he able to command his men to attempt the impossible? Do you enjoy doing what you do for him?"

He answered as sharply as he dared speak to any woman, "I clean his boots. He doesn't expect me to lick 'em!"

They entered the cottage and she led the way to a room with its own cheerful fire already alight in the grate. He felt her watching him as he slipped off his heavy pack and leaned his rifle against a cupboard. It was like undressing in front of her. His eyes moved to the neat bed and he tried not to picture her there.

"I think Major Blackwood is the finest man I've ever met." He said it so simply and firmly that she stared at him. "As for men getting killed, we all know the risks. I've seen a lot of good chums go. But you hope for the best."

"Mr Swan tells me that your major has been decorated, or will be very shortly."

Payne hid his surprise. So that was it. She had met him already and formed an opinion of him which in no way fitted the man.

"I was there, miss." His eyes were faraway, seeing it again. "A lot of fellows went west that day. We started with a colonel in command but after the major fell what was left of us was in the hands of a junior lieutenant. I knew it was going to happen—I'm sure he did too. But the Aussies were being shelled by one of our own ships." He was leaning against the mantelpiece, his face warmed by the fire. "He stood up, calm as you please, framed against that bloody sea—begging your pardon, miss . . ."

She said quietly, "I hear much worse. Please tell me. I want to know."

"Well, the ship ceased fire, then Johnny Turk started shooting at him. Even *they* couldn't miss. I thought he was done for. When I saw his wounds I could have wept. But we made it." He looked sideways at her. "Never thinks of himself. I sometimes wonder why he went into the corps at all. I once heard him say, because it was expected." He forced a grin. "Like me, I suppose. We never knew nothing else."

Mercifully, Jack Swan appeared and beamed at both of them.

"All shipshape, Harry." Then he looked at the carpet. "Sorry about the kid."

Their eyes met, and there was understanding and compassion in them that the girl had never seen before between such hardened men. Why had she told him about David Blackwood? She had only ever told her mother, and she had died in an influenza epidemic. Even her father didn't know. And yet she had told David's brother, a perfect stranger; and once she had almost asked Jack Swan about serving with David in China.

She said uncertainly, "I must go. I have a class of two waiting." She looked at Payne. "Enjoy your stay." Then she was gone.

Swan said, "Come into the kitchen. The missus has done some mulled wine for us. Just the stuff to give the troops, eh?"

Payne said, "Why does she have it in for the Blackwood family?"

Swan shrugged. "Didn't know she did. The estate owns her father's house, but then it used to own just about everything around here." He reached into a cupboard above the stove. "Now tell me all the news about the mob. I hear old McCann's a bloody sergeant-major now. God, the corps must be desperate!"

Payne shook his head. Once a Royal Marine, always a Royal Marine. But he was thinking of the girl's face, her expression of shock when he had described the moment the major had been smashed down.

He raised the thick glass mug and said, "Here's to the lads who couldn't get back, Jack!" He thought of the sobbing officer with the sticks. "God, what a bloody mess it all is."

They drank in silence.

Jonathan Blackwood's appointment at the Royal Marines Headquarters was not until afternoon, so having arrived early at Waterloo station he decided to walk the rest of the way. He had always had a wary respect for London, but he had never grown to appreciate it like many of his brother officers.

If he had expected some sign of war he was soon surprised, as he crossed Westminster Bridge and paused to gaze at the handsome towers and terraces of Parliament and the nearby abbey. He had heard that air raids had been carried out the previous year by German airships, the Zeppelins, but they had become almost nonexistent now, too vulnerable to the massed antiaircraft batteries around the capital, and the increasing success of the Royal Flying Corps.

The thing that struck him more than anything was the mass of servicemen in every major street. Some were with their girls and others lurched tipsily from one pub to another.

He had thought he might find here the same tension so obviously in Plymouth and Southampton, but he had been mistaken: he was surprised by the outwardly carefree and jocular behaviour of soldiers and sailors alike.

He walked on. On this cold January day he felt fitter and stronger than for many months, and he supposed his regular walks around the estate were having the right effect.

He lingered in the silence of the abbey, looking at the many plaques and statues: noble figures in splendid uniforms, men remembered if not for their lives then for their brave deaths in every quarter of the globe. Sound echoed and carried, and the many visitors seemed to be holding their collective breath as they stared around at the abbey's treasures. He left, feeling oppressed.

A troop of Horse Guards clattered past, their young faces pink in the bitter air, and their officer saluted him with his sword. He watched them until the buildings swallowed them up, seeing himself in their youth, their obvious pride in their uniforms and their service which he had once known, and could now barely recall.

The Royal Marines section of Admiralty was in Tothill Street, down towards Petty France. When he showed his identity card to the military police he glanced at a clock and marvelled where the time had gone. He smiled. And he was not even breathless.

"This way, Major Blackwood." A bored civil servant who showed neither curiosity nor much interest led the way to the first floor. "Please wait. I shall announce you."

There was a long wall mirror near the double doors, no doubt a necessary fixture, so that visiting officers could adjust themselves and their uniforms before facing the imposing might of the adjutant-general. He thought suddenly of Waring, his contempt for the strutting Brigadier-General Nugent at Mudros. But Nugent had not been the only one to vanish into oblivion after the evacuation of Gallipoli. Even Sir Ian Hamilton the G.O.C., whom Nugent had quoted with such relish, had been dropped. Kitchener had been lost at sea in the cruiser *Hampshire,* and General Sir John French, who had commanded the British Expeditionary Force on the Western Front since the beginning, had been replaced by the experienced General Haig. French, a cavalry officer of the old school, had been defeated by his own insensitivity to the war's mounting barbarity, and after the disastrous battle at Loos where the British losses had been almost double those of the enemy, and for no gains at all, he had bowed to the inevitable.

"Please go in, Major Blackwood."

There were two men in the high-ceilinged office. Jonathan had only seen the adjutant-general once or twice, but he was not a man one would easily forget. Tall and formidable, his chest adorned with four rows of decorations, he seemed to tower over his companion. It was hard to imagine him a young lieutenant, creeping beneath the deckhead of some small cruiser.

Major-General Sir Herbert Loftus was instantly recognisable. Without waiting for the adjutant-general to get down to business, he strode forward and gripped Jonathan by the hand. "This is a happy day for me! To see you looking so well after what you have gone through is far better than any late Christmas present!"

Loftus was well known throughout the corps, and there was no class of cruiser or capital ship in which he had not seen service. His record of arms read like the corps' history itself. Egypt, Africa, China, India; the campaigns had been as blustery as the man himself. Although young for his rank, his hair and neat moustache were completely white, so that by comparison his skin was like tooled leather. *A Royal Marine's Marine*, they called him. He had once been heard to say that he could win no greater honour.

The adjutant-general coughed politely. "When you are ready, Herbert?" Then he smiled and the severity vanished. "I was in doubt as to the value of this interview, Blackwood. Now I see it might hold some merit."

Major-General Loftus nodded. It was obviously high praise from the great man.

They sat facing each other, the faint beat of a military band muffled by distance and the stout walls of Caxton House.

The adjutant-general crossed his hands on his empty desk top. Jonathan doubted if he ever allowed it to be littered for long. "Open the batting, Herbert."

Loftus began, "Another naval and marine division has been raised to fight on the Western Front."

Jonathan saw his superior frown. Loftus was perhaps being too frank at this stage.

The major-general was unmoved, and stared unwinkingly at him. It was what he remembered most about Loftus afterwards: eyes so blue and intense they had seemed to go right through him.

"There is to be a new offensive, probably in the spring. That is not so far away as it seems on this cold afternoon. We need every trained man we can find. I shall command the division as a whole, under the direction of Sir Douglas Haig of course. A full-scale attack in the old Somme area must be successful before the weather breaks. I happen to know that Haig has certain doubts about the French support, and our attack is intended to remove the pressure from our main ally."

Jonathan opened his mouth and then decided against

interruption. Perhaps he was even more out of touch than he
had realised. Only weeks ago the papers had been full of the
great battle of Verdun, and the fierce French resistance. Their
proud rallying cry, *They Shall Not Pass,* had seemed a rare bea-
con of hope and victory in all the blackness and misery.

"Speak out, Blackwood. You have to know anyway."

Jonathan looked down at his hands. Clenched into fists
again, like a warning.

"The French held the line at Verdun, sir. The enemy captured one of the fortified positions, but only temporarily."

Loftus said quietly, "As in your campaign at Gallipoli, censorship is severe. But the truth will out, as it did when a
handful of journalists revealed the dreadful losses you had
really suffered, while Sir Ian Hamilton's releases to the press
had always been filled with optimism." Jonathan waited. He
had at least learned why Hamilton had been relieved. Loftus
watched him impassively. "They held Verdun certainly, after
months of bloody fighting and the threat of disgrace and
ignominy for any French general who failed to hold his sector. But to date, as far as I know, nobody is aware that when
the Germans eventually broke off the engagement, there were
half a million dead in the field." He watched his words going
home. "Also our one worthwhile ally, the French army, was
in a state of chaos and mutiny."

How could any offensive succeed if an army was in a state
of revolt?

Loftus answered the unspoken question. "Much has been
done to seize and remove the ringleaders. In some instances
the French artillery was ordered to fire on its own lines. But
morale has never been lower. They need—no, *must have* the
pressure removed. Sir Douglas Haig has promised to break
through to the Belgian coast, and destroy the German bases

there between Nieuport and Zeebrugge, which are being used for U-boats. I hardly need to tell you that that further tightens the enemy's hold on French supply convoys."

Somewhere outside a clock chimed, and Jonathan realised he had been here for a full hour. It seemed to have passed in minutes.

Loftus glanced questioningly at his superior, who offered a curt gesture in reply.

He said, "There will be one additional Royal Marine battalion, which will be separate from my main division. It will be infantry, and will also contain some of the heavy howitzers for support. It is only a matter of time before the R.N.L.I. and R.M.A. become one, but time we do not have. There's nothing in battle that succeeds like competition and reputation. You know the corps, and every man jack in it knows your family's reputation . . . In short, I want you to command it."

Jonathan felt the room closing in. Wyke had hinted at this, because he had known better than most what he had gone through during the months on the peninsula, and in the agony of those that had followed.

Loftus said, "You will be made up to lieutenant-colonel brevet, of course." But he did not smile, and his eyes were like reflections from an arctic berg. "I know your family has given more than most already for this damned war. I cannot order you to take this appointment." He shrugged. "I simply happen to believe that you can do it—and you are possibly the only one in the corps who can. And soon, I think you yourself will come to accept that."

A voice seemed to shriek in his skull. *Tell them, for God's sake. You can't do it. Fate is against you. Next time there'll be so many more depending on you.*

He was almost shocked to hear his own voice in this vast, quiet room. "I hope I can justify your faith, sir."

It was madness. He could almost hear Waring's infuriating laugh, mingled with the cries and curses of hand-to-hand combat.

Loftus showed no surprise. "I served under your father for a time. Not an easy man, if I may say so. But you—you're like your brothers, especially David. I knew you'd accept."

The adjutant-general glanced meaningly at the clock above the painting of Trafalgar. Nelson had just fallen but the painter's emphasis was on the scarlet-coated marines firing from the hammock nettings, while one of their sergeants ran to help the little admiral.

"Your presentation will be at the end of the month, Blackwood. Make sure your new rank is in evidence on that day, won't you?"

He must leave here, if only to make himself realise what he had just done. From major to lieutenant-colonel at the stroke of a pen.

The adjutant-general was saying, "The presentation will be at Eastney Barracks. I am afraid *I* shall be representing the Colonel-in-Chief."

Loftus said dryly, "Can't be helped. The salmon season begins the day after. One can hardly expect His Majesty to miss that."

The adjutant-general glared at him, then said, "I did have doubts, Blackwood." He thrust out his hand. "But no longer."

It was over.

There were two different redcaps in the reception area and one hurried towards him, his eyes brimming with eager curiosity.

"Sir? The adjutant-general's car is waiting for you."

It was starting already. He said, "I want to get to Waterloo, Corporal."

The redcap sounded indignant. "Oh, no, sir. I am instructed

to tell you that the driver will take you straight home."

Home. It was a long time since he had thought of Hawks Hill as that.

"Then thank you. It'll make a change. I hope he can find the place in the dark."

The M.P. shook his head. "When you get to be the adjutant-general's driver you'd *better* know such things, sir."

There was another surprise even as the long khaki staff car slid smoothly to the bottom of the steps. He heard footsteps on the tiled floor behind him and without turning he knew it was Wyke. It was this appointment of which he had been trying to warn him; his father had probably told him.

Wyke seemed uncertain now, still testing the strength of their friendship and unsure of the proprieties of rank.

"I just heard, sir! You've accepted!"

As David had often said, it was like a family. Secrets were not possible for long. He shook Wyke's hand warmly and then embraced him with all the affection of a brother.

"It's so good to see you, Christopher! You'll never know."

Wyke seemed suddenly shy.

"I wanted to ask you, sir, before anybody else shoved his oar in. I know it isn't proper procedure . . ."

Together they walked down the steps to the car. The light was already fading over London; the driver had the door open and his hand up in a stiff salute, and suddenly there was no more time.

Jonathan said, "I would take it as an honour if you would be my adjutant. Is that what you wanted to ask?"

Wyke's face was one great grin. "Thank you, sir. Yes, it was!"

"I'll be receiving orders soon now. There'll be a lot to do."

The prospect did not seem to daunt Wyke.

"See you on the thirty-first, sir. The champagne is on me!"

He was still saluting as the car rolled away into the traffic.

Harry Payne stood back and eyed Jonathan critically.

"Tailor did a good job, sir. Just the ticket."

The last day in January was a perfect one, as if it, like the ceremony about to begin, had been planned to the last detail.

It was strange, he thought: he felt far more at home at Eastney Barracks than at Hawks Hill. He had completed training here, and as a young subaltern had gone from here to join his first ship. It seemed like a lifetime ago.

Below the window he could see the length and breadth of the parade ground, usually crisscrossed by marching squads and platoons of men, their efforts cursed or approved by motionless N.C.O.'s: drill with rifle and machine-gun, light artillery or merely the mysteries of fixing and unfixing bayonets with perfect timing.

There was a guard of honour there now, for the adjutant-general, and the guard commander was moving slowly along each rank to make certain that nothing could be faulted. On the opposite side of the square the band played lively music of the sea. Beyond a painted rope the visitors stood closely packed, for warmth as much as anything, for the barracks faced the English Channel and the breeze was like a knife.

There would be some familiar faces here today, but a lot would be missing. There was a new colonel commandant now, Roger Tarrier's father having been sent to a grander appointment in Scotland on the admiral's staff. Payne had been complaining about the award not being presented by H.M. the King as the corps' colonel-in-chief.

"They queue up at Buckingham Palace for next to nothing!" he had said indignantly. "I expect most of the medals he hands out are picked out of a hat!"

Jonathan watched uneasily as more visitors appeared.

Perhaps the Palace might have been better, although not for
Payne's reasons. Here he would stand alone, unsupported by
others who had faced death and probably viewed these cer-
emonies as far more harrowing. There were women too:
officers' wives, local dignitaries. The mess bills would be heavy
after this.

He leaned forward sharply so that his forehead banged
against the cold glass.

"Who are *they?*"

Payne moved up beside him, hearing the edge in his tone
and, worse, knowing what had taken his attention.

He followed his glance and found a large group of marines
standing apart from all the rest. There were nurses too, their
blue and scarlet capes lifting slightly in the breeze, like the
Union Flag that flew above the old square clock tower.

"They wanted to come, sir." His eye fell on the new rank,
the crown and pip of lieutenant-colonel. Pity his brothers
couldn't be here today, or Titch for that matter.

Jonathan tore his eyes from the group by the wall. Several were in wheelchairs, others on crutches. His men, to be
left like this . . .

Payne repeated, "They wanted to, sir. They don't blame
you for what happened." He wanted to add, *They're proud,*
that's all. They want to share it with you. But it was useless, and
he knew it.

Another movement at the opposite side behind the band.
It was the barracks adjutant, riding his magnificent white
horse very slowly like a knight about to take part in a joust.

Payne said gently, "Nearly time, sir. Starter's orders."

Jonathan turned and said, "*You* should have been given
something."

Payne smiled, relieved that he had not pursued the matter of the wounded spectators.

"I can wait, sir."

When he looked out again the guard of honour had moved into open order, bayonets fixed, their officer with his drawn sword at the carry. People shifted and pointed, some waving to familiar faces.

"I don't know if I can go through with this." Only when he saw Payne glance at him did he realise he had spoken aloud.

The door opened. "Ready, sir."

After the warmth of the room the cold bit into him like ice. At the top of the fine stone steps he looked straight across to the sea, today hardly moving but for a low, undulating swell. It was a view known to sailors down the centuries: Spithead and the Solent and the green hump of the Isle of Wight like an unfinished backdrop.

Unexpectedly Payne saluted, his face expressionless.

"Good luck, sir. You'll be right as ninepence, you'll see. Just remember, the lads'll be looking to you today."

Then he was gone and Jonathan's escort, a smart young lieutenant who was probably still undergoing training, fell into step beside him.

Unbeknown to Jonathan, he was glancing at him whenever he could, noting the flecks of grey in his dark hair, the tight crows-feet about his eyes. Suffering, strain and anxiety were all there, but the lieutenant saw only the hero, who had been prepared to throw away his life to save men under fire. The man he would most like to be.

"Band, *ready!*" Jonathan saw the glitter of instruments, the buglers moistening their lips in readiness.

"Guard of honour! Pre-sent . . . *arms!*"

The rifles slapped out in salute, a faint cloud of blancoe above the ranks as each gloved hand made the air ring to their crack. The bandmaster's baton began to beat time, and as the massive figure of the adjutant-general strode into view, followed closely by Loftus and the new colonel commandant, "A Life on the Ocean Wave" blared out and echoed from the old redbrick walls as it had for so many years.

Through the guard of honour Jonathan saw Sergeant-Major McCann, standing quite alone and rigidly at attention.

His youthful escort whispered, "Right on time, sir!"

Jonathan watched the general moving along the guard, pausing to speak to the officer-in-command and to a sergeant whose medals had caught his eye.

"Ready, sir?"

Jonathan gave a brief nod. It was happening so quickly it would soon be over. God, he thought, his escort was so nervous his teeth were chattering. Together they marched across the square, and as the band ceased playing and the guard were stood at ease, he could feel the silence like something physical, like the deafness he had experienced when Waring's booby-trapped Bible had exploded.

Major-General Loftus and the commandant were standing slightly behind the general, who was positioned on a carefully painted white disc. Nothing had been left to chance. He saw Loftus's bright blue stare and knew this was his idea: in the corps there was no better way to reward gallantry and to show off the man he had chosen to command the new battalion.

The adjutant-general returned his salute and peered closely at his uniform to make certain he was displaying his new rank. Then with great care he took a document from his pocket and put on a pair of small gold-rimmed spectacles. It made him seem slightly more human.

Jonathan glanced at the men beyond the other barrier. Corporal Wakeford was one of those in wheelchairs. He had no legs, but was nodding and making what appeared to be cheerful comments as the general's resonant tones carried easily to the spectators. There were others he had thought dead, and two who could have been at Hawks Hill, their bandaged eyes peering upwards as if they could see him.

And around the corner of the wall Payne watched it all, and knew exactly what this public display was costing so private a man. Jonathan looked as pale as death, and Payne wanted to be there with him, in his place: aboard a ship, or on some bloody firestep with all hell showing its teeth.

Then he recognised a familiar figure by one of the ornamental cannon. It was the hard man: the undisciplined machine-gunner Bert Langmaid, of all people.

Payne joined him and murmured, "Thought you didn't believe in this sort of stuff."

Langmaid glared at him. "I don't, see? But he's different. Not a bad on'." He relented slightly. "For a bleedin' officer, that is!"

The adjutant-general was coming to the end. Jonathan tried not to think of all the missing faces, so young in the flash of artillery fire.

He had barely heard a word of the citation. *Over and above the line of duty . . . With no thought for his own safety showed courage and heroism of the highest order . . .*

More faces moved towards the general and a leather box was being held out towards him.

Some of the spectators pressed forward to see better, and as a gap appeared in the crowd directly opposite him, he recognised the bearded figure of Pitcairn, the village doctor. He was deeply moved, for although he had often attended the Blackwood family Pitcairn had never considered himself, or been considered, a friend to his father. And there was someone else with him. He blinked against the hard light. She was wearing the same green coat with the fur collar, and even at this distance he saw her emotion.

Then, very slowly, she raised a small handkerchief. It was only for him, and said more than any spoken word or message could ever do.

In the next second he was falling back two paces and saluting, the ribbon of the Distinguished Service Order about his neck.

"Band—ready!"

But in those few moments before they broke into another lively programme a single voice roared out from the crowd.

"Good old Blackie!"

The effect was immediate, and to him awful. Cheering and shouting rebounded across the parade ground, so that the bandmaster had to wait while some of his own men joined in.

The adjutant-general said over the uproar, "See you in the mess, Herbert. Went rather well, apparently."

Major-General Loftus paused a moment longer. He said, "I told you, Blackwood. You're the man for the job!" He followed the general towards the stone stairway, others in his wake according to rank and status; then he paused and looked back, shading his eyes against the hard glare from the sea. He saw his new lieutenant-colonel walking amongst the wounded marines, and felt the pain like his own when one of them clapped Blackwood across the back.

The girl in the green coat had disappeared. He had noticed the quick exchange at the close of the ceremony, the raised handkerchief like a signal. He was strangely pleased about it, whoever she was. Where he was going, and with the task ahead, Jonathan Blackwood would need all the help and all the comfort he could find.

TWELVE

It was not until April that Jonathan Blackwood returned to
Hawks Hill. During the intervening ten weeks the new battalion had been under canvas outside Salisbury where
officers, N.C.O.'s and men had been put through every kind
of training. The instructors for the most part were already
veterans and knew exactly what it was like to be under fire,
and the hard necessities of day-to-day survival.

The battalion showed plenty of promise and Jonathan had
made certain that everyone, high or low, had pulled his
weight. Digging trenches and shoring them up with the primitive materials they might expect to find on the battlefield so
that they would not collapse under the first bombardment,
crossing tangled barbed wire with ladders, duckboards, or
advancing in full kit and wearing the hated anti-gas respirators were all part of it. Other days were used for physical
training, or long route marches over rough country until the
marines had come to hate the instructors more than the
enemy they were being trained to fight.

It had been Jonathan's first experience of the other con-
flict, the paper war which every senior officer was plagued
by. But his adjutant, Captain Christopher Wyke, and his new
second-in-command Major Ralph Vaughan had cut down the
daily load considerably and given him time to acquaint himself with every squad, platoon and company of his command.

Major-General Loftus had visited the training camp twice
but had not interfered, although he had obviously had a hand

in the choice of an army unit which was doing the same kind of exercises. A battalion of the East Surrey Regiment was usually ready to act as the enemy, and the tough rivalry and the confidence it bred helped a great deal, although Jonathan sometimes suspected that these men forgot what lay inevitably at the end of the mock battles and forced marches. Competition and comradeship had become the only object. The long casualty lists might have belonged to another world, a part of something unreal.

On his final visit Loftus had hinted that a massive attack would begin sooner rather than later on the Western Front. The weather had improved, the flooded trenches and bogged-down roads—what remained of them—were almost passable.

"Give your people a week's leave. They've earned it." He had been climbing into his car at the time and had added in an almost matter-of-fact way, "Take some yourself. I hear you've been overdoing it lately." He could just as easily have said, "It may be the last chance you'll get."

Jonathan had often recalled that bright, cold day at Eastney, over two months ago. To him it seemed yesterday. Her face in the crowd, the signal to him which had excluded everyone else. He had not seen her since; she had vanished with her father while he had been meeting some of the wounded marines, and might have been only another dream. He had wanted to call at her home, or at least speak to her father about her, but immediately he had rejected the idea. In a small village, in peace or war, there was always ready gossip. Just a simple visit could so easily compromise her position after he had gone.

Why delude himself anyway, he thought angrily. She had been in love with David, who had known nothing about it. Why had she told him even that?

On his return to Hawks Hill and after a restless night, he

got up early and went for a walk, towards the dark copse where in childhood they had stalked dragons or fought pirates. He paused on the winding pathway and took several deep breaths. How good it felt and tasted. April in Hampshire: the distant trees enveloped in millions of buds so that they seemed shrouded in a fine green haze, and the hillside itself below the copse alive with a swaying sea of daffodils. He began to walk on but stopped as he heard the far-off twang of a cuckoo. He had already heard several: they were always early visitors to Hampshire.

In the quiet morning, the familiar doubts suddenly assailed him again. He should have told Loftus, explained. And what would he have said? The question repeated itself over and over, and there was never any answer.

He stared out over the peaceful countryside. Little had changed here for centuries. Would it ever be torn apart like the fields of Flanders?

It was impossible, unimaginable; but over there, too, they must have thought it could never happen. Whole acres covered with shell craters, villages once like these obliterated from the map.

And those men he had sent on leave, proud of what they had accomplished together, ready for anything. Suppose he broke down this time, failed them utterly and came back like one of those shattered figures at Hawks Hill. He lowered himself onto a grassy hump and made himself face the other prospect: death, or mutilation in its most grievous form as he had seen too often.

These men who had been forged into a weapon, proud to be in the corps, eager to show the army what they could do; they were all depending on him. Because of a family name, and all the weight of tradition that went with it. The whole Blackwood family seemed to be rising from the ground to drive him on, no matter what failings or weaknesses he might imagine within himself.

A dog was barking a long way off. A million miles from his life and the dread which he must conceal from everyone.

"Good morning, Colonel! You *are* an early bird!"

He lurched to his feet, surprised she was here, guilty at what she might see in him.

She was wearing a cool-looking flowered dress, with the same country boots showing beneath it. The smile on her lips was uncertain and questioning.

"Is something wrong? If I've come at an awkward time I do apologise. . . . It's just that we heard you were back." She tossed the long chestnut hair from her face. "This is always a nice walk, isn't it?"

He was suddenly certain that this was no casual meeting. She had been coming here to see him.

He said, "I wanted a place where I could think. I was sorry I missed the chance to talk with you at the barracks. You'll never know what a difference it made to me—your being there, I mean."

She looked at him directly. "Well, you were going to be pretty busy. I could see that. And besides . . ." She seemed to change her mind. "My father was very pleased."

Had it been David she had seen receiving the D.S.O. on that last cold day of January, instead of himself?

He asked, "May I walk with you a while?"

She was searching his face for something. Or someone.

"It's your land. Or will be again when this terrible war is over." Then she changed the subject once more. "When I found you just now, lost and miles away in your thoughts, I saw the young boy you used to be. Wistful. Full of hope, perhaps."

He said suddenly, "I've thought about you a lot. Ever since

we met on this path." He hurried on as something like a warning showed in her face. "I used to ask myself, what colour were her eyes? Blue or grey? I was even wrong about that. They're green."

She seemed disconcerted, thrown off guard.

"Like my mother's. You don't remember her, do you?"

"Of course I do."

They began to walk, but he was careful not to brush against her.

She asked abruptly, "Are we going to win this war, Colonel Blackwood?"

"Please call me Jonathan." He glanced at her fine profile, the tiny pulse beating in her throat. Then he answered her without hesitation. "Nobody's going to win."

"You mean that, don't you? When I met you I imagined you would be quite different about it. I felt so badly afterwards. Not because of the medal—I expect you've earned that a dozen times over—but because of . . . things. What Harry Payne said about you."

That's the first I've heard of it. But he said nothing, watching each emotion, afraid of losing or forgetting it.

"Down at the barracks too. Those poor men . . . they have nothing left. Like the ones I teach. I sometimes think some of them must hate me because I'm whole, or because I'm safe at home."

"I don't think so," he said, but she did not appear to hear.

"You went amongst them. I saw what it did for them, and what it was doing to you."

They walked on in silence, pausing only once to listen as the cuckoo called again.

"Is it true you're leaving soon?"

He replied quietly, "So they say."

What was the point of it? There was no future for him:

how could he even dare to think of it? So that they could
snatch a few hours or days together before he was lost to
Armageddon, or worse, come back to her like some horror
from the grave?

She said in a small voice, "People will miss you around
here." She said it with barely controlled emotion, so that her
soft Hampshire accent was more pronounced. She did not
wait for him to answer but said, "What were you thinking of,
when I found you by the path?"

"About all this, I suppose. What would happen to it if . . ."

She put her hand on his arm. "Don't say it! Don't even
think of it." There was anguish in her voice, and he supposed
it was for David. "You should find some nice girl who understands your sort of life . . ."

He glanced down at her hand. Small, well-shaped, and
strong. With skin like hers she would soon be brown when
the summer came.

He said steadily, "I've found her. But like David, she
doesn't know."

"I told you that in confidence."

"And I told you this—Alexandra."

When he looked again there were patches of colour in her
cheeks.

"You mustn't talk like that."

"I know. But I just did." He paused, and plunged on. "I'm
34 years old, and like my brothers and all my family I've
always served the corps. I was closer to David than anyone,
but I can never be like him. Or like any of them." He could
not stop now; was afraid to stop in case she turned away from
him. "When I take my men to Flanders it won't be me who's
leading them, it will be the Blackwood family. And I don't
think I can deal with it. It's all such a . . ." He groped for the
words. "Such a bloody waste."

She waited, but he said nothing else. They walked on.

They paused by the fence with the rickety stile and she said, "I must go back now." There was a silence, then she went on, "I'm 26 . . . and until a few minutes ago I thought I knew everything. You've proved me wrong in almost every aspect of this war. Men who treat you like a friend when they've hardly anything left . . ." Her voice caught, but she persisted. "And those who lead them into battle, or direct it from a safe distance. I always thought they must be callous, and wanting only glory."

He reached out to touch her hand but she pulled away. "No, please. It's all too quick. I must have time to think."

He was losing her. But she had never been his to lose.

He asked, "May I see you again? Just to walk with you?"

"I shall be at the hospital tomorrow." Then she said, rather desperately he thought, "We can be friends, can't we? Is it not enough?"

He smiled. "I feel better already."

He watched her climb the stile, and on the other side she turned, her eyes halfclosed against the sun. Then she smiled in response.

"My *friends* call me Alex!" She did not look back, although he watched her out of sight.

When he reached the house he could not convince himself that it had happened, or that he was not reading too much into ordinary words and gestures.

Tomorrow then . . .

He found Payne in the stableyard with an army motorcyclist, his goggles pushed to the top of his cap. The rider saluted and pulled an envelope from his pouch, and he sensed Payne watching him grimly as he signed for it.

He hardly saw the motorcycle go, puttering down the drive into the silence as he tore open the envelope.

She had green eyes, and he could call her Alex . . .

The paper seemed to mist over as he tried to hold onto her picture in his mind.

Payne asked quietly, "Trouble, sir?"

He looked at him and beyond him to the high copse and the golden sea of daffodils. It had been only a dream after all.

He was surprised how calm and empty he sounded.

"The battalion embarks for France in five days' time."

Doctor Alfred Pitcairn finished washing his hands and dried them vigorously on a towel. He was a neat, wiry man who looked more like a university professor than a country G.P. He glanced at his list of housecalls and did not look up when his departing nurse called a greeting to someone in the passageway. The door opened and closed again. Alex was home.

She came in and crossed to the desk where her father heard all the woes and symptoms of people he had known most of his life, and those of their offspring as well, although there weren't too many of those left in the village.

"Hard day, Daddy?" She moved to the open window and stood looking out at the garden.

"The usual. Some decent food would do them more good than I can. They're going to ration bread now, I hear, as if things aren't bad enough."

She said suddenly, "How much longer do you think it will go on?"

He put on his jacket. "I've almost stopped asking myself that." She sounded troubled. "What is it, Alex? Your work?"

She did not answer directly. "I went to see Colonel Blackwood today. I thought I should apologise for dragging you away after the presentation." She paused. "He was very nice to me. Not at all what I expected."

Doctor Pitcairn sat down and began to fill what he had always called his cutty pipe. There was more to it than that, he thought.

"Are you making comparisons, Alex?"

She said defensively, "What do you mean?"

"Your mother told me, you know. We had no secrets. I decided to say nothing about it." He watched her sensitive face. "But at the barracks I saw it all there again. Try to forget him, Alex. You'll meet some other nice young man, you'll see." She moved about the room touching things so familiar that she no longer even noticed them. "And talking to his brother isn't going to help."

He watched the pipe smoke drifting through the window. She was a lovely young woman, he thought, so like her mother as she had once been, and yet there were no men in her life, apart from that youthful infatuation with David Blackwood and the cheerful young subaltern in the Rifle Brigade. Even if he had not been killed, nothing would have come of that. There was no one else, certainly not locally. The men still at home were farmers working on the land; cider and darts in the pub, and after marriage far too many children. He wanted something more than that for Alex. She was not a headstrong girl, not with him anyway, but she was solitary and very private. He had been surprised when she had asked to be trained to teach blind children, but he no longer doubted her sincerity. When she was not at Hawks Hill she helped partially sighted veterans to train others who were completely blind.

She was looking at him now but her gaze was far away.

"He asked if he could see me again. I think he's lonely, and can't talk to his men about things."

He put down his pipe and said quietly, "John Potter the

grocer was in here just now with a poisoned hand. He said Colonel Blackwood's batman was in the shop today, buying a few things."

"Harry Payne. Yes, I've met him."

"He says they're off soon. Very soon . . . inevitable, I suppose."

"But he's only just got here! He's not ready for it!"

"I know. I was talking to one of the army surgeons. He said he knew Jonathan Blackwood in hospital in Plymouth. He was pretty badly wounded . . . worse than I realised."

"But they can't make him go, Daddy. Not after that . . ."

He walked round the desk and held her closely. "He's a Blackwood, Alex. You know what that means. Besides which, they need men like him, if only to bring this bloody thing to an end."

"But the Americans are in the war at last. They'll make all the difference, won't they?" She looked at him despairingly. "It can't last forever!"

"It takes time," he said. "The Americans may not be so eager to throw lives away for nothing." He had almost added, *the way we do,* but the expression in her eyes had been a warning. "Perhaps the orders will be changed." It sounded so inadequate that he was suddenly angry with himself. "Are you going to see him before he goes?"

She wiped her eyes with her handkerchief, the same one she had raised to Jonathan on that cold bright day. An army lorry was rattling through the village, filled with soldiers who were singing lustily as if they hadn't a care in the world.

"Take me back to dear old Blighty . . . !"

"I said I would."

Doctor Pitcairn glanced around his untidy consulting room, imagining life without her to chat to about everything under the sun. It was as selfish as it was natural, he thought.

"I'll use my bicycle," she said. "It's quicker." She kissed him. "Don't worry about me, Daddy. I can take care of myself. And anyway . . . it's nothing like that."

He smiled sadly. It was everything like that.

She was surprised to find Jack Swan moving a metal trunk down the curving stairway, assisted by one of the orderlies. She blurted out the reason for her visit, very aware that the sergeant on the desk and the white-coated orderly were both gaping at her.

Jack Swan was breathing hard from carrying the heavy trunk, and took far too long to answer.

"Just missed him, my dear. Motor car came about an hour back." He saw her shocked surprise. "All a bit of a rush."

She said in a whisper, "Gone? Not coming back?"

The sergeant said unhelpfully, "There are a lot of troops on the move, I hear."

She looked past him. The sunlight was still there, throwing patterns through the trees; but she saw none of it.

Wheels grated on the drive and she ran to the door. But it was an ambulance, the red crosses like blood in the sun. The sergeant folded his newspaper and grunted, "'Nother one, Fred. Fetch the duty orderlies."

Jack Swan lowered his voice. "He left you a letter, miss."

She was still staring at the driveway. She had thought it was the car, bringing him back.

"Letter?"

Swan glared as men hurried past, their faces like masks as they prepared themselves for what they were about to see.

"Come into the kitchen. You'll be more private there."

He closed the door very quietly behind her and sat impassively on a chair outside.

For a long time she stared at the envelope with its unfamiliar handwriting before she was able to tear it open, imagining him at his desk even as Harry Payne had been packing their kit.

My very dear Alex: I am sorry we cannot have our walk tomorrow . . .

She saw tears falling on the letter. This time they did not stop.

Captain Christopher Wyke sat at a trestle table, his face set in a frown of concentration as he checked through yet another list of equipment and stores. He could feel the warmth of the filtered sunlight through the sloping side of the tent, and was conscious of the incredible silence after all the bustle of training. On this fine morning the camp was all but deserted, save for the H.Q. platoon and a few military policemen.

His father, the major-general, had been delighted that he had secured the position of adjutant to the battalion.

"With a commanding officer like Blackwood an adjutant's job is a sure step toward promotion!" The Old Man had added with a chuckle, "Or to a nervous breakdown!"

He had certainly felt a sense of pride when the battalion had paraded in the early morning, ready to march the 22 miles to Southampton. They had looked fit, and some of them were obviously glad that the waiting was over.

I was like that before the Dardanelles.

The Royal Marine Artillery detachment had also left, but had taken the easier road in lorries supplied by the army. With any luck they would eventually be united with the promised howitzers when they reached France.

"But you look far too young to be a captain!" The girl named Hermione had been all over him at that last party at the Savoy.

He smiled, the strain dropping away from his face as he

remembered her passionate kisses, the warm pressure of her body.

Maybe he *was* too young for his rank. Maybe they all were. That was the thing about advanced promotion, his and everyone else's for that matter. If the war ended tomorrow they would probably drop back to their original ranks. It happened often enough,

But the war was not going to end tomorrow; and although there had been comparative stalemate on the Western Front the French army was now ready to advance, with only the victory at Verdun recalled by thousands of conscripted soldiers, and not the chaos and disgrace which had followed it.

He stretched his arms, and winced. The wound still throbbed occasionally, but he had almost forgotten the intensity of the pain throughout his journey home on the hospital ship. Now it felt more like an old bruise after being kicked. That last fight was clearly fixed in his memory, however, with Blackwood's face as he had helped drag him to safety always there.

Now they were together again, this time not by accident, but because of the new battalion.

He smiled again, recalling their discussion regarding extra marines. He had said, "No need, sir. We have all the men we asked for, everyone a volunteer."

Why should he be surprised, he wondered. Even that slovenly hulk Bert Langmaid was with them. For good or ill, he was still not certain.

This time tomorrow there would be another battalion in their place, one which had been unlucky on the Western Front. Their numbers had been reduced by sixty per cent in one savage advance. Here they would be stiffened with new recruits, put together once more, and then maybe sent back.

So many came here, and to places like this: regulars, territorials, volunteers, yeomanry, and now the conscripts.

He allowed his mind to drift into more pleasant memories of the girl Hermione. He was sure his mother and father would approve.

A shadow fell across the tent flap and his friend, Lieutenant John Maxted, who commanded the H.Q. platoon and would be one of the last to leave, came in.

"Are you busy, Chris?"

Wyke waved him to the one remaining chair. "Take a pew." Maxted was a funny chap, he thought, always calling him "sir" after his advanced promotion to captain, until he'd explained that it was only necessary to behave with such formality when duty required, or, as he had put it, laughing, "When you're dealing with someone you really can't stand!" He said now, "Ready to leave, John?"

Maxted tugged at his Sam Browne. "I suppose so. Won't be sorry to quit this place."

Wyke took out a silver cigarette case and offered him one. He even managed to do that elegantly, Maxted thought sourly. Nothing seemed to dampen his confidence. The family name, he supposed, like Blackwood's heritage of courage and honour under fire.

If only . . .

Wyke tapped his cigarette on the case with studied ease, but he had guessed something was wrong. Maxted had proved his worth in the field, and had done a lot to encourage some of the greener subalterns who had joined the new battalion. He was a decent fellow, reliable too. It had to be said that John Maxted did not have enough imagination to be afraid; so what was the matter with him?

"Something up, old son?"

Maxted stared past him. What would Wyke say if he told

him? Perhaps it was really Wyke's fault, always talking about that other life of girls and champagne, and restaurants of which he himself had never heard.

She had laughed at him when he had admitted he had never had a woman before, but it had been too late even then. He had had opportunities, some of which he had not even recognised. But the fear of doing the dishonourable thing, and getting a girl "into trouble" as his mother would have termed it, had always dissuaded him.

This girl had changed all that. It had been unplanned: a wild, uncontrollable passion. At first he had been shy until she had started to slip out of her clothes, then something like fire had seemed to consume him while she had guided and coaxed him into intercourse.

She had said afterwards, "You'll be better next time."

He realised that Wyke had asked him something. "Just wondering about France."

It sounded so lame that Wyke said gently, "If you ever want to discuss anything, off the record so to speak, old son . . ." He saw his friend's doubt and anxiety. "I'll never forget what you did for me."

The shutters came down behind Maxted's eyes. He had thought it a mere irritation when he had first become aware of the soreness. There was some pain now, and it was not going to disappear. One night he had had to stuff the corner of his blanket in his mouth to stifle his sobs of anguish and despair. She must have known she had been diseased.

A corporal bobbed his head through the flap.

"Colonel's comin', sir."

"Thanks." Wyke waited for the man to leave. "Chin up, John we're going to need all our wits before long."

He was still puzzling over it when Lieutenant-Colonel

Blackwood entered the tent. He looked around with an inde-
finable air of finality, like someone saying good-bye.

"Maxted all right, Christopher? Seemed a bit fed up, I
thought."

He seated himself in Maxted's vacated chair and crossed
his legs. Wyke always noticed how he tried to hold his back
clear of anything rough or uneven. It must have been hell
for him.

"Nerves, I expect, Colonel."

"They've given me a motor car." It seemed to amuse him.
"My M.O.A. is furious. He can do most things but driving isn't
one of them!" He smiled, but there was a trace of something
else in it, some unhappiness. "I'd like you to ride with me.
Should be quite a pleasant drive."

So that was it, Wyke thought. He didn't want to go back
to it; but he knew he couldn't stay behind.

The corporal reappeared. "H.Q. platoon ready to move
out, sir."

Wyke stood up. "I'll see them off, sir. We'll meet up at
Southampton. At least I'll be arriving there in style!"

Jonathan heard the car pull up nearby, the sudden stamp
of boots as the last of the battalion began to march out. An
N.C.O. bawled, "Sling yer bund'ooks! March at ease!" and he
tried to remember the man's name. It seemed necessary,
although he had served with plenty of officers who had never
bothered to remember anybody.

She might have got his letter by now. He tried to recall
each part of it, from the moment when she had found him
sitting by the path. Their path. Smiling at him over the old
stile. Friends . . .

What might she think? Most likely regret what she had
told him, unwilling to become involved with someone she
would never see again . . .

"Oh, God!" He thought of the Scotch Payne had packed, and suddenly needed it. *What is the matter with me?*

"Is the colonel in there?"

He stood up, angry and ashamed. It was probably the driver.

He heard someone answer, "Yeh, mate, inside."

A burly military policeman blocked the entrance. "Beg pardon, sir . . ."

"What is it, Corporal?"

"Didn't want to disturb you, sir, seein' as you're leavin' soon . . ."

He waited. New orders? A despatch from headquarters?

The redcap answered awkwardly, "I didn't think you'd allow it, sir, but there's a young lady at the perimeter fence. Says she wants to see you." He added doubtfully, "I can easily get rid of 'er if you like."

"No, I'll come at once." He walked out into the sunshine where Wyke was standing admiring the car and watching his gear being packed into it.

She was by the guard hut, her hand shading her eyes while the long chestnut hair ruffled in the warm breeze. The redcaps stared from their little hut but Wyke, with rather more sensitivity, took one look and then turned towards the car as if he were afraid of disturbing them.

She said, "An ambulance gave me a ride."

"But how will you get back? What will people think?" Empty, meaningless questions. "You came all this way!"

"I shall be all right. I'll manage."

He wanted to hold her, press his face into her hair, tell her everything. The next moment they were walking together, across the hard-packed earth which had been stripped of grass and pounded flat by many thousands of marching feet. She slipped her arm through his.

"I couldn't just let you go without seeing you. I got a train to Salisbury. There were lots of army ambulances there. I—I brought your letter with me." She looked up at him, her eyes very clear and bright. "It was a beautiful letter."

"It's all true." He hesitated. "Alex . . . I've never met any-one like you before. Never wanted anybody the way I want you. Perhaps it's as well we're leaving when we are."

He felt her fingers tighten on his arm as she said, "I saw some of your men marching along the road just now. They looked fine." She did not repeat what the ambulance driver had said to his stretcher bearers. *Poor sods. More bloody cannon fodder!*

She said, "And I have never met a man like you. I was a fool to behave the way I did. And now we are being parted." She shivered but there were no tears. "Write to me when you can. I'll write too."

Another car was driving in past the guard hut. Officers: the first of the incoming battalion.

Jonathan turned her in his arms. "Don't forget me, Alex."

I must go. He had seen men break down at times like this, but he had never before known how easily it could happen. "Do something for me, will you?" She nodded, her hair partly hiding her face. "Take that walk again. I'll be with you, even if you can't see me."

He lowered his mouth to her cheek but she turned slightly, so that their lips brushed, and then sought one another's.

She said in a small voice, "I haven't had much practice, I'm afraid." Then she touched her cheek as he stepped away from her, and walked towards the waiting car.

Only after he had gone did she realise that the tears on her face were not her own, but his.

THIRTEEN

After all the urgency, the battalion's arrival in Southampton was something of an anticlimax. Nobody seemed to know what to do with the marines, and out of desperation Jonathan Blackwood decided to contact the Royal Navy directly and without persisting in the accepted channels. As he later explained to Wyke and his second-in-command, Major Ralph Vaughan, the delays were caused by suspected enemy mine-laying in the Channel off Boulogne, the favoured crossing point for troops to France. The naval operations officer had speculated that the Royal Marines would be sent on a longer but probably safer route to Le Havre.

Vaughan muttered, "Bloody bad organisation, that's what it is." He was a burly, aggressive officer whose face had been badly battered in the boxing ring, where he had represented the corps in many interservice contests, and he was greatly respected for his qualities as a leader. The marines admired him, and were wary of his hot temper. He went on, "Didn't do all that damned training to end up on the bottom of the Channel, what?"

The battalion, the Fifty-First as it was now officially titled, had settled in where it could: in the loading sheds of the docks, in empty railway waggons, even in makeshift tents, and queues formed throughout the days at the mobile kitchens where men consumed bully beef, sausages and baked beans by the hundredweight. They grumbled about the food, but not too much. Every man knew he was receiving a larger ration than any civilian could hope for.

While his officers tried to keep the marines occupied and out of trouble, Jonathan had attempted to discover the true situation on the Western Front. The news for public consumption was optimistic. A rising star in the French army, a general named Nivelle, had the solution to the bloody and costly stalemate. There was to be a further Big Push, in which all of the French army's divisions on the Western Front would participate. The enemy's front line would collapse, and the others would soon follow suit.

But after the promises at Gallipoli and a similar brand of optimism from the G.O.C. there, Jonathan was doubtful. He recalled, too, Loftus's frankness concerning the Verdun mutinies.

As he went about his daily rounds and visited the navy over the water at Portsmouth, Alexandra Pitcairn had been much in his thoughts. He had written to her, very conscious of the strict censorship and the eyes that would read every word, and even dared to hope that he might be able to see her again before the Fifty-First was eventually ordered to France.

At the end of April he was surprised to receive a summons to Portsmouth, where he found Major-General Sir Herbert Loftus waiting at the commodore's house in the dockyard.

They shook hands gravely. "Better meet here, I thought. If they saw me at Eastney or somewhere it would hardly take a genius to put two and two together." Loftus seemed on edge, his mind elsewhere. Then quite suddenly he said, "This is strictly confidential—secret, if you like." His blue eyes fixed coldly on Jonathan. "Later on, you can use your own discretion."

He already knew; it was like an icy hand closing around his heart.

Loftus said directly, "I think you've anticipated me, Blackwood. The French attack has completely failed, and there is a real mutiny this time. Can't say I blame them, but it leaves us right in the dung heap. You will embark your people this evening. There will be escorts available—the C-in-C Home Fleet has promised that at least. I am informed that Sir Douglas Haig's original plan to relieve the pressure on the French is to be executed, but remember, Blackwood: your battalion is to take a *supporting role only*, at least until my whole division can be properly deployed."

With characteristic brevity he shook hands again. "Good luck, Blackwood. You have a fine lot of chaps—all turned out very well."

Back at Southampton Jonathan found the two allotted troopships already warped alongside the terminal jetty, from which proud liners had sailed in peacetime to every quarter of the Empire. He skimmed quickly through his instructions before sending Wyke to gather all the senior officers, the company commanders, and one most unsoldierly captain named Alton, who although listed as being in charge of the Royal Marine Artillery detachment had up until a few months back been the manager of an arms factory. His appointment, like his commission, was temporary, and had been granted specifically so that he could supervise the howitzers he himself had helped to design, and which he would know better than any regular gunner.

Later, when the company commanders went to their men with the news of embarkation, Jonathan was aware of their raucous reception even in the cramped boat-train office which had become his personal H.Q., and where Harry Payne had set up his camp bed. There was wild cheering. They were leaving at last. That was all they knew; all their officers knew. What they really thought, he reflected, was anybody's guess.

It all seemed to happen very quickly after that: like his

departure from the camp at Salisbury, teeming with life one minute, deserted the next. Where they had walked together; where they had kissed. Wyke had never mentioned it, never asked questions, although he was probably as curious as all the others. *The Colonel's lady. Old Blackie's bit of stuff.*

Eventually he sat down to write the last letter. The tramp of boots had been swallowed up, and even the camp bed had been spirited away.

My very dear Alex . . .

He glanced around the empty office. At least this letter would escape censorship: a naval signals officer at the docks had promised to post it "ashore," as he had put it.

He sat in silence, staring at her name. The rest of the page was as empty as the future. When all this had begun he had been a mere captain. With the Blackwood name and tradition of service, he had been a captain of promise. Now he was a lieutenant-colonel, brevet or not, with all the responsibility of the rank. He had more men under his personal command than in the whole of the mighty *Reliant*'s ship's company. And why?

He heard Payne hovering outside the door in case he was wanted.

He had been selected because he was known, and not merely because he knew how to lead men to their deaths; how to die without making a fuss. He thought of Hawks Hill and what might become of it if the worst happened. His cousin Ralf Blackwood had been a major in the R.M.L.I. when he had last heard: he had been involved in several scandals, usually over gambling or women, but he had remained in the corps, and had shown an unexpected courage while serving under David in the Boxer Rebellion.

He was sealing the short letter when Payne came in.

"All your kit's aboard, sir."

It would be a strange twist of fate if, after all, Ralf were to be the last of the Blackwoods.

"I'll just drop this letter off."

"Wish I could deliver it meself, sir."

Jonathan shot him a quick glance. You never really knew with Payne. It might have been an innocent comment about preferring to stay at home; or was there already speculation about his clumsy intentions towards her?

He took a last look round. Either way, it made no difference now.

Per Mare, Per Terram, he thought. After the sea, it was back to the land, and the next horizon.

The girl sat on the grassy bank of a tiny stream, her knees pulled up almost to her chin. Jack Swan, his face round and red like a polished apple, leaned against his little trap while the donkey munched grass unhurriedly by the side of the track. Alexandra Pitcairn had been watching the easy way the ex-marine had been cutting and shaping sticks. He had explained that there was a shortage of proper canes for the soldiers who were recovering from their leg wounds. And in any case, he said, it was a nice day for it.

Swan puffed at his weathered pipe and watched the girl through the smoke. She made a fine picture, he thought, enough to turn the head of any squaddy. Her hair was tied back to the nape of her neck and he could see the tan on her throat and arms where the spring sunshine had made its mark.

"You've had another letter from th' colonel, you say, miss?"

She looked at him warmly. "Yes. I'm not certain of the date."

He asked, "He all right, miss?"

"All right?" She frowned. "I'm not sure. He and his men seem to be in reserve, whatever that means."

Swan grinned. "That means that the brass don't know what to do with 'em. The army don't understand us Royals. Never have."

Us Royals. It was much as Harry Payne had told her. Once you were in the corps you never really left. it. She discovered that she had pushed off her shoes, and as the hot breeze fanned her legs she was pleased that she could speak to this man about the family. Probably the only one who understood. She slid her feet into the stream and yelped. After the warm air and dusty grass it was like ice, but she held her feet submerged. It made her feel vaguely sensuous, wanton.

Jonathan's letters told her very little. He described picturesque villages in France, children marching beside the marines, waving and calling out to his men, who understood not a word. She had become accustomed to his handwriting, so that he seemed less of a stranger. But there was so much he had not told her, or could not.

Like rumours of mutiny and harsh reprisals in the French army. It did not seem real, especially here in this quiet place. Even the big house was invisible from this part of the estate.

Swan looked up at the great copse and said wistfully, "When all the farms were doing well we thought we might clear that lot—plough it maybe. Can't be sure of anything any more."

Who did he mean by *we*, she wondered. The old general, or she allowed her mind to explore it—Captain David Blackwood?

Swan was watching her, almost as if he knew what she was thinking. She asked, "When you were with David Blackwood in China, was that where he won his Victoria Cross?"

"Bless you, no. He got that for a big battle in Africa, the

capture of Benin. That was before we got sent after them Boxers."

"What was he like?" She lowered her lashes to hide her interest.

"A good officer, never drove the men too hard. But woe betide anyone who took his manner as weakness. Captain David'd come down on him like a ton of bricks!"

He looked up as a church bell rang far away in the village.

"Time to move on, miss. We're so short handed here I don't know what we'll do if they take any more off the land."

He seemed to recall what he had been saying and gave a quiet chuckle. "Mind you, Captain David was a bit of a lad with the ladies. Took after his father, I shouldn't wonder!"

She tried to cover her surprise. "Jack—what will happen over there?"

He stared at her, vaguely conscious of the use of his first name, and of the fact that she had so neatly changed the subject.

He answered, "Well, miss, it was April when the Colonel left, an' now it's near the end of May. According to one report in the newspaper, the Germans have had enough. They couldn't take another battle like Verdun and this last bloody set-to with the whole French army. An' with the Yanks in the war, old Jerry might decide it's time to throw in the towel."

She stared into the stream, at her own small feet so pale against the loose stones.

"But you don't think that."

Swan said slowly, "I'm not really the one to ask. I did my soldierin' against spears and muskets, brass cannon an' screaming natives. Hardly the Somme, or Loos. I've spoken to a lot of the poor fellows who come here to try and get over what's happened to them. They're not bitter, as you might expect. Nor do they act like the world's rejected them because of how they are or how they look. It's as if they've rejected *our* world."

She watched him as he loaded the last of the sticks onto his cart. Why had she never spoken to him like this before? Why hadn't anybody?

Swan tapped out his pipe and heeled the ash into the track with great care.

"Fact is, miss, I don't think they know how to stop it. If they lose an attack the general staff seem to think that to try something different would show the enemy we've lost our guts, begging your pardon, miss. So they do it all over again!"

He touched his hat and clambered onto the little cart.

"Nice talking to you, miss."

She watched them until they had topped the rise. A man and his donkey, like a picture in one of her books when she had been at school. She pulled the neck of her dress away from her skin and felt something like guilt as her fingers touched her breast. Was that how it might be? Could be?

She recalled how she had deliberately turned her head so that their mouths had met in a clumsy kiss. The awareness had been there; but experience? Not at all. Not a bit how Swan had described Jonathan's beloved brother David. *A bit of a lad with the ladies.*

Perhaps she was the strange one. She had not been teaching Braille for more than a month at Hawks Hill when she had seen the other side of men. It had been before the place had been enlarged, when the flood of wounded and shell-shocked officers had scarcely begun.

It had been a day much like this one, heavy with the scent of grass and flowers, the air full of birdsong. She had been sitting in a small ward using both hands on the fingers of the man who sat with her, moving his bandaged head and eyes from side to side, listening to birds he would never see again. Or merely trying to remember, as she worked his stiff fingers in her hands.

She had suddenly been aware of his arm encircling her waist, and she had lightly scolded him and thought nothing more of it.

In the next instant she had been thrown back across the bed, while he held her with a grip so hard she had almost cried out. She had forced herself to lie quite still while he had pressed his face against her, gasping staccato sentences about the smell of her perfume and her body. Then she had begun to struggle, and heard herself scream as the man tore the front of her blouse apart and pulled at her until his fingers were digging into her breast. One of the other blind patients had come in with an orderly and it was all over. While they were pressing the emergency bell she had tried to cover her nakedness: her skin was raw where he had clawed it. Looking back, almost the worst part had been the immediate aftermath. The two blind men had circled one another, hitting out and shouting every obscenity they could think of like a pair of sightless gladiators.

After that, the duty sergeant always had an orderly close by when she was in the ward alone. It was not possible to blame them all, or be wary of them all: she could not even dimly imagine what shattered thoughts and images preyed upon their minds. "There were many failures, where memory and interpretation were too broken ever to retain anything again, but other men who worked with her and not against her while she had taught them the mysteries of groups of raised dots had given her an indescribable sense of pride even as they had saddened her.

She put on her shoes, and was walking down towards the village when the thought hit her like a slap. Suppose Jonathan should return like that, shattered in mind or body; or the war and its brutalities fuel his hunger for something she sensed he had never known? If he touched her, what would she do?

She walked on, oblivious to the whistles from passing lorries and other army vehicles. She was used to it: everyone was. When she reached the house she could hear voices in the surgery. Her father's practice had become his whole life, and he would see anyone at almost any time if he thought it useful.

There was a familiar envelope on the hall table, stamped with the Crown and the words "PASSED BY CENSOR."

She took it and went straight up to her room, and opened the windows to catch the scent of the garden. Then she sat on her bed and tore the envelope. For just a moment she stared at her dressing table mirror and touched her breast again as she had by the little stream. It was like looking at a total stranger, as the question came once more to her mind.

When she unfolded the letter she saw his now-familiar hand, as if she could hear his voice. *My very dear Alex . . .*

When she looked up again the stranger was still there. Lips slightly parted, eyes devoid of shame.

As usual it was a short letter, as if he could not bring himself to speak his mind.

"We are in a quiet village now, not even as large as Alresford . . ." There was a blue smear in the margin, as if the censor had been trying to decide if they were using some kind of code, and had obviously given them the benefit of the doubt. *"My men are in good heart and have settled down very well in rather primitive conditions. I received another letter from you today. I shall reread it when things are quieter."* Quieter? Did that mean they were closer to the front? *"I long for the day when I shall see you again. You are never distant when I think of that meeting we had at . . ."* The name *Salisbury* had been deleted.

He had ended, *"From your friend and admirer, Jonathan."*

A letter so gentle and yet so uncertain. Would she ever know the other man, the one she had imagined she could reject in David's memory? The man she had seen at Eastney among high-ranking officers, on whom his men would depend; trust, even when their very souls were committed to hell if so ordered.

And he trusts me. It was almost as if the mirror's reflection had spoken. Then she put the letter in her drawer with the others and went downstairs.

"Did you get your letter, Alex?" Her father was squinting at a pill bottle, his glasses on the top of his head. He blinked at her. "Ah, I see that you did. Good news, I hope?"

How old he was getting, she thought, his little pointed beard was almost white now. What did he really think of her correspondence with a soldier, an officer and a Blackwood to boot?

"I think, Daddy . . . I *think* there's going to be another great battle."

But when she looked, he had gone back into the surgery. Later he would play chess with his old friend Proudfoot the vet, and refight the campaign again.

Something like ice seemed to brush her skin, which before had been pleasantly warm. When she went to the window all the birds had stopped singing. There was only silence.

Dear God protect you, Jonathan. I want you back.

"I'm going up to Hawks Hill, Daddy."

"Don't be out too late, my dear!" But he didn't leave his surgery, and she was glad. She didn't want him to see her face.

The heavy staff car lurched and dipped through countless potholes and shattered cobbles, which lay about the road like petrified loaves of bread.

It was obvious from Wyke's silence that he was shocked by what he saw: a small market town reduced to gaunt walls and smashed window frames, the air heavy with dust and smoke and something foul which the driver had laconically described as the aftermath of a gas attack. A town abandoned, bombarded and fought over, looted and then destroyed, first by the enemy and then by the French. The Germans had fallen back a few miles for fear of being separated from their main divisions by the ambitious counterattack which had gained almost nothing; and there were many crudely made crosses in overgrown fields, where rotting carcasses of cattle still lay as evidence of the fighting.

Jonathan recalled how he had described their own position as "a quiet village." That was true. But it too had been abandoned, and after they had travelled all the way from Le Havre, mostly on foot and then in the final stages by a battered fleet of London double-decker buses, the sight had made some of his men stare with astonishment and disgust. The village lay about eight miles from the front line, the Messines Ridge to the south, or as far as the troops were concerned, to the right of the Ypres salient. Names and places already fought over again and again: a desert of pain and murder, rusting barbed wire, huge shell holes, many of which were still filled with water despite the warmth of early summer. Others retained the stenches of battle, and thick oozing mud like quicksand. Flanders.

Most of the marines were more used to the careful cleanliness of ships and barracks, where the life, if rigid and spartan, was something they all understood. But after shelter was rigged in some old barns and roofless cottages they got down to work, throwing out pickets, much to the amusement of the soldiers at a nearby field-dressing station, digging latrines, and preparing the mobile kitchens where they would display no lights and give no hint of their strength to any reconnaissance aircraft or spy. And that first night after their arrival, they had stood in silence and watched the inferno that seemed to cover the whole front line. It went on for two hours, the ground shaking and the bellies of the clouds lit with vivid red and orange flashes and drifting flares. A picture from Dante; and many of the marines were wondering how anything could live in it, while the heavy artillery roared out and the shells screamed over the village at eight miles' range. And yet it felt so near they had almost imagined the heat of each screaming salvo.

After a few days, incredibly, they had got used to it. Reports came and went on the field telephones or brought by filthy dispatch riders, one of whom had been chased by a Fokker fighter plane, the road sparking with bullets until the soldier had managed to throw his motorbike into a ditch.

A military policeman waved down the staff car and strode up to inspect the occupants. The redcap looked so alien in his steel helmet, and Jonathan was well aware that his own men hated the new headgear, clumsy, heavy, and impractical as it was. In time they would even get used to that, he thought. The redcap saluted, and then glanced round as four more of his section clumped along the battered road with a soldier in handcuffs, his face bloody as if somebody had struck him.

He said sharply, "Deserter, sir. He's for the chop." He said it with such venom and hatred that Jonathan stared at him, recalling some of the men he had seen in Plymouth and at Hawks Hill, as deeply wounded as if by shrapnel or bayonet.

They were waved on and Harry Payne remarked to their driver, "That pig can afford to be brave, eh? He's got the whole division between him and the Jerries!"

There was hate there too. He was thinking perhaps of his kid brother, who had vanished in this terrible place. Nothing left even to bury.

The driver glanced up at the eyeless window of a house, or what remained of it. There was a soldier sitting by it with a pair of binoculars, who waved casually and then continued scanning the sky, looking for aircraft, observation balloons, anything.

The driver climbed down and remarked, "If you 'ears a football rattle it's a gas attack, gentlemen. Masks on, pronto. Nasty stuff, is gas." He said it with no particular emotion. Just an ordinary soldier, by now one of the old sweats who had somehow survived. He pointed at a collapsed building. "Wine shop," he grinned, the strain and anxiety falling away. "No drink now, o' course. But Brigade H.Q. is under it." He indicated a sandbagged doorway. "In the cellar!"

He took out a cigarette and watched the two officers duck into the doorway, then he said to Payne, "What's your lot then?"

Payne unslung his rifle. "Royal Marines."

The soldier drew slowly on his cigarette. "Takes all sorts, dunnit?"

"Will they really shoot that poor bugger?"

"Yeh. 'Appens all the time. Sometimes, nearer the front line, the bloke's shot by 'is escort so they don't 'ave to risk their own lives getting to the rear. The officers know. But nobody sees it, right?" He paused. "I was in the first high jinks at the Somme last year." He shook his head. "Strewth—is that all it is?" Then he said dully, "In with a division, out with less than a company, an' damn all to show for it!"

Inside the wrecked wine shop a group of soldiers were sitting at a trestle table with field telephones, signal pads and mugs of tea. One, a sergeant, stood up.

"'Tenant-Colonel Blackwood, sir?" He pointed to the cellar door. "Brigadier's down there, sir."

Jonathan glanced in passing at a colourful calendar advertising lemonade, which was propped against a steel helmet. It showed a scantily-clad girl with a saucy smile saying, "My Jack always likes his glass of Austin's!"

Wyke said, "Not the only thing he likes, by the look of it," but his voice was empty. The ruined villages with their deathly stillness had obviously affected him deeply.

The date on the calendar was the fourth of June. David's birthday, or would have been. Did she still think of him? It seemed incredible that David had never noticed her when he was at home on leave; it was a small place, and she would have caught any man's eye. Jonathan did not altogether believe in his brother's reputation where women were concerned: during the siege of the foreign legations in Peking there had been a rumour about David and the wife of some German diplomat, but he himself had always thought it only that. A rumour. Old Jack Swan might have known, but he would be like a clam as far as loyalty to David and the past were concerned.

Down the stone steps and through a smelly anti-gas curtain. The cellar was large, and filled with maps and clips of signals brought by dispatch riders or runners close to the trenches. The brigadier, a lean officer with cold, searching eyes, looked up from his maps table.

"Blackwood? Good chap. I'm Ross." Short and sharp, like the opening and closing of a rifle bolt. Two of his red-tabbed staff officers were poring over plans and neither glanced up at them. "Here we are." He was leafing through his personal log. "Fourth of June."

There were newly pierced holes in his shoulder straps. He must have been promoted right up from lieutenant-colonel:

Jonathan could even see the old imprints where the rank had been.

"I was ordered not to involve you yet." He slapped some dust from his jacket. "Filthy place!"

Jonathan leaned carefully against the canvas back of the chair offered to him and crossed his legs. It made him appear relaxed, confident. He was neither.

He said, "Major-General Sir Herbert Loftus told me when we left England . . ."

"All changed, I'm afraid. His own division is not quite ready for this sector. Sailors and marines, not the best of mixers in my experience." He watched Jonathan's expression, searching for something. "Your adjutant-general has given it a qualified sanction, but Sir Douglas Haig has personally taken charge. He will brook no argument, but then he's probably right. Your Fifty-First battalion will close up to the support lines. I'll make certain that your men are properly guided to the rear positions."

"All taken care of, sir." One of the red tabs had spoken but still did not look up.

"Well done, Harry." The brigadier looked at Wyke. "Take this pack, Captain. Guard it with your life." He added off-handedly, "You can get some tea. Outside."

Wyke needed no second telling. He left the cellar.

Ross leaned forward in the dimness and stared at the bright scarlet and blue ribbon on Jonathan's tunic.

"Hm. Heard about that, Blackwood. Just what I bloody well need at the moment!"

"When do you expect to go into action, sir?"

"June the seventh. It's all been well planned, but we've had to advance things. The French might easily throw in their hand if we don't ease the pressure." He jabbed his map with one finger. "Here: the Messines Ridge. Once we've taken that, all we have to do is thrust through the enemy's line about 35 miles, and we'll be at the coast." He must have seen the doubt in Jonathan's eyes. "We have the weather for it . . ." He hesitated for the first time. "Not like last year. So let's make the most of it."

Jonathan leaned over the map and tried to restrain his apprehension. It was almost exactly the same as the last time. But how could it be? Who would see sense in it if the plan was faulty?

Last year the goal had been the same. The British had attacked on a front twenty miles wide. After four months of indescribable savagery they had only been able to advance about three miles. Four months: and the cost to the British army in that exhausting struggle had been 400,000 casualties.

I must have missed something.

"Don't worry too much, Blackwood." The brigadier was peering at his watch. "We've got a few surprises for them this time. It's all in that pack I gave your chap. Just get the Fifty-First into position. When the first attack is completed, we'll need trained and disciplined men in the line. In short, your marines."

The building quivered and more dust drifted down from the ceiling onto the steps.

The brigadier said, "That's on the Sixty-Third Division's sector. They've been having a rough time, but there are no real problems."

Jonathan straightened his back with effort and listened to the thunder of artillery.

"Do they get many deserters, sir?"

Ross regarded him coldly. "There will always be a few cowards, Blackwood. Even in the Royal Marines, I daresay."

He held out his hand. "Good to have you with us." He could have been talking about a mess party. Or was that to cover his own doubts?

Outside it was still sunny, and Wyke was waiting for him as he walked slowly towards a chipped war memorial. It depicted a French soldier with a trumpet to his mouth and the Tricolour streaming behind him. There was a camel too, and a list of names from some forgotten campaign. Now the memorial itself had been devastated by a war which seemed to know no bounds.

Wyke said, "The brigadier seemed pleased, sir."

"I'm depending on it." To the driver he said, "Take us back, please," and to Wyke, "Officers' conference right away." The words recalled Waring and his arrogance, and he added, "Senior N.C.O.'s as well. I want them all to know where they are and exactly what's expected of them."

They drove back to the "quiet village" in silence, staring out at the devastation, the ruined houses, the simple crosses tied together and lining the roadside. It was impossible to know what it had once looked like.

He said abruptly, "Tell the platoon commanders to collect all the letters home by noon tomorrow. We shall move up to the support lines at dusk."

He would write to Hermione, Wyke thought, and the colonel would write to the unknown girl with the lovely hair. And Maxted . . . He frowned. Must find the time to speak to him, and soon. Maxted had been in action, and a lot of the recruits would be looking to him. Maybe he had been jilted by someone. The thought amused him.

I'll soon shake him out of that!

Jonathan climbed down stiffly onto the road.

"My very dear Alex." He could see the words in his mind as

clearly as if he had already written them. *"Tomorrow we are going up the line in support of a full-scale attack on a ridge near Ypres."* He smiled. The censor would love that.

Wyke saw the smile and felt his own tension draining away like sand. After witnessing the silent devastation he had been uneasy and depressed, but the colonel's apparent confidence strengthened him in some way, and he was able to comfort himself with memories of Hermione, and pleasantly sensual thoughts of how and where he would propose to her.

That night Jonathan lay on a blanket and stared at the stars through the beams of a roofless cottage. They seemed so distant, so remote, so peaceful: so untouched by the rumour of war.

He could not sleep, although he had been drinking the Scotch Payne had produced like the magician he was, and several times throughout the night he had heard the steady tramp of marching boots, going "up the line" as they called it. Thousands of men, making their way to an inevitable rendezvous.

He had written to her immediately after holding his conference with officers and N.C.O.'s. She would receive the letter in a few days. By then it might be all over. For many it would be over for ever.

There were no heavy bombardments this time. There was only a dull, ominous rumble from another far-off sector of the front.

The scene was set. Only the actors had to appear.

FOURTEEN

The four companies of the battalion were paraded in a loose and untidy formation while their officers and senior N.C.O.'s carried out a final inspection. Nothing must be forgotten or overlooked. Nobody knew what their next billet might be, and once on the march they had to be completely self-dependent.

Some of the heavier equipment would be carried in hand-carts, but each marine would be loaded down with the rest: full pack, and a small one for essential items like mess tins, water flask, ammunition pouches and extra bandoliers, entrenching tools, rifle and bayonet, all topped by the new steel helmet.

A little apart from the main body of men, the H.Q. platoon was having a similar inspection.

Private Bert Langmaid watched his two assistants with a suspicious eye while they lashed the heavy machine-gun and boxes of ammunition into one of the little carts. With a snort he crunched over the broken ground and released two of the straps. "Remember that next time, my son!"

"That man!"

Langmaid swung round and glared at the officer. He was the second-in-command of the platoon; probably because nobody else would have him, he thought. Second Lieutenant Brian Rooke was nineteen years old and very sure of himself. He had a pink, pouting face and was rarely seen to smile, and then only if it was at some joke made by a senior officer. He came of an old Royal Marines family and his father had recently been appointed colonel commandant of a new training establishment.

"That's not the correct way to do it!"

Langmaid replied bluntly, "'S the way *I* does it." He watched the officer's flush of anger, and knew the other marines had stopped their activities to listen. A bet or two might be laid on the outcome of Langmaid's latest insubordination.

Ned Timbrell, now appointed platoon sergeant, marched quickly to the scene and saluted, his heels clicking together as if he was on the square.

"Did you hear what this man said, Sergeant? I want him put under arrest!"

Timbrell had taken to his three stripes as if he had been doing it all his life, as he had always known he could.

He said, "We've at least an eight-mile march, sir. To arrive on time we'll be doing the first bit when it's still light."

"I can manage without the statistics, thank you, Sergeant." Rooke was angry but enjoying it in some strange way.

Timbrell kept his temper. "Private Langmaid is the best machine-gunner in the battalion. We're lucky to have him."

"In *your* opinion!"

Timbrell clenched his fists and pressed them against the rough serge of his trousers. *Stupid little sod.* But he said patiently, "We might be spotted by a Jerry aeroplane, sir. A column on the march with all this gear would be easy meat. Couldn't miss!" Oh Christ, he thought, here comes the platoon commander.

Lieutenant John Maxted asked sharply, "What's going on? We shall be falling in in two hours' time!"

Rooke felt on safer ground. "That man there, sir, is insolent! And the platoon sergeant seems to think he is fit enough to tell me my duties!" He pointed at Timbrell's ribbon: the

Distinguished Conduct Medal, a rare decoration even at the Dardanelles. "I'll not be treated like a child because of *that!*"

Maxted said hotly, "Then stop bloody well acting like one!" To Timbrell he added, "Get the men to work again!"

Timbrell saluted but did not even blink at what he had just witnessed. As he marched past the machine-gun party he muttered fiercely, "If you drop me in it again, Bert Langmaid, you'll live to regret it!"

Langmaid deliberately loosened another strap on the cart. "Well, Sarge, don't 'e know nothin'? Who does 'e think'll defend the column? It takes long enough to mount the gun and load it, without 'avin' it tied up like a . . ." He could not think of a suitable comparison and said, "Little bastard— thinks 'is shit doesn't stink because he's an officer!"

As Timbrell strode away Langmaid turned to his two assistants and gave a great grin. "One of the sappers told me the life of a second lieutenant on this front is about six weeks." It amused him and he even patted their shoulders. "If that little prick crosses my sights I'll soon shorten the bleedin' record!"

Almost two hours later Maxted went to one of the cottages, which had a crude sign painted outside: *Adjutant, Please knock before entering.* Some wag must have done it in the night, for there was no door left to knock and not much of the cottage either. Maxted looked round at the emptiness of the place. Only a map case and Wyke's personal belongings for the march remained.

"H.Q. platoon's ready, sir. They've been stood down for a meal, as ordered."

Wyke said, "I've just had young Rooke in here to lodge a complaint against you."

"I thought he might. Pompous idiot! If he treats the men the way he did just now he'll get what he deserves."

Wyke studied him for a moment and then said quietly, "What is it, John? You know you can tell me."

Maxted thought of the pain, which was getting worse by the day. He asked, "Will it go any further?"

"No. The Colonel won't know either. He has enough on his plate without this sort of trivial behaviour. But Rooke was right—you know the rules well enough when the men are listening and watching."

Maxted stared at him wretchedly. Rooke came from one of those old corps families, like the Blackwoods and Wyke. He tried not to think how hard his own father had had to work so that he himself could go to a good school and gain the right of entry into the corps, the one thing he had always longed for. Now that would soon be in ruins. When the truth came out he would be disgraced, court-martialled and dismissed from the corps: everything gone. The others would change their tune then. Even Christopher Wyke would turn his back on him.

I were better dead.

And what of his parents and his sister when the scandal was exposed? He felt suddenly sick.

Wyke was saying, "I'm worried about you, John. Would you like to see the M.O. at Brigade?"

His own response was startling in its fury. *"No, I don't!"* What do you want the men to think? That their lieutenant is a coward? Afraid for his own skin? Is that it?"

Wyke sat on an empty packing case. "Whatever you say, John. But nobody would ever be stupid enough to think that about you."

He watched Maxted slam out into the hazy sunshine. All very peculiar, he thought. Then he listened to the rolling thunder of another artillery bombardment which was making the air quiver, and was surprised that it no longer disturbed him. But that was exactly how the old sweats felt about it. Unless you were in it, you took the guns for granted. He began to buckle on his belt and holster. Well, almost. . . . He reached for his respirator haversack, hesitated, and opened his breast pocket, in which he carried a stainless steel shaving mirror. The old hands always maintained it would deflect a stray bullet from the heart. Unlikely, but it gave some comfort. He took out the little leather case he also carried there and opened that. Inside was a lovely photograph set in a fine silver frame, which Hermione had given him on his last leave. The frame had come from Garrard's, she had said. She must feel the same way about him. He studied her face and her mischievous smile and carefully replaced it.

Two marines were walking past the doorless cottage, their boots heavy on the rubble.

One was saying, "We're off soon, Wilf. What d'you reckon to it?"

His companion said harshly, "Don't think we'll see this ruddy place again!"

The guns seemed suddenly louder and more menacing as the unknown marine's comments lingered behind him.

Wyke's hand was still pressed to his pocket, and in his mind he tried to see the girl more clearly. He whispered her name aloud. "Hermione." But it no longer seemed real. Only the distant thunder remained

The young lieutenant of the Sixtieth Rifles touched Jonathan's sleeve and said, "This is it, sir. The brigadier's in the command dugout." Then he was gone.

It had been an eerie experience, groping along the narrow communication trenches and being handed from one guide to the next. Jonathan stared up at the sky. Still dark, but at this time of the year dawn, when it came, would be sudden. He thought briefly of the battalion, now safely delivered to the main support lines. What would most of them think of this? The awful stench, the awareness of the enemy, the compulsion to whisper even though there were at least two lines of trenches ahead of them. They had passed sentries like silent statues, who had barely given them a glance; other inert shapes lay where they could, men worn out by continuous combat, trying to rest wherever and whenever the opportunity presented itself. It was almost impossible to believe that there were so many thousands of troops on either side of this place: men who were waiting for the attack, their minds empty of everything but the inevitable.

"They're here, sir!"

Jonathan ducked through a canvas curtain and paused to accustom his eyes to the cramped clutter of the forward command dugout. Brigadier Ross was drinking tea by a map table, and the place seemed to be full of people. The air was cold and tangy, and the smell of damp clothing mingled with that of something like bleach, which Jonathan had already learned was the aftermath of chlorine gas.

Ross inclined his head curtly.

"Got here then, Blackwood." He laughed, a bleak sound. "Have some char." He wore his smart cap, probably so that his men would instantly recognise him and know he was here with them. Closer to the front line the cap would be a real gift to any sniper with a telescopic sight.

Someone called, "Good to have you with us, Colonel!" Several others grunted with what might have been approval. They were all tense, on edge.

"Last one's arrived, sir!"

"About bloody time."

A figure stumbled into the dugout and showed his teeth. "Sorry I'm late, sir . . ." He turned and stared at Jonathan, his face filled with disbelief. Then he crossed to him and seized his hand. "Remember me? Christ, I thought you'd been knocked off!"

Jonathan felt the warmth of the man. He was a major now.

"Of course I do. Ben Duffy—your father builds boats in Perth!"

They stood in silence, isolated from the others in memory. The peninsula, the snipers, Sari Bair, Gaba Tepe, the Anafarta Ridge and all the other objectives which had been denied them. The final cost did not bear recollection.

Ross commented dryly, "The Anzacs are here with us, on our right. The Canadians are next after that." He gave a thin smile. "Melting pot of Empire!" They all looked toward him while he studied them, assessing them. Then he said, "Tomorrow morning is the moment, gentlemen. Many of you know this sector well. Only *too* well." Someone gave a contemptuous cheer. Ross seemed very relaxed, not even annoyed by the jokes or the mockery.

"Ahead of us lies the Messines Ridge, higher terrain of course, with a good field of fire from the enemy's viewpoint. They've had plenty of time to prepare. They realise we must attack before winter when, as we know, the whole front will become bogged down again. We know about their trench system, deeply built and very strong. Time and time again, gentlemen, we have put down an artillery barrage before each attack, only to have them pop up from their bunkers as soon as we cease fire and try to advance. Result—catastrophe."

A ruddy-faced major stepped up beside him and said, "I can tell you what *we've* been doing." His badge was that of the Royal Engineers.

Someone commented, "About time you did something,

Nobby," and the others laughed. Jonathan glanced at the brigadier but he showed no resentment. Like an indulgent schoolmaster, or a referee before the big match, going along with their biting humour.

The sapper officer beamed. "On the morning of the attack there will be a careful and calculated bombardment of the enemy's front line. As usual, they will take to their bunkers and wait for the infantry's assault."

They had all fallen silent, and some of them were watching him steadily, not with affectionate derision now but with a quiet concentration and intensity, as though they did not dare to hope that this time it might be different. Young faces made old with strain and exhaustion and the experience of death, which those at home could never appreciate. Sons, lovers, fathers.

The major said in an unhurried tone, "We have been digging saps right up to and beyond the German front line, and we have laid the biggest mines there in military history." He glanced at the brigadier, who gave a spare gesture of approval. "Each mine consists of over twenty tons of explosive." He allowed the words to sink in. "As soon as the bunkers and dugouts are filled, we'll blow them to smithereens!"

The brigadier said, "Thank you—er, Nobby. That was very graphic. Well done." He became grave. "We will advance on our whole six-mile front, and the reserves will reinforce the line."

Jonathan thought of the R.M.A. detachment with its two massive howitzers. No wonder they had not been brought into close support, and that more carefully controlled artillery was being used. One great howitzer shell, each the size of *Reliant*'s main armament, would drop from full elevation and not much accuracy at this range, and might have blown up the mines and all the sappers with them.

"According to the experts the wind will be behind the attack, so with any luck our people will be spared the risk of gas."

The Australian said in a hoarse whisper, "You remember my colonel, the bloke you liked? Well, he was gassed out here a month or so back. Some new liquid stuff." He touched his eyes. "Completely blind, poor bastard."

A voice called, "First light, sir!"

"You are dismissed, gentlemen." The brigadier beckoned to the Royal Marines. "I thought you might like to see it for yourselves." Jonathan, with Wyke behind him, followed the brigadier to an observation position protected by bullet-riddled sandbags and slabs of concrete. It was only then that he realised that this part of the line cut through the remains of some demolished building.

He did not know quite what he had expected: something like that other front when he had been an observer for the Royal Marines. He watched in silence as the light spread across the scene like a slowly developing film, revealing its picture of desolation and horror. To the left there had been a thickly wooded area, still shown on his map, and lying almost in line with the ridge. Now hundreds of shell holes, some as big as craters, filled the area, and of the wood nothing remained but scorched and blackened stumps like rotting teeth. He saw barbed wire against the paling sky, some blasted away by shellfire, but not enough to warn the enemy that another Big Push was imminent, and beyond that to the right there were masses of it, tangled and impassable unless great efforts were made to remove it. Like a forlorn monument, standing with its tail in the air, was an aeroplane, the British markings still clearly visible. Jonathan rested his binoculars on a hard sandbag and peered at it. It was nose-down in the middle of the huge mass of wire and he guessed that the pilot and observer were still inside. The fuselage was riddled with bullet holes, probably put there by bored sentries on both sides letting off steam.

He knew Wyke was beside him with his own glasses, and heard him gasp as he saw the scattered remains of corpses: in the wire, beyond it, everywhere. Some were so broken and torn or decaying that only their rusting helmets gave any clue to nationality.

Wyke was recalling what the Rifle Brigade lieutenant had told him when he had asked him about the stench.

He had replied casually, perhaps indifferently, "Corpses, old chap. We bury our dead as best we can without getting chopped in the process—then bang, at the next bombardment they come flying back into the trench. Bits of them, anyway."

Jonathan had overheard the conversation. The lieutenant was not callous, not brutal; he was merely trying to retain his sanity.

He had observed the same black humour at work even in the comparative safety of the communication trench, which was so high and so narrow that it would bury men alive if it collapsed under shellfire. He had seen an arm protruding from the top of the trench, with a torn khaki sleeve and a clenched fist, devoid of flesh, raised against the sky like a last rebuke. Some sapper or signals unit had run a telephone wire through the ragged fingers as a sort of macabre defiance, but mainly to disquiet newly joined men who had to run their own fingers along this line every night to ensure there were no faults. As Payne had been heard to remark, "Right lot of little comedians round here, and no mistake!"

The enemy front line swung away to the right with the British trenches attempting to follow it. Once there had been grass here. Jonathan stared at the charred tree stumps and thought of the copse at Hawks Hill. How many had fallen in this one sector? How many would die tomorrow?

Somewhere, a machine-gun opened fire and the first sunlight glinted on something beyond the ridge. Like a tiny insect, flying in tight turns to avoid drifting balls of smoke, dirty stains against what would be a clear summer morning.

He heard the impartial tap-tap-tap of the plane's machine-gun, although what it was shooting at was impossible to judge. They had seen two of them on the march here. The war's new dimension: a private aerial world for brave and reckless young men who had been schoolboys not so long ago. One had drifted away in flames and crashed in a field. The other had flown slowly away, like someone bored and cheated by the ease of the kill.

Ross said quietly, "In your view, Colonel, do you think it can be done?"

Jonathan let his binoculars drop across his respirator haversack and tried not to think of the Australian colonel, Ede, who had been blinded.

"It can be done, sir, now that we know about the mines."

The brigadier waited for some further comment, and then snapped, *"But?"*

"I know this is a different sort of war, sir, but at Gallipoli the major fault was the failure to exploit any small gain or success we had. The enemy was always given too much time to prepare, or to hit back."

"That kind of folly is not unknown on the Western Front! But this time there is an impressive plan to make certain we maintain the impetus. If we fail before the weather changes . . ." He did not need to elaborate. He said sharply, "What do people call you?"

"Well, Jonathan, or Jono, sir." It was startling how this cold-eyed man could change tack.

"Jono it is then. Unlike some, I need to know my officers.

And it seems you'll be just that, until your Major-General Loftus can bring his ponderous division into play." He sounded pleased about something. "Now I'm off to breakfast." The air cringed to the first artillery strike of the day. Further up the line the German guns had reawakened too, and the sky was soon hazy with drifting smoke.

Ross began to descend the crude ladder. "Glad you met someone you knew." He turned and looked up at him. "I fear the Anzacs may get the worst of it tomorrow."

Major Vaughan, who had also accompanied Jonathan to the dugout, said in a whisper, "Do you really think they can do it, Colonel?"

Jonathan waited for the next salvo to pass overhead, with a sound like a giant tearing up canvas. Then the fall of shot: columns of smoke far away, earth and debris erupting high into the air. There were men under that bombardment.

Eventually he answered, "I think they might, Ralph." He looked at Vaughan's battered face. "But what then? You noticed the brigadier made no mention of the French."

"Well, yes. I thought it a bit odd."

"It means the French have told Haig that it's all his show. We're on our own."

A shell burst directly over the line and shrapnel ripped into the command post and along the support trench. The Germans might be seeking the reserves. As the echo of the explosion died away Jonathan heard someone screaming inhumanly, like some tortured creature.

"Stretcher bearer!" But the scream had stopped.

He saw concern in Vaughan's eyes and smiled. "But it's not the first time, is it?"

He liked Vaughan, as much as he allowed himself to like anyone amid the hazards of war, but it was pathetic to see how he brightened up at a few cheap words of optimism.

He saw Harry Payne. "Can you rustle up some breakfast, d'you think?"

Payne almost winked. "Got some eggs, sir."

Around them the land was in torment, exploding under towering columns of smoke. Eggs? But he knew better than to ask.

"I think we'd better go back," he said. "Getting noisy around here."

He walked into the communication trench and stared up at its high side, black against the sky. The horizon.

Tomorrow, then.

Captain Christopher Wyke groped his way to the forward command position and found Lieutenant-Colonel Blackwood alone in the observation post. The whole front seemed unusually quiet, unnerving. As if the enemy out there in the damp smelly darkness knew what was planned and was merely waiting to open fire.

What if the mines which were supposed to herald the full attack failed to detonate; or some German sapper had rendered all or some of them safe? He said quietly, "Battalion at stand-to, sir. Ready to move forward if needed."

Jonathan had his pipe in his teeth but it was not lit. As at Gallipoli, it was always a comfort when he got the chance to smoke it. God knew they were rare enough.

"Thanks, Christopher. Tea?"

Wyke realised that Payne was also here, covering his cigarette with the palm of his hand. "No, thank you, sir."

"I think you should. It's one of Payne's specials."

Wyke took the mug from the shadows and sipped it. Special was right. It must be one-third rum.

"Won't be long now." Jonathan was using his binoculars, but it was like staring into nothing. That would soon change.

All along the six-mile front men were crouching low beneath the firesteps. If the mines worked as planned, there was a chance that any soldier could be injured by flying rocks and all the other debris which must litter no man's land from end to end.

He had the gradient, the distances and the obstacles on this particular sector fixed in his mind like a map. Gallipoli had taught him that, and far more than he would have thought possible.

"Are the lads all right?"

Wyke had to drag his mind back to reality. "Pretty good, sir. Bit restless, not much else." He thought of the machine-gunner Bert Langmaid; he had been the only one not wearing his steel helmet. Instead he wore his old Broderick cap on the back of his head, more like a Jack than a Royal Marine. But nobody had bothered to mention it, and that would probably irritate that great lump of a man more than a proper dressing-down. He recalled Maxted with his H.Q. platoon, slumped against the side of the trench smoking quickly in sharp, nervous drags. They had not spoken. It was not the time.

Sergeant-Major McCann had been smoking his pipe and talking very quietly with the new colour-sergeant, Bill Seagrove. Wyke had come to know the sound of so many voices, even in the dark like this. Dialects from all over the country, with many young faces which would never have been seen in the corps but for the war. Errand boys and waiters, farm hands and bus conductors whose jobs were now in the charge of women and girls.

Eventually, Wyke asked what was uppermost in his thoughts. "Do you think the mines will work?"

Payne groped over to him with his jug and answered for them all.

"Put the kibosh on this little lot if they don't!"

Jonathan tried to see his watch but it was a waste of effort. It would be ages yet before the artillery opened fire. At least it would seem that long. So many moving along those foul communication trenches: old sweats and boys, the hard cases like Langmaid and McCann shoulder to shoulder with the others who would crack if things went against them. An army made on the barracks square and fashioned into fighting men in the dirt and lice of Flanders.

Jonathan said, "If nothing happens . . ." It was as if he were thinking aloud. "I still believe the attack will go on." After all, what else could they do? He recalled the Australian Major Duffy when they had first met, in another dugout at Anzac Cove. *I'm just a soldier, but I tell you now, it can't be done.* Chilling words, but all too true: Was this to be another heroic failure? He gripped his pipe so hard with his teeth that it was a marvel he did not snap it.

Wyke seemed to need to talk as the minutes ticked past. Somewhere far behind this position the gunners would be consulting their maps again, fuses to be checked, each shell to be treated as something holy as it was thrust home into every eager breech.

He asked, "Will you stay on in the corps after the war, Colonel?"

Jonathan saw something in the darkness. A careless match, or somebody trying to look at his watch. But not in the front line. It was as if every man there was either asleep or dead. Soon he would see the crashed aeroplane again, the tangled wire. He considered Wyke's question, surprised that he had never doubted it before. Even in the presence of death no such idea had occurred to him. Now it did, and Wyke had innocently laid it bare without knowing what he had done.

He tried to make light of it. "I don't know. I shall be so

used to power by then, maybe I won't want to drop the rank and its privileges. I might try something else."

Wyke sounded surprised. "Even if I drop to lieutenant, I wouldn't want to quit the corps. My father says . . ."

Jonathan smiled. Yes, the major-general wouldn't want the boat rocked. Like his own father, and all the others before him. He pictured Hawks Hill as he had last seen it. Not the poor shambling officers, or the ambulances and the tired-looking nurses, but the other part of it. That sea of daffodils, the unchanged hedges and birdsong. A sense of continuity if you had the wit enough to see and use it.

He thought of her hand on his arm, her skin already tanned when they held one another so briefly at Salisbury. She was a local girl. She would not want the upset and separations of service life, or the pressure of engagements which were part of an officer's progress.

He shook himself, angry at the futility and the utter hopelessness of it.

"Bit lighter, I think, sir." Payne was patting his pockets, checking his weapons and equipment.

Jonathan levelled his glasses once more. Again, it was like a film developing: a creeping monochrome of various depths and shades. First the Messines Ridge, as if that was where the world ended. Then the darker brush strokes: burned trees and the empty spaces where the shell craters would eventually reveal themselves. As if the film had been spoiled or badly exposed, or the image were too terrible to focus fully upon.

Flash . . . flash. The guns began to fire, their wrath making his ears cringe as they tore over the trenches. Sharp, vivid explosions lit up the enemy lines and the upended aeroplane. Somewhere a machine-gun and then others began their harsh rattle, as they probed for raiding parties or a full-scale attack.

Jonathan said, "Test the line to Major Vaughan, Christopher. Just in case!" There was a sharpness to his voice, and he could feel his senses heightening with the bursting shells and the raking fire of automatic weapons.

"Answering, Colonel!"

Jonathan turned to speak to him and then saw the whole post laid bare with yellow fire as the first of the massive mines exploded. The roar of the next mine robbed him of any thought but the total destruction it would bring to the enemy's front line. The artillery had opened the range to concentrate on the German support lines even as more mines ripped away the dawn, the flames revealing the tons of falling earth and rocks, burying hundreds in tombs that had once provided confidence and shelter against the British guns.

He thought of the R.E. major who was no doubt watching his handiwork. In mufti he would look more like a prosperous farmer than an explosives expert.

Payne murmured, "God Almighty, something worked for once."

Jonathan glanced at the paling sky. No sun today, it was far too cloudy. It would be wrong to have sunshine. That belonged elsewhere, away from fear; away from death.

He said, "Tell Major Vaughan to be ready to move to the first support line. Any minute, I shouldn't wonder!"

Two more huge mines hurled tons of earth into the air. One appeared to explode immediately behind their front line. The R.E.'s must have been working like moles to get so close, for both sides maintained listening posts for something like this. Some puny sunlight broke through the motionless clouds, but no man's land remained in smoking shadows, as if the earth itself was ablaze.

There was a momentary lull, and above the far-off artillery fire he heard the sudden shrill of whistles. Six miles of whistles, the scene the same in every trench. He could see it clearly enough: he had been there. The soldiers dragging themselves up from the firesteps and onto the parapet, staggering like old men under their weight of gear and weapons, led and urged on by their officers. A whole division in this sector alone. Very faintly, before the machine-guns took up the challenge, he heard them cheering, wildly, hopelessly, as the well-sited guns found the prongs of the attack and cut into it like a steel wire.

"Shall I tell the major, sir?" Wyke sounded breathless, as if he had been running instead of crouching over the field telephone in its webbing case.

"Not yet." He lifted his glasses and tried not to swallow as a mass of running infantry was caught in cross fire from below the ridge. Men were falling like slaughtered animals; others pressing on from behind seemed unable to climb over the piles of dead and wounded alike, and they too were seen to fall. A handful of men, almost hidden in smoke, had somehow got through. Jonathan saw their arms jerk like puppets and then they threw themselves down by some tangled wire as their grenades exploded. One of the machine-guns had been knocked out, and like a surging wave another mass of infantry charged through the gap. He was losing the picture as the lines of khaki figures vanished into the smoke, but not before he had seen many others fall, and the bayonets cut down any foolish enough to plead for mercy or surrender.

More whistles, and the artillery was firing again to cover the leading infantry when they reached the breached line. Then more grenades, the handy little Mills bombs that could wipe out anyone left alive in a ruined trench, or be tossed into smoking dugouts to silence any survivor.

The next line of men was climbing onto the parapet, and whistles from the Anzac sector sent more reinforcements into the attack.

Jonathan said evenly, "Tell him now, Christopher. Get them moving." He had to repeat it for Wyke to hear above the clamour of weapons and grenades. Amidst the carnage and thickening smoke he saw some of the wounded trying to crawl to safety. One, all alone, was on his hands and knees creeping in a circle, unable to see.

Jonathan could hear Wyke's voice on his handset, cracking with excitement and perhaps relief.

"Yes, sir! That's right, sir! They're through! *The enemy's falling back!*"

Patches of red and white flitted through the corpses and destruction: medical corps stretcher bearers with their familiar armbands. The crawling man tried to turn round as the stretcher bearers lurched and ducked towards him. Jonathan made himself watch, as he had at the peninsula; he must forget nothing. The man had no face.

Tap-tap-tap. Such an inoffensive sound above the smoke, beyond the reach of their desperate, struggling figures. Two young men in a private dogfight. What could they know of this horror?

"Come on there! Tell off by platoons! Move yer bloody selves!"

Sergeant-Major McCann, concerned as always that his marines would not let him down in the eyes of mere soldiers.

They were slowing down in the cratered waste of no man's land. Sappers and machine-guns were moving up to the captured trench before the enemy counterattacked. It would be a long day. Then night would hide it all again, when only the teeming horde of rats would appear to profit from it.

Major Vaughan clumped into the observation post, sweating fiercely. "All in position, Colonel." He banged his hands together as if it were cold. "What a show, eh?"

"We should be quiet for a bit, Ralph." He felt drained, as if he had been out there where so many had fallen. "The ridge should hold off an attack on this sector."

He heard somebody screaming. A lost soul amongst the dead, waiting for help, for anyone who might care.

He took a mug from Payne, unaware of his troubled expression. He could smell the rum without effort, and knew that he must ensure that his men had their ration a little earlier than usual. But just for the moment he needed solitude, if only to convey that he, at least, did care.

At the end of that June day Jonathan received his orders from Division. The Fifty-First would remain in reserve.

The attack had been a complete success, and the advance along the whole front had been at least two miles. For that modest accomplishment they had paid the price of 25,000 thousand lives.

FIFTEEN

━━━━━

The two girls sat on the grass in the walled garden and admired the baskets of strawberries they had picked throughout the afternoon. Alexandra Pitcairn swept her chestnut hair from her face and plucked at her blouse. "We've done well. I'll take some up to the hospital later on."

Her companion, Kitty Booth, was dark and vivacious, like a fairy-tale gipsy girl. She had her skirt pulled up over her knees and said, "What wouldn't I give to be able to strip off everything and run naked into the sea!"

Alexandra smiled—She had always liked Kitty even though they came from very different backgrounds: she was not afraid of hard work, and had turned her hand to anything she could get when everyone had been against her. She had met a young corporal when the county regiment had had a couple of battalions under canvas at Eastwood Farm. It must have seemed like another world to her, as she had been only a naive eighteen when the soldiers arrived. All those young straight-backed men in uniform, parading and marching, walking out in Alresford where there were a few ale houses and inns.

Kitty and her corporal had fallen in love: as simply as that. Her father, the police sergeant in Alresford, had seemingly been in favour. A regular soldier with prospects, he said, she could have done a lot worse. They had spoken with the vicar, exchanged letters with the corporal's parents. It was all arranged.

Then without warning the regiment had been ordered to France. Two months later the corporal was killed in action, and a few months after that Kitty gave birth to a little girl.

Everything had changed for her, and infuriated by the shame it might cast on his career in the county police her father had turned her out of the house. *I'll have no slut in my home!*

If Kitty still brooded about that she never mentioned it. Alexandra's father had, characteristically, offered her a room, and in exchange she had worked about the house. It was per-haps the first time that Alexandra had seen her father in a different light, not merely a dedicated country G.P. but as a radical, and a man above all who cared for his fellow human beings whether they were sick or well. It was fortunate that she had still been living at home, otherwise she knew some of the more spiteful gossips would have suggested that the doctor was keeping a woman "who was no better than she ought to be," after the death of his wife.

Kitty had always opened her heart to the doctor's daughter, although she did not visit so often now that she had a respectable job in the town working in a milliner's shop, where her ready smile had become a great asset to the owner. Her newborn child had not lived long enough for Kitty to know it. Like her dead corporal, it was something that remained locked in her heart, still precious and private.

In town, as here in this small village, the gossip surrounding her had died. After nearly three years of war, hers was not the only loss of innocence, and there were too many families concerned with their own bereavement to condemn her one indiscretion.

She lay now on the grass with her chin propped in her hands.

"Thought you were going out today, Alex?"

"I was going down into Alresford, to buy some perfume if there is any."

Kitty's bare legs moved back and forth like scissors, and her eyes were thoughtful.

"So there *is* a fellow then."

"Is that what they say?" She was used to Kitty's directness; maybe that was why they had always got along. But it was a shock all the same.

"'Tis what *I* say." She blew some of her hair from her mouth. "You can tell me, you know that. Should, after all we've been through together."

Alex put a strawberry to her lips. "It's quite silly, really."

"Was that why you were going into town? To see him? What's he like? What does he do?"

"He's—he's a soldier, Kitty. But he's not here, he's gone over. You know." Kitty was so worldly, she thought with a sudden rush of embarrassment. Younger than herself by about five years, but she always felt so uninformed and ignorant by comparison.

Kitty said, "I know, right enough," and the silence was suddenly grave. Then her mood changed again like quicksilver, as it always did. "And you want him, is that it?"

To her own annoyance Alex knew she was blushing. "I don't know. I never really knew how it could be. How I could feel . . ." She tried to put it into words. "I just want to see him again. He's never bored with what I say, and he's good to be with . . ."

Kitty was on her knees beside her, one sun-warmed arm around her shoulders. "Tell Kitty, Alex love. You've done more than enough for me. Maybe I can repay some of it now." She paused, examining the lovely, innocent profile. "He hasn't—well—you didn't—"

"No. I never have." She thought wildly of the blinded officer who had attacked her. Maybe that was how it always was, all she would ever know. "I'll be an old maid, you'll see."

"Oh, don't be daft, girl!" Kitty studied her, weighing the words and the moment, not wanting to stem the rush of confidences. "You're thinking: maybe he won't come back, maybe he'll be killed, is that it? Afraid you'll be all alone again."

And I have been alone, more than anyone will ever know.

"I want him." She gazed intensely at Kitty, with eyes that were clear green in the sunlight. Like the sea, Kitty thought, although she had never seen it. "What is it like?" She saw the younger girl's mouth twitch. "Don't mock me, Kitty!"

Kitty took her hand in hers and patted it as she would a small, uncertain animal.

"Like nothing else. My Bobby and I used to do it in the fields when he could get out of camp. He used to make me so excited I couldn't wait, I wanted it that bad." She watched the fine colour flood Alex's face. "There now, I've shocked you, haven't I?"

"No. I'm just shocked with myself. I didn't know, you see, and I still don't."

"Where's your soldier live? Somewhere you'd not be known?"

Alex laughed with amusement and despair.

"He lives here."

Kitty released her hand and exclaimed, "That one who was here? The colonel?" She breathed out noisily. "My God, girl, you've got a nerve, an' I love you for it!"

Alex said quietly, "He's had a bad time. Far worse even than my father realised. At first I thought he was afraid of going back, but I don't think so now. He's troubled about something, and he thinks his men might suffer because of him."

Kitty stood up as the church clock chimed. "Must get back, I promised to take the baker's kids for a walk when they come out of school." She paused in collecting her baskets. "You're entitled to some happiness even in this rotten war, Alex. Just be careful, and listen to me." She walked away, and then paused. "If you only knew what it was like, and how much I envy you!"

For a long time Alex remained there, watching the sun on the redbrick walls, going over what she had said, how she had been able to discuss something so private. Even thinking about it made her cheeks burn. *I couldn't wait, I wanted it that bad.*

She turned suddenly as her father came out of the back door, his spectacles on the top of his head, and she knew she was blushing again, as if he could read her thoughts.

The doctor glanced around vaguely: "Oh, she's gone, has she?"

"Is something wrong, Daddy?"

"Quite the reverse, my dear." He held up a London newspaper, which she knew the army dispatch riders always brought him when they could. "There's been another battle. Near Ypres, as far as I can make out." He did not see the anxiety on her face as he lowered his glasses to peer at the front page. "It's official. They drove the enemy back and the general staff say that the German army is almost beaten, and after this victory will be," he squinted closer to read the exact words, "will be little more than a disorganised rabble!"

He smiled at her. "Thought you would like that." He folded the paper under his arm and tugged out his watch. "What about some tea before I go out again?"

She scarcely heard him. There had been no mention of the Royal Marines at all. He was safe. It was almost over.

She thought of her talk with the irrepressible Kitty, and was surprised to discover that she was no longer ashamed.

The Royal Marines commandant-general slammed through the doors of his Caxton House office and thrust an aggressive hand out toward Major-General Loftus, who stood up as he entered.

"God damn it, Herbert, I'm sorry to have kept you waiting!" He hurled his cap and swagger stick onto a chair. "I've been all this time at the damned War Office. Looking for somebody who actually understands what's going on in Flanders, and in this damned coalition government, is like looking for a pork chop in a synagogue!" He calmed down slightly but he was still fuming. "Care for a drink?" He stabbed a bell button and a marine appeared in the doorway in seconds.

Loftus pulled out his newspaper with its glaring headlines about the Germans' impending defeat, and spread it on the desk.

The general scowled. "I know. I've seen it. I sometimes

think the enemy is on *this* side of the Channel." The marine returned with a tray, decanter and two glasses, then backed out of the door as discreetly as a butler. Loftus took a glass and peered over it, his blue eyes very hard.

"They promised me, sir. The Fifty-First was to remain independent until my Grenville Division could move up to the front."

"Well, Herbert, your division isn't going, not yet anyway. They need reinforcements everywhere, not least to prop up our Italian allies in the Alps, and of course the Russians are nearer to bloody revolution than they've ever been. I happen to know that the prime minister wants to get rid of Haig, but as I discovered at the War Office there's no alternative to Haig's plan, and who would replace him in any case?"

Loftus put down his empty glass without having even tasted the whisky. "I heard as much, sir. Lloyd-George has never liked the G.O.C. . . ."

The general waved him down. "That's not the point, Herbert. All this optimism, this pie in the sky about the Germans is rubbish. One more push will *not* cause their collapse, and in any case the army can never cover 35 miles to the Belgian coast before the weather breaks. How could *anyone* be so blind as to promise to complete the first fifteen miles in under two weeks? You've read my report. We lost all those men for a mere two or three miles. It's not a battlefield, it's a bloody cemetery!"

They were silent, each immersed in thought, while the muted murmur of London penetrated even to this office. Then Loftus said, "So Blackwood's battalion remains under army control."

"Yes. I did everything I could, but . . ." He shrugged. "They did agree to allow the battalion to fall back to the French coast for a rest period. The R.M.A. will remain to support the next big push." He stared at his glass. "End of next month. Top secret, of course."

Loftus thought he had misheard. "But it isn't even the end of June yet, sir! Our people gained an advance, albeit a small one, but the whole point, unless I misunderstood my orders, was to follow up the success before the enemy could regroup and make good his line."

The general refilled the glasses. "I know, and you didn't misunderstand. Haig intends to follow up when he's ready, not before. There's an even worse enemy than the general staff, Herbert. The weather. That land has been fought over so often it would become a bog. The army has put some new tanks into the field and they seem to have done well enough, especially from the tactical point of view. Nobody wants to be rolled flat by one of those brutes, and they offer good cover for advancing infantry."

Loftus said, "But in last year's weather they would have been useless."

The general turned over some papers without seeing them. "Absolutely."

Loftus suggested, "I could spare another company, sir. All marines."

"Good thinking." Then he said sharply, "In your opinion, Herbert: should I pull Blackwood out, put somebody higher in command?"

"No, sir. He's the right man for the job."

"I think so too." He smiled. "Can't bump up his promotion any more—they wouldn't stand for that!"

Loftus said, "My Grenville Division is based at one of the big camps at Étaples near Boulogne, about fifty miles from the front at Ypres. The Fifty-First can withdraw to there for a rest and training period. If there's to be no attack until late July, it might be useful, for both the battalion and the division." He tried to smile, but it was impossible. "Keep the discontent and mischief to a minimum at least."

The general nodded absently. "Pig of a place, I'm told, but I'll make certain your total authority isn't challenged, until the advance anyway."

Loftus said, "I think we should bring Blackwood to London, sir. His adjutant too. Bright young chap, very useful. I've seen his reports."

The general studied him keenly. "Had to say that, didn't you? His father is a friend of yours." He smiled. "See to it then. I expect Blackwood is a little bitter about the change of plans—I would be, in his place. Make the necessary arrangements. His second-in-command . . ." He frowned, groping for the name and face.

"Major Vaughan, sir."

The general's eyes crinkled briefly. "Yes, him. Saw the young devil fight a few times—knocked the hell out of everybody. Well, he's earmarked for promotion to half-colonel. Do him good to be left in charge for a while." He reached for the decanter. "Blackwood isn't married, is he? I'd have heard."

Loftus's face was impassive. The general certainly would have known: he missed nothing.

"No. Not married, sir."

"Pity. Plenty of time though. Have to think of the future." He sighed: "Well, keep him in London, where I can have an eye on him. We'll be able to get him back to his men soon enough if the balloon goes up prematurely, and it might do him some good as well. Bit more life than down at that god-forsaken place in Hampshire."

They both looked at their watches and the general said,

"Leave it to you then, Herbert. I must be off. Dining with the fourth Sea Lord tonight. Useful of course, but it does tend to mess up one's other arrangements."

The marine orderly entered with Loftus's cap as if to a signal. Loftus accepted it with a wry smile.

"I know, sir. Hell, isn't it?"

So Jonathan Blackwood's life was arranged.

A few days later Alexandra Pitcairn was sitting in the garden, depressed after a long session with one of the patients at Hawks Hill. He was a young subaltern, no more than nineteen, who had been blinded in France when a flare pistol shot from another officer's hand had exploded. There was no hope of his recovery and he lacked any sense of purpose, and even her efforts to explain how successful the Braille training could be had made no impression upon him. It often began like that, until she was able to win a man's confidence and remove from his own mind the stigma of cripple.

She had let him talk for much of the time, his young husky voice telling her what it had been like. How he had lain for two days in a shell hole before anyone had found him. He told her about his girl, how he had hoped to marry her when it was all over. His parents had been to visit him at the previous hospital, and his mother in particular had kept saying he was not to worry, that everything was going to be just as it was. It was no help at all.

Once he said, "I wish they'd left me out there to die!"

She had held his hands in hers, wanting somehow to reassure him. But even that was different now. Once they had been only instruments, coaxing minds out of darkness into understanding. Now they had become hands, human, physical things, not to be ignored when she had tried to move stiff fingers, and guide them to learning.

There had been no word from Jonathan Blackwood. She had told herself countless times not to be so silly. He would write again when he had the opportunity. She was amazed by the hunger she felt for the briefest message, anything that might sustain her.

"So this is how the idle rich carry on!"

She looked up and saw Kitty Booth grinning over the gate. Kitty came into the garden and sat beside her.

"Bad day, my dear?"

She sighed. "I get so tired sometimes—and the work just goes on and on. And I think waiting . . ."

"No word, then?"

"No. I . . ." She hesitated. "After I told you about him I thought perhaps I was imagining it, because I wanted to."

Kitty smiled. "Don't you even think such things! Anything I can do?"

Good old Kitty. "My father's up at the hospital, giving the medical officers a hand." She forced a smile. "You could make us some tea . . ." Then she broke off and stared beyond Kitty's shoulder. Her face was suddenly ashen.

Kitty exclaimed, "What is it?"

She could neither breathe nor speak. The gate was half open and the post girl was leaning her bicycle against the wall beyond it. She opened her bag.

"Telegram, Miss Pitcairn."

"Oh my God—*no*—"

The post girl pulled it out and they saw the official stamp.

Kitty said sharply, "I'll take it."

The post girl waited. She had delivered so many, and yet she had never got over seeing the anguish on the faces of the recipients.

Alexandra held out her hand but it was visibly shaking. "No, it's all right. He wouldn't want . . ."

But her eyes were almost blinded with tears. Kitty opened it and read the brief message, then she put her arm around her friend and whispered, "He's coming home, Alex love. He's not hurt—or anything."

Eventually she wiped her eyes on her sleeve and took the telegram with unsteady fingers. It seemed a long time before she could read it.

My very dear Alex. I am coming to London. Please meet me. Letter following. With love, Jonathan.

The word *love* seemed to steady her more than anything.

"He's coming home, Kitty!" She hugged her, and then the post girl, who grinned and said, "Well! Must be quite a man, I'm thinkin'!"

When they were alone and Kitty was at last brewing the tea she asked, "What's London like, Kitty? I only went once, when I was a child."

"I don't know—I've never been. Don't have that sort of money." But she smiled. "You will get his letter soon, I shouldn't wonder. You will go to him, won't you?"

Alex nodded, fingers gripped tightly together as the young subaltern's had been.

"I—I want to ask you things, Kitty."

Kitty said softly, "You won't need to ask me. But I'll tell you whatever you like."

"What will he do? Take me to a theatre, or one of those restaurants they're always talking about? Where would I stay? What . . . would I do?"

Kitty looked for the biscuit tin. "He *loves* you, Alex. He's not some fumbling lout at the village dance. He's Jonathan Blackwood, and he's trying to tell you."

Doctor Pitcairn wandered through from the hall, and they both fell silent.

"You know, I think the nights are drawing in already.

Doesn't seem possible." He smiled at Kitty. "Anything unusual happen today?"

Alex turned her face away and heard her friend reply casually, "Can't think of anything."

The doctor was so immersed in his notes that he hardly noticed.

"That's good. Now let's have some tea."

The London rail terminus of Waterloo was busier than ever, or so it seemed to him: packed with people saying good-bye, or waiting nervously to welcome someone home from the war.

Jonathan had arrived far too early, just in case he missed her. She would have received his letter but had not had time to reply to it. There was another possibility, of course. She might have changed her mind, or recognised the danger in what she was doing.

He had been to the R.T.O.'s office to check on schedules, and had managed to avoid two Royal Marine captains he knew who were returning to Portsmouth.

Beyond the rank of ticket barriers the trains lay waiting to leave, or came to a halt amidst clouds of steam with doors flinging open like fins along their full lengths. The passengers were mostly in army or naval uniforms. At the gates military police stood double-banked, their eyes everywhere as the inspectors took or clipped the out-thrust tickets while the crowds surged through: looking for deserters, men overstaying their leave, or others who were improperly dressed. By the sharp contrast in their appearance Jonathan recognised those from a barracks or some training depot: smart as paint, eager to get on leave. The veterans, in stained uniforms and scarred boots, were dull eyed, empty of expression as they stared around until a familiar face or waiting family emerged from the crowd. There were trolleys piled with kit bags and sailors' hammocks, a boozy-looking chief petty officer with a party of boy seamen on their way to complete their training. Some appeared to be no more than about fourteen.

Jonathan thought of Harry Payne with regret and a certain sadness. He had asked him what he would do on this brief leave, and Payne had been vague.

"Might look up an old pal. If not I'll beg a place at Eastney. I'll give the gate my whereabouts, 'case you need me." One thing he did not intend to do was visit his mother and stepfather.

Wyke had said he was going to see his young lady, then take her to meet his parents. He had seemed very confident that it would turn out well.

Both Payne and Wyke had probably guessed why he himself wanted to remain alone. He had heard no rumours around the battalion, so obviously the pair of them, like Swan, knew a secret when they saw one.

He recalled the depression and dismay when the Fifty-First had received its new orders for moving to the French coast. They had been ready, keyed up to the limit after the army's success at the Messines Ridge, and the order to wait while reinforcements and more artillery were brought up had seemed like madness, particularly to company commanders who would eventually be expected to lead their men against a rested and well-prepared enemy.

He saw some women from the Salvation Army with collecting boxes, and others handing out pamphlets to the passing throng. No one took any notice. He was reminded of the trio of soldiers he had seen on his way here, still wearing khaki uniforms from which the badges and ranks had been stripped. They had been standing near the Savoy Hotel playing their instruments, a mouth organ, a concertina and a flute, and there had not been a whole man among them. One had an arm missing, one a leg, and the third was badly scarred in the face. They had not been openly appealing to the passersby, and in turn, no one had appeared to notice the khaki cap upended on the pavement.

Take me back to dear old Blighty . . .

They had seemed to be in good spirits: maybe it was enough merely to be back in dear old Blighty, away from the mud and the blood and the lice and the smell of death. He had been deeply moved, and had stopped and put some notes in the cap, probably more than they usually collected in a week. The one with the concertina had given him a broad grin and said, "First time I've ever 'ad a blinkin' colonel on 'is knees to me!" His one eye had fixed on Jonathan's D.S.O. "Give the bastards 'ell, sir!"

He had hurried on towards Waterloo Bridge, but his thoughts lingered on the Savoy. What it would be like to take her there, openly, and without shame: to have her waited on and fussed over by the staff, and all the while he would be watching her, bringing the dream to reality.

He had strode on, angry with himself. It was only a dream. Suppose he had asked her to go there with him? What sort of man would she think he was? There were so many regulations now about hotel registration and food allowances it would have been very soon apparent that they weren't married, and that would have made her feel so cheap. Her distress would have been unbearable.

She would probably reconsider and take the next train back in any case once she found out what he had arranged: accommodation at a town house belonging to one of David's friends, who had inherited wealth and property in Norfolk and very seldom used the London house unless there was a race meeting somewhere in the area. He had always insisted that David or either of his brothers use it as a *pied-a-terre* if in the city, and Jonathan had gone there upon his arrival in London.

At least they would have a base, he thought, trying to justify himself, somewhere to talk and be alone together.

He was so uncertain that every time a train moved he realised how nervous he had become. There had been something in the tone of Alex's precious letters which had kindled hope, where before any thought of her had been a delusion; a warmth had crept into her written words so that they might have been spoken by her voice in his mind, and he was able to see her vividly whenever he had read them.

Suppose she misunderstood this latest clumsy attempt to reach her, to salvage something if not of the future then the present, and believed he only thought of her as a passing fancy?

Porters were shouting, women were frantically embracing departing men, and steam was puffing towards him around a bend in the track, which suddenly seemed to be lines of blinding silver in the sunlight beyond the covered platforms.

It was the one, it had to be. He glanced at his watch. Right on time: the good old Southern Railway.

"I say—Jonathan Blackwood, isn't it?"

He turned and saw a vaguely familiar face: a man wearing a smart, well-tailored suit that made him look like a prosperous lawyer. That was it. He plucked the name out of memory.

"Mr Collins! How good to see you." He *was* a lawyer; had handled his father's complicated business affairs and the repayment of his many debts after his death.

The other man was going on about the weather, the war, and the crowds. None of it made sense. He could hear the train grunting up to its platform, saw the inspector opening the gate, the redcaps taking a sudden interest.

"Meeting anyone I know?"

"No, I don't think so." He knew he sounded curt, but he couldn't help it. The train had stopped: all the doors were banging open like the previous arrivals. He turned to say something else but the lawyer had gone; probably in a huff, he thought, to wait in the buffet and see for himself who was coming.

He stared down the platform in vain. Crowds of sailors and more troops were nearly through, with the few civilians among them immediately apparent. A soldier was being questioned by two redcaps, his face like death. The other crowds pressed closer to the gates. The last farewell.

Khaki uniforms hurried past. Some saluted, others looked in the opposite direction.

Back to the house then. Another long evening drinking and staring at the sporting paintings that filled every wall, watching him. Men with guns, men with dogs, and unlikely looking jockeys on improbable horses.

He thought with envy of Wyke: showing off his girl, all the fear and the danger forgotten.

She was coming towards the gates. She wore a white blouse and a dark green suit and hat, and carried a small leather case, and she passed through a bar of unbroken sunlight where the glass roof had fallen in after a zeppelin raid. For those brief seconds she seemed to shimmer in his vision. Then she was through the gate, smiling and waving, watched by one of the inspectors with admiration.

He held her tightly.

"I was beginning to wonder." He studied every detail of her face. As he had expected she was very tanned, and her eyes were shining with excitement and emotion.

She said, "You're staring." Then she lifted her face to his. "I've been thinking about you all the time. I feel so wicked, coming here like this."

He kissed her gently, but this time she did not turn her mouth to his lips. It was enough to see, hear and hold her; the beauty of her face, the curve of her throat, the very freshness of her was more than he had dared to imagine.

He took her bag and immediately she protested. "Oh, you mustn't! You're in uniform!"

He said lightly, "I don't have to keep saluting this way."

She asked, suddenly and abruptly, "How long?"

"Six days. I have to see some people at headquarters tomorrow." He already knew what the next question would be.

"Where are we staying?"

He knew it was important. It was something she had wondered about, perhaps dreaded. He explained as best he could, thinking how convenient, how premeditated it all sounded, and was surprised when she said calmly, "I hoped it would be something like that. A hotel might have been . . ." But the mood changed instantly as she held up her left hand. "But I came prepared, just in case!"

It was a plain wedding ring, and suddenly he wanted to hug her.

She said, "I won't have people gossiping about my colonel." And as an afterthought, "I went all the way to Alton for it, so you needn't think—"

"I was thinking only that you came. I don't know how you managed it, I don't know how you explained. I only know that I'm overwhelmed." He steered her around luggage and trolleys and waved to a cab. "I'm taking you out to dinner tonight, by the way. Not a big place, and not full of red-tabbed generals and politicians. I've had just about enough of those lately."

She held his arm tightly. For only a second the bitterness had shown itself. But the strain was much less evident, falling from his face even as they walked and spoke, and the quiet confidence she had always sensed in him was unimpaired. If she had harboured doubts, they were now gone.

The cab rattled over the bridge and down towards Trafalgar Square, and she leaned over him to peer out and up at the little admiral.

"How lovely!" she said, with the unsophisticated pleasure he found so appealing. "Just like the picture on my pencil box when I was a child! I don't remember ever seeing it before."

The cabbie, who sported a ferocious walrus moustache that would have put Sergeant-Major McCann to shame, chuckled. "Where's your wife been then, Guvnor? In the nick?"

And although they both laughed, Jonathan saw her flush and nervously turn the wedding ring on her left hand.

Down a narrow street, and the cab came to a halt. She got out and gazed up at the house, her apprehension returning. The front was narrow but it was three storeys high, with splendid wrought-iron railings and a fanlight over the dark blue door. The brass knocker, typical of the owner, had been made in the form of a fox mask and riding crop.

"You said it was small."

He said, "Well, I suppose—by London standards, it is."

"You see?" she said. "I'm just a country girl." Her face clouded suddenly. "Out to dinner? I'm not well dressed enough for that—"

He put his fingers under her chin and smiled down at her. "If you wore a stoker's boilersuit you'd be the most beautiful woman I've ever laid eyes on."

He said it so seriously and with such sincerity that she could find no answer. At that moment the door opened and the elderly housekeeper peered out.

Jonathan said, "It's kind of you to be here, Mrs Scully."

"A pleasure, Colonel." Her eyes moved to the girl. "Ma'am." As she closed the door behind them she said, "I've made up the rooms, sir, and there's plenty in the pantry. You won't need any more until . . ."

But Alexandra was staring up at the curving staircase, at the paintings, the freshly-polished, elegant furniture. He had never brought a woman here before; it was quite obvious. But she guessed that others had, and no questions had been asked.

More to the point, he had not brought her here out of subterfuge, but to protect her and any reputation she might have when she returned home again.

Six days. Was that all? She climbed the stairs slowly, missing nothing. They would be days she would never forget.

As her first night in London drew to a close Alexandra sat in her room and went over everything they had done together, wondering why she was not completely exhausted. He had taken her to see Buckingham Palace and then for afternoon tea at the Grand Hotel, where nearby a band playing in the square had entertained servicemen and civilians alike. To her eyes there seemed so many uniforms, but otherwise the war and the shadows it cast seemed far away. They had returned to the house so that she could rest and change into the one special gown she had brought, then he had taken her to a small restaurant in Piccadilly: a place with comfortable booths and red velvet draperies and cushions. All the waiters had seemed quite ancient, and Jonathan had remarked that the younger ones were probably in the army. But mostly he let her talk: about her mother and her life, her past, and the thoughts she had never before shared with anyone.

He had seemed nervous, even shy, more so than she had expected, but his attention to her, his willingness to escort her wherever she wanted to go, and his companionship moved her in a way she had never known.

They had walked back to the house and she imagined that he was glad of the darkness: his arm must have ached from all the salutes he had had to return. He had commented, "They just want to see the lovely girl beside me!"

She brushed her hair and felt the slightest breeze, saw it stir the curtains. She had opened the windows wide for, as many people had remarked, it was the hottest and most humid day yet.

She thought of him in the adjoining room. Undressing; perhaps having a drink before he turned in. Not once, beyond his very apparent affection, had he made any advances or behaved in a manner which might have offended her.

Five more full days. It would go like the wind. What had she really expected, perhaps secretly hoped? That he would have insisted upon more? She opened the drawer in the dressing table, where she had put the nightgown Kitty had offered her.

It was mine. I never had the chance to wear it. You take it with you, Alex love.

She stood quite still and held the nightgown against her body. Beautifully laced and daringly cut, it had been for the wedding night Kitty had never known. Against it her own cotton gown looked like a smock. She wrinkled her nose and then pulled it over her head and gazed at herself in the mirror, strangely excited and shocked by her nakedness.

Maybe you think it's a bit of a cheek, Kitty had said, and blushed. *If you do—well, I'm sorry.*

She put on the silk nightgown and adjusted it so that it

fitted her body to perfection. What would she do if he knocked or spoke to her through the door, or opened it? But she knew he would not.

She lay on the bed in the darkness. When she had looked in the mirror it had been like that other time. She had smiled, and the girl who had smiled back had been a stranger. A woman in love.

The air was so humid that she had to push down the sheet, and she thought she would never be able to sleep as each precious memory flowed back into her mind. But she did sleep, more peacefully than for a long time.

And suddenly she was awake, her heart beating furiously although she did not know why. Even as she sat up the curtains were lit with a fierce, vivid flash, followed a second later by a roar of thunder that seemed to shake the foundations. She opened the curtains and looked out at the dark city, feeling the warm, moist air on her bare arms and shoulders. More lightning revealed the neighbouring roofs and chimney pots, stark against the black sky, and she withdrew hurriedly. Someone might see her like this. There was going to be a real storm, perhaps a cloudburst. She thought of Hampshire. That might stop the farmers complaining, for a while anyway.

Then she froze. Perhaps that had been the sound which had awakened her, and not the storm. She strained her ears and heard it again: a voice calling out, pleading incoherently. She did not hesitate but pulled her dressing gown around her and listened at the connecting door. It was Jonathan, and he seemed to be weeping, crying out.

What must she do? Pretend not to hear? There was nobody to call, and the housekeeper had gone long ago.

The connecting door was locked, and she went out into the passageway, her progress lit occasionally by the violent flashes. Outside his door she was unable to move. If only Harry Payne were here, or somebody else.

Then she knew she wanted nobody else to see him this way, and opened the door very carefully, waiting for another flash to light up the room. There was a small lamp on a table, and she felt for the switch and was momentarily blinded by the sudden light. Jonathan lay face down on the bed, his head buried in his arms, wearing only pyjama trousers; and she stared for what seemed like minutes at the jagged, star-shaped scars on his back.

The crumpled jacket lay like a wet rag on the carpet and there was an empty glass overturned beside it. The thunder tore the night again and he flung himself upright in the bed, his eyes wide and anguished. She knew he could not see her. He was somewhere else.

He was trying to shout but it came out as only a whisper.

"Stand-to! Face your front! Hold your fire, damn you!"

She spoke to him gently and a slow recognition crept into his eyes.

"It's all right," she whispered. "You were having a nightmare. I came to help."

He stared at her, then groped feverishly about, she supposed for his pyjama jacket. She sat on the bed and put her arms around him.

"There. I've got you. You're safe now."

"Mustn't see me like this." His face was buried in her hair. "It's—wrong."

She stroked his shoulder, and then the savage scars on his back. "You're like ice."

He was still trying to see her face. "So sorry about this. You were having—such a nice time—"

Humble, she thought, like a small boy who had disgraced

himself. She released him gently and said, "You can have this to put over you." Her fingers were shaking, and she fumbled impatiently with the cords of the dressing gown and slipped out of it. She faced him in the lamplight, her eyes quite steady.

"Is this what you want, dear Jonathan?"

He reached out and took her hand, and very slowly drew her onto the bed beside him; and propped on one elbow he gazed down at her, probably imagining it was only the beginning of another tormenting dream.

As his hand caressed her she heard herself whisper, "This was meant to happen," then his fingers were exploring the silk and lace, sliding the ribbons from her shoulders so that he could uncover her.

It was like being someone else: the smiling stranger in the mirror. It was not happening to her but to someone else. His fingers stroked each nipple, then his shadow was above her as he slipped the nightgown from her body. He was touching her everywhere, kissing her skin and allowing himself to explore her, so that she could only guide his hands and invite his body to a deeper intimacy. Their mouths were joined, her tongue touching his while her blood and pulse seemed to pound with the thunder. His hand went down, strong, insistent but strangely tender.

She gasped, "I've never—"

He was looking down at her, his breath mingling with hers, his face youthful once more. She whispered, "Whatever I say—whatever I do, don't stop. I love you, Jonathan!"

She cried out as he entered her, and the sudden pain seemed like one last resistance. Then as she received him the pain faded, like the thunder which had given them to one another.

The storm over London culminated in a heavy downpour. But in the room above the wet and streaming street, they heard none of it as they lay exhausted in a tight embrace. As if, even in sleep, each was afraid of losing the dream.

SIXTEEN

The Fifty-First battalion left the camp at Étaples and marched towards Flanders once again. Three days later, despite an attack by two German scout planes, they reached their new reserve position, which was even more desolate and ruined than their original one. They found a cellar in one of the houses where Jonathan and his H.Q. platoon could set up their telephones, but all the drains were shattered, so if it should rain even modestly the place would be flooded.

Shortly after their arrival Brigadier Ross and two of his staff came up, and while the latest intelligence pack was handed over to Vaughan and Wyke, Jonathan took the brigadier on a tour of his command.

"Can't tell you how glad I am that you're back with us, Jono." The brigadier's eyes flitted from freshly dug defences and new latrines to the machine-guns, mounted so that they would be ready for an air attack offering either bullets or the terrible splinter bombs that could cut down twenty men at a time if they were not under cover.

All the marines, busy in their shirtsleeves, were careful to have their anti-gas respirators slung around them, and Jonathan guessed that a lot of them probably feared that most inhuman form of warfare more than anything. He had already seen gassed soldiers being led back to the rear lines, eyes bandaged, each man shuffling uncertainly with his hand on the shoulder of the one in front.

Ross said briskly, "Good leave? Much about us in the newspapers?"

Jonathan had come to like this crisp, sometimes intolerant man. "They're more or less saying it's all over, bar the cheering."

"They would." Then he added angrily, "As I said before, we should have kept going. It's one thing to lose so many men, but for no good purpose it's unthinkable."

He pressed Jonathan no further for details of his leave and for that Jonathan was grateful: it was not something he wished to share, except with her alone. Every day some new discovery, a fresh awareness of one another and a new arousal of passion. He had taken her to a music hall, one he had heard Wyke mention, to museums and shops and to Westminster Abbey where they had sat in silence, hands clasped. Strangely, with her it was a place of peace despite its towering grandeur and its many memorials to the dead.

He still found it difficult to believe that it had really happened. How she had held him, her hands cool against the scars until even he was no longer ashamed of them. She had been shy, but once that had been overcome her desire had matched his own, and with her hands and lips and then her entire body she had left him weak and gasping, only to be roused again, and again.

Now he was back. He had put her on the train before he had gone to gather his kit. Harry Payne had arrived at the house, rather subdued and not his usual talkative self, and curiously Jonathan was glad of this too. He needed privacy, in the little time that remained to him, to cling to every memory of her.

She had shed no tears when the train had begun to move, but had watched him steadily from the open window until the carriages were hidden by the curve in the track. At the house he had found a letter among his freshly laundered shirts, and a neatly folded lace handkerchief: the one she had used as a private signal at Eastney.

Brigadier Ross said, "The date stands, I'm afraid. Thirty-first of July. A massive artillery bombardment before dawn . . . Division tells me there'll be over three thousand guns. Never knew we had that many. Your R.M.A. will be amongst 'em, but I fear heavy casualties. Jerry knows all about it. No damn mines like the last advance." He shot him a quick glance. "You'll hear anyway. I'm afraid your Anzac chum Major Duffy didn't make it."

Jonathan stared at a solitary bird overhead. From where, he thought, and to what place that would be safe?

"I think I knew, sir . . . His father will miss him. He builds boats."

Ross remarked, "Is there a country where men still do simple, ordinary things?" He peered at his watch. "Must get back." He looked at him searchingly. "You look well, Jono. Good thing, too. I'm going to need all the reserve battalions once we get going."

They shook hands, observed by a few of the marines and surrounded by the remains of a dead village.

After he had gone Jonathan found Major Vaughan working through the battle orders.

He looked up with a puzzled frown on his battered face. "All these guns, sir. After the last advance at the Messines Ridge I would have thought the enemy would have had enough of it." He opened his stiff-backed map case. "It all seems to hinge on this place, sir, although it doesn't seem to warrant much attention strategically. I have to confess I'd never heard of it."

Jonathan glanced down at the map. Passchendaele. It meant nothing in particular to him.

"I think they intend to remedy that, Ralph."

He felt a sense of urgency, the need to write to her again, reveal all his thoughts and to hell with the censors. Leave out nothing. So she would remember too, and cherish everything as he did.

It must have taken true courage to do what she had done, after the sheltered life she had always known. He saw her now, facing him in the lamplight while the storm had burst around them and the nightmare of the Western Front had come alive as he had tried to fend it off, unable to hide from it even in sleep.

He sat on a broken fence rail and slowly filled his pipe.

Vaughan remarked in an undertone, "He's different in some way. Don't you think?"

Wyke smiled, recalling the girl with the chestnut hair who had visited the colonel at Salisbury. She must have done that for him, and his own Hermione would soon do as much for himself. He and his parents had taken her to a charity ball at Claridge's in Brook Street, and as his mother had commented afterwards, "We're all very lucky, Chris. She really *fitted in.*"

In one of the temporary dugouts, Sergeant-Major McCann was drinking his rum ration with several of the sergeants. He looked up and wiped his considerable moustache as Sergeant Ned Timbrell ducked through the canvas curtain.

"Tot ready?"

The new colour-sergeant, Bill Seagrove, folded a tattered magazine and said, "Meant to tell you, Ned. There was a bloke at the camp asking about you. Forgot to mention it at the time—we was all a bit pushed as I recall."

Timbrell looked at him over his mug, his black-olive eyes steady. "Wot did 'e want?"

The sergeant-major watched with sudden interest. There was an unusual rasp in Timbrell's tone.

The colour-sergeant said offhandedly, "Not one of our lot. Said he was from your neck of the woods. Blackfriars—that's London, isn't it?"

Timbrell tried to push it aside. After all this time. . . . Nothing could happen now. But Blackfriars—it was too much of a coincidence to take for granted.

"Wanted to see you about something." Seagrove shrugged. "Wouldn't say what."

"Did you tell 'im anything?"

Seagrove grinned. "Course not. Think I'm daft?"

Timbrell swilled his empty mug in a bucket of stained water and left the dugout.

"What's up with him, Sarn't-Major?"

McCann said, "Probably 'is bookie's after 'im!"

They all laughed, and standing in the rutted street Timbrell clenched his fists. Not after all this time. It wasn't possible. The gaping corpse sliding into the Thames and drifting silently away . . . must be all of ten years, or bloody near.

Lieutenant Maxted called, "Got a job for you, Sergeant!"

"Right away, sir!" He hurried over. This was more like it. His world, and—one he understood. The rest was just a memory of the slums. Not real any more.

The air vibrated to a burst of artillery fire and Maxted said tightly, "Not us this time. Nearer to St Julien." Why the hell should he care, he thought. He was in agony. He couldn't last out much longer without help.

Harry Payne ducked across the street and made his way to the cellar. Better safe than sorry. The Germans had been known to get their snipers right behind the lines. He had noticed the way Maxted kept his sergeant talking out in the open. Brave? Reckless? It would be plain stupid if the crosswires were already on him.

Payne thought of the girl he had seen at Waterloo. He had

been on a train from Portsmouth, returning from leave to join the colonel when he'd seen them. He had already guessed that a woman was involved, and he had suspected it would be Alexandra Pitcairn. The colonel wasn't the kind to pick up some tart or a showgirl at a stage door somewhere. Well, ruddy good luck to him. He himself had gone to the small house near the barracks where an old mate had once lived. He was dead now, had gone down in a cruiser after hitting a mine.

His friend's widow had come to the door, flour on her hands and smudges on her face. She had been surprised, embarrassed, but had made him welcome. A really nice little piece, he thought; he had been best man at their wedding.

It was creepy that his friend should have been the one to go first: he had been nothing more dangerous than a drummer in the ship's band. It made no difference to the sea, apparently.

Payne could hear himself saying it as if she were right here with him. "Look here, Peg—I've always been pretty fond of you, you must have known that. Why don't we make a go of it? Get spliced, all right and proper."

She had taken it very calmly. "You know we had a kid?"

"That's all right," he said, "I'm good with nippers."

"She's with her gran in Gosport. Won't be back till tomorrow." She glanced at the distant Union Flag that flew above the redbrick tower at Eastney. You could see it from almost everywhere in Southsea. "I still expect to see him coming down the road," she said. She had made up her mind. "I'll think about it."

But Payne had not gone to the barracks. Once, she had cried out her dead husband's name in the night. But the rest had gone like a fairy-tale.

He thought of the colonel's remarks regarding promotion.

Might be worth it after all now that he had someone to care about him, a ready-rolled family of his own. He could do a lot worse.

Payne found the colonel sitting alone in a dugout, a half-empty glass of Scotch in his hand. He gestured to the bottle.

"Have one yourself." Payne thought he looked oddly at ease, his features unlined and free of tension.

"Cheers, sir." There was probably no other officer in the corps who would treat him like this.

Jonathan raised the glass. "A week's time, Payne."

"Sir?" He had known it was too good to be true.

"Up the line. First reserve."

Afterwards, Payne thought it had been like hearing a door slam shut.

Captain Wyke covered the field telephone with his hand and said, "Major Vaughan has just reported, sir. The battalion is standing-to."

Jonathan held his watch against one flickering lantern. "I'm coming up. Tell him from me that every man will wear his helmet." He gave a quick smile. "Even Langmaid."

He glanced around the cellar. The reserve position was three miles back from the line, but if German artillery retaliated some of the shells might easily fall here. It was wrong to get too casual about it. About everything. And if the much-vaunted attack failed? He shrugged. Then this battalion would become the front line in a matter of hours.

Harry Payne asked, "Care for a wet, sir?"

Jonathan shook his head. He could just do with a drink, but had seen enough officers who had walked amongst their men stinking of it. Later he would have one. Maybe more than one.

They went out into the cool clammy air. It was half-past

three in the morning. Another twenty minutes and all those guns would open fire. What had Ross said? Three thousand of them?

He clambered down into the command trench, which they had finished only days ago. Anonymous shapes, here and there a glowing cigarette covered by a man's hand. They had to relax while they could.

"Mornin', sir!" That was McCann.

"Cloudy start, sir!" Corporal Geach's unmistakable Yorkshire accent.

It was surprising how well he had managed to get to know these men, or most of them anyway. The extra company Loftus had sent over to him to reinforce the battalion was something quite different: all recruits, straight from their depot. Even their young company commander, Captain Conway, was leading his men into battle for the first time. Two months ago he had been in charge of the marine detachment in a battleship undergoing repairs at Malta.

Jonathan moved his holster slightly and made certain that the respirator haversack was unclipped.

He heard lieutenant Maxted giving orders to his N.C.O.'s, his voice very curt and severe. Nerves, perhaps, or even fear. Maxted had already seen enough in his young life to know what to expect. To dread.

Jonathan started as something tapped on his helmet and again on his shoulders. The next instant a heavy downpour had begun, lashing at the crouching men, beating against the front of the trench, the noise loud and angry in the darkness.

He licked his lips. The rain was not merely uncomfortable, it was dangerous. Voices were cursing and blaspheming along the trench and he heard one of the light machine-guns being covered to protect it.

But the weather, the strain of waiting, and all the other discomforts were forgotten as with a great, unending roar the British artillery opened fire. Men pressed themselves against the streaming trench and covered their ears as the noise continued like one endless explosion. High explosive and shrapnel of every kind and calibre. In the searing red and orange flashes Jonathan consulted his watch again. It was just after ten minutes to four. Right on time, as Ross had said it would be. He forced himself to look at it, to try and estimate the fall of shot and the extent of the barrage. But it was impossible. The clouds which had opened their bellies as if to delay the attack were so low that he could see them glowing brightly in the bombardment. It was like being covered and surrounded by fire.

He became weary with the incredible din, his mind too dulled to grapple with anything. And all the while the rain hissed and rattled down like bullets. The trench was already filling with water, and most of its occupants were soaked to the skin.

When the bombardment stopped, the land over which the troops would have to advance would be so churned up by the heavy shell-fire that they would be slowed down even more by the craters and the mud. He knew this gunfire would be audible even across the Channel in England. Somehow that made it seem even more unreal.

He tried to recall the quiet house and the night she had come to him. She would be at home now, remembering also. How had she explained her visit to London? She had said she had some days off due to her, but it would hardly excuse her absence, and he had no doubt that her father would take a dim view of the truth.

In the letter she had left at the house she had written, *I love you so much, my darling Jonathan. I'll never leave you as long as you need me.* It was like hearing her speak, as they had so often in the nights which had gone so quickly.

The barrage continued without respite, and as the time passed and dawn came the sky remained as dark and threatening as night. Then men clapped their wet hands to their ears as, with one final roar, it all stopped.

Jonathan found himself listening as if he expected to hear the attack. The infantry climbing from the firestep and onto the parapet, the shrill of whistles, the advance into the heavy rain. He could hear the machine-guns now, rattling steadily: their gunners were probably unable to miss.

Independent artillery opened up to the rear and he saw the glowing explosions spurting beyond the German lines.

Wyke called to him, "Brigadier, sir!"

Jonathan took the handset and pressed it to his ear. He had not even heard it buzzing in its case.

"Sir?"

Ross was as crisp as ever. "Attack's begun. First objectives are taken. This bloody rain! If we get the chance to exploit this . . ." He broke off as one huge explosion made the air shiver. Then he continued, "There are two cavalry divisions in reserve. Be ready to move, Jono!"

Jonathan handed over the handset, suddenly sickened at the minds that could still order horses into barbed wire and machine-guns.

If this rain got any heavier the tanks would be helpless to move, but cavalry were certainly not the answer. He thought of the young officer who had saluted him with his sword. Perhaps he was here too. No breastplate and shining helmet, only a hell of mud and wire unlike anything he had ever known.

While Harry Payne held a shaded torch for him he opened his map, even though it was etched onto his brain. Somewhere ahead was Pilckem Ridge and slightly to the right the beginning of the Gheluvelt Plateau. According to the map the front itself was crossed in many places by brooks: they would be rivers of mud if this continued. It would be hard going. Once across the main Menin Road they would divide the attack: Polygon Wood and then Passchendaele. After that, a smart left-wheel and on to the coast.

He thought of the Australian from Perth. *It can't be done.* Now he was out there somewhere in the mud with all the thousands of others. For three miles' gain at the very most.

The field telephone buzzed again. This time it was one of the brigadier's staff officers.

"Whenever you like, Colonel. Bring up your men. The second wave has just gone over. The support trenches are vacant. Good luck." The line went dead.

Jonathan wiped his mouth with the back of his band. On a wall at the Naval and Military Club in London there was a large framed reproduction of a scene at Waterloo: a young, red-coated officer waving his men to the attack. The painting was entitled *The Whole Line Will Advance!* and it had always stirred his imagination as a boy when his father had taken him to the club.

He said sharply, "Pass the word. We're moving up. A Company will lead."

He stared up at the hard, sharp line of the trench they had dug and would now have to abandon. How many more horizons?

Sections, platoons and companies began to trudge forward to find their way into the first line of communication trenches. Men bowed down by their weapons and kit. Men soaked through and caked with mud. Men who splashed through the narrow, uneven earthworks, looking neither right nor left or even at the clouds above them. Sometimes they had almost to crawl to keep below the defences where the sides had fallen away, and in other places the trenches were so deep that any heavy shell could bury them alive.

They had gone only about three miles when they reached the rear support lines, but at every slippery step they were aware of the mounting wrath of battle, rising in massive, separate explosions that deadened even the sharper clatter of rifles and machine-guns.

Another communication trench was reserved for walking wounded being sent back to a dressing station: a different army, bandaged, splinted, and bloody. They were clinging to one another like punch-drunk fighters, but still managed to smoke their cigarettes as they went.

One had got into the wrong trench and was trying to force his way past the oncoming marines.

Someone called, "What's it like, mate?" The hatless soldier did not hear him but struggled on, his eyes staring from deeply-shadowed sockets. Beyond reach and reason.

Sergeant-Major McCann said angrily, "Well, it ain't no bloody picnic, that's pretty obvious!"

Surprisingly, there were those who could still laugh at his sour frustration.

Jonathan walked with some of the H.Q. platoon, and guessed that they were watching him. Reading their own fate in his reactions, perhaps. He thought of the small boy with his father at the club, and wanted to laugh. Or weep.

The whole line will advance!

The support lines of the sector allotted to the Royal Marines were well constructed but had been heavily damaged in an earlier artillery bombardment, and the H.Q. command dugout was like a slum.

An infantry major handed over the position to the marines with almost guilty haste.

"We couldn't dislodge them from the Gheluvelt Plateau." He jabbed the map with his scratched and muddy fingers. "The Jerries will counterattack, so you'll probably be needed in the front line a bit sooner than expected. My lads are being pulled back to rest and eat. I suggest you get your men fed whenever you can."

Everyone ducked as a shell exploded in the air beyond the trench, and they heard splinters and shrapnel smacking into the mud and piled sandbags. The major indicated the remains of a copse or small wood. "German machine-guns there. Lost a lot of men trying to get through the wire. If you take over the front we'll need more wire there too." He sounded doubtful, as if he thought marines unsuitable here.

Jonathan beckoned to Wyke. "Senior officers, *now!*" Then he said, "We'll manage."

He turned to watch as his own men hurried past the dugout, weighed down as before but moving swiftly, aware of the nearness of danger. The air cringed to the shriek of artillery, the sharpest being some French seventy-fives far over to the right.

To Major Vaughan he said, "Light machines here, Ralph. I want the heavier one on our flank. Sentries on the firestep too."

Another shell tore overhead and must have exploded near one of the communication trenches: great clods of earth and tree roots burst into the air and there were muffled cries, probably from some of the troops they had just relieved.

"Hot soup, if you can. More use than rain-soaked food." He looked at McCann's frown of concentration as he wrote in his little book, the way he grinned as he added, "Double ration of grog, too."

When Vaughan returned with two breathless runners Jonathan said abruptly, "Take over, Ralph. I'm going to look over our position." He shook his head as Wyke began to follow. "No. Keep the team together."

Payne pursued him, watching for deep holes or broken lengths of the duckboard that served to keep the trench dry and prevent noise in the night. The light was still more like dusk than day, and the air was filled with drifting smoke and the awful stench of rotting corpses exhumed in the last artillery barrage. Once, Jonathan stood on the firestep and peered at the next line, and the one beyond that. The front line was completely hidden in smoke and torrential rain, and beyond there was only the enemy. He could just make out the Plateau, and the telltale blink of machine-guns. Mud everywhere, corpses and human remains scattered like garbage, or discarded pieces of statuary broken in battle. In one bright flash he thought he saw someone moving, then he looked away, his stomach contracting. Rats, countless numbers of them moving busily amongst this carnage, oblivious as stray bullets sang through the air or ripped into the ground nearby. In a second flash he saw a face staring at him, but it was another corpse, a Tommy trying to get to the rear. Below his belt there was nothing left, and yet he was still able to stare as if he did not believe it.

Sentries leaning against the trench did not turn as he passed. Other men sat in the few remaining dugouts or beneath crude canvas sheets. A dead soldier lay on his back, uncovered, his eyes screwed up at the moment of impact. The rain had almost covered his boots and one arm, which had been trodden into the mud by hurrying infantrymen. A man abandoned by his comrades. Friends were vital in the trenches, but dead men were soon forgotten. They were things, not people.

He reached the sector where Vaughan had placed the new company from the missing Grenville Division. Young, worried faces beneath the steel helmets, eyes blinking with each savage explosion. Their commanding officer, Captain Alton, lifted a hand in salute and then dropped it. "Sorry, sir. My sergeant over there told me not to do that. A giveaway for snipers!"

Jonathan glanced at the sergeant in question and nodded in acknowledgement. The stripes on his muddy sleeves and the assured way he was standing amidst the chaos and the litter of death marked him down as an old sweat. One who would not break, no matter what. But there were precious few like him here.

He asked, "Where's your other machine-gun?"

"I was waiting to be told what . . ."

Jonathan interrupted curtly, "You command this company. Think it out, and *do it!*"

He turned back along the line. God, he thought, I'm beginning to sound just like Beaky Waring.

Harry Payne splashed along behind him, lost in thought and yet aware of the nearness of danger.

He felt the rain running down his spine between his webbing and extra ammunition pouches. It was like ice, which made no sense. A few days ago they had been working in shirtsleeves, sweating even. Payne thought of the house in Southsea, close to the barracks. So warm in his arms, so eager; and with her shyness gone she had wanted only to please him.

He had once thought of setting his cap at her, but he'd never been much of a one for anything serious. She had changed all that. He squinted at the colonel's shoulders as he strode along ahead of him. What about him, he wondered. How serious had it been for him?

Later they sat in the dugout consuming mess tins of soup which was surprisingly hot, although none of them could identify the taste.

More shells were bursting in and over the sector. The ground shook and writhed under the onslaught, but whistles were heard above the barrage. More men were going over the top, out into the torn battlefield and oblivion.

The rain, like the German counterattacks, was unremitting. For two days the enemy tried to regain their lost positions and were fought off. At the front the infantry waited their turn, while in the support trenches the Fifty-First made ready to take over the line.

Jonathan had done what he could to prepare his officers and senior N.C.O.'s. That they would be in action was now beyond doubt. The only doubt was the final outcome.

He had reported to Brigadier Ross and had been told that the delay was over. Losses had been greater than expected, gains fewer than hoped.

Jonathan had asked without cynicism, "How many this time, sir—after two-and-a-half days, I mean?"

Ross had given him that piercing look. He had not tried to lessen the blow, nor had he called him Jono.

"Around thirty thousand, as far as they can tell. More reserves are coming up, but I don't like this weather." A telephone had buzzed, and Jonathan had left him and made his way back to his men.

That night after dark, the Royal Marines moved forward and took over the line.

Alexandra Pitcairn stood by the open kitchen door and watched the rain dripping from the trees and drifting over the garden.

Behind her, her father sat at the table, the London newspaper spread out to catch the light.

"Another big attack, Alex." She said nothing, and he began
to read excerpts to her. "'After a series of daring and undis-
closed tactics, the Second and Fifth Armies, fighting in
appalling conditions, have continued to put pressure on the
enemy's front. The advance began after a bombardment by
our artillery, described as the greatest man-made explosion
ever seen. Troops of the Commonwealth forces are fighting
side by side with persistent gallantry . . .'" He paused and
looked at her shoulders, and her fingers gripping the door
handle. He had not questioned her about her relationship
with Jonathan Blackwood, or what had happened between
them in London. If he had been able, he would have prevented it. But she was not a child; and he was only grateful
that she had told him some of it.

They must be expecting heavy casualties despite the newspapers' optimism, he thought. More huts had been
constructed at Hawks Hill, and he had heard that all hospitals from here to the coast had been warned to prepare to
receive unspecified numbers of wounded. Even at Hawks Hill
they had been told that shell-shock cases and blind patients
would have to take second place.

He looked at the paper again and cleared his throat.

"The G.O.C. has spoken of his pride in these men from
overseas, and has welcomed the additional support of the
Royal Marines under his command."

She gripped the handle so hard she felt it breaking her
skin. She had known, as Jonathan had, even when they had
been so free of care in London during those six precious days,
that such peace and such happiness could not last.

She had lain awake in the quiet nights here, touching her

breasts as he had done. Imagined him gazing down at her: the smile, the hunger, so dear to her. It was the lover she remembered, not the man tortured by experiences she had seen mirrored on the faces of patients at Hawks Hill.

He had written recently with such disturbing longing and passion, untouched by the censor although it angered her to think of some stranger sifting through his words, reading his most secret thoughts and hopes.

And now he was there, with all those others of whom he had spoken so often. And it was raining. He had feared that too.

New casualty lists were appearing daily, and she had forced herself to read every one. She had never forgotten the horror of that moment which had so suddenly changed to joy when the post girl had delivered his telegram. Now, every day, she heard voices around her like ghosts, as other villagers read the lists.

"That's the butcher's son!" or "That's three of them gone in one family!"

She had been there today, standing in the rain, surrounded by the voices. She had broken away from them and whispered fiercely, "Not you, darling Jonathan, *not you!*"

Her father was saying vaguely, "You must try not to worry, dear."

She swung round, her eyes desperate.

"I love him, Daddy! Don't you understand? *I love him!*"

She heard her own despairing cry. Like a small voice in some vast, terrible wilderness.

SEVENTEEN

Overnight the rain had stopped but, Jonathan guessed, only temporarily. At dawn the battalion stood-to below the firestep, wretched in their sodden uniforms and having had no hot food, only bullybeef and lukewarm tea, the latter well laced with rum.

He watched a marine cleaning the mist from a trench periscope before refitting it against the sandbags. It was better than nothing. A more effective gadget had been left behind by the relieved infantry: a large shovel with two holes punched in it for a man's eyes. Caked in mud, it would blend well with the parapet, and make a fair shield to deflect a bullet.

Jonathan climbed onto the firestep and peered through a gap in the sandbags. He could sense the mood of his men, their disgust at the front line, strewn with decomposing bodies and with many more who had dropped to the enemy's fire even as they had responded to the urgent whistles. The stench and the constant reminders of violent death made some of the marines vomit, or stand closer to their companions as if for protection.

The churned-up waste of no man's land grew sharper in his binoculars as he moved them very slowly. There was no sunlight, only clouds, but any observant marksman might see even the smallest movement.

There was their own barbed wire. A few ragged shapes fallen across or into it, in one of the counterattacks, he supposed. There was hardly an open space where men had not been killed or abandoned as beyond aid.

A strange grey light was playing on the shell holes, and the charred stumps of roots that stood out from the mud like horns.

They were trees that had been flung here by the first bombardments.

There were several gaps in the wire. He recalled what the departing major had said about it and the doubt in his voice. He had been right.

The Germans directly opposite them had probably been in the line a long time, and were tough and experienced infantrymen. It would take only a handful of such troops to wriggle through the gaps and fling grenades into this trench. It would have to wait; there was enough to shore up and reconstruct without bothering about the wire for now. Several of the trench walls had completely collapsed, the sandbags just so much sodden debris, and here and there he had seen half-buried bodies, or a pair of boots protruding to mark where a man had been shot or blown up.

He saw some tin cans swaying very slightly in a damp breeze, each containing a few pebbles or pellets. Anyone trying to cut through the barbed wire in the dark would disturb them, and the sound of rattling cans would be enough to alert any sentry.

He shifted the glasses again. Mist or smoke clung to those craters which had earlier erupted like volcanoes, hurling many tons of earth into the air, but he could faintly make out the slight rise in the ground and the black stumps of more trees. That was the enemy's wire. Beyond it was a machine-gun position. Someone had described it as well sited. The mud-covered corpses were evidence of that. Immune to rifle fire, and too close to the British front line to call down artillery support, it could best be taken in a night attack. But first, through their own wire.

Major Vaughan climbed up beside him, catlike for so big a man.

"Pig of a place, sir."

"Where no birds sing."

"Sir?" Vaughan glanced at him curiously.

Jonathan gripped his glasses tightly. He saw something move, only for a second: the pale shape of a face, alive amidst all this carnage, under one of their heavy-looking helmets. Studying his enemy. The start of another day.

"Fritz is up and about, Ralph."

Vaughan said uneasily, "Well, the wind's still in our favour. No gas." He wiped his mouth with a dirty handkerchief. "It might carry some of the stench away. I couldn't even do justice to a steak-and-kidney pie with all this filth about!"

An anonymous voice called, "I could, sir! Just try me!"

Jonathan moved away from the observation hole. Holding together. Trying not to show fear. More testing than fear itself.

Somewhere behind the lines the artillery commenced its morning bombardment. He hoped that communications and powers of observation were better than at Gallipoli, where ships had shelled their own troops. What was the target? Surely not Passchendaele? Any news that came from there told only of stalemate, bloody advances and even bloodier counterattacks for just a few yards. The Germans retained the Gheluvelt Plateau, and despite constant attempts to dislodge them had held their line.

Jonathan considered the state of the immediate front: a place so full of craters and mud that even if they reached the enemy's front line troops would be further hampered by the havoc caused originally by their own artillery.

He climbed down into the trench. "We'll need a wiring party tonight, Ralph." He saw Wyke watching them and thought suddenly of Livesay as Vaughan asked, "Volunteers, sir?"

Perhaps Vaughan and Livesay had learned their trade together.

He shook his head. "One section should be enough. The companies in the line will need to rest. Better select men from our H.Q. platoon. Maxted will be the best guide." He touched the major's wet sleeve. "They'll only get jittery if they think it's so important that it needs the second-in-command to organise it." He realised suddenly that Vaughan had been thinking just that, and that he might be asked to go out there with them.

At least it should be a lot safer than at Gallipoli. There, the ground had been so hard on their front that it had been impossible to move without making a noise.

All the same, most of these men were untested by close combat, and it was no joke to stand out in no man's land and be prepared to remain stock-still if an enemy flare or star shell burst overhead.

Vaughan was saying, "There'll have to be an officer, sir."

"Ask Maxted. They're his people."

Machine-guns chattered into action from below the ridge. The combination of mist and smoke concealed even the flashes. But the bullets were here right enough, cracking into stones and spurting mud into the trench. As the invisible guns traversed on their fixed arcs, the bullets hummed so closely overhead that it seemed the gunners could see their target. The marines on the firestep pressed themselves into the earth, fingers gripping their rifles, their soaking, muddy figures becoming a part of the slime and filth of battle.

Soon afterwards German heavy artillery opened up, hurling shells in high trajectory to fall with enormous vibrations, which were more a sensation than sound.

Maxted appeared. "From Brigade, sir!" He stared at the collapsed trench, the protruding boot. "The enemy's bombarding the support lines. The reserve troops are getting the worst of it, and a supply column too!"

So the brigadier had already guessed. A mostly untested battalion in the line, the supply and reserve infantry bogged down in a heavy bombardment. It meant only one thing: the enemy would attack.

Jonathan said, "Warn all positions. Machine-guns under cover until the last moment. Ralph, have more ammunition brought up." He saw each word striking home like a fist.

"Now, sir?"

Jonathan had already turned away. "We'll need grenades." He could feel his words going along the line of men nearest to him. He did not need to see their faces.

Old Blackie says the bastards are coming! We'll kick their arses for them!

The new men fiddled with their clips of bullets; the older hands felt for their vicious trench knives or handmade cudgels. A few had even ground their entrenching tools so that they were razor sharp and lethal.

Jonathan saw Harry Payne frowning as he checked his rifle and opened one of his pouches, remembering how Payne had broken all the rules and gone out into no man's land at the Dardanelles, just for his sake. He could feel the pressure of the long Turkish knife right now in his boot. Very deliberately he took out his pipe and gripped it in his teeth. It was too damp to fill and light even if he had wanted to. It was only an act. For all of them.

"How'll they come, Sarge?" Nervous, unsure.

Then Sergeant Timbrell's harsh Cockney voice. "Well, they're bleedin' Germans, ain't they? They're bound to 'ave a bloody brass band leadin' them across!"

Jonathan climbed onto the firestep again. The enemy guns were firing higher now. Another bluff, to convince them it was too dangerous to show their faces over the parapet. He swallowed hard to moisten his mouth. "Pass the word, Sergeant-Major. *Fix bayonets!*"

He wiped his binoculars with an already damp piece of cotton four-by-two. They kept misting up in this wet, lifeless air.

Payne murmured, "You watch yourself, Colonel."

Jonathan looked down at him and smiled. "You too."

Then he was pressed against the same observation hole, cursing the mist and trying to recover his bearings.

He saw the sloping ground and dead trees, but there was a difference. Not mist this time. Men. Hundreds of them, coming out of the wire, hunched and moving in long crouching lines.

He shouted to Vaughan, *"Stand-to!"* He blew sharply on his whistle and heard it repeated along the twisting trench. *"Here they come!"*

He found that he had drawn his revolver. There was not much point, if they got near enough to lob their grenades; it was only an automatic reaction. A machine-gun was firing from the left front, bullets scything over the parapet like maddened hornets.

The enemy soldiers were loping forward, bayonets quite grey in this strange light. He even found time to notice that they were not burdened by unnecessary kit, so confident were they that they would overwhelm this trench or live long enough to retire to their own lines.

He watched them weaving about, some falling headlong as if hit by soundless bullets. But it was the other enemy, mud, which had dragged them down. It might warn his own men what to expect. He saw the light machine-guns with their wheel-shaped magazines wavering slightly while the marines tested the range and waited for the order. The bigger machine-guns he could not see from this command position, but he guessed that Bert Langmaid and his mates were also waiting with cold anticipation.

The German infantry were shouting to one another, and he saw a great mass of them swerve towards the gap in the English wire. Men caught midway through the wire were easy targets as the dangling, scarecrow figures there had already demonstrated.

Jonathan moistened his whistle with his lips but they were like dust. On either side he saw the bayoneted rifles waver and guessed what some of his young marines were thinking. A few shots banged out; some of the Germans were firing from the hip even as they stumbled over the pitted ground, but nobody moved.

Seventy-five yards, fifty yards. *Dear God, let it work!*

The whistle's blast brought instant response as rifles and light machine-guns ripped into the oncoming infantry, so that those halfway through the gap in the wire slowed down and peered round for alternatives. From either flank the heavy machine-guns opened fire with deadly effect. The gaps were filled with falling men, and heaving piles of bodies as others trampled them down in an effort to escape the well-sited guns. One running soldier paused and raised his arm, and prepared to hurl a grenade at the marines' nearest length of trench. Then he seemed to pivot round before dropping to his knees in the mud, his mouth making a black, terrified hole in his face just seconds before his grenade exploded beside him. It cut down a handful of men, and their cries were lost in the insane clamour of weapons.

Two more grenades reached the parapet and Jonathan heard shots and then weak screams as they exploded, mercifully outside the trench.

"*Cease firing!*" Jonathan thrust his revolver back into its holster as like a tide broken on the beach the enemy began to recede. There was firing here and there, but they were eager to reach safety beyond the wire, so that their own line could rake the British defence and force their heads down.

He heard men gasping for air as they wedged fresh clips into their rifles, or slammed magazines and belts of ammunition into the machine-guns.

Vaughan said harshly, "Determined bastards!" He too was breathing fast and heavily. "The gaps in our wire were some help after all!"

"Only in daylight, Ralph." He glanced round as Wyke called, "Four casualties, sir. One of them dead, Private Ellerman, and another going fast!"

"See what you can do for them. But there's bound to be artillery brought into it, so the wounded will have to wait until darkness before we send them back." He knew it sounded hard, callous to some of the new men, but all he must think of was what they had just done. They had repulsed a German attack, probably of company strength, with more waiting in reserve in case they had managed to bomb the front-line trench.

The rain had begun again and he heard Harry Payne murmur, "Oh, sod it!" Jonathan watched two men carrying a stretcher past the dugout, blood-soaked canvas draped over it. They saw McCann and one asked, "Where do we put 'im, Sar' Major?"

McCann retorted brutally, "Tip 'im over the back. No time for a state funeral just now!"

Jonathan knew what those close enough to hear would think, the youngsters anyway. McCann was good, damned good, but here, as on any barracks square, the sergeant-major was rarely seen as a friend.

Another bombardment made the yellow water in the puddles and shell holes quiver as if it was being boiled from
below. More guns joined in from either side. The Germans
were trying to find the supply column again and maybe the
promised reserves. The British gunners were trying to crush
any more attacks before they could begin.

Hot soup was coming from somewhere, hunks of half-
stale bread packed with bullybeef and mustard. The marines'
jaws worked on it busily, their tired eyes and stubbled chins
so much at odds with their habitual smartness, something
highly prized in the corps.

The corpse of Private Ellerman sprawled over the rear of
the trench, his clothing in bloody tatters where the grenade
had riddled him with splinters, with all the others who had
died here over the days, the weeks and the months. A man
or a good mate to a *thing,* and now just another liability to be
endured.

Two more marines were to fall, but the constant bombardment seemed to have beaten the men of both front lines
into a kind of dulled torpor. The two marines had been hit by
well-aimed solitary shots. A sniper somewhere, watching for
a careless moment, a face or shoulder showing just seconds
above the parapet, the sandbags and makeshift defences they
had built from fallen trees and piles of what had once been
the bricks of a small village here.

Jonathan ordered his men to stand down, and the sentries
to be careful of their own safety.

He sat in the command dugout with the map outspread
on an old packing case, and wondered when the enemy would
strike next, and where. Vaughan was struggling with a tough
hunk of bread, and he was sharing a mug of tea and rum with
Lieutenant Maxted. Even down here they could hear the
screams and anguished moans from the wire, where so many

of the German infantry had been abandoned. There was nothing anyone could do for them, even if somebody was crazy enough to crawl out and try to help. It was more than likely that he would soon become one of the dead.

Sergeant Timbrell ducked through the rough curtain and handed Maxted a small bag.

Maxted looked at him without understanding and the sergeant said dully, "Personal belongings and identity tags, sir. An' a few francs."

Vaughan said, "Put them in the book. There may be time to send letters to . . ." He did not go on.

Timbrell said, "I've detailed the section to draw their gear at sunset, sir." He had to repeat it before Maxted looked up at him again.

"Oh, good. Thanks."

Jonathan said, "Are you in charge tonight, Sergeant?"

He replied, "Yessir. I done it before. We won't let you down—they're all good marines."

Jonathan indicated the earthenware jug. "Have a tot." He watched the foxy-faced sergeant as he poured a full measure of rum into an unwashed cup. Anything was better than just sitting, listening to the distant roar of guns. Some were probably Captain Alton's great howitzers, hurling their challenge with all the others. How could men stand it? How many had sat here or in miserable holes like it and listened to the relentless thunder, always expecting a box barrage to move over and then fix upon their particular part of the defence line? At the other end of the trench and behind them in the next support line, men were already unable to lie down except on the firestep. Water was knee-deep in places, and the rain showed no sign of stopping.

If only there was somewhere he could find solitude, even

for a few minutes, so that he could read a few lines of her letters.

Maxted said sharply, "I'd like to take charge tonight, sir." He stared at the sergeant. "I don't see why you should take all the risks!"

Jonathan put the letters to the back of his mind. "I thought you already had an officer?"

Timbrell looked down at the jug. "Mister Rooke, sir." He made another effort. "I 'spect 'e'll be up to it, sir."

Jonathan watched them gravely. *Rooke would not be missed* was closer to the truth.

Like an intrusion they heard Rooke's petulant voice as he snapped, "I don't care what you've done, *Private* Vickers! Just follow my example and do as you're told!"

Timbrell scowled and turned to leave but Maxted said evenly, "Have your rum, Sergeant, if the Colonel doesn't object."

Outside in the steady downpour Maxted found the subaltern, hands on his hips, glaring at the marine in question.

"Over here," he said. The pain was devouring him, and he knew why he had just volunteered to take charge of the wiring party. It had been wrong; he knew that. Others would suffer because of it.

"Sir?" Rooke squelched across the mud and sagging duckboards. "Is everything all right?"

Maxted found that he hated this pompous, self-satisfied little prig who would one day be a general. Upbringing and influence. Unbeatable. He asked quietly, "Must you always try to make the men look like peasants? Vickers is a good man. Brave too."

Rooke gave a small smile. His complaint to the adjutant had obviously worked. Maxted was almost subdued.

"There *are* standards, sir."

Maxted stared up at the sky, the rain cleansing his desperation and his anger. "Remember what I told you. Or you might get yourself shot in the back!"

Rooke gaped at him. It was not what he had expected. "Shoot *me*?" He sounded outraged. "An officer?"

Maxted gave him a contemptuous glance. "In their place, I think *I* would!" He lowered himself into the dugout and sat down, rain making puddles around his boots.

Vaughan said uneasily, "Well, I suppose he's got to learn sometime."

Sergeant Timbrell picked up his rifle and gave his lieutenant a quick smile. "Thanks, sir."

Maxted stared emptily at the curtain after Timbrell had departed. *Thanks.* So simply said. And for what? For allowing them all to be killed, to die decently like the corpses they had tipped over the parapet?

While I pay a much higher price even than death . . .

Sergeant Ned Timbrell climbed carefully up and onto the parapet, every sense and nerve straining to detect danger. It was like being suddenly naked, alone in this terrible place, without cover and completely vulnerable. He could feel the rest of the wiring party moving to the parapet, doubtless ready to drop out of sight if he were suddenly shot down by a sniper. He could still taste the rum on his tongue and wondered if it might be his last. He made himself stand quite still, his ears and mind reaching out like signals from a wireless set.

It might conceal their movements and hide any unexpected sounds, but the unending chorus of groans and pitiful whimpering from the German wounded and dying grated on his nerves. They seemed not only men who had fallen in the attack through the wire but all those others who lay dead in the mud, becoming a part of the ground they had once fought over.

Timbrell pushed the mysterious caller at the base camp from his mind. It could not matter now. One lapse and they might all be lying with the rest in this haunted place.

He bent over. "Ready!" He did not call him *sir,* even though he guessed that the subaltern was close by in the darkness. Sod him, he thought.

It was strange about Maxted. Always a cool one under fire, and ready to help anyone who needed it. He was growing more moody and intolerant by the hour and Timbrell guessed that the adjutant had noticed it as well. He said hoarsely, "Up you get, you layabouts!"

They climbed out of the trench where their comrades were already in position, ready to cover their return if the worst happened. Timbrell picked out each man, everyone a black shadow; but to him they could have been lit by torches.

Corporal Geach was almost the last. "Hey-oop, Sarge! The rain's stopped!" Then finally came the second lieutenant, peering round like a terrier after a rat. If he were a dog there would be plenty of things to hunt out here, Timbrell thought.

"Sir?"

Rooke touched his mouth with his hand. "You just carry on, Sergeant."

Timbrell drew a deep breath. *What they all say.*

They gathered around him so that he could speak in a whisper.

"We go through the wire at the two main gaps. We'll withdraw after we've done the wirin'. Nothin' fancy. Just like I told you. Corporal Geach and I will mark the gaps with white tape. Don't want to lose any of you, eh?" Nobody even grinned.

They began to move away from the trench. Only three of

them were armed with their rifles, with every loose piece of gear on the weapons from piling-swivel to webbing sling laced and taped tightly into place. There was less chance of them making a noise with these precautions. The drums of barbed wire were carried by two pairs of men, with a stout spar through the middle and leather gloves to offer some protection.

As they crept and slithered closer to the wire, the sounds of men in agony became louder and more insistent. It was unnerving. From time to time there was a shrill cry as one of the marines trod on what he had thought to be a corpse. Once a German soldier reared up on his buttocks, hands clawing at their clothing as they stumbled past.

Timbrell thought savagely, it could be us. Could be us!

A corpse pirouetted like a ragged puppet as if to watch them pass. He must have been there since the wire was originally laid out. Not enough flesh or bones left to hold the thing in position.

Timbrell peered round for Geach, but with his party he had already been swallowed up in the darkness. Timbrell halted and stared ahead. There were fewer groans out here. He shivered despite his toughness. Nothing between them and the Germans except their own wire somewhere ahead. Very carefully he cut a strip of white tape with his trench knife and knotted it around a metal staple where the gap began. Cut by an enemy patrol or blasted away by artillery, it had probably been severed so many times that it no longer really mattered.

Something bumped into him. It was Vickers. "Sorry, Sarge." Timbrell nearly laughed. Such politeness amongst this hell. Like Old Bill.

"Get on with it." He could rely on these men. By sounds alone he could feel their purpose as they got busy with pliers and crowbars, while those with the drum of wire wove this way and that. The barbs seemed incredibly loud as the first long strand was paid out, but from experience Timbrell knew that the noise would be lost out here. Like being in a boat and attempting to board a darkened vessel at night. Every movement, even the sound of the rudder, was like a thunderclap.

Second Lieutenant Rooke said curtly, "I'll see how Geach is getting on. It's all taking too long."

Timbrell bit his lip. "I'd think again 'bout that, sir." His wiring party were hunched in the midst of it like dumb beasts, probably listening, cursing the officer for wasting time.

"Now look here, Sergeant . . ."

Timbrell hissed, *"Still!"* This was the first real test.

The flare exploded some way off to the right, probably in the sector where their line linked up with the Royal Warwicks. But the Germans had often used flares before, piece by piece along the length and breadth of no man's land.

Timbrell glanced at his men, shining so brightly even at this range that it seemed impossible they could not be seen. The same searing brightness illuminated the cratered land beyond and around them, the gaping corpses and the bright-eyed rats. Even the great coils of cruel wire held a kind of beauty.

Timbrell was aware for the first time of something which he had thought had no place here. It was pride. Pride for these men he had helped to train, whom he had chased and bullied where necessary, and had allowed to buy him a beer when the worst of it was over.

After an eternity the flare faded and died away. It took far longer to accustom their eyes to the all-engulfing blackness that followed.

Private Vickers said, "Hey, Sarge, he's buggered off!" He sounded amazed.

"Good riddance, and you never 'eard me say that, see?"

Another flare fit the scene and Timbrell saw a wounded soldier staring up at him, his eyes like stars in the drifting flare. Timbrell saw the gaping wounds, black in the glacier light. How could a man still be alive? Man? He was just a boy, like young Barlow had been.

Timbrell whispered, "Die! Why can't you die?"

The boy's mouth opened and closed but he did not speak, nor could he probably. But one hand lifted very slowly as if it were part of someone else and tried to seize Timbrell's sodden tunic. Then just as suddenly it fell back into the mud. Only the pleading eyes remained before the flare faded away.

"Keep at it, lads!" He saw them pulling at the wire; they knew what he was going to do. They had all seen what they were not supposed to see. Not an enemy soldier, but a horribly mutilated boy who was refusing to die.

Timbrell knelt down and put his hand on the inert shape. *Rules of war.* Not out here, there bloody weren't. He felt the shoulder jerk only feebly as he drove his trench knife into him, ending it.

He trudged back with the wiring party. The drums were almost empty. It did not seem possible. He turned back as if he expected to see him there. Why should it bloody matter? He was a Jerry, like all these sprawled in the darkness, gasping, crying out for help which would never come. Timbrell shook his head. But for some reason it did matter. Aloud he muttered, "Leastways it does to me!"

Dark shapes were standing amidst the few remaining bricks of this unknown village. Instinct told him it was Geach and his party.

Vickers said wearily, "Beat us to it, Sarge!"

But Timbrell was staring round, suddenly anxious.

"Where's that soddin' officer?" There were no medals for losing even a second lieutenant.

"*Still!*" As the flare burst high over the wire a machine-gun began to chatter from the enemy line. Once again Timbrell felt the same strength of pride at the courage and sheer guts of his men. Not much farther. Twenty yards at the most. Then helping hands, slaps on the back and mugs of rum for all of them. He moved his head very slowly and felt his hair rising on his neck as one of the corpses stood up suddenly amidst the sprawling tangle of wire.

Someone said in a fierce whisper, "Jesus, it's him, Sarge!"

It couldn't be. In the same instant Timbrell knew that it was. Then it came to him. Rooke had not gone to find Geach. *It's all taking too long.* He had found himself a place to hide.

Unknowingly, the wiring party had passed him in the darkness and had sealed him inside this barbed metal trap.

"Get me out of here!"

Timbrell tried to think clearly. One stupid move, and that machine-gunner and then all the others would be turning them over like a reaper in a field. He moved as quickly as he could to Geach. "Take them back, Corporal!"

Geach peered at him. "Not likely, Sarge! What do you take me for?"

"Do as I say, *now!*" He added heavily, "They'll be on us in a minute."

He froze as Rooke's voice echoed shrilly over the ground. "That's an order, Sergeant!"

Geach exclaimed, "Well, I'll go to the foot of our stairs!" Then he said, "I've got it, Sarge." To the others he called, "Single file you lead, Jury!"

Timbrell watched them melt away. All but one. It was Vickers.

"Nothing you can do." He slipped and fell across something stinking and rotten, but Vickers dragged him to his feet and said, "See? Can't manage without me!"

It was like a new nightmare. The pair of them rigid as if on parade, their legs slowly sinking into the ooze and filth, while Rooke peered through the wire at them, gripping a length of it, his eyes wide with mounting terror.

Timbrell was astonished as he listened to his own voice. Inhumanly calm and patient, when every fibre was screaming for him to turn and run after the other:.

"You'll be all right, sir. But we can't do nothin' now. Stay under cover till we can get to you." He winced as Rooke began to scream, "Don't you dare to leave me! *I'll see you shot!*"

Timbrell looked up at the black clouds. At any second they would pop off another flare. Then the guns would start up.

Surprisingly, it was Vickers who said, "We need the proper wire cutters. Our tools are for bending and shaping the bloody stuff. Remember? You were telling me how to do my job."

"That's enough." Timbrell backed slowly away from the wire. Geach would be in the trench by now, and even the colonel would know what the hell was going on.

"Come back!" Rooke must have dragged at the wire with sudden desperation because several of the little tins jangled noisily, so that even the dead and wounded seemed to be listening.

"Bloody fool!" Timbrell and his companion began to stumble back towards the invisible trench, everything gone from their minds but escape. The flare seemed to explode directly above them, but for several long seconds nothing happened. Timbrell saw men rising from the parapet to help them and heard Rooke's screams grow wilder until the guns opened

fire, traversing back and forth, no doubt expecting to catch a whole section of men out in the open.

They were almost into the trench when Vickers gave a sharp cry and fell down amongst the others. Timbrell followed him and tried to hold his limbs still as Vickers reached out for him, like the kid had done. He was actually grinning. Before he fainted all he said was, "Blighty one, Sarge!"

At dawn, Rooke's riddled corpse was still hanging on the wire.

Alexandra Pitcairn climbed the steps to the main entrance of Hawks Hill and thrust open the door. Even inside the reception area it felt cold and damp and she could see her breath hanging in the air like steam. In the village they were all saying it was the worst September they could remember. It was unbelievable to think it would be October in only a week's time. People talked about Christmas, but few were looking forward to it. Rationing and the shortages of even simple items were bad enough, but the deteriorating weather made it a poor outlook.

The duty sergeant smiled at her, "Bit parky, miss." Then he said, "Old Jack Swan wanted me to tell him if you dropped in. I'll have one of my lads find him for you."

She sat down in a high-backed porter's chair, one of the few original furnishings in this part of the house. Even the worn leather felt damp through her coat. She unbuttoned it slowly. It was past its best, but like her long boots it was an old friend, and even if a new coat were available it would be no match for a Hampshire winter like this one was.

She had heard her father discussing the need for further medical accommodation for the endless tide of wounded men from the Western Front. All the military and naval hospitals had long since been filled to overflowing, as were the large civilian hospitals in the southern counties. But it was still not enough.

More long huts had been constructed by the army here, and some of those which had originally been intended for rest and recuperation from operations elsewhere were now transformed into surgical wards.

She thought of her own patients. All of them had been sent to other places, many of them to the north of England. How must it be for these young, sightless survivors from the war who had just begun to recover their faith and hope, to be suddenly shifted elsewhere? They would know no one, and be very aware of the strangeness, the different dialects and accents. It would be like starting all over again. She had still not decided what she herself should do. She helped her father whenever she could, but he seemed troubled and at times distant. He asked her little about Jonathan; perhaps he was indifferent, or too depressed by his own work to care.

Jonathan wrote whenever he could, but the post was irregular and the letters usually came in packets. Enemy action in the Channel and North Sea had cut down sea passages or ensured that the vessels were used for more urgent cargoes.

She had read every letter several times, and ached to know what he was doing and where he was. She had sent him a photograph of herself with a lock of her hair in the folding case, and she wondered if he had received it safely. Her own letters, now written freely and without reserve, would draw them closer across the miles.

She recalled the August evening when she had heard the guns as she walked up towards the copse: like a distant thunder below the horizon. The Western Front had suddenly touched her even at Hawks Hill.

She stood up abruptly and walked to the fire, staring at

herself in the unpolished mirror over the mantel. She wrinkled her nose at her reflection. Her hair was all anyhow after the mist and rain outside and the scarf, with which she had covered it.

I look a real sight.

Behind her the orderly sergeant was sitting at his desk, apparently reading a newspaper, but she knew he was watching her. She smiled to herself. What would he think if he really knew?

"Here he is, miss."

She turned, startled by his voice. As if he had read her thoughts, or she had spoken them aloud.

"Hello, Mr Swan." They shook hands. She never called him Jack in front of the military intruders, as he referred to them. It might take away his last piece of authority.

Together they walked down the familiar passageway, but the notice was no longer on the door of the little ward where she had helped men to see words once more in their broken minds. It merely stated *No entry without escort,* and she wondered what terrible injuries lay concealed there.

There was nobody about, and Jack Swan stopped by a side door. "I don't know if I'm doing the right thing, miss. Now that you're here I'm not so sure."

She clutched his arm. "Tell me. Is it about the Colonel?"

"Bless you, no, miss. But . . ." His eyes moved along the passageway and his face was troubled. "Only found out by accident. You know the rules here." He made up his mind. "In one of the new wards there's an officer from the R.M.L.I." He saw her frowning. She did not understand. "The Fifty-First, miss."

"Jonathan's battalion."

"Yes, miss. I did manage to see him myself. To make certain . . ." He did not elaborate, and he could see he had no need to. "But I said nothing about you, of course."

By the time they reached one of the new wooden wards she was shaking as though with cold, but she knew it was something more than that. Once through the door, and then another where an army nursing sister sat at a table sipping tea, it was no longer a part of Hawks Hill. It had become a hospital.

The sister smiled at her. "Of course I know you, miss Pitcairn. Your father, too."

Swan said, "Lieutenant John Hunter, Sister. Is he well enough to talk?"

She looked at the girl in the shabby green coat. "A friend of yours, perhaps?" She did not press the point. "He's still sedated—they removed several splinters from his body. But with luck he should be all right. He's a hardy young man."

Swan said stoutly, "He's a Royal Marine!"

Alexandra heard nothing of the exchange. She was thinking of the terrible scars on Jonathan's back, recalling how he had almost broken down when she had stroked them.

The sister glanced at her little watch. "I can give you five minutes. The M.O. and matron are doing their rounds shortly."

Swan saw how visibly she was bracing herself, the tanned hands clenched into fists so tightly that the knuckles were bleached.

"I'll be here, miss. Case you needs me."

The sister led the way between the beds. The light was hard and bright as it came through some of the windows, more like a cold dawn than nearly dusk. She bent over the bed to one side.

"A visitor, Lieutenant Hunter." Then she pulled out a stool and said in an undertone to the girl, "Not too long now."

The lieutenant had very fair hair, almost white in the hard sunlight.

"I don't want to trouble you," Alex said. He was staring at her as if she had dropped suddenly from the sky. "I wanted to ask you about somebody." She was already out of her depth. "In your battalion."

She saw his eyes cloud over, and something like fear looked out at her.

"I—I may not have seen . . . There were so many, you understand—"He seemed to sense her desperation. "I might not even know him."

She took his hand in hers and said, "Lieutenant-Colonel Blackwood. I have to know. Is he all right?" She wondered how she had managed to say it, and did not see the relief flooding into his face.

"Oh, gosh," he said boyishly, "The colonel!" and blushed. "Yes, he's fine. *Was* anyway, when I picked up this basin of Krupp steel."

He was safe. He was safe. She realised that the patient in the bed opposite was watching them, smiling as if he knew what she had come about.

"There was a terrible battle." She felt his fingers move inside her hand, like frightened creatures trying to escape. "It went on for days. I don't know how many men we lost, let alone on the whole front." He stared at her and then whispered, "Don't they *know* in England, miss? It's like a slaughterhouse over there."

She squeezed his hand to reassure him. There were so many things she wanted to ask, but rounds were about to begin, and his voice was becoming slurred with drugs and exhaustion.

"May I come again? I work here sometimes." But he was

asleep, his face, like the hand in hers, that of a young boy.

She stood up and smiled at the man in the opposite bed.

An orderly was coming along the ward, but he stopped motionless as he saw the expression of horror on her face. The man's smile had not moved. Nor would it ever again.

She walked quickly from the ward. *Don't they know in England? It's like a slaughterhouse.*

At the door she turned and forced herself to look back. Curtains had been drawn around the bed to hide the terrible smile. There would be another occupant there tomorrow.

Swan seemed quite shocked when she returned to him.

"Why, miss, you're crying! I should never have . . ."

"No, Jack, you did the right thing." Outside the air was like a knife, and she felt herself shivering. She said quietly, "Somebody should cry. For all of them."

EIGHTEEN

Captain Christopher Wyke sat on an empty ammunition case and watched with tired interest as his colonel completed a careful shave. The water was cold, and he thought how painful each stroke of the razor must have been.

Jonathan wiped his face and throat with a towel which was none too clean, and felt more alive and alert. He had been told to report to the brigadier yet again. What this time? Another desperate attack before the weather stopped any hope of success?

The battalion was in the reserve trenches, or what remained of them. The walls had collapsed as soon as they tried to shore them up again. It was like hacking through solid mud. The little *beeks* or brooks that crisscrossed this part of the front had, as expected, swollen in the torrential rain to become rushing rivers and spread across the pockmarked battlefield, turning it into one huge morass. It was now a constant danger, a risk even to try and move across it, let alone force an advance.

From every sector the news was the same. Tanks were bogged down and useless, like stranded whales. Wounded men drowned in it; mules, guns and limbers vanished as if they had never been. And all the while, the rain fell in torrents, and icy winds swept through the waterlogged trenches where soldiers and marines alike shivered, often knee-deep in mud.

Secretly, Jonathan knew that the offensive should have been halted, at least until the weather improved. It was what they had said last year too. But they had not waited, and by the end of the August offensive the casualties had already risen to more than 80,000.

The Belgian coast, the original goal, had been just over thirty miles away when they had started. The whole advance had probably captured three miles of that, and nobody really believed any more that the plan was going to work. He listened to the distant *crump-crump-crump* of an anti-aircraft battery. Probably trying to shoot down a German reconnaissance aeroplane, not that there was much left to see or photograph from the air. The front line was now some four miles from Passchendaele where the Canadians were fighting to hold what they had gained, as were the Australians at Polygon Wood.

The Fifty-First battalion had taken part in the last advance at Broodseinde. At the beginning they had been held in reserve, then later they had been ordered to make a diversionary attack to divide the enemy's defences. It had been

unfortunate that the weight of the enemy's immediate counterattack had fallen on Captain Conway's company of raw
recruits.

There had been no real line left to defend, and attacker
and defender had fought hand to hand, with knife, bayonet
and grenade, often disappearing completely in shell holes
brimmed with rainwater. By the time reinforcements had
struggled up from the reserve trenches more than two hundred marines, including Captain Conway, had fallen.

Place-names meant nothing any more, and the maps with
their ranges and plotted fortifications could have been from
another war entirely. Jonathan had become very aware of the
mood of his men. There was no longer much sign of fear,
except during one gas attack, but that had changed to insane
cheering when the wind, perverse as ever, had veered to drive
the deadly clouds back over their attackers.

He sensed the closeness as well as the bitterness, as each
day was followed by another. They no longer spoke of the
next leave, and time had shrunk to tomorrow and no further.
Everything was shared, even the pathetic possessions of someone who had just been killed. In other times, impossible to
believe now, they would have saved them or sent them home
to the family of the deceased. Now when a man's body was
disposed of, his only memory became a bar of chocolate, a
few cigarettes, and maybe a watch.

The Germans still held the higher ground, and had taken
to using carefully timed shells that exploded directly above a
trench or a wiring party out in the open. When that happened there was no body to bury, no belongings to pass
around. It was oblivion.

Sometimes the mail got through; sometimes it did not.
But Alexandra's photograph with the lock of hair arrived in
perfect condition. Jonathan had seen men break down, col-

lapse completely merely from looking too long at such pho-
tographs, reminders of a world most of them now believed
was gone forever.

In the reserve trenches there were still a few dugouts
where men could hide, eat and sleep. In one of them Jonathan
had held that particular letter to a candle while Vaughan and
Wyke had leaned against one another, their greatcoats stiff
with clay, their gloved hands thrust into their pockets in an
attempt to find warmth.

*My darling Jonathan . . . At Hawks Hill it is raining now. When
that happens I pray for you. May God keep you safe. . . . I feel so
selfish, for I want you all to myself. To offer myself to you and none
other, to have you take me as your need demands. For that is how I
want it to be, forever . . .*

Jonathan glanced around for his trench coat. It was still
raining. He recalled exactly when the first heavy drops had
fallen on his helmet, and then on his shoulders. They should
have known then that there was no more hope. He stood
up and watched Harry Payne cleaning his razor and shaving
mug as if he were in the barracks, or on the China Station.
Perhaps that was what made the marines different from
the others. Routine, the comradeship born in cramped ships'
mess-decks; whatever it was, it was right here in bloody Flanders.

He and Wyke had seen some infantry returning from their
rest periods behind the lines: they seemed to have no such
talisman. Faces like masks, eyes sunken with fear, they had
gone marching up the tracks, the duckboards and finally in
the mud. Then they were nothing, merely a part of the whole,
like the blackened trees and the abandoned, flooded trenches.

Wyke said suddenly, "I think Lieutenant Maxted is ill, sir.
I offered to send him back to the dressing station but . . ."

Jonathan looked at him. "Well, it's too late now. Three

days' rest." He waved one hand around the filthy, dripping dugout, "In these palatial quarters. So we'll be on the move fairly soon."

There was an edge to his voice. "I need every available officer right?"

Wyke nodded. "Right."

Harry Payne waited to catch him by the anti-gas curtain. "No Scotch left, Colonel." He sounded as if he had been betrayed. "Managed to get some Froggie cognac from the Sussex Rifles."

Jonathan grabbed his wet sleeve. "You are a bloody marvel." He turned up his collar and listened to the rain hissing into the trench. A mouth organ was playing plaintively from somewhere along the line and he remembered the wounded soldiers by the Savoy Hotel.

I don't want to die! I just want to go home!

He stopped suddenly and thought of her beside him in the little restaurant. He had hoped she would like it; it had been small, intimate, friendly, and they had treated her like a princess. It had been wonderful to see the pleasure in her eyes, which had been shy and uncertain.

He heard Payne sloshing along behind him, lost in thoughts of his own. The mouth organ pursued them.

Don't want to go to the trenches no more
Where whizzbangs and shrapnel they whistle and roar
Take me over the sea where the Alley-man can't get at me . . .

"All right, sir?"

Jonathan turned and looked at him. "Sorry. I was somewhere else." The air cringed to a tremendous explosion. A long way off, but it made wet earth and stones splash down beside their boots. Then he said very steadily, "It's such a bloody *waste*. But they can still sing and yarn about it."

Payne held his breath, not daring to interrupt. The colonel was speaking to her, not him.

Jonathan took out his briar pipe. "I once thought I would be afraid. But I have something stronger now . . ."

He turned back into the rain and Payne did not hear the rest of it. Payne had not had an easy life, and he had built a shell around himself so that he would be neither shocked nor hurt. He had thought he could never be moved by anything ever again. He was wrong.

It was midafternoon when Jonathan eventually returned from Brigade H.Q., slowed down by a sudden bombardment across a stretch of torn land where two villages had once lain astride the Menin Road. The road had led directly to Ypres, or "Wipers" as the Tommies had nicknamed it. Now there was nothing left to distinguish it from the rest of the battlefield. With Payne close on his heels he had passed some of the field dressing stations where men were lying in the rain with dull grey faces while they waited for the overworked surgeons to attend to their wounds. It could have been no worse at Waterloo, he had thought. An old trench, long abandoned, had been near one such field hospital, and he had seen medical orderlies laying out corpses before putting them in that for burial. Even worse, there had been men trying to put the right limbs with the various remains, like some grisly and horrific jigsaw. A padre had been with them, his clothing black with rain and mud, his little book in his hands. From his appearance he was in constant demand, like the doctors and stretcher bearers.

He had found the brigadier in his new H.Q., another cellar, which the sappers had emptied for him and installed some kind of drainage at the same time.

Ross had been using one of his telephones, a half-eaten

sandwich and a bottle of red wine nearby on a trestle table amongst his maps. He had waved Jonathan to a scruffy-looking deck chair, while his batman poured a generous glass of wine.

Ross had put down the telephone and taken another from his brigade-major. "Sorry about this, Jono. Damn rude of me. But try the wine—pretty good stuff." He blinked as the ground shook to a solitary explosion and added dryly, "Considering." Before he began his next telephone conversation he had indicated a thick official envelope. "I've read it, but it concerns you in many ways." His voice was very matter-of-fact, but Jonathan knew that nobody could be that calm in his vital position. Ross had turned to grope for his sandwich and said, "Thank you for letting me know, Sir John. Yes, I'm afraid it does look that way."

Jonathan, reading, had barely heard him over the ever-present rumble of cannon-fire. It was an official despatch, probably from that same great office at Royal Marines Headquarters in London. It seemed unreal, a message from another planet. All the way from the adjutant-general, through Major-General Sir Herbert Loftus who was still at base camp on the French coast with his untested Grenville Division, on to corps H.Q. and eventually here, to this smelly Flanders cellar. Surprisingly it had only taken a few days to arrive. He had massaged his eyes to ease the strain, to try and make sense of it. He was reading about somebody else, even though the despatch heading was his own name and rank.

He was going mad. It had to be. His battalion, weakened by the heavy casualties in poor Captain Conway's company, was resting. He had left them as soon as he had shaved . . .

Ross had still been speaking on the telephone, and another was already buzzing in its case until a hand reached out to silence it.

Crump-crump-crump. The Archies were at it again. Some
German pilot and observer circling around again to watch out
for reserves moving up; more artillery. Nothing could move,
nothing heavier than a man anyway. Jonathan had removed
his helmet and run his fingers through his unruly hair.

Concerning Lieutenant Colonel (brevet) Jonathan Blackwood,
D.S.O., R.M.A. Officer Commanding the Fifty-First Battalion. This
officer will be relieved from his command when convenient and will
return to Eastney Barracks for transfer to London. In due course
arrangements will be made for his replacement to be appointed.

It was unbelievable. He could picture her face when he
eventually wrote and told her.

He had seen Ross watching him, some breadcrumbs
uncharacteristically on his medal ribbons.

"Well?"

"Do you know what it means, sir?"

"I know the army. There's not that much difference, no
matter what they say." He had sat back in his chair, fingers
interlaced, his features expressionless. Then he had said, "Staff
appointment in all likelihood. Makes good sense. To them."

"It's a bit of a shock, sir."

A hand had come out and their glasses were refilled.

"I know what you're worried about, Jono, probably more
than anything else." There had been a massive thud and distant shouts.

Ross grimaced. "A dud. Bit of luck for us."

Jonathan had felt the others looking at him. He said quietly, "There's to be another push, isn't there, sir?"

Ross had glanced at his big map, which hung from a sal-
vaged coat stand. Probably from the same place as the deck
chair.

"It has to be." He had picked up his swagger-cane and
pointed deliberately. "Poelcappelle, about five miles north-

west of Passchendaele. A better gradient—would be drier if we have to halt there before the winter takes over. My staff tell me it's chalk there, ideal for cutting out better defences, as the Germans are always quick to discover."

"When, sir?" He had tried not to imagine her at the station, running to meet him.

"Four days." He had seemed to come to a decision. "Look, Jono. You're not God. Neither are you irreplaceable. From what I know of you, you could have been killed a dozen times already, just as it could happen to any of us. If you consent I can have you out of here tomorrow. Nobody will or could blame you—you've done as much as anybody, and probably more than most. Men will die and keep on dying until it's finally over, and neither you nor I can do much about it." He paused. "You have a competent enough second-in-command, I'd have thought? And they do need officers of your calibre where it counts. Not a silly lot of old duffers bewailing the South African War or the Crimea."

It had gone suddenly quiet. As if the last bugle had just sounded. Jonathan had thought of Wyke and Vaughan, and Maxted who was quietly going out of his mind. And all the others, old and new, whom he had come to know. Men he had seen suffer and die; others who had rallied, even cheered when he had needed them.

He had asked, almost abruptly, "What would you do, sir?"

Ross had eyed him coldly. "In God's truth, I don't know. In your case, I would at least consider it."

Another telephone had made itself heard.

Jonathan had found himself on his feet, his dark hair brushing the cracked ceiling.

"I have considered it, sir." His whole being had protested. He was betraying her: their love, their hopes, everything. "It does say *when convenient.* I'll stay until it is, if you don't mind, sir."

The brigade-major had held his hand over the telephone. "It's corps, sir."

"Tell them to wait!"

The major added unhappily, "It's the general, sir."

Ross had repeated testily, "I said *wait!*"

Without any sign of relief or emotion he had held out his hand. A firm grip, like Captain Soutter's had been.

Jonathan had heard himself say, "I know it will eventually come through in orders, but as a favour please let it remain between us until then. It might be misinterpreted, and I never want any of my men to think there was any doubt about my staying with them."

When he reached the reserve sector again he was still struggling with his conscience and the aftermath of what he had done.

He saw the usual groups of marines, either queueing for food or curling up somewhere to eat it. Huge vats of baked beans and sausages, fannies of steaming tea, hardtack biscuits covered in thick treacle. It was not a banquet, but it would fill their bellies and make them feel like men again. More ominous was the heady aroma of rum. Preparing them.

N.C.O.'s straightened up as he passed; the lump of Bert Langmaid, sheltering beneath a groundsheet while he spooned the hot beans down his throat, merely glanced at him. McCann and Timbrell, Geach and Seagrove the colour-sergeant who was still feeling his way. A quick nervous smile from some of the younger ones, a cheeky grin from the old sweats.

In only a few days they would be up the line again, attacking a small, unimportant place of which none of them had ever heard. They might question the reasons and the sanity of it, but they would do it. Not for King and Country, not because "England Expects." But for the corps, and mostly for each other.

He paused, staring along the frieze of muddy figures.

How could I leave them now? Alex . . . try to forgive me.

When he ducked into the dugout the other officers, who were eating their first hot meal for days, looked up expectantly with a question on every face. Harry Payne put a plate in front of him and darted him a quick glance. He had some idea of what had happened, and he could guess the rest. He need not have worried after all. There was nothing to show the cost of that decision.

He was the colonel again.

Before dawn on the ninth of October the Fifty-First battalion was in position, crouched low in the collapsed and shattered trenches, finding what cover they could, as much from the heavy rain as from their own shell-splinters. The bombardment had gone on for two days, and it was impossible even to guess how many thousands of shells had been fired. Some of the guns must be getting worn through, and there was a real danger of shells falling short onto the waiting troops and marines.

Poelcappelle was on their left front and Passchendaele somewhere to the right. There could be little left of either.

Jonathan leaned against an upended ration cart and peered at his watch. He saw the others doing the same and could sense their apprehension, dismay even, that they were being ordered to advance in these impossible conditions. He hoped he had managed not to reveal his own hopelessness, which had grown steadily since their return to the line. News of the unrivalled courage and determination of the British infantry had been matched only by their casualties. Days ago, when they had been resting, the infantry had forced an advance despite the awful weather and the enemy's stiff opposition, and gained one mile along the whole front. At Corps H.Q. it must have seemed like the long-expected breakthrough, and a cavalry division had been brought up for the anticipated collapse of the German centre. Their assault failed, and most of the horses had been killed by machine-guns. Their surviving riders retreated on foot.

Jonathan stared into the rain. He could feel the water like ice around his ankles, and recalled a memo he had seen. Any man reporting sick with trench feet would be dealt with as a malingerer, until proven otherwise. He moved his frozen toes and tried to smile. What would they say if *he* reported sick?

"Runner, sir!"

A small soldier, his breath puffing loudly, lurched through the collapsed firestep where the H.Q. platoon had mounted its machine-guns.

Jonathan ducked under a canvas screen and switched on his torch. Vaughan and Wyke stood outside, cursing luridly as more mud tumbled down while shells hurled up columns of smoke and earth in no man's land. The West Riding Division, blooded on many occasions, would be waiting and watching. This bombardment was to lay waste the heavy barbed-wire entanglements along their sector.

Jonathan stepped out into the rain. He was shivering badly; the wind was colder than he had first thought. Or was it the wind?

He handed a folded message to the runner and said, "We go over the top at five-thirty."

He knew from the silence that they must have dared to hope for some last-minute reprieve.

He said, "Brigade reports some machine-gun pillboxes to

the left front of us. The R.F.C. spotted them when the sun showed itself a couple of days ago. The infantry haven't a hope in hell of getting through with those in position. They haven't fired a round as yet—we'd have seen them—but they must know about the attack. They'll just sit there and wait."

More shells burst to the right, the flashes giving life to the funnelling smoke and reaching up to touch the clouds with fire.

He continued without expression, "I'd like to send a separate party over before the real attack begins. They'd stand a fair chance of reaching at least one of the pillboxes." The enemy would be on their toes for the main attack, he thought, but they were doubtless in their deep bunkers now, making the most of their protection and comparative dryness.

It took a physical effort to control his sudden anger as the realisation struck him. The Royal Marines were to be a useful diversion, just in case the main attack was delayed by circumstances or the weather. Had Ross been trying to prepare him for that, or had he known nothing about it?

Vaughan said, "I should like to lead with my company, sir."

"Yes. I intended that you should. You have a lot of seasoned men."

It was a kind of madness, this matter-of-fact manner in which they were discussing mass murder. Perhaps it really needed officers like Beaky Waring. No fear, no hesitation: he hadn't had the brains to see beyond his duty.

Maxted said dully, "I can take the raiding party, sir."

Jonathan was about to deny the request, then recalled what Wyke had said. He wished it was light enough to see Maxted's face.

He said, "Choose your men. I'll want you an hour before we go over." He turned away, although they could not see him. *And why not?* By the end of the day they would all be killed, or left out in the rain to die like those Germans in the wire.

"Major Hayward?" He saw a shadow move. "Oh, there you are, Peter. Thought you'd caught a bus home."

Somebody laughed. Actually laughed. It unnerved him. "You will take B Company next." He touched Wyke's arm and felt him tense. "H.Q. will keep with C Company. We can set up a field telephone when we get into position." They looked up as more shells screeched over the trenches. He wondered what had happened to Captain Alton's howitzers. Sunk beneath the mud with all the other abandoned waggons and weaponry: a battlefield junkyard.

Maxted was saying, "I shall need two good N.C.O.'s."

Timbrell called, "Count me in, sir. More my line than swimmin' across!" A tall sergeant named Harriman said, "Me too, sir."

"Twelve good men." He seemed to be thinking aloud.

McCann guffawed. "No such animal in the Royals, sir!"

Jonathan had tried to prepare himself for just such a moment as this when he had read her last letter. It was never far away. And then it was *now.*

Someone was murmuring, "God help me, God help me," over and over again fervently, like a prayer.

Another voice rasped, "For Christ's sake, Ted, stow that claptrap!"

Wyke was peering at his map with the aid of a torch while a marine held a sodden greatcoat over him to hide the light: the coat had been abandoned here, so it was assumed that its owner was no longer in need of it.

He felt someone beside him and knew it was Maxted.

"All right, John?" He hoped he sounded calmer than he felt. How could he ever describe it? A kind of lightheadedness, with anger and despair surging around in his mind.

Maxted hesitated. "I just wanted to say . . ." He stared down into the blackness as if to seek out the right words. "To say sorry, for the way I've been . . . you know."

Wyke nodded, not understanding, but aware that it was terribly important to his friend.

"We've all had about as much as we can take, John. I know I have. . . . We don't seem to be getting anywhere. It's more men, more men all the time. I haven't slept since I was on leave." He attempted to grin but it was not possible. "Not much then either, I have to confess."

Maxted sounded surprised. "Really? I always thought you of all people—"

Timbrell came down beside them. "Ready, sir. Grenades are primed, seven-second fuses. Four each." He could have been instructing recruits.

"Coming, Sergeant." Maxted gripped Wyke's hand, and the grit and wet rasped against their skin like some kind of bond.

He said quite calmly, "I think we'll not meet again, Chris." Then he was gone.

Wyke heard the colonel speaking with Maxted: a level tone, now so familiar, even dear to him. But he was unable to forget Maxted's calm farewell, as if there were no way out. A man under sentence of death, and now quite able to accept it.

A few minutes more and Maxted's party were up and over the broken parapet, sliding into mud and groping around shell holes with little more than the artillery to keep them on course.

The enemy did not return fire, nor even release a flare. The guns had succeeded in keeping their heads down if nothing else.

It was hard work: every yard was covered by shattered debris and huge spreads of soft mud. Maxted wanted to cry out as the exertion made the pain sear into his groin like a branding iron.

He tried to empty his mind, and wondered what his parents would say if they could see their precious son now.

He remembered when he had first mounted a guard at the barracks. The sunset bugles, the flag coming down very slowly, the salutes and the time-honoured ceremonial which affected even the old hands. He had been a part of it. It had been his dream. He gritted his teeth as the agony stabbed through him again.

He felt Sergeant Harriman beside him, keeping pace, arm over arm: a true light infantryman.

"Did you see, sir?" His whisper was almost lost in the downpour.

"What?"

"That last shell, sir. Saw it in the flash." Even he sounded shocked. "The bloody gunners 'ave missed it! The wire's still there!"

Maxted took a deep breath and started forward. He retorted savagely, "Not our problem! Let's get on with it!"

He was speaking to himself in quick painful gasps. *Must be time. Can't see my watch. Must remember to pull the pin from the grenade. . . .* He collided with a huddled corpse and thought suddenly of Second Lieutenant Rooke. Probably still hanging on the wire. His whole frame shook with silent laughter until the pain stopped it.

A red flare burst lazily over his right shoulder and Maxted pressed his face to the ground, tasting the filth and the stench. The flare was a signal, and even as the artillery fell silent for the first time in days he vaguely heard the shrill of whistles right along the line.

"Come on!" He wiped his face with his sleeve. "They'll be up to the wire in a minute!"

In answer a machine-gun began to chatter urgently, and so loudly that he froze with disbelief. They were almost on top of it, the noise of the gun's rapid fire only yards away. He fumbled with his grenade satchel, and almost dropped one of them into the mud in his haste.

"Right, lads! *At the bastards!*" He tugged the pin and heard the strike lever rattle away as he thrust the live grenade into the satchel. Then he was on his feet, swaying in the mud, his coat caught in some broken barbed wire, while he swung the satchel round his head like David's sling. He gave a great gasp as the satchel flew from his grip and he tore himself free of the wire. How long? Seven seconds, wasn't it?

He heard bullets fanning past him, some smacking into the mud. Then he felt a great blow in the chest and knew he could taste blood as he began to slide down the side of a shell crater.

Sergeant Harriman threw himself down as the grenades blew up in one ferocious explosion. The machine-gun fell silent, and through his deafness Harriman could hear them screaming faintly.

He pulled himself to the water-logged shell crater and knew that it was hopeless. Maxted was still sliding deeper: he would die either way.

The icy water was up to Maxted's waist now, and he felt the freezing relief drive away the agony which had brought him close to suicide.

Down, down. It was almost over. He was free.

Sergeant Harriman, with a couple of his men, heard him cry out. Not from fear or pain. Only two words.

"Thank you!"

And then Lieutenant John Maxted, aged twenty-one, died of his wounds.

The whistles shrilled, and scrambling like old men the marines went over the top. Several fell before they had even reached their own wire, but then there was a vivid scarlet flash followed almost immediately by a loud explosion.

Wyke gasped, "They've done it, sir!" He felt like cheering despite the danger and the horror of it. "If they can knock out the other ones. . ." He fell silent and Jonathan said, "Well?"

"Just something he said. He knew he was going to die."

The sergeant-major shouted above the roar of guns and the clatter of lighter weapons, "Brigade's on the line, sir! The wire's still there! West Riding Division is in trouble!"

Jonathan said, "Tell them we've knocked out one pillbox." Their faces lit up to another bang. "Belay that. *Two* pillboxes."

In the red glow McCann looked like one of Satan's fiends. Hayward's company had vanished into the smoky darkness. Surely it must get lighter soon.

Major Dyer's C Company, bayonets fixed, waited on the firestep for the order. The survivors from Conway's company were detailed to carry ammunition when they went, and a young R.M.A. lieutenant named Jason Ellis had taken Maxted's place with the H.Q. platoon.

Payne tugged at his chinstrap and muttered, "Not before time," as the rear artillery began to fire long-range onto the German support lines. "Give 'em a bloody headache!"

There was so much smoke that it was hard to tell how the first wave was getting on. Machine-guns were firing again, but on the other sector, where men would be dying, screaming as they fell into the wire they had been promised would be destroyed.

Wyke glanced towards the colonel as his face glowed in
profile in another explosion. "Are we going now, sir?"

Jonathan turned. "There's nothing here for us." Then, as
if afraid something might change his mind, he raised his whistle, and throughout the company other whistles replied.

"Over the top!" For a few seconds more Jonathan pressed
his fingers into the half-frozen sand of a torn sack. Inside his
mind a voice cried out like a lost soul. *I'm afraid. I'm afraid.
Help me.*

But the voice which answered refused to acknowledge it.

"Forward, Marines! Forward!"

Then with the others he was running and wading through
the mud, past and over the bodies of men he had known,
ducking and twisting as rifle-fire sang amongst them. Here
and there someone fell, and he heard McCann bellow "At
'em, me beauties!" One marine swung round, his teeth bared
like a wild animal's as figures loomed through the smoke,
until Timbrell shouted, "It's us! You bloody madman, Bid-
mead!"

Slowly and with relentless care, the strengthening light
spread itself across a vast, devastated panorama. Marines ran
from cover to cover, one pausing to empty his rifle into a
small hole where some Germans had been cut off from the
other wire, where they had probably been sniping at the
infantry. Then a grenade, tossed as casually as a man throws
a ball to his young son, finished it.

Dyer was yelling, "Reload! *Reload, damn you!"* Then he fell,
blood spurting from his throat as the life left him. The last
stretch. Marines flung more grenades to keep the defenders'
heads down; and Jonathan heard the snap of cutters as the
remaining wire broke under them, and they were through.

If the Germans in this one of a network of trenches and
bunkers attempted to take cover they were driven to earth,

where the grenades turned their holes into traps of blood. Others caught on the firestep fell back under the bayonets, the knives and the other murderous weapons that turned civilised men into beasts for as long as they could use them.

Then bruised, bloody and gasping for breath, they fired into the air and cheered. It had become lighter still, and nobody had noticed it. Ralph Vaughan, his helmet gone, a bloody wound on his cheek, was coming toward him. *"We took it, sir!* Reinforcements should be here at any moment!"

But Jonathan was staring round. "Where's the adjutant? He was with me."

Payne said roughly, "Here, sir." They stood aside as Jonathan slipped his arm around Wyke's shoulders and tried to lift him. He had fallen on the parapet, his horizon, and lay with one out-thrust hand still gripping his revolver.

Jonathan said harshly, "I want him taken to a dressing station!" He was staring around at the other world as order and discipline took over.

Vaughan said, "No use, sir. He's gone."

Jonathan stood with effort. One bullet. That was all it took. It had gone through Wyke's breast pocket, puncturing the steel mirror he always carried there, and the photograph of his girl.

Vaughan suddenly exclaimed, "Colonel! You've been hit!"

He glanced down at his leg and the blood pumping over his boot. He had felt nothing, and even now it was more like the bursting of an old wound.

He gasped, "Don't let me fall, Harry. Not now, after everything they've done!"

The marines parted to let them pass, some with their eyes averted when they saw where the telltale blood had marked him down. Payne held him tightly, his eyes stinging when some of his men saluted, or reached out and touched him.

He had called him *Harry*. And it mattered.

Stretcher bearers were already picking their way through the mud and the bodies of the living and the dead. Occasionally they would stop and retrieve one. But not too many, it appeared.

Vaughan waited until they had forced the colonel onto one of the stretchers.

"Go with him, Payne. He'll need you even more now."

Jonathan opened his eyes as a medical orderly fastened a shell dressing around his leg. The rain, which had not stopped, made him feel clean again.

To Vaughan he said, "Take care of them, Ralph. It would have been yours anyway."

Vaughan said nothing, deeply moved although he did not understand.

Payne watched the orderly's grim features as he made the dressing fast, until eventually the other man became aware of his hostile scrutiny and raised his head. Then he grinned, and gave a thumbs-up.

Jonathan tried to see more clearly through the pain and the rain on his face. "What's happening?"

Payne slung his rifle, and hung the colonel's helmet on the muzzle. Then he fell in step with the two stretcher bearers, and thought what a short distance they had come, only a few hours ago. Yet so many lay dead on every hand.

He cleared his throat and answered quietly, "Going home, sir. That's what."

POSTSCRIPT

In November 1917 the great push along the Ypres front came to a halt. The British armies did not succeed in taking the higher ground, where the exhausted troops might have found some relief from the freezing mud and relentless rain. The coming of winter and the disastrous weather proved to be as savage an enemy as the barbed wire, the gas and the perpetual bombardment by artillery.

Despite all the suffering and death the army never broke, nor was it defeated. There was simply no way forward any more; neither was there hope of a new offensive. When the June attacks were begun Zeebrugge had been 35 miles from the Ypres sector. When the offensive of 1917 ended in November, it was still over thirty miles away.

No armies had ever fought in such conditions before, and their record of courage and sacrifice remains unmatched. In less than five months the British armies fighting alongside their Empire cousins lost another quarter of a million men, killed, maimed and missing. It is almost beyond belief that in that same short period of the war another 35,000 men vanished altogether, drowned in the sea of mud, forgotten, and left to die alone and undiscovered. A missing army, and a lost generation.